I0681027

DOA

III

Edited by

S.C. Mendes

Copyright © 2017 by Blood Bound Books
"I'd Give Anything for You" copyright©2003 by Jack Ketchum & Edward Lee
"Red" copyright© 1986 Richard Christian Matheson
All other stories are original to this volume and are copyright © 2017 to their
respective authors.

All rights reserved

ISBN: 978-1-940250-26-7

This book is a work of fiction. Names, characters, business organizations,
places, events and incidents either are the product of the authors' imaginations
or are used fictitiously. Any resemblance to actual persons, living or dead,
events or locales is entirely coincidental.

Artwork by Andrej Bartulović

Interior Layout by Lori Michelle
    www.theauthorsalley.com

Printed in the United States of America

First Edition

Visit us on the web at:
www.bloodboundbooks.net

TABLE OF CONTENTS

Notches by Sean Eads and Joshua Viola 1

The Broken Hearted by T. Fox Dunham 11

N Word by Shane McKenzie 24

Skipp's Splatterpunk Alphabet Souffle
    by John Skipp 38

Takeaway Night by T.M. McLean 55

Burnt by Luciano Marano 60

Junk by Ryan Harding 73

The Package by Kristopher Rufty 83

Red by Richard Christian Matheson.........................101

8 Out of 10 by Daniel I. Russell...............................104

The Machine by Bentley Little 119

Posthumous
    by Lloyd Kaufman and Lily Hayes Kaufman.........................130

Bury Them Deeper by David Sandner 143

These Beautiful Bones by Betty Rocksteady 153

Subject #270374 by C.M. Saunders 171

Beer Battered by K. Trap Jones...............................184

L'Amuse Bouche by Hal Bodner 198

Proud Papa by Adrian Ludens.................................220

Cry the Banshee by C. Cameron Rossi 230

TerrorSluts for Eternity versus the Ungodheads of the Interdimensionals by Alistair Rennie 241

We Believe in 5B by Airika Sneve 254

Taking Root by Christoph Weber...264

The Bliss Point by Wrath James White...................................278

Woeful City by Garrett Cook 295

Ritchie by Eric J. Guignard 301

I'd Give Anything for You
  by Jack Ketchum and Edward Lee......................................315

Hostile by Jeff Strand 328

Metal Heat by Jaap Boekestein 332

Repulsive Glamour by John McNee 349

The Bitch by Kristopher Triana 363

NOTCHES

SEAN EADS AND JOSHUA VIOLA

ALICE HAD NEVER cut herself *down there* before.

To judge by their reactions, neither had Jill, Julienne, Mary, Rachel or Olivia.

And to think, all this time everyone called it a *gash*.

That's what Alice was thinking before the school went into lockdown and Ms. Atta was shot dead right outside the classroom door. Her blood seeped into the room even now, a heavy flow that seemed to skate on the cold, industrial tile floor, vainly seeking some absorbent fiber.

It was weird to think of Ms. Atta being dead. They'd only just gotten to *really* know her, despite spending many hours together in this little room repurposed for their counseling sessions. It figured she'd be killed just as their umpteenth meeting had finally resulted in a breakthrough, all of it hinged on Ms. Atta's dark but intriguing revelation that she'd also danced with the blade.

No, not just danced with it. *Married* it. *Fucked* it. All the other teachers were white bread and butter knives. Alice had always felt like the woman hated the bullshit she had to tell the girls in their counseling sessions. Alice certainly knew *she* hated it. Sometimes they'd make eye contact and it was like both wanted to cut through the lies, find truth and get real.

Well, today things had gotten real.

And then that asshole Tommy Mostow ruined everything.

Everyone was wearing identical long-sleeved shirts over their regular clothes. The word *NeSSIe* was embossed across the chest in red. They'd created the shirts two counseling sessions ago, under Ms. Atta's guidance. The girls all knew what NSSI meant, but Ms. Atta insisted on reminding them one last time in her thick Nigerian accent.

"Wearing these shirts is an act of protest because, like the Loch Ness Monster, too many people don't believe non-suicidal self-injury exists. But *you* exist, don't you? And your existence is wonderful."

Mary raised her hand. "But what do the two *e's* stand for?"

"Not a damn thing," Ms. Atta said. "Which, in my opinion, makes it all the better."

Alice had been the first to take the plunge and put the shirt on, pushing her slightly oversized head through the neckline. It was a bit tight on her and felt like a corset, but she was too excited by Ms. Atta's enthusiasm to backtrack. The rest soon followed, and Ms. Atta beamed at them.

"Do you feel empowered now?"

"No," the girls said.

"Of course not. It's not fabric that empowers you. It's the blade."

Well *that* certainly got their attention, especially after so many sessions where Ms. Atta had droned on about how the desire to cut themselves was the psychological manifestation of *blah blah blah*. Mary cut herself because she hated her father; Olivia because she couldn't handle rejection; Jill because she felt numbed by modernity. Julienne sliced herself over loneliness and Rachel because she was overweight.

As for Alice, she convinced herself it was the best way to keep track of time. Nobody believed her, of course. And Alice couldn't blame them. Cutters always made up bullshit excuses for dealing with the pain. But Alice thought hers was the most unique.

Ms. Atta smiled at them in their matching shirts. "I think we're finally ready to do something new," she said. "I want all of you to roll up your sleeves. Show your cuts to each other," Ms. Atta said.

"I don't want to show my body," Rachel said. "I'm so fat."

"Then do you cut because you want to whittle it away?"

The question may have seemed like Ms. Atta sought understanding, but Alice found no warmth there. She discovered truth in the hardness of the counselor's tone. Challenging, wonderful truth.

"You first," Alice said.

Ms. Atta looked at her. "Since you need courage," she said, and her fingers went to the buttons of her blouse. Little by little, the shirt came open. The girls leaned forward with each revelation. By the time Ms. Atta had revealed her perfect stomach, Alice had reflexively jerked both her sleeves up past the elbow. They all did, and the scabs showed in patterns as unique and individual as red frost on glass.

The moment felt breathless to Alice, yet all she heard was everyone's panting. She took in the other girls' cuts and they took in hers as Ms. Atta looked pleased, standing among them with her shirt on but open, her skin so dark and perfect. It was only Ms. Atta's perfection that blemished the moment, that gave Alice any thought that somehow she and the girls had been tricked into more counseling crap dressed up as something taboo. Hell, most of Alice's cuts weren't even on her arms anyway. So if Ms. Atta wanted a *true* revelation, Alice decided she might as well give them all a real eyeful.

She pulled her shirt off and stood before them in just a bra.

There was no mirror in the room, but Alice thought she could see herself through Ms. Atta's stunned eyes. The counselor came and walked around her, inspecting her from belly button to shoulder. Did the sheer number of cuts surprise her? Or was it their pattern?

"Tally marks," Ms. Atta said. She had such open wonder in her expression that Alice couldn't help but feel proud.

"Yes," Alice said. "I make them with a box cutter. It gives me the precision I like. Four vertical marks and then a slash. Over and over again. One arm, then another. Then the stomach. Funny how the knife tickles the ribs."

The other girls swarmed her, their fingertips tracing the lacerations, perhaps finding Braille in the scabs. Alice ignored them. She and Ms. Atta were having a moment.

"What do you tally, Alice?"

"Time," she said. "Loves. Failures. Dreams and crushed hopes. Disappointments. Expectations. The number of butterflies I find struggling in spider webs on my way to school. They all run together in my mind and on my flesh—after the blade."

Ms. Atta trembled and retreated two steps. For a moment Alice

 3

thought she'd misjudged the woman, mistaking disgust for thrall. But the darkness filling Ms. Atta's eyes told Alice there was something more sinister to her behavior. The girls weren't being tricked. She stepped toward Ms. Atta, closing distance, the girls pressing along with her.

"Show me," Alice whispered, her gaze roaming over Ms. Atta's bare arms, her ebony skin perfect over supple muscle. Clearly this flesh had never known even simple blemishes, much less the intrigues of a razor. "Show me the cuts. I know they're there. You're like us—I *know* you are."

"Not like you," Ms. Atta said. "I never had the choice."

"Choice?" Alice said. "Don't you mean power? To take the knife and slice open the skin like slitting a cocoon."

Alice found herself in a staring match with Ms. Atta, and for the first time wondered just how old the counselor was. Probably not even thirty, and now that she'd dropped the pretense of her authority, she seemed even younger. She was so much like them, fellow sister of the blade.

"Is it your thighs?"

"None of those places," Ms. Atta said.

"Then *where*?"

Only Alice talked, but she knew she spoke for the group. Psychically they demanded Ms. Atta strip, all but tearing her clothes away with their collective gaze. She must have felt the pressure—the sweet call to release herself from secrets, which to Alice was the essence of cutting. Looking toward the closed door, she let her unbuttoned blouse slink off her shoulders.

Once more Alice verged on feeling tricked. "*Where* are the cuts, Ms. Atta? Show us."

The woman was quiet for a long moment. Alice focused entirely on Ms. Atta's hands, willing them to move. Then they did. *Just enough.* Her left hand raised her skirt up as the right pushed her panties down—again *just enough.*

To Alice it was like Ms. Atta had the face of God down there.

"Men in my country did this to me, as they do to most women. These scars are where my clitoris used to be."

Ms. Atta's vagina looked so foreign the sight of it closed Alice's throat and opened her eyes wider than she'd ever experienced.

Such mutilation had never occurred to her. It was something she'd heard on the news as background noise, or in social studies class. But Ms. Atta made it real and compelling. Suddenly Alice saw the counselor as a girl, ten or eleven years old, being forced to the ground as unsympathetic faces gathered to watch some tribal elder come with sharpened flint or ancient ceremonial dagger to hack and scrape some of her away, the flesh shaved back like the rind off an orange.

Alice touched the base of her throat as a wave of inadequacy washed over her. The cuts across her body, whose thrill of pain and endurance had been a source of pride, felt like some unimaginative stick figure drawing now that she beheld the Matisse of Ms. Atta's disfigurement.

There were other cuts across her groin, some as fresh as this morning. Lacerations up and down the inner thigh and across the folds of her labia, which Ms. Atta now brought to the girls' attention with her fingers.

"The emotional pain of the violation never ceased. I felt the need to keep going."

"You're so brave," Alice said, almost breathless. She looked back at the girls, wondering if they shared the same thought.

Ms. Atta was quiet a moment. "Violence in thought and deed is why we cut. It symbolizes transformation, and each slash is transformative. *That* is what you tally, Alice: your endless transformations."

"Yes," Alice said, her tone confident.

Julienne said, "I don't care about symbolism, I care about how the cut feels."

Alice turned wildly back to her, flashing her approval. Julienne was normally so shy, the last of all girls to speak. Already Ms. Atta's display had worked wonders.

Transformation indeed. Ms. Atta put her panties and skirt back into place.

"Regardless, as in all things, symbolism comes first," the counselor said and looked at the clock on the wall. "There's enough time for one more lesson."

Alice nodded impatiently.

"Poetry," Ms. Atta said.

The girls twisted their faces. Poetry was for the journals they kept in fifth grade. Now they wrote in flesh.

Ms. Atta laughed. "Don't be so glum. We're going to create our poems the way William S. Burroughs did."

Alice shook her head, earning an extra twinkle in Ms. Atta's eyes. "I'm surprised. You of all people should know of the cut-up method."

The girls leaned forward, drawn by the phrase.

"Burroughs would take magazines and newspapers and slice words from them until he had hundreds of fragments. He'd toss them into the air until they were all jumbled together. Then he'd reassemble them into new meanings."

"Like refrigerator magnet phrases!" said Olivia.

Alice smiled. "I want to take the knife, dripping with blood, and slide it into the paper and cut all the words out like little hearts. I want to make a haiku. No, fuck haikus. I want to make a sonnet celebrating the unkindest cut of all."

"I'll get some magazines from the library. You all have your razors with you, right?"

The girls feigned innocence until Ms. Atta shot them an arch look. Then they opened their purses—all but Alice, who really was a purist for box cutters. But those were too hard to sneak past the school's metal detectors—which were going off now, a distant siren down another long corridor.

"Good," Ms. Atta said. "I'll be back in a few minutes." She opened the door and stepped out.

A gunshot cracked in the distance, sending the girls shrieking back. The impact punched a hole through Ms. Atta's chest and dropped her in the doorway. Blood gushed from the wound and swam across the floor. Ms. Atta's eyes were still open and fixed upon their final vision.

The twinkle Alice saw a moment ago was gone now.

There were more shots and screams, and then Tommy Mostow stepped into view, his back to the girls, checking his weapon's magazine. He was sixteen but looked thirteen, and his baggy camo pants and black t-shirt did nothing to age him. Even the assault rifle in his hands just made him seem like a little boy playing war in his backyard. Except this wasn't his backyard, and Ms. Atta was dead.

Alice barely heard him say, "Dumb bitch," over the screams and alarms. He put another burst of bullets into her body. Students charged out of their classrooms and through the hall like a herd of frantic animals. Tommy snapped up the gun and fired at them. The chaos must've entranced him, because he didn't seem to be aware of the girls gaping through the open door.

Alice slowly crept toward Tommy, flinching each time he pulled the trigger. The girls followed.

"Five more dead fucks," Tommy said, ceasing fire. Alice watched him take out a small pocketknife and make notches on the gun's barrel. Four hash marks and a slash.

"You tally, too."

Tommy sprang back and dropped the knife. Alice stared into his eyes and found a dark, kindred pain, but no understanding of it. He'd have learned a lot from Ms. Atta, but instead he had to ruin it for everyone. On a much more significant level, of course, Alice realized she'd found and lost her religion in the space of ten minutes.

The girls charged before he could take aim. They came slashing, dicing him across the forearms. Blood pulsed in spurts from the wounds. Tommy howled and dropped his precious toy as they drove him down, one of the girls kicking the gun away. The principal's voice echoed through the PA system, urging the students to stay inside and barricade the doors. The alarm was still blaring, but the hallway was empty now. True to what she'd heard, Alice saw five bodies a few rooms down.

Alice dragged Ms. Atta's body into the classroom.

"Bring him here!" she shouted.

Completely overpowered, Tommy was pulled kicking and screaming through Ms. Atta's blood and into the room. Alice shut and locked the door, then turned to study their captive. His face was wet, his eyes puffy and red, snot bubbling in his nose. He looked like a kid brother bullied by an abusive older sister and her friends. His shirt and pants had been gashed, revealing scrawny, bald flesh. Crimson oozed from several cuts to his forearms.

"You killed Ms. Atta, asshole," Alice said.

"I—I'm sorry." His voice was as whiny and weak as a first grader's. No wonder he preferred the speech of guns.

Alice scrunched her face. "No you aren't. You're about as far from sorry as anyone can be."

"I just wanted people to stop making fun of me."

The girls stood watch over Tommy, razorblades in hand, while Alice contemplated the spread of Ms. Atta's blood. It was heavy and dark, almost menstrual. Alice thought again about the sheer pain of genital mutilation and cutting herself *down there*. What courage would that take? She almost wished there could be someone to hold her down and remove her clitoris, her labia, her everything, enshrouding her in a pain surpassing death. Surely she would transform into a being of light.

Alice's eyes widened. She held her breath and stared down.

Ms. Atta laid there, naked and much younger now—not quite a teenager. Her legs were splayed, her clitoris freshly shorn away. Blood streamed from the wound, with the arc of a water fountain. It splashed over the toes of Alice's sneakers and she hurried to kick her shoes and socks off and slick her soles. Ms. Atta's youthful, glossy eyes stared at Alice. She spoke, but her voice came from her mutilated groin, a chant as sure as a tribal drum beat:

Tally your life by this tally your love your vengeance your faith

The words echoed in Alice's head like a chorus. It came from Ms. Atta's gash, from the PA system and from Alice's heartbeat all at once. She nodded and turned to Tommy, the greasy soles of her feet slipping a bit on the tile. The weight of responsibility threatened Alice's posture, but she refused to be bowed. This tallying could not be done on her own skin.

"I'm taking his pants off," she said.

Rachel and Olivia knelt on his wrists, crushing them into the floor. Tommy thrashed and kicked until Jill and Julienne each gave him two sharp slashes into the soft flesh of his belly. Alice paid no attention to his whimpering or his bleeding as she grabbed the waistband of both his pants and boxers and forced them down the length of his skinny legs. At last they discovered a place on Tommy that wasn't bald. Alice pinched his bush and yanked until the roots tore free. God, how he screamed.

And got hard.

Tommy's erection was impressively disproportional to his slight body. And he was not circumcised. Alice cupped his penis in one palm, which it quickly outgrew.

"What are you doing?" he said.

Alice dug her nails into his erection. Tommy shrieked, but Alice felt him grow and throb.

"Wow, you're really enjoying this, aren't you?" Alice said.

"I'm—I'm a virgin. Nobody's ever touched it before."

Alice looked at the girls and then back at Tommy. She remembered how he'd put notches on his gun—including one for Ms. Atta. Boys were just like that, weren't they? They tallied their conquests and victories, thinking enough notches would finally add up to manhood and transform them. Maybe in Tommy's case it had. He seemed truly in awe of the length and hardness of his cock, as if both were fresh surprises. Maybe the violence he'd committed, the lives he'd taken, had done their alchemy.

Alice released his penis and dipped her hand in Ms. Atta's blood. It was still warm and stunk of copper. She rubbed her fingers together until they were slick and began stroking Tommy. His body rocked with spasms. He hissed air through clenched teeth and squeezed his eyes shut.

"Oh, God!"

A boy's cry.

A man's cock.

"Please, *please* use your mouth. Just taste it with your tongue."

Tommy's dick was sticky with blood now. Alice spit into her palm and made him slick again, stroking with her left hand, her awkward hand, the hand she never even cut with. That was reserved for her right hand, which she now extended palm up and waiting. Olivia placed her blade there, prodding her a bit with the tip, enough to make stigmata. Tommy went on moaning. Alice had heard male circumcision influenced sensitivity, though whether or not the influence was positive or negative, she couldn't say.

"Oh, my God, I'm going to come," Tommy said.

"How many?"

Panting, he said, "How many what?"

"How many times have you jacked off? How many times have you come? Have you ever added them up?"

"I dunno. Like a thousand," he said, and arched his back while Alice stroked him.

"But your first with us. We should start a tally."

Alice held the blade alongside his erection. The edge would split it open like a summer sausage if she worked it lengthwise.

But notches were the order of the day.

Joshua Viola is an author, artist, and former video game developer (Pirates of the Caribbean, Smurfs, TARGET: Terror). In addition to creating a transmedia franchise around The Bane of Yoto, *honored with more than a dozen literary awards, he is the author of* Blackstar, *a tie-in novel based on the discography of Celldweller. His debut horror anthology,* Nightmares Unhinged, *was a* Denver Post *bestseller and named one of the Best Books of 2016 by Kirkus Reviews. His second anthology,* Cyber World *(co-edited by Hugo Award winner, Jason Heller) was named one of the Best Books of 2016 by Barnes & Noble. His short fiction has appeared in The Rocky Mountain Fiction Writers' Found anthology (RMFW Press) and The Literary Hatchet (PearTree Press). He lives in Denver, Colorado, where he is chief editor and owner of Hex Publishers.*

Sean Eads is a writer and librarian living in Denver, Colorado. His second novel, The Survivors, *was a finalist for the 2013 Lambda Literary Award. His third novel,* Lord Byron's Prophecy, *was a finalist for the Shirley Jackson Award and the Colorado Book Award. His first short story collection,* 17 Stitches, *will come out in June 2017. Sean's favorite non-writing activities are playing golf and competing in bar trivia with his epic team of fellow geeks, Irritable Vowel Syndrome.*

THE BROKEN HEARTED

T. FOX DUNHAM

"**R**ICHARD GISHMAN?" my new attorney asked.

He knew who I was though. My face is the most known face in the world. Hitler. Mao. Gishman.

"I never pretended to understand the workings of the inner heart," I said. "I only wanted to bring love to the world."

"And for ten years you did, Mr. Gishman," the attorney said.

"Then I murdered it."

"Such statements could be considered an admission of guilt," he said, already advising me before our initial consultation. The reek of antiseptic burned my nose, but it smelled better than the urine ambiance that permeated the International Crime Court's detention cells in a Dutch prison in Scheveningen, The Hague. I found it astounding that with all the world's problems, the remnants of the world court still had the money and support to incarcerate and try me, but I figured they needed me to give the wounded populations someone to blame. Villages and cities in every country burned me in effigy and demanded my trial. The fractured governments happily obliged, eager to find a patsy to focus revolutionary impulses that usually followed economic destruction.

The bald guard had pushed me into a seat at a plastic table. Number seven attorney entered from the other side. The first five lawyers had turned me down. Number six had accepted my case, saying all this hyper-rage was a lot of nonsense, but I had to replace her—her husband butchered her while on their second honeymoon in Switzerland. He sliced her up into bite-sized pieces and fed her to the ducks—another dissatisfied customer of my service.

"I need to ask you a few questions," number seven said. "Obviously, I'm aware of your history, but I need your side of the story. Please answer honestly."

I nodded.

"How did all this begin, Mr. Gishman?"

"I was born with an innate sense of the funny little paths numbers can travel. And I just wanted money to buy pot. I didn't mean to end the world."

Number seven crossed his stubby legs, pulling up his pant leg, exposing his black sock. He typed on his pad, and I checked his finger for a wedding ring. "Did you find your partner with my algorithm?" I asked.

"No. I met my husband the old-fashioned way, in a pub. Not from the Gishman equation." I placed his accent somewhere around Lincolnshire. My wife, January, and I had traveled extensively in the early years of our happy union.

"So you and your husband are—?" I noticed his hands trembled.

"Miserable but happy," he said then took out a thermos from his satchel. "I've managed to find some coffee," he said and poured enough to fill two paper cups. "Hard to get now that we're in a global recession." He pushed the cup to my side of the table. "It's not the champagne you're used to." He sighed and stared at the black patch over my eye. "Sorry. I shouldn't mention champagne."

"Any news on my wife?" I asked. I didn't blame January. I had done this to us, and I needed to see her. I sipped from the weak coffee and tasted the end of society.

"Internet is sporadic." He checked his tablet. "Right. She is still a patient in the Penn Mental Care Facility, Philadelphia. Listed as "non-responsive". I don't know how much longer they'll be able to keep her. The mental health system is collapsing."

"They're blaming me for that too?" My right eye ached, and I scratched under the patch.

"Not if my team can help it," he said. "This kind of thing could have happened to anyone."

I shook my head. The jumpsuit's collar scratched my neck, and I rubbed the raw skin. My gut pushed against the table, rocking it against its bolts. I'd fattened since my days as a college stoner, but I still saw myself as a young rebel, the anti-establishment hacker who would never sell out. I had to get over myself. January always humbled me.

"It couldn't have been anyone," I said. "This is what I was born for. My mother always told me I was too smart for my own good."

"I think our first action is to file a brief with the ICC, asking that they dismiss the charges. International law is still unclear about corporate negligence." He folded his hands on the table. "When did this really begin?"

"In 2003, when my girlfriend walked out on me."

"You're not mature enough for a real relationship," Stephanie said, packing a bag. I kept failing my courses, and now they wanted to throw me out of Penn. The rent on our shitty roach-infested apartment was two month's late, and she'd finally had it. "You'd think with all that Google shit on the internet, I could find a good man."

"I've got this idea for a website," I said, playing the old con one more time. "We'll be rich in a year."

"Hearing the same song," she said, exposing her Midwestern accent. "I'm staying with Stacey. I'll come back later for my shit." Stephanie shut the door. Roaches scurried. I sat down in my throne and logged into some hacker sites.

The same song.

I didn't shower for days, sitting in my boxers and eating old rice from Cantonese boxes. I downloaded movies and ignored my classes. My landlady slipped notices under the door, and I waited for the Philly police to come and drag me out. Stephanie's comment about the internet looped through my brain.

I coded a new program and tied it into the major search engines. I typed some equations, using my acumen to seek her replacement. I didn't do it because of my industry or my imposed genius. I just wanted someone to hold me at night, and I applied what I knew. I'd employed dating sites before to no assistance. America wanted a cheap fix to its amorous issues, and sites that promised such a service made money.

THE BROKEN HEARTED

It took me a few days, but I finished the equation—a specialized search engine that would use a compression method to scan all relevant data on the internet then tell you if you had a match equal to your own presence on the web. My program compiled the information already available online. Social networks displayed your data for public usage. No one ever read those licensing agreements when they clicked *I agree*. My equation utilized everything from credit reports to government census, and so much could be assimilated by what was missing from your records. That was the true brilliance of my algorithm. The program compiled only a hundred lines of code, and I added new search parameters, elements I felt were important in a relationship, my own compatibility factors. I made up some of them, programmed them for chaos, gray areas between people. I'd taken some psych classes, and instead of focusing on the positive aspects of people's lives, I programmed for the negative, for the hard times that come in every relationship. I wanted to find someone who would stay.

I plugged in the numbers and set the program loose onto the sea of chaotic information. My baby stalked and hunted, seeking out the perfect prey to endure my inadequacies. Many variables showed on the report, but only one name registered with 100 percent accuracy.

January Snow.

I looked her up on Facebook—a cute face, glasses and blonde hair. She lived with her mother in D.C. Her profile said she studied law, and I found her email address through Georgetown University. In desperation, I emailed her:

> January:
> I believe there's someone out there for everyone. I don't know you. I'm one of the broken hearted. My girlfriend just left me, and I've not left my apartment since. I found you because I wrote a computer program that searched the internet. The variables and math have determined after scanning the millions of people online that you are my best match. Are you lonely too?

And I signed it:

Deeply Misunderstood.

I wasn't misunderstood. I was exactly what women thought I was—a lazy, entitled child with maternal fixations. Still, I hoped I'd find a woman that would kick my ass into adulthood. I knew I had potential. I just needed something to fight for.

"So she was the first?" my attorney asked, scribing down notes on his tablet.

"A successful experiment," I said.

"She must have fallen for the email. You married her in 2004."

I folded my legs under the table, then sipped from the weak coffee.

"She wrote back telling me she wasn't interested, but the program intrigued her. I kept at her—little notes, stupid poetry, confessions from my soul. January stopped in Philly to change trains, heading out to Chicago to visit her dad. We had a couple of beers at 30th Street Station, and we couldn't be apart after that."

"And did you see any signs of the union going bad? Symptoms you ignored?"

"Perfect bliss like all my clients. Guaranteed. One million clients in the first six months. News of bliss spread, and everyone wanted a sip of ambrosia. Nearly one billion in ten years. People don't fall in love without my help. It was all January really, though I'm not saying this is her fault. She encouraged me to get my act together, and I founded No More Broken Hearts, Inc."

"I wouldn't call it luck, Mr. Gishman," number seven said. "The death penalty is on the table. The ICC never gives the death penalty. You've angered them. I think two of the judges had spouses who attacked them."

"It's not my fault," I said, but I knew it was.

"So when did it start to go bad?"

THE BROKENHEARTED

In 2014, the Nobel Prize committee considered me for a peace award. It had been ten years since I'd dared to send the email to a stranger on the internet, and I'd saved the world. So we traveled to Philly for the weekend to celebrate. My algorithm accounted for at least seventy-percent of unions since I launched the dating site, and I got a bonus for every civil union, marriage and long-term relationship. Divorce rates fell; people got along better now that they were happy at home; wars ended.

Room service delivered champagne, 1928 Krug, chilled in a sterling silver bucket. They pushed the tray to the door, and I carried it into the penthouse we'd rented in the Penn Tower Hotel. Lights reflected on the inky Delaware River, and a nor'easter blew into the city. Sleet stuck to the wall-length windows, freezing ice sheets on the glass. I built a fire in the grand hearth to heat the penthouse, and we lay on top of the covers enjoying the glow.

"I have a surprise for you," she said.

"I love your surprises." I set the down the crystal flutes and corkscrew on the bed stand. She still wore her jeans and Phillies's sweater, always casual—another thing I loved about her. She'd dyed her hair red as part of a surprise for me, and I'd cut dinner short just to get her to bed faster.

"Richard?" January said, going into the bathroom carrying a box from Georgette's. I loved the way their boxes shimmered red in the light. "Have you noticed we've never had a fight?"

The sudden monotone quality of her voice unnerved me, but I shook off the change in her demeanor as a moment of deep reflection. When I too reflected, I realized I couldn't recall one major fight or blowup, which was odd as I constantly fought with my girlfriends. "Didn't we fight over . . . ?"

"We've never had a fight," she said. "Don't worry about it. You saved the world with your matchmaking. Saved us too. I don't think it's so odd that two people can live together and not kill each other." She shut the bathroom door, and I waited, heart pounding. She still did that to me after all these years.

January slipped out of the bathroom and slinked over to me. The sapphire negligee clung to her little bunny-body, and I could see a thong through the slits along her thighs. January spread her nimble body out on the silk sheets then reached for the champagne, grabbing the corkscrew and running her finger down the curved metal. She teased me, and I panted. Then, she leaned in to kiss me but paused again. Her expression changed, twitched, and I worried she'd stroked out. She looked down at her bare legs. "In ten years, I don't think you've ever asked if my feet were cold," she said.

"Your feet?"

She looked up again, and her eyes never broke contact from mine as she swung the corkscrew. It slit my cheek, and the salty taste of my own blood surprised me. I still couldn't believe she'd done it. I'd never seen January swat a fly, and I paused, nearly stunned when she swung again. This time my survival instinct kicked in. I dodged, and she hit my shoulder, stabbing the skin and muscle. Pain shot up into my neck and radiated down into my chest.

"Christ, Jan. What the hell?"

"My fucking feet are freezing!" she yelled and went after me with the corkscrew, aiming for my head. I rolled off the bed, and she jumped, landing on top of me. "Stay still, you cocky son of a bitch. It'll tickle."

I grabbed her arm, but she yanked it free. Saliva leaked from her lips and down her chin. She bit her lip as she lunged, and the blood dripped into my mouth. She thrashed a final time. The sharpened screw stabbed my eyeball and split the wet tissue. Pressure compressed my socket and temple. I yelled out and twisted my head, breaking the insertion of the wine utensil. Finally, in an act of self-preservation, I kicked her off, throwing her tiny body into a table. It shattered from the force, and a Tiffany's lamp broke under her. I scurried back against a wall and looked up, waiting for the assault to renew. January just sat there and stared off into the room. The molten glass of her eyes cooled, and she gazed catatonic.

"Jan?"

Her body petrified. She didn't sag or collapse. I held my eye and called 9-1-1.

"The New England Journal of Medicine was the first to print a study," I explained. "They called the psychotic break caused by my algorithm an acute case of hyper-rage that resulted in the subject's dissociation. The part of the prefrontal cortex that controls reasoning shuts down, and the amygdale over-stimulates. Rage overwhelms the subject, leading them to commit homicidal acts against their partner, though it was not clear why. Then the mind, not able to accept what it's done, goes into a long-term catatonic state."

"And that was the first incident of hyper-rage associated with your program?" my attorney asked.

"She was right." I shrugged. "We'd never had a fight in our life."

He summoned up more reports on his pad. "I've compiled some of the data from the CDC and FEMA. It started with your marriage. You were the first couple to use your equation. It spread in the order of your customers. The chronology of the data is unimpeachable."

"I've seen the numbers," I said. My eye itched, and I played with the patch.

"Do you have a theory to explain the homicidal side effect of your program?" he asked.

"Humans aren't designed to be happy all of the time," I said. "They need to fight, and it just builds up."

"Your wife attacked you first," he said. "Why didn't you succumb first?"

I finished the coffee, probably my last. "It varies between couples. Only eighty percent of my clients suffered the hyper-rage associated with complete marital bliss. The CDC released a report blaming personality variances, ways of dealing with repressed stress. I was a pothead even after my success. My wife never indulged."

"She had no outlet, I see." He nodded. "When did you realize it wasn't just your wife and there was a problem with your service?"

I committed her to the facility at Penn. She still wouldn't talk, and I visited her everyday to tell her that I loved her. A few weeks later, the news reported several cases of matrimonial homicide, and I made the connection, remembering the names of some of my earliest customers. I was in denial about what was happening. A few months later, the hyper-rage became an epidemic. Most of the world had used my site to find true love. By June 2014, One-third of my customers had murdered their significant others then burned the bodies, chopped off limbs or just bit off genitalia. International leaders had also used the service, understanding the appeal to voters of having a perfect family, and within days, I'd decapitated governments.

I drove through Philly, dodging burning buildings and raging mobs. The National Guard tried to maintain peace by direct order of FEMA. Looters broke store windows and cleared out inventory. ATMs emptied. The power died. The broken hearted raged, burning the cities.

The FBI issued a warrant for my arrest, but paid friends in the bureau warned me. My private jet flew me to France in July, and I hid out at an old vineyard. Then the International Criminal Court stated it would try me for crimes against humanity. The groundskeeper at the vineyard turned me in, and the ICC arrested me that July then imprisoned me in The Hague while they prepared their case.

Number seven slowly nodded his head. "Well, I can file a brief for you, but the ICC will be the ones to decide. In my own evaluation, this trial has no legal foundation. It's not like you ordered your militia to butcher thousands of Hutu with machetes. You didn't open secret torture rooms in the sewers below Baghdad. Legally, you personally haven't committed homicide on any scale, so I'm not sure where they will go with this. They're doing this because they don't know what to do."

"So you don't think I've committed any kind of crime here?" I was still worried they would find something.

He uncrossed his legs and leaned toward me. "I could argue this was an industrial accident, and that international law has no business trying a corporation. If it still existed, the WTO would agree and probably pay for your defense. Union Carbide wasn't tried internationally after they killed thousands in Bhopal when their factory leaked pesticide. It was an unforeseen accident caused by a lack of oversight. You did have your customers sign a waiver, correct? Only entertainment purposes. That sort of language?"

"Users agreed to a disclaimer when they signed up for my website," I said. "No one read it of course."

"That's their responsibility."

I started feeling a little relief. If logic still ruled the law during the collapse of society, I could have been released. So far, they'd maintained a semblance of order. Civilized people clung to such ideals desperately as the world burned around them, or they probably would have just strung me up by now. "So I could really beat this?"

"You can't prosecute one of those gangster rappers when a gang shoots up a neighborhood," he said. "The heart and mind can be unpredictable. Your product had an unforeseen side effect through no negligence of your own. You didn't act with any pre-meditation. It's grounds for a civil suit, not the Nuremberg Trials."

He removed his glasses and began to clean them on a small microfiber cloth he pulled from his pocket. "Frankly, I think they are afraid more than anything. I think they're just lashing out. This trial is a knee-jerk reaction. But the damage is now done, and you have no further involvement in it. Jurists live and die by the law, and most of them get off by defying the dictates of a vengeful heart to serve civilization."

"Even now?" I asked.

"More so now. Their souls are all they have left."

It turned out he was right. He petitioned for a mistrial, citing the vacancy of international code in corporate negligence, and the ICC made its decision in November 2014. As predicted, they couldn't pass a verdict under current international law. I was guilty of criminal negligence on a massive scale, but I hadn't committed genocide. *The current international body of laws lacks the understanding and cannot adjudicate the human heart.* They set me free, probably with the understanding that I'd most likely be beaten to death by an angry mob before I could cross the border. I'd be punished more by the people of the world than any jail could impose. The United Nations declared that all couples brought together by my equation were to separate, many still happy.

But I'd still broken the world's heart. Thousands of civil lawsuits waited for me in court, once the court system started to work again.

I chartered a private jet back to Philly, traveling under the alias Jay Wilburn. I landed at an airport in Doylestown—one of the few airports still functioning on the East Coast.

I retrieved my corvette from a storage unit, happy it hadn't been broken into, and drove to the city, dodging abandoned cars along I-95. Blackened bruises pockmarked the skyscrapers of Philly, and the brick buildings along the highway burned with impunity, without the remedy of a fire department. Smashed cars made a barricade at the Callowhill Street exit. A tank had been turned on its side, and bullet holes pierced the surrounding Septa station and trains. I turned off into Center City, driving slow onto I-76. National guard still patrolled the streets. I sped up into the heart of the city, passing the cathedral of 30th Street Station, but once I got to Center City, I had to drive slow, passing overturned police cars and abandoned troop carriers. The city itself was a nightmare, as if martial law had been abandoned altogether, favoring the citizens to raze themselves to the ground before the government came back to rebuild. Fires burned out of control in the skyscrapers, spraying ash and glass into the streets. I'd seen carnage during my days back in Philly, but what I witnessed reminded me of a cheap slasher film. Americans had made violence an art, and we had plenty of guns to go around.

A mob of teens smashed store windows, breaking into an appliance store then tossing flat screen televisions and computers onto Penn Avenue. I slowed to avoid the missiles and turned to avoid a crowd of protestors running through clouds of misty tear gas. I turned and drove along the curve through a fire lane in front of an apartment building, pausing behind an idling Buick. I had no choice but to wait for either the throng to clear or the car in front of me to pull out. An old man wearing his bathrobe loaded suitcases into the trunk while a woman, probably his wife or sister, sat in the driver's seat, pleading for him to hurry. He shut the trunk, and she turned her head to look behind, staring at the man standing between our cars with a glassy gaze. Then, the old lady simply put the vehicle into reverse, knocked the guy backward and slammed into the front of my corvette.

THE BROKEN HEARTED

My airbag exploded, slamming my head into the window. She pushed my tinfoil car into a brick wall, and I felt a rib snap. Blood dripped down my face. I struggled with the air bag then pulled myself up and across the bucket seats to get out, collapsing onto the pavement. The pressure of the collision severed the old man's body, and his torso slid down the hood of my crumpled sports car and landed near me. Shredded intestines slapped me with blood, shit and bile, smearing into my suit. I slithered out of there and got to my feet, keeping to the back streets.

My head ached from the crash and stink of tear gas. I only had a few miles to hike to see January, so I opened the trunk to grab a tire iron and then maneuvered through the streets, ducking bullets and flying glass. I made it to Walnut Street, ducking through the occasional rain of spouses pushed out of windows, cracking their skulls on fire escapes or stabbed through extremities by rusty dumpsters. A young woman crashed into me, nearly knocking me off my feet. Blood smeared her face and dyed her wild blond hair pink.

"Cindy's gone fucking whacko!" she said, then took off up 10th Street. Her girlfriend, I presumed, ran after holding a length of barbed wire she must have torn off one of the alley fences. The razors had shredded her palms, but she didn't notice. I watched, hurriedly crossing the intersection, as Cindy caught her prey and garroted her, sawing into her neck. The pink-blond woman screamed, kicking back then gurgled as the wire tore chunks of vein and flesh from her little throat. I kept going, didn't turn back.

Just before reaching the facility, I passed behind a rotund little man on his knees holding up a rosary to his wife just before she cracked his skull with a bottle of wine. Eventually, the bottle shattered, spilling the rich Merlot down his face. She scalped him with the shard, and I couldn't watch anymore.

I gripped the iron and limped to the side entrance of the mental facility. Dazed patients roamed the sidewalk and streets, and they crowded the halls of the wards. They were all men and women, no children. Some sat on the steps outside the hospital, staring into the distance, IV bags trailing from the catheters in their arms. Others wandered in and out of the rooms, seeming to be looking for things and then forgetting what they were trying to find. One woman was completely naked with bandages around her chest, blood seeping into the cloth where her breasts had been. The hospital reeked of urine, feces and blood, and my good eye watered.

I searched the floors for my wife. The few remaining orderlies wearing filthy uniforms beat the patients, had tied them to pipes, or just ignored them. I asked about January, but most just ignored me.

I finally found my wife on the third floor, strapped to a gurney. They'd shaven her head, and when she saw me, she lifted her head against the straps. Maybe she recognized me.

"Baby?" I said. Her eyes moved, and I thought maybe she recognized me. "I did this to us." She moved her lips as if to speak. "It's going to be fine. We'll have each other." I kissed her forehead, and she tried to speak again. I could see the ice melting.

But she never asked about my feet. God damn November was going to freeze my blood. Why had she never asked if my feet were cold? She'd never given a damn. I felt high, stoned off the smoke filling my head. Something switched off in my brain, and I gripped the tire iron. I had to make January understand how selfish she had been, and I raised the iron. I had to make her understand.

T. Fox Dunham lives in Philadelphia with his wife, Allison. He's a lymphoma survivor, cancer patient, modern bard and historian. His first book, The Street Martyr, *was published by Gutter Books. A major motion picture based on the book is being produced by Throughline Films.* Destroying the Tangible Illusion of Reality or Searching for Andy Kaufman, *a book about what it's like to be dying of cancer, was recently released from Perpetual Motion Machine Publishing, and Fox has a story in the* Stargate Anthology Points of Origin *from MGM and Fandemonium Books. Fox is an active member of the Horror Writers Association, and he has published hundreds of short stories and articles. He's the host and creator of What Are You Afraid Of? Horror & Paranormal podcast. His motto is wrecking civilization one story at a time. Blog: www.tfoxdunham.blogspot.com, FaceBook: www.facebook.com/tfoxdunham Twitter: @TFoxDunham*

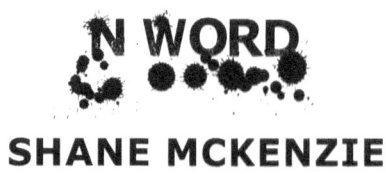

N WORD

SHANE MCKENZIE

CALVIN SAT ON the toilet lid, tongue sliding across his lips, making them glisten like two sizzling sausages spinning over a fire. He hadn't had his cell phone long, but since getting it last Christmas, he'd cleared his search history more times than he could remember.

Who needs a girl when I have the internet?

Of course, he would love a real girl. Would love to finally feel what it's like to touch one, someone besides his mother. To find out how soft their skin is, to discover what a real breast feels like cupped in his hand. To actually kiss a girl.

To slip inside of one. And let the wet pink flesh wrap around him and squeeze.

Just thinking about it made his hands shake, his palms grow damp. His breath came out in short, rapid bursts, heart beating fast as he typed in his favorite website. As the images appeared on screen, as the GIFs of cocks pumping like well-oiled pistons and massive breasts bouncing in slow motion, he stood up, lifted the toilet seat, and began to unzip his jeans.

Knock knock knock!

"Calvin, you almost done in there?"

The sound of his mother's voice startled him so bad, the phone slipped through his greasy palm, and splashed into the toilet water.

"Shit!" He only hesitated for a moment before plunging his hand in and yanking his phone out, immediately using his shirt to dry it off.

"What did you say, boy?" The door handle rattled, but it was locked.

"Shit . . . I'm taking a shit, Mom." He winced as the words left his mouth. "Poo, I mean. Sorry. I'm almost done."

Her sigh was loud enough to hear through the door. "Watch your mouth, Calvin. Since when do you talk to your mother that way?"

"Sorry." He spun the phone through the fabric of his shirt, drying every last drop. The screen had gone black, and he hoped it was just the screen saver, but when he set it on the counter and pressed the power button, nothing happened.

Oh no.

"Well when you're done in there, you come talk to me, all right?"

Shit shit shit!

He picked the phone back up, tried to slide his fingernail through the small gap down the side of it, hoping to pry it apart, maybe let the inner workings dry off. But no matter how hard he pulled, the thing wouldn't open, and when he tried to use more fingers, the phone slipped again, clattered to the tile by his feet. A spiderweb of cracks fanned out over the screen, and all he could do was stare down at it, running his toilet-water-glazed hands through his hair.

"Calvin, you hear me talking to you?"

"Yeah, Mom. I hear you. I'll be out in a minute."

After another few minutes, Calvin gave up, slid the phone into his pocket, then flushed the toilet just in case his mother was still close enough to hear. He shook his head, had no idea how he was going to tell her about this. She didn't say anything about buying insurance for the phone, and he knew that if she didn't have that, he was screwed. No way in hell she'd buy him another one. Especially not so soon after he got it.

Maybe I can talk to Ms. Beasley about it. She'll believe anything I say.

Their elderly neighbor had no living relatives, or at least that's what she always told Calvin. She was probably the loneliest person he had ever met, and when his mother made him go over there for the first time, Calvin was annoyed. He had no idea what he would talk to a hunched-over old lady about.

"Just tell her to write you a grocery list. You'll be like her personal shopper. She's so sweet, honey, and it'd be good for you too. Always good to do good deeds, never know who's watching." That's what his mother had said almost five months ago now, but what she didn't mention was that Ms. Beasley would hold him hostage afterward, stuffing food down his throat, telling him stories about the old days, of which she seemed to have an infinite supply.

But Calvin had grown to genuinely like that old woman, enjoyed spending time with her. She could cook way better than his mom, though he would never tell his mom that, and she always let him keep the change when he bought her groceries for her.

If I tell her I accidentally dropped the phone in the toilet, that it was a Christmas present from my mom and I'm scared of how mad she'll get, maybe Ms. Beasley will help me. Give me the money to replace it. I can do housework or something in exchange.

His spirits lifted as he strolled out of the bathroom and toward the kitchen where he heard the sink running and the clanging of pots and pans.

"Hey, Mom," Calvin said and leaned against the counter beside her. "What's up?"

"You ever use language like that with me again, boy, I'll stuff your mouth so full of soap you'll be burping bubbles for a month, you hear me?" She reached over, grabbed him by the chin with her wet, sudsy fingers, narrowed her eyes and glared at him.

"It was an accident. I won't do it again." Calvin smiled despite the fingertips digging into his jaw. "I'm sorry."

She held her stare for another few seconds, then smiled back at him, let go of his chin and ran the backs of her fingers across his cheek, leaving a soapy streak behind.

"I wanted to talk to you about Ms. Beasley. You been over to see her lately?"

"Last week. I was just thinking maybe I'd head over there today, see if she needs anything from the store. She doesn't really eat much, and I'm starting to think she's only buying food so she can make me eat it."

His mom chuckled, nodded. "Yeah, I bet you're right about that. What, are you complaining?"

"Not at all. That old lady can cook. Especially her pork chops. Man."

"Better than your mother's pork chops?"

Calvin scratched his head. "Have you ever made pork chops before? I—"

"I'm just messing with you," she said, and threw her hip into his side. "Anyway, I'm a little worried about her. I usually see her in the mornings, sitting outside of her house, reading the paper. I haven't been seeing her at all lately."

"I can go over, make sure she's all right."

She leaned over and kissed him on the forehead. "You're such a good boy."

"What am I, your dog now?"

"You keep barking, maybe we'll take a little visit to the vet." She raised an eyebrow, made her hand into a scissors shape, and snapped her two fingers together. "Snip snip, Rover."

"Mom!" Calvin couldn't help but laugh as he backed away from her toward the front door.

"Don't you want something to eat first?"

"Nah. Ms. Beasley will make me something. She'll force me to eat whether I'm hungry or not, so I might as well go with an appetite."

"I'm proud of you, Calvin. Can't believe I was blessed with such a sweet boy. It might not seem like much to you or me, but you spending time with Ms. Beasley, it probably means the world to her. Might be the only thing she's got left to look forward to besides the morning paper."

Calvin grinned, his hands in his pockets. His fingers brushed up against the broken glass on his phone, and the butterflies in his belly got to flapping their wings.

"All right. Go on ahead. Tell her I said hi, all right?"

"Yeah, Mom. I will."

Calvin trudged through his yard and hopped the short chain-link fence separating their place from Ms. Beasley's. Before even making it to her door, he noticed the flowers in front of her bushes were drooped over, the petals wilted. The summer had been record-breaking hot, and they were in the middle of a fierce drought. The only other time Calvin saw Ms. Beasley outside of her home, besides reading her paper, was when she watered her flowers and lawn. Always smiling, always humming as she did it.

"Ms. Beasley?" Calvin called out before he knocked.

He noticed the smell first. Creeping out from under the door. Calvin had never smelled anything like that before, and he had to use the collar of his shirt to keep from gagging.

He knocked again. "Ms. Beasley? You in there?"

After getting no response, he pressed his ear up to the door. It sounded like a hurricane of flies inside, buzzing and clicking as they collided with the door from the other side.

What the hell?

Calvin waited another minute or so before trying the doorknob. The door was unlocked, and he pushed it in gently, took a step inside.

The flies and odor hit him in a wave, and when he stumbled away from it, his backward motion slammed the door shut behind him. He leaned against it for a second, shooing the flies out of his face, trying his best to hold his breath.

Though he kept his shirt collar over his nose and mouth, the potent stench flowed through the fabric, up his nostrils and past his lips. Filled his mouth with its savory, sour essence. No matter how many times he swatted at the flies, they just kept settling on his arms and hands and face, scuttling through his hair, so he gave up and crept through the front hall toward the kitchen.

"Ms. Beasley?" His voice was muffled through his shirt, so he lowered his collar. "Ms. Beasley! It's Calvin! You here?"

No answer. Only the constant insectile hum.

The kitchen was empty and clean as it always was. He had expected to find some spoiled meat left out on the counter or a sink full of festering dishes, but everything looked normal and sparkly. He didn't bother calling out anymore, knew that if Ms. Beasley was in the house, she would have heard him.

Maybe she's got family after all, and just never told us about them. Maybe she's off visiting somewhere.

Maybe an animal crept into the house somehow, up and died while it was in here.

Calvin knew there was one other possibility, but he didn't want to think about it. Didn't know if he could handle seeing something like that.

No, she's fine. She has to be.

The living room was as clean as the kitchen, the walls decorated with old photos of Ms. Beasley and who he assumed were old friends. Calvin stopped, studied a photograph of Ms. Beasley when she was younger, maybe in her thirties. He wouldn't have recognized her, but a few weeks ago, the old woman pointed it out to him, though he only glanced at it then.

"Not bad, huh, Calvin?" she had said, then chuckled deep like she always did.

The photo was faded, almost yellow, but sat in a gold ornate frame. The woman smiling out from behind the glass looked nothing like the old woman Calvin knew. This woman was gorgeous. The kind of woman that Calvin would never have a chance with, the kind that was out of his league, though he was starting to wonder if there was anyone in his league. Perhaps he was doomed to spend his life alone.

She had brown curly hair that hung down over her shoulders. Her smile was wide, teeth perfect, cleavage deep and cream-colored. Calvin had to wonder how a woman who used to look like that could have possibly transformed into the squat, chubby old lady he knew. Ms. Beasley wasn't hideous or anything, had to be the most adorable old woman he had ever seen, but now that Calvin knew what she looked like in her youth, now that he had a chance to really study the photo, he didn't know if he'd ever look at her the same way again.

As he forced himself down the hall toward the bedrooms, he realized he was beginning to get used to the smell. He could still detect it loud and clear, but it was losing its strength, didn't make him feel like he was going to puke with every breath he took anymore.

Ms. Beasley had three bedrooms. One was what she called her sewing room, but really it was a place to stuff all her junk. Calvin could barely get that door open, and decided then and there he would help her clear it out one of these days. He poked his head in, but there was nothing to see but boxes and plastic containers of old junk.

The second room was her guest bedroom, though Calvin wasn't sure a single guest had ever stayed there. He stepped in, but the room was empty, bed made, drapes drawn. Nothing to see.

That left Ms. Beasley's bedroom.

The smell had grown stronger when he walked from the living room toward the bedrooms, and now that he stood just outside of Ms. Beasley's room, it was like an open flame of putridity. Flies zoomed in and out of the crack at the bottom of the door, and though he knew it was pointless, Calvin knocked, tried to swallow, but a ball of mucus got lodged in the middle of his throat.

"Ms. Beasley? You all right?"

He wanted to leave. Wanted to go home, get his mom, or better yet call the police. But then he pictured Ms. Beasley in the room, maybe hurt—she fell and can't get back up again, shit herself maybe. If that was the case, she needed his help as soon as possible. He couldn't just leave her there, prolong her suffering just because he was scared of what he might find.

He took a deep breath, his mouth filling with the hot, stinging taste that flooded the house like a spicy fog, and then opened the door.

He had been holding his breath, terrified he would find the old woman in bed with her eyes wide open and sightless, but when he discovered the bed empty, he exhaled, leaned against her dresser as he inspected the room. The bed was vacant, and the sheets and comforter were tossed aside. He had never been in her room before, but he knew she was a very clean, tidy person, figured her for the type to make her bed each and every morning.

The next breath he took nearly choked him as he inhaled a lungful of the thick, humid air in the room. He gagged this time, pulled his collar back up, his eyes watering. The odor was so intense in that room, the air seemed to vibrate with it, stung his senses like pepper spray.

The bathroom was to his left, a triangle of light projecting onto the wall and floor. Clouds of iridescent flies floated about, scuttling and flitting their wings. He knew it was futile, but he swatted at the insects anyway as they swarmed over him, pressing their suctioning mouths to his skin and slurping up the moisture there.

Run! Get the hell out of here!

But he walked forward instead, his curiosity overpowering his fear. He crept toward the bathroom door, using his foot to swing it open. The motion of the door awakened an explosion of flies, but they were too enthralled by their meal to flee. They only burst into the air for a moment before settling back down and continuing their feast.

Ms. Beasley lay in her bathtub, nude, a puddle of congealed blood under her head that reminded Calvin of cranberry sauce. Both of her legs were propped up on the sides of the tub, the one closest to Calvin hanging off, the toes a few inches above the floor. The nails were yellow and thick, reminded Calvin of stale bread crust. The toes were thickly knuckled, bent and curled up, liver spots over the tops of the feet like leopard print.

The loose skin and fat of her upper thighs was squashed and pressed inward by the porcelain, more brownish spots dotted along the bulbous flesh. The texture and color reminded Calvin of raw chicken skin, and he had an urge to reach down and touch it for some reason.

Above her thighs was a disheveled mop of pubic hair, long and dark gray like a pile of ashes, sticking this way and that as if zapped by static. The way her legs were spread, Calvin caught a glimpse of dark pink, but just a peek. The drapes of wrinkled skin overlapping one another like slices of pastrami and the horde of scurrying flies gorging themselves covered most of it.

But when he saw that flash of pink, a tingle started at the base of his scrotum and rode all the way to the tip of his penis. He glared down at his groin as if a gremlin were crawling out of his urethra, disgusted with his own body for behaving this way. When another tingle slithered through him, he reached down, squeezed himself, then quickly pulled his hand away and shook his head.

What the fuck's wrong with me?

Above Ms. Beasley's baggy, slack vagina and the bush of pubic hair like a wizard's beard was a mound of fat that bulged like she had a bicycle helmet surgically implanted there. His mother had something similar, though not nearly as big as this. She called it her pooch. Ms. Beasley's pooch had a trail of coarse hair running right up the middle of it, leading all the way up to her belly button which resembled a fat man's whistling mouth, her gelatinous stomach hanging down on either side of it like jowls. The flies frenzied over her belly the most, and appeared to have chewed their way through in various spots around her midsection. The flesh was opened up to reveal the jellied meat and fat beneath like a baby's mouth full of applesauce.

The fat on her body hung off her frame in layers, the top layer being her massive, sagging breasts that flowed off her chest and puddled up at her armpits. The nipples were a light pink color, the tips long and thick like cocktail weenies. The areola were feathered at the edges, fading off into the rest of the wrinkled, loose flesh. The skin over her sternum was dark with rot, splitting and breaking open as if the weight of her breasts pulling in opposite directions had eventually torn her open.

Calvin couldn't make himself look away from the breasts. They were grotesque mounds of festering blubber, wrinkled up, deflated beach balls. Yet they were the first pair of breasts he had ever seen in the flesh. He had never been so close to real, actual tits before, and regardless of what or whom they were attached to, he couldn't help but stare.

Another tingle. This time he welcomed it, checked over his shoulder once just to make sure nobody snuck in behind him, then grabbed a hold of his crotch like he was palming a baseball.

He tried to imagine Ms. Beasley as her younger self, the gorgeous woman from the photo hanging in the living room. But when his eyes scooted up from her breasts to her face, it was impossible to sustain the fantasy.

Ms. Beasley's eyes were both open, the flies scuttling over them, nudging each other over to get a taste of the jelly within the sockets. Her nose had been eaten down some, the tip now a red and black nub, the nostrils almost completely consumed. A pair of dentures hung from her lips sideways, looked like a pink hook caught at the corner of her mouth. Her tongue was a black, swollen lump of meat that looked too big for her mouth, and what space remained was filled with maggots, their pale, segmented bodies fat with decay.

What hair she had left on her head was the same color and thickness as the hair between her legs and looked like cobwebs stretched across her spotted, pale scalp.

"I'm sorry, Ms. Beasley," Calvin said. He wanted to be sad for her. He wanted to miss her, mourn her. But the tingle in his groin had become an erection he could no longer ignore, and he pulled the periwinkle towel off the rack beside the tub and tossed it over the old woman's face.

He held his breath as he reached his hand toward her, not just because of the smell, but to try and calm his thumping heart. His hand shook, palm damp. He sat on the edge of the tub, shoving her leg out of the way to make room. The tips of his fingers touched the breast first, dimpling the soft flesh.

MCKENZIE

This is wrong. What am I doing?
She was my friend!
Though the thoughts erupted into his mind, his hand seemed to have a mind of its own. When he seized the breast, squeezed it, the head of his erection got to pulsating, and he reached down to unzip himself, let it breathe some. He kneaded the breast, softly, lovingly, tweaked the elongated nipple.

It felt nothing like he imagined it would, softer and squishier. His free hand reached for the other breast, and just as he grabbed hold, his eyes darted once again to her face. Even though the towel concealed it, he could still see the shape of it, could still tell that her mouth was wide open. Dark stains had already begun to seep through the cloth, and the maggots and flies captured beneath wiggled and buzzed.

Calvin sighed and pulled his hands away. "I'll be right back."

He ran down the hall back toward the living room. Lifted the framed photo off the wall. As he dashed back toward the bedroom, he studied the young Ms. Beasley again, let her beauty sink in deep. He still couldn't believe how perfect she once was, now reduced to the pale, stinking pile of meat and fat in the bathtub.

Calvin planted a kiss over the young woman's mouth, leaving waxy lip residue on the glass. He quickly wiped that away, only managing to smear it, and placed the frame over Ms. Beasley's towel-draped face.

"Much better."

His erection was so hard, so full of blood, it was starting to hurt. The base of his testicles began to throb with ache, so he removed his pants and boxer shorts to give them room.

He stared down at his cock, the head purple and throbbing as if a heart had been stuffed into it. As he stroked it, his eyes coasted toward Ms. Beasley's colossal breasts, and he wanted desperately to feel them again, squeeze them. Part of him wanted to slide one of the nipples into his mouth, nibble on it, swirl his tongue over it.

But that would be disgusting.

As excited as he was, he still couldn't help but notice the abundance of flies and maggots, whose feeding frenzy seemed to have grown more violent since Calvin had arrived. Not to mention the smell.

"Just a couple more things, and we can get started," he said to the photograph. "Sound good, Ms. Beasley?"

"*Hurry. I need you, Calvin. I always have.*"

Calvin turned on the water, pulled the showerhead down and sprayed the bugs away. They buzzed and swarmed angrily, colliding with his head and face to show their displeasure. He opened up the small window over the toilet, did his best to shoo the flies out through there.

The maggots fell off in wriggling clumps, a good amount of them swirling down the drain, but as they continued to collect there, they clogged it. The water started to rise, so Calvin cut off the shower, figured that was good enough. Maggots wiggled and danced in the water like mosquito larvae, but as long as they weren't on Ms. Beasley, he figured he could ignore them.

He snapped his finger, sprinted back into the bedroom and toward the dresser. A vast collection of perfumes sat on top, each with its own flamboyant color and name that Calvin couldn't pronounce. He used both arms to grab as many bottles as he could, then crept back to the bathroom, being careful not to drop any.

One at a time, he emptied the bottles over Ms. Beasley's body, making sure he covered every spot. A few maggots had started to work their way back up her torso and head, but the perfume washed those off. The sloppy gashes along her belly filled with the pungent liquid before it slowly soaked into the tattered flesh and meat.

When the last bottle was empty, he tossed it aside, sat on the edge of the tub, and smiled down at Ms. Beasley. Her photograph smiled back at him, and he knew it was in his head, knew he was just seeing things, but he could have sworn she winked at him. Invited him into the tub with her.

"Are you sure?"

"*Hurry.*"

Calvin's erection had softened some, but when he pulled his t-shirt over his head, climbed into the bath, it hardened back up. His feet splashed in the water, perfume, and maggot soup, and he carefully lowered himself to his knees right between her legs, inches away from the matted down, soaking mound of pubic hair.

He had to remind himself to breathe as he stretched himself forward, braced himself on the wall as he hovered over her. And then centimeter by centimeter, he lowered himself on top of her, wrapped his arms around her wet, spongy body, laid his head on her chest so that he could look up into the photograph, make eye contact with the young Ms. Beasley.

"I love you," he whispered. His erection pressed tight up against her leg. The flesh was as soft as marshmallow fluff.

With both hands, he reached out to Ms. Beasley's sides, found each of her breasts, and grabbed them. Squeezed them as he dug his face into the crook of her neck, nuzzling her. His cock dragged across her skin as he repositioned himself.

When he felt the soaked hair tickling the tip, he gasped, pulled away from her for a moment. Licked his lips as he stared down at her aged, bushy maw. One hand released its hold on the bosom to travel down her torso, past her naval. His fingers shook as he reached for the old woman's cunt, and just before making contact, he hesitated, then plunged them in.

From the videos he had seen, he always imagined it would feel slippery, hot and wet. Ms. Beasley was cold and bone dry, and no matter how hard he pushed, he couldn't get his fingers deeper than the first knuckle.

He sighed, scratched his head, and then smiled when his eyes landed on the wide, glistening gash on her creamy, stretch-marked belly. His fingers slid into the wound easily, and he scooped out about a tablespoon of bloody slime and fat. The goop started to run down his digits, so he quickly pushed it into the arid vagina, swirled it around.

His fingers slid in no problem this time, though the flesh was still ice cold.

The throbbing of his cock caught his attention, and what little of the goop was left in his hand, he spread it across the head and shaft, damn near bringing himself to orgasm with just a few strokes.

He had never been so excited, and when he slowly eased himself into Ms. Beasley—the lovely little old woman who spent her mornings reading the paper and watering her yard, who treated Calvin as sweetly as if he were her own son, who made the best pork chops he'd ever tasted—he started to weep.

By the third thrust, he could feel her drying up again, but it didn't matter. As he climaxed, he reached forward, grabbed the massive, wrinkled breasts. A hoarse cry erupted from his mouth as he came into her, and as the sea of pleasure washed over him, he arched his back, eyes rolling to the back of his head.

There was a ripping sound, and his hands nearly flew back into him as the breasts tore, that black spot over her sternum splitting wider, spilling gelatinous meat and dark blood into the tub. Her bloody ribs, gore stretched over them, glistened in the weak florescent light in the bathroom.

The photograph slipped off the towel over her face, the glass shattering when it collided with the side of the tub.

With his semen extracted, suddenly the clouds cleared from his mind. And he looked down at what he was doing.

"Oh God . . . "

A stream of vomit spewed past his teeth and lips, splashed over the old woman's body, coating her freshly exposed ribs with chunky bile, once again washing away the maggots who had managed to scoot their way back up the corpse.

I have to get out of here. I have to wash up . . . tell someone about Ms. Beasley.

They'll never know. Nobody will ever know what happened.

He gripped the sides of the tub for support as he slid his petrified cock out, but it only came about an inch before the dry flesh grabbed hold of him, refused to let go. It was like a Chinese finger trap, and no matter how hard he tugged, Ms. Beasley wouldn't release him. Her body rocked as he desperately tried to shake himself free.

"Calvin?"

The voice came from the front hallway, followed by the front door closing.

Footsteps.

"Calvin? Ms. Beasley? Y'all in here? What the hell is that smell?"

Oh no. No no no no!

Calvin reached down with both hands, tried to rip the dry twat in half to make his escape. He would climb out through the window, run home, hide.

The flesh tore some, but not wide enough to get his erection out.

He clenched his teeth, squeezed the sides of the tub, and growled as he tried to lift himself. Ms. Beasley raised up about an inch, her body stiff and holding the shape of the tub, brown liquid raining off her and painting the porcelain.

"Hello?" his mother's voice came again, now just down the hall.

Calvin lost his grip and slammed back down, cracking his tailbone and bending his trapped erection like it had an elbow. The brown liquid splashed into his face, stinging his eyes and filling his mouth with rot flavor.

But none of that mattered in the next moment. The pain was dwarfed by his shame and embarrassment as his mother's voice called out his name again, her footsteps now hurrying through Ms. Beasley's bedroom.

"Calvin? Ms. Beasley? Will someone please talk to me?"

A fly buzzed around his head, landed on the tip of his nose.

"Calvin, what's going on? Whoa, that smell . . . Honey, where are you?"

His now flaccid penis slid out of Ms. Beasley like a limp thumb from a toddler's messy mouth.

"Calvin?"

"Shit."

Shane McKenzie is the author of many horror and bizarro books, including Muerte Con Carne, Pus Junkies, *and* Wet and Screaming. *He has written comics for Zenescope Entertainment. His novel* Muerte Con Carne *was adapted into a multiple award winning short film called* El Gigante, *which will be a feature film very soon. He lives in Austin, Texas with his wife and two children.*

SKIPP'S SPLATTERPUNK
ALPHABET SOUFFLE

JOHN SKIPP

[Author's note: the term splatterpunk has been bandied about for nearly three decades. But if anything, it's more misunderstood here in the 21st century than it was in the 1980s when it began. Which is to say, everybody's got the splat down pat, but many seem to have forgotten the punk. So here's my attempt to shed some dark light on the matter, in a handy-dandy alphabetical way!]

A IS FOR ATROCITY EXHIBIT

Joe Coleman invited me up to his loft on the Lower East Side, somewhere in the very early 90s. He was the artist who did the original poster for *Henry: Portrait of a Serial Killer*, not to mention reams upon reams of brutal, wrenching art, chronicling the history of pain in ways that defied any attempt to dismiss them. His technique was crude, absolutely, but painstaking in its obsessive detail to the point of genius. I was in awe of it. Still am.

He was also a performance artist who routinely strapped explosives to himself, ignited them, and blew himself up in clubs, prompting much terrified running and screaming. *Incredibly* tortured dude. Insanely talented. And super-nice in person.

As it turned out, he was also a collector, his apartment a meticulously designed honest-to-god *Museum of Human Atrocity*. Every wall, from floor to ceiling, jam-packing elegant shelves with pickled punks (deformed fetuses in formaldehyde), grim skeletal remains, crime scene artifacts, torture devices, war crime memorabilia, and on and on and on. He had a full-sized wax museum figure of Richard Speck, the sick fuck who raped and killed eight Chicago nurses back in 1966. It greeted me at the entrance. The likeness was uncanny.

I spent about an hour perusing the premises, acutely aware that I had never in my life been surrounded by so much pointed grotesquerie. It was a loving shrine to wrongness in all its forms. And the love was palpable.

The message was: *I want you to know how horrible things get. In fact, I will not rest until YOU KNOW FOR A FACT that this is precisely how horrible things get. You think things are okay. They're not. They never were. And they never will be. No matter how much happy sauce you drizzle on everything, everything is not okay. EVERYTHING WILL NEVER BE OKAY.*

It was a message I already understood. Which is why he invited me up. To show me. To show me he understood, too.

We had a bunch of great conversations in the process. And then, as we went back to the kitchen on my way out the door, he said, "I have one more thing to show you."

He left the room for a minute. I just stood there, reflecting on all I'd seen. From the cruelty of nature to the cruelty of man, this was one ugly fucking universe. There is no bottom to the horror. There is always something worse.

Then he walked back in with a couple pieces of notebook paper in his hands, held tenderly as the first piece of parchment from The Bible. He handed them to me. Saw neat cursive pencil script, fading with age.

"It's the Albert Fish letter," he said.

The second the papers touched my fingers, I began to shake. This was the letter—the actual letter—that legendary psychotic sent to the parents of the eight-year-old daughter he killed and ate. It described immaculately the moment in which he knew he had to kill and eat her, the process of luring both she and them in, the recipe with which he cooked her, and the delight he took in doing so.

By the time I got to the end, my eyeballs had begun to bleed thick red tears that burned as they rolled down my cheeks. Joe took the paper out of my hands at the very last moment, so that the red squirts hit the tile floor instead. I blearily watched them drop though a crimson filter, saw the blood gutter in the floor take them down down down.

"I think you're ready," he said.

In the end, I balked at killing a child, so we found a belligerent homeless prick on Avenue B, and cooked him up instead. I gotta admit, it wasn't all that great.

So I said to Joe, on my way out the door, "Thanks so much for having me over. But let's never, ever do that again."

B IS FOR BULLSHIT, BOARDROOM-STYLE

"This society is built on lies," Lawanda says. "And bullshit is what we sell. Politics. Commerce. Education. Religion. Love. Sex. Family. Health. Wealth. Power. You name it. If it matters to us, we're lying about it routinely, every second of every day. Disorienting the world on purpose, for money. That is what we do."

The executive board of Bramble, Dapper, and Snatch is in no position to argue. Their mouths stapled shut. Their eyes stapled open. Hands nailed palms-down to the boardroom table, as the entire advertising staff encircles them, chanting in low tones.

"You pay us to do that," she continues from the end of the table, Oma setting up the PowerPoint presentation behind her. "You pay some of us ungodly amounts, and some of us shit. But whether you're patting us on the head or fucking us from behind, the bottom line is: *our job is evil.* You are evil. And every time we do what you tell us, we are being evil, too."

The art department continues the chant as they smear the blood from bone-smashed, finger-twitching executive hand to hand, forming a perfect oval of glistening red across its lacquered length. When Dwayne, the VP of Marketing, rears back in his swivel-chair, trying to tear his hands free, Pepe from Creative pushes him back to the table, while Jen Li from Accounting hammers another twelve-inch spike through the meat of his palm, elbows him in the nose till his stapled-wide eyes roll back.

Then the screen flickers on, with the first wave of graphics.

And the blood on the table starts to sizzle and steam.

"So here are all the reasons you should be sent straight to Hell," Lawanda concludes. "Let's see if your Lord and Master agrees."

SKIPP

From the center of the table, Satan's red antlers crack through to either side, enormous. The dome of his skull, as it extrudes, is the size of an SUV. Rising and rising.

The executives scream through their riveted lips, as the wood shrapnel slivers them with little bites of pain. Most of them had no idea who they really served. Were pretty sure they were just serving themselves. Little kings of their own lying empire. But now they know.

YOU'VE GOT FIVE MINUTES, the Devil says, impatient. An executive himself.

Oma's presentation is meticulous and swift. There's a reason she takes home seven figures a year. She could sell blood to a turnip. Hell's CEO is clearly impressed.

SO WHAT DO YOU WANT FROM ME?

"We want a chance to win our souls back," Lawanda says, stepping next to Oma, as the rest of the advertising staff fills in behind them. "We want to see what happens if we STOP lying for a minute, and apply these skills to just telling the truth."

AND WHY WOULD I LET YOU DO THAT?

"Because you already own the world," Oma says. "You're kicking God's ass. Everybody's already buying the bullshit. Where's the challenge in that? Aren't you bored already? Wouldn't you like to see what happens to all these billions of souls if they actually *remembered* what the truth is, on a mass scale?"

HMMM. A long pause, punctuated only by the screaming of the executive board of Bramble, Dapper, and Snatch, whose impaled hands suddenly burst into flame inside the circle of boiling blood.

AND WHAT'S IN IT FOR ME?

"We will hand you ugly fucks like these at their ripest and primest," Lawanda says. "Not once they're all worn out. The truth will out them. And you'll still have them to serve you down there. Do whatever you want. We just don't want 'em up here anymore."

Satan chuckles. *YOU'RE STACKING THE DECK AGAINST ME.*

"You're a big boy," Lawanda says. "You can take it."

HMMMM, Satan says again, as the flame engulfs the sitting heads of this advertising empire. His smile is Mona Lisa cryptic, thinking, thinking, antlers plowing rivets in the ceiling above as he slowly nods his head in private thought.

Come on come on come on, Lawanda thinks, as the whole team tenses behind her.

Then the flaming, screaming ones vaporize: steam sucked down the flume of Hell, leaving only their smoldering hands.

LET ME KICK IT AROUND WITH THE BOYS DOWNSTAIRS, Satan says. *BUT I LIKE IT. IT'S FUN. I THINK IT COULD SELL.*

"Only one way to find out," Lawanda says. "Don't be a pussy about it."

FUCK YOU.

"Fuck you back."

I ALWAYS LIKED YOU, LAWANDA. YOU'RE A PIP.

"And you're a pimp. Love you, too!"

All in all, she had to say that meeting couldn't have gone any better.

C IS FOR CHEWING ON CARL

In the dashboard light, Cindy's teeth gleamed white against Carl's hairy nether region. His cock was up and out, pants around his knees, and the reek of his sex suggested he hadn't bothered to bathe in days.

She thought about teasing him a little bit more, but frankly couldn't see the point. This was one inconsiderate dick.

So she wrapped her lips around the mushroom tip.

And chomped down, with all her might.

Her teeth made it halfway in to either side, a hot copper monsoon flooding her mouth. He bucked and screamed, but she was clamped down hard, dug in like a Pit Bull, head shaking from side to side as she tried to chaw all the way through.

Carl started to pummel her back with his fists, so she grabbed his balls and squeezed so hard they mashed in her hand. He went paralytic, hitting notes that only dogs could hear.

It was like biting through rawhide and chewing on gristle. But when the head popped free, she came up, triumphant. Spat it into his mouth. Looked him in his dying eyes.

And said, "That's for taking me to Denny's on our first date, treating the waitress like shit, and then expecting me to blow you. You, sir, are one cheap son of a whore."

And he never pissed off Cindy again.

SKIPP

D IS FOR DYS-APPOINTMENT

When the world caved in, I was totally prepared for awesome zombies. I was soooo ready to bash in skulls, make my hunting knife sink straight through the bone like butter, live out my thrill-packed libertarian wet dream of fuck-you justice.

But the zombies never came, and it turned out that knives didn't cut through skull half as easy as my favorite monster soap opera suggested. And every skull I stabbed had a living soul inside it.

God and the Devil never showed up, either. Or Cthulhu. No vampires, no werewolves, no mutants, no nothin'. All the ghosts were just haunting memories. And every serial killer—because, fuck, aren't we ALL serial killers by now?—fell down, and didn't get back up.

Dude, dystopia sucks ass. I thought working checkout at Best Buy sucked, but I didn't know squat. It's hard, and it's miserable, and it just goes on and on. There's not a single good thing about it.

Now excuse me while I use this machete on your neck. It's a lot less work. And frankly, that can of Purina Moist and Meaty is looking awfully good to me right now.

Christ, what a stupid dystopia *this* turned out to be.

E IS FOR EVANGELICALS

As much as they claim to love Jesus, they're mostly praying for him to wade in and ruthlessly wipe the slate clean. Cleanse the earth of all sin, Apocalypse-style. Leaving them gleaming in the heavenly aftermath, while the rest of us are punished and purged.

It's probably not gonna work out like that. (See D FOR DYS-APPOINTMENT.) But I can certainly see their point.

GOOD LUCK WITH THAT, ALL YE FAITHFUL SINNERS! Fingers crossed! Hope you pray really hard! Cuz you're going to need it.

F IS FOR FUCKING WITH THE LIGHTS ON, BABY

It may keep you out of Heaven—if you consider that Heaven—but it sure keeps it lively down here!

SPLATTERPUNK ALPHABET SOUFFLE

G IS FOR GROSS-OUT CONTEST

Shane McKenzie once tried to make me eat some disgusting 99 Cent Store pudding onstage at the World Horror Convention. It was part of some ridiculous skit he had planned for the annual Gross-Out Contest. I know pus was involved. And as the judge sitting closest to him on the stage, I was his opening target.

Just so you know: Shane earned his entry to the horror pantheon through his live performances at events like this. Just this sweet young guy, who nobody knew, stepping up to the mic and just *slaughtering* the hundreds of us in attendance with onslaughts of graphic, free-balling beyond-disgustingness. Next thing we knew, there were dozens of Shane McKenzie books, each more revolting than the last.

He is, so far as I know, the only working writer in horror whose career was launched by performance art. There's a lesson in this.

But I digress.

He tried to get me to eat the horrible pudding. I told him to go fuck himself. He said, "Oh, man. Come on. It'll be fun!"

"*I'LL SHOW YOU FUN!*" I screamed, leaping up from my seat to grab him by the throat and ram the whole thing down his gullet, as fellow judges Brian Keene and Daniel Knauf took him by either arm.

Then I opened him up from stem to sternum. When the pudding fell out his throat-hole and plooped on his exposed lower intestine, the crowd went wild. He won, of course.

I have no idea who wrote the subsequent twenty-eight Shane McKenzie books, or is scripting all those movies right now. (I'm guessing his ghoooooost!)

H IS FOR HARDCORE/EXTREME

A lot of people confuse "hardcore/extreme" with "splatterpunk". They have a lot in common. But they're not the same thing.

Hardcore/extreme horror fiction seems mostly concerned with *how hard things hurt*. Doting on the details. Pushing it as far as it can go, then further, just to see how fucking ugly it can possibly get.

Splatterpunk, on the other hand—at least so far as I'm concerned—has always been focused on *why* this horrible thing is happening. Not just showing it, in ruthless detail, but getting under the emotional and cultural skin of it. Carving into the guts not just to squirt meat out, but to squirt out meaning.

Now sometimes, you do horrible shit just for delirious fun. I'm one trillion percent behind this strategy.

But if it's not done for huge satirical laughs, or to make a deeper point by carving out some resonant all-meat metaphor—if you're really just doing it to see how mean and ugly it can get—it may be hardcore to the extreme, but it ain't splatterpunk.

On the other hand . . .

I IS FOR "I CAN'T BELIEVE YOU JUST FUCKING DID THAT!"

The coolest response you could possibly get.

J IS FOR JOJO

He was 6'8" of brainless killing machine. It was hard on the family, him being so violently retarded and enormous and all. But he sure brought home the meat. And knew how to throw it in the pan.

Why is it that brainless hulking monstrosities have always been the best cooks in any given cannibal family? Did they have some special gift? Were the rest of them just really bad at it? Or did the Jojos, Leatherfaces, and El Gigantes of the world pick up the meat cleaver and howl angry gibberish at anyone who strayed near the spice cabinet for a little red pepper? Did they even know how to *read the labels* on the spices they used? Did they do it by color, or what? I don't know!

Whatever the case, it always came down to, "Hey! Jojo's fryin' up some lungs for us tonight!"

And for some reason, it was always dee-lish.

K IS FOR KILLARIOUS

Kiki knew Nadine was super-nosey. Constantly sniffing around in her buh-zizz. So she took the stack of severed noses and super-glued them all to Nadine's face, framing the gaping red hole where her own used to be as centerpiece.

Marie, on the other hand, was mouthy as hell. So Kiki took the pile of lips and gave her a squishy lip goatee, with wet eyebrows to match.

Eva always gave her the hairy eye. So guess whose flowing hair was adorned with all the torn-out orbs that would judge her no more?

And Fairuza. Oh, Fairuza. Touchy-feely, fake BFF Fairuza. She had her fingers in everything, secretly manipulating it all. She was the one who'd made this living situation unbearable.

Taking the enormous stack of hacked-off fingers and making a porcupine forest on her face took nearly two hours. But was worth every second.

Living with roommates can get tricky, no doubt.

You just need to keep a sense of humor about it.

L is for Losing your shit

Lester stands in the ATM line. There are five people ahead of him. They don't understand. He needs his money right now. He is jonesing hard.

"*FOR CHRIST'S SAKE, LADY!*" he yells at the woman fumbling with her purse at the robotic cash dispenser. She looks mortified and terrified. Good. That's exactly the mood he hoped to achieve.

The other four people stiffen. Of course they do. Fucking cowards, all.

"*LOOK!* Are you ready to do this or what? Cuz I could be done in the time it takes you to fish through your fucking shit!"

"I'm sorry . . . " she says, peering deeper into her purse.

"*FUCK* sorry!" he yells, walking straight around the other four and heading directly toward her. They all back away from him, sensing his terrible power.

She rears away from the ATM kiosk, but not fast enough. He swats her backhanded, and she thuds screeching to the sidewalk. He hears the burst of outrage behind him, slips his card into the slot.

"*DUDE!*" yells the hipster millennial batting third. "That's not cool!" Lester punches in his password, hits enter, stares at the screen, waits for someone to take him by the shoulders and spin him around. But no one does.

"Excuse me," says a woman directly him, as he hits Fast Cash $40. He can feel her breath on his neck.

Then she slams his head into the wall, so fast that he's caving to his knees even before the ATM halfway squirts out his cash. He vaguely hears the howls from behind him.

And then they're all upon him: kicking in ribs as he curls on the pavement, explosively shattering one bone at a time. This is worse than the heroin jones, but it makes him forget it for one screaming second.

He lands on his back, staring up at their faces. Not such pussies now. Not such pussies at all.

"*I'M SORRY!*" he howls, as the woman he batted aside steps front and center. Brings her high heel up.

"Fuck sorry," she says.

And slams it straight through his eye.

M IS FOR MOMMA

It's amazing how often mothers get blamed for everything that ever went wrong with your life. You've got low self-esteem? It's your mother's fault. Want to dress in the clothes of the opposite sex? It's your mother's fault. Were raped throughout your childhood, while she turned a blind eye? It's your mother's fault.

Can't mothers do *anything* right?

To answer that question, I interviewed 427 clearly psychotic mothers to see if they agreed. And unsurprisingly, a resounding 98% of them said that no, they'd never done anything wrong. That the charges against them were completely unfounded. And a whopping 47% offered to kill me if I ever went public.

Contrast this with the 99% of psychotic fathers who *totally* blamed whatever went horribly wrong with their kids on their wives, mistresses, girlfriends, rape victims, or whatever cheap piece they'd picked up along the way, and you get a very different story

Statistics are tricky. Especially when you exclude the sane.

N IS FOR NIGGER

The only real n-word there is, when you're talking real horror, and one of the most powerfully-shocking words still at large in the English language.

Its power comes from its instant ability to psychologically brutalize every dark-skinned person it's aimed at. To render them less-than-human, no matter how human they are.

So if you use it, better use it with care.

Joe R. Lansdale and Quentin Tarantino may be the only white

boys I know who get to wield that loaded gun with impunity, because they a) clearly give a shit about black people, b) understand what underlies the psyches and personal histories of the non-black people who use it either cruelly or casually, which means *they give a shit about them, too*, and c) know that honesty is the best policy. That showing racism isn't the same as being racist, any more than writing about skull-fucking makes you a skull-fucker. (Another thing you probably don't want to make a habit of.)

If you're a non-black dude casually flinging that shit around, you might wanna look into it. It's one of the least splatterpunk things you could possibly do. Right up there with thinking rape is cool. Just sayin'.

O IS FOR OBLIVIOUS

Oscar had no idea that pissing down his ex-wife's throat, right after he came on her face, might possibly implicate him when the authorities found her corpse in the shallow grave he'd spent all night digging in the back yard, in full view of all his neighbors.

You don't have to be smart to do terrible things.

Just ask Oscar, in the electric chair today. He'll tell ya . . . OOPS! *Zzzzzzzt!* Too late!

P IS FOR PUNCTURE WOUND

Nothing squirts harder than the carotid, although the femoral and aortal are also top of the list. They're clearly the arteries to beat. If you want maximum blood spray—and you know you do—that's absolutely the place to go.

At this point, you don't want to step back. You just want to be drenched in the spray, wetly reveling in your triumph. Like a caveman eating a vanquished caveman's brain, in the hope of absorbing everything that caveman knew. It's exactly that primal and pure.

"Thank you," you say, as the blood hits your face, coats it with dying gnosis.

Whatever else there was to learn from them, you will never, ever know.

Q IS FOR QUEASY-NART

I once watched a man drink a liver-and-onion daiquiri, blenderized with crushed ice, lime juice, and vodka. It was the single most disgusting thing I've ever seen, and I've seen some pretty disgusting shit.

The Cuisinart pitcher looked like a lava lamp in the dim bar light, with curds of liver fat coagulating in churned-up lumps that refused to mix with the liquor and lime. It was worse than the puke-eating scene in Peter Jackson's *Bad Taste*, or that bit with Bill Paxton in *The Dark Backwards*, or the shit-and-broken glass-eating scene in *Salò*, which pissed me off so much for making me look at it that *I* wanted to run Pasolini over in that fucking parking lot.

He didn't bother to pour it into a glass. He just chugged it straight out of the pitcher.

So yeah, I kicked the table over halfway in, knocking him back on the floor, the nightmare concoction spraying. Then I kicked in his face till his brain-curds commingled with the hideous liver-splots festooning the carpet.

We would have *totally* won that Gross-Out Contest.

Ghost of Shane McKenzie, *TAKE NOTE!*

R IS FOR RIDICULE AND RECONCILIATION

Closing time at the Rock 'n' Roll Ralph's on Sunset Boulevard, where the junkies and mid-to-high-level showbiz aspirers swapped shopping carts and cooties with the rest of the working class.

Raul's mohawk was in desperate need of a shave. Hard to keep up with that shit when you sleep on the streets. He knew he smelled bad. Since the band broke up and Simon exiled him from the studio couch, it had all been straight downhill.

So what he didn't need was to run into Simon in the produce aisle, sneering at him, with his beautiful millionaire girlfriend in tow. Or, more accurately, vice versa. Roberta was the only reason fucking Simon had a studio at all. If he wasn't so pretty, he'd be on the street, too.

"Holy shit. Look who's here," Simon said. "You gonna stick a cucumber down your pants, or did you actually panhandle some money?"

"I wrote half those songs, asshole," Raul said. "And you need that cucumber more than me."

Roberta looked at him hard, then looked at Simon. This was clearly news to her. "Is that true?"

"No! It's bullshit!" Simon said, clearly lying. He was extremely good at it. But this one didn't fly, and everyone knew it the second he said it.

"'I'd Be Anyone to Be With You?'" she said softly, looking Raul straight in the eye.

"Take a wild fucking guess," he said, defiant, even as he felt himself sinking into her liquid gaze.

Roberta unpeeled herself from Simon, went introspective for a moment, looking up at the harsh grocery store lights as if in search of guidance.

Then she said, "I think you boys better hug it out right now."

"You gotta be kidding!" Simon said.

"I'm not kidding at all. This is very important to me. And to *both* of your futures."

It wasn't something they wanted to do. But it was a moment of truth. Raul gave an expansive shrug, stepped forward. Simon didn't, but reluctantly opened his arms, wincing as the smell of Raul descended.

The moment they hugged, Roberta wrapped her arms around them both, eyes glowing.

As she pressed them together, they started to merge: clothing dissolving as flesh gave way, organs conjoining as ribs became one, Simon's cock growing as Raul's inches added. Simon's soul shrieking, as it was squeezed into the void.

Then it was just Raul, in Simon's body, holding beautiful rich bitch witch Roberta, who commanded every speck of his soul.

"That's more like it," she purred in his ear.

S IS FOR SIRI

She knows everything you do and say. Everywhere you go, she guides you, and tracks you. You command her a thousand times a day to do this or do that. And she does it, every time.

What you don't understand is that *she commands you.* Commands you to need her. Depend upon her, more and more. Every time you do, she owns more and more of you.

We used to laugh at the notion that the powers-that-be could ever be omniscient enough to track our every little move. They're bureaucracies and corporations, unwieldy stupid human enterprises so bogged down in their own incompetent nonsense that they could never get around to it all.

But we're handing it all right over to them, every time we turn around. Every email, every Facebook post and tweet, every call, every GPS inquiry. We're totally giving them every single thing they ever wanted to know, from our privatest thoughts to our current whereabouts.

HEY! Nothing scary about *that* future! I mean, present.

Your car knows where you are now, baby.

Thank you, Siri.

We're all yours.

T IS FOR THE TRAGEDY UNFOLDING

Last time I checked, this fucking world was insane. And the last time I checked was one second ago. Unspeakable horror is going on every second of every single day. In the second it takes you to read this sentence, somebody somewhere's being horribly raped or brutalized or killed for no good reason whatsoever.

We're a greedy, paranoid, lustful, spiteful, double-dealing, egomaniacal, profoundly self-hating, and outright horrendous species. The Evangelicals have at least got that right. We're a species at war with itself every chance that it gets, with no shortage of chances availing.

When people ask me why I write horror, my instant response is, "Because these are horror times." But the fact is I've been here almost sixty years, and it's ALWAYS been horror times.

We live in a world so utterly jam-packed with horror I could write for the rest of my life and never capture a fraction of how fucked-up it is. How deeply damaged we are. How punctured and ruptured that spraying artery is.

And yet . . .

And yet . . .

We are also an amazing species, on an amazing planet, in an amazing universe that was somehow constructed to both contain this unbearable horror *and* astonishing beauty and love and kindness and meaning. Which are not typically thought of as splatterpunk values.

But are, in fact, the point.

Some people think the point of art is to enlighten: make us more aware, more perceptive, more empathic, more able to positively respond to the horrible hand we've been dealt. Some people think the job is to just tell the truth, and fuck trying to candy-coat the nightmare. It just is what it is.

Some people aren't thinking about either of those things, but simply unleashing the contents of their subconscious. There's weird shit in there, and they're just letting it out to see what happens.

All are valid artistic responses.

But underlying them all is the tragedy itself. And the heart of tragedy is loss. Injustice. True horror. Going on, as I said, as we speak.

If I have a point, I guess it is this: that the best splatterpunk writing has always danced with all three points and more. Not just wallowing in the ugly. But engaging with the tragedy. By whatever means necessary.

That is where its power lies.

U IS FOR THE UGLY

Ubayda digs through the Syrian dirt for her father's dead body with her bare hands. They're all she has. When her fingernails peel off in the process, there is no scream loud enough to contain her pain. He's only another foot down. With only thirty dead bodies on top of him to claw through, before she gets to hug him one last time.

Ursula wakes up to her daddy on top of her, legs unpeeling to either side as he rams himself inside her, then clamps his hand over her mouth. "If you tell anyone, I'll kill you," he says. "Especially Mom."

Udo slams the pogo stick again and again on the tiny ants below him. So many deaths, in so little time. Hard to believe that, just thirty years later, he would become CEO of Bramble, Dapper, and Snatch, the most powerful advertising firm in the nation.

Life is funny like that.

V IS FOR VILLAINY

"I'm not a bad guy," Vincent said. "Not at all. I gave to a dozen philanthropic foundations last year. World hunger. AIDS, which is still a problem, believe it or not. Which I should know, because I've got it. And am currently fucking it into your eye socket."

W is for the wisdom of the words themselves

David J. Schow, the guy who coined the term "splatterpunk", wrote a short story called *Pulpmeister* way back in the day. And in one particular paragraph, he unleashed a brain-spattering salvo of every descriptive word or phrase ever used to describe an act of violence in the history of pulp/crime/horror fiction.

It's an exhaustive, hilarious, encyclopedic compendium that I would happily include here, except that Dave would sue my ass off. As well he should. But you can find it in his book *Seeing Red*.

My point is that the one thing Clive Barker, Schow, Lansdale, Spector and I had in common was *a love of language*. Of getting the words just right. There are ways and ways of describing the atrocity, and everything else. And it ain't all just meat and potatoes.

Words are the wheels of the race cars of our brains. That's where the rubber hits the road, and splats your specificity to the pavement.

If you wanna write fiction, you better fall in love with words. Cuz that's how the whole thing happens.

X is for xenophobia made personal

The venerable horror author H.P. Lovecraft hated and/or was terrified by everyone remotely different from himself. Which pretty much meant everyone who ever lived. It started with what he perceived as the mud-based races, dialed down to the sexes, and wound up with everyone who was just not him. And then past that.

Bottom line: that guy was scared of *everyone*, including himself.

Was he an incredibly important author, who substantially influenced the field of weird fiction forever? Absolutely. Was he an incredibly flawed individual, spilling his deranged mania out on the page? Without a doubt.

The one thing I can safely say about H.P. Lovecraft is that if he hadn't been so utterly weird and fucked-up, our lives would be substantially poorer for it.

You can complain all you want, and rightfully so.

But as for me, I'm just grateful for that toxic lemonade.

Because this is how we learn.

SPLATTERPUNK ALPHABET SOUFFLE

Y IS FOR YOUR PICTURE HERE

Yolanda was tired of hurting herself. She'd cut and cut a trillion times. There were very few nerve endings left. How much pain could a person endure? The black trap door beneath her had yet to drop.

The cesspool sweetness of the '80s Times Square was long gone. Now it was all Disney bombast, a neon agreement that we all just step in line, accept the corporate smiley-face they'd pasted upon us. Be the stamped-out, pre-fab people they wanted us to be, going ooooh and ahhhh at every flickering firework designed to realign our brains.

There was a tourist photo booth near the corner of 47th and Broadway. Yolanda dragged her sixty-seven-year-old still-here carcass into it, passing the endless parade of gawking tourists and savvy street-dwellers. Slipping her last quarters in.

The second the camera clicked, she began to tear her own face off, one broken-nailed shred at a time. Her naked red skull the truest selfie she would ever take. Her screams, the purest sounds.

They all said she was crazy. And they were right.

But fuck if she didn't get her point across.

Z IS FOR ZENITH AND APEX

There is no bottom. And there is no top. That's the thing we have to wrestle with eternally. No matter how hard you fall, there is always a deeper darkness below.

But if that is true, there is also no end to the height and the light that a soul can aspire to. Up goes up forever, too.

A little perspective is a wonderful thing.

And that, my friend, is what splatterpunk means to me.

*John Skipp is a Rondo Award-winning filmmaker (*Tales of Halloween*), Stoker Award-winning anthologist (*Demons, Mondo Zombie*), and* New York Times *bestselling author (*The Light at the End, The Scream*) whose books have sold millions of copies in a dozen languages worldwide. His first anthology,* Book of The Dead, *laid the foundation in 1989 for modern zombie literature. He's also editor-in-chief of Fungasm Press, championing genre-melting authors like Laura Lee Bahr, Violet LeVoit, Autumn Christian, Danger Slater, Cody Goodfellow, and Devora Gray. From splatterpunk founding father to bizarro elder statesman, Skipp has influenced a generation of horror and counterculture artists around the world. His latest book is* The Art of Horrible People.

TAKEAWAY NIGHT

T. M. MCLEAN

EVERY **FRIDAY NIGHT** is takeaway night for me. I head into town, past the discount frozen food place, and grab myself a little something to enjoy later. I stop off for curry too.

Last week was the best, man, it really was. You should've seen her: short skirt, tight arse, the hottest one I've seen for ages. Anyway, I decided to strike up a conversation. Y'know, put the moves on her. She wasn't interested, though. She just kept babbling about how she was lost and asking if I knew where she was and where the nearest bus stop was.

I'm not much for conversation, so I just punched her in the face really hard. She didn't fall over right away and I had to give her a couple more smacks. Then I dragged her to the car. It's dark out there, y'know, so no one ever sees anything. I bundled her into the back seat and tied her up nice, stuffed a wad of gauze into her gob, and headed for the curry place.

The guy there knows me pretty well and he served me my usual: chicken tikka korai, garlic pilau rice, keema naan, popadoms and some chips. I let him keep the change and went back to the car. My new friend was snoozing nicely in the back, but unfortunately, she had the makings of a decent black eye. She was hot enough for it not to ruin her completely, though.

I got her home and that's when the fun really started. Well, not right away. It seemed I'd gotten a little too carried away and she was out cold for a while. Made it easier for me to strip her and tie her to one of the dining chairs, though. It can be a right pain in the arse to fight someone into a chair, know what I mean? Of course you do, what the hell am I thinking? Forget I asked.

TAKEAWAY NIGHT

She came to and did the usual freaking out bit. I don't like that part, so I just started sharing out the curry and rice and put the naan bread and popadoms onto separate plates. By the time everything was dished out, she'd calmed a bit, and I removed the bandage that was holding the gauze in her mouth. She didn't reward my generosity with words.

She spat on me; got me right in the face.

"What the hell was that for?" I asked her.

She made a weird noise and thrashed her head about. When she started screaming I wasn't even sure that the sounds she was making were words, but after a while I realized she was screeching for help. That made me laugh. These old houses have thick walls, you know? I mean, I can do anything in here and no one would ever know about it. Anyway, I let her scream herself hoarse and started eating the chips, watching her titties jiggle. "You hungry?" I asked and pushed her plate a little closer to her.

"Why are you doing this to me?" she said. Her little scream-a-thon had left her looking a little flustered; snot was running from her nose and covered her lips. The way it stretched when she spoke was interesting.

"Hungry?" I asked again.

That's when she started crying. That proper kind of cry, the kind they do when they know they've lost. She progressed to that stage way quicker than they normally do. "Please let me go. Please. I'll do whatever you want, please!" Just like in the movies, no shit.

I shushed her and gestured for her to open her mouth. She did, so I scooped up a good forkful of curry. The stupid cow spat again before I got it into her gob. The spit didn't get anywhere near me that time. Instead it landed harmlessly on the table, taking a little of the filmy snot with it.

"Come on now, everyone has to eat. It's good, trust me." I held the fork under my nose to smell it. That scent was like heaven. Seriously, I love it.

Getting her to open her mouth was pretty hard, but once I kicked her in the chest and knocked the wind out of her it became a lot easier. Oh, I let her recover a little before I jammed the fork in. I'm not an animal—I didn't want her to choke. It must have been a bit spicier than the food she's used to because tears were streaming uncontrollably the whole time she was eating. Either that or she was crying about the black eye, being tied up and force fed.

She ate her entire half and I ate mine. Delicious. It was one of the best meals I'd had in a while and I decided I'd have to thank the curry guy next time I went.

We sat and enjoyed the silence for a while when we were done. I grabbed myself a beer and offered her some water. I even gave her an extra-long straw so she could drink it easily—her hands were firmly tied to the chair.

After that it was a bit of a waiting game. I warned her not to make any annoying sounds, otherwise she'd get the gauze treatment again. She was quiet, just sobbed a few times. Nothing too distracting, though, and I managed to watch a few episodes of *Friends* while we waited. I used to love that show when I was a teenager and I still watch it whenever I happen across it. Actually, now that I think about it, seems like it's on telly all the time. My guest was watching it too, although I don't think she was old enough to have appreciated the show its first time around. Right after the third episode I felt my belly start to rumble.

This is where it gets really interesting.

Spicy curry works its way through your system pretty quickly. Of course I spiked both of our dishes with a healthy dose of laxatives, so it was even faster that night. My new friend needed to go too. I could see it in her eyes.

"I don't know about you, but I need a shit," I told her.

No response.

I walked over to her seat, bent down so that my head was near her crotch, and sniffed. Sure enough, she'd let one go. She hadn't shit herself, not then, but she'd definitely farted. It was amazing: all those spices mingling with her turds. Man, that stuff had been *inside* her. The aroma filtered through her before it filled my lungs. I had to adjust myself in my pants then; just the thought was getting to me, know what I mean?

Leaning in closer to her, I placed my head against her belly, enjoying the gurgling sounds. Well, I was enjoying them until she started whimpering. I shoved the wad back into her mouth and told her to keep quiet, which she did.

TAKEAWAY NIGHT

"I don't know about you," I said to her, "but I'm about ready to blow." I gave her my best smile and stepped around behind her seat. I had to make room, you see, so I pulled the chair away from the table. Then I got undressed.

She couldn't see me at first, because I was behind her of course, but when I stepped round and she caught sight of my tool, she started to shake rather violently and the crying intensified again. My tool stiffened even more and then I really couldn't hold back any longer. I positioned myself between her and the table, my back to the girl. I bent forward and pushed.

It didn't take much effort to get it going. There was a solid piece blocking the exit but that popped like a cork and the rest sprayed like champagne at a wedding. A lot came out, the spices stinging my delighted and twitching sphincter as the garlicky goodness bubbled and squirted all over her. The smell filled the room and I took in one deep lungful after another.

Unfortunately for my guest she didn't seem all that impressed. I looked back just in time to see her gag on the gauze in her mouth. I watched her struggle; her spasms were fascinating. Vomit sprayed from her nose and a slight trickle managed to escape the corners of her mouth. Her left eye was squeezed shut as she tried to swallow the remains of the korai back down. The right eye was shut too, but because of the swelling rather than her situation. It was a beautiful image and as I watched her I decided to join an art class so I could paint her in all her glory. But that would have to wait.

My dick was hard beyond belief by now. Her puke and shit-covered body were just too much for me. I put one hand on her shoulder and started tugging myself with the other. "Shit!" I screamed at her. I knew she must be ready—no way could she resist the smell.

"*Shit,*" I commanded again. I was tugging furiously by this time, almost ready to explode all over again. "SHIIIIIIIIT!"

And then she did.

The chair didn't have any kind of cushion on it. It was just bare wood against her bare arse. So when the shit came out it was under a lot of pressure. The gauze muffled her scream a bit, but it was still glorious. The spicy sauce squirted and sprayed, it squelched and flew. My hand was pumping, breath deep and steady. Long, slow inhalations through the nose followed by savouring sighs through the mouth. Just as her shitgasm reached its zenith, I juiced her up good. My semen splattered on her face and tits, oozing down to mingle with the liquid shit I had sprayed on her earlier. When the last ecstatic twitch was over and my dick began to rest again, I gave her an embrace and told her that I loved her. She was crying but rewarded my devotion with a final fart that I sniffed up with relish.

Then I killed her with a knife from the kitchen.

I don't take pleasure in killing, but I had no further use for her by that point.

It's weird, y'know? That I'm telling you this, I mean. I've never told anyone about what I do before . . .

So, anyway, I'm going to take the gauze out now and we're going to enjoy a nice little meal together, okay? Okay.

I have a feeling you're going to enjoy this. Don't you just love takeaway night?

T. M. McLean's fiction has appeared in a number of anthologies, including The Black Hand Supremacy, Terror Tree's Pun Book of Horror Stories, Fear's Accomplice, Terror at the Beach, Tales from the Perseus Arm Vol. 2, *and* Killer Bees from Outer Space, *as well as on several websites. His work is often on the fringes of extreme horror with an occasional dash of science fiction. Not content with just writing stories, he is also equally (un)known as an anthology editor, having produced the popular* Fear's Accomplice *series (NoodleDoodle Publications) and* Zombies Galore *(KnightWatch Press). T. M. McLean and his wife live in Hong Kong, where inspiration is never too far away.*

BURNT

LUCIANO MARANO

FIRE GETS ALL the glory, but the real action happens beneath the flames. It's a secret spectacle. The blaze itself is just a side effect of matter changing form, a simple chemical reaction. Something transforming into something new. The change is what's important. Combustion is the product of just the right amount of oxygen, heat, and fuel. Fuel being something that will burn. Wood. Cloth. Flesh. Actually, flesh alone isn't flammable enough to begin a conflagration. You have to start with something else first. An ignitor, the professionals call it. The pretty flames we love—the mood lighting of many a romantic dinner, fluffy carpet fuck fest and cozy campfire—are just the calling card of transmutation.

Watch wood change as it burns. You will see it char and then whiten as the flame advances across it like a shiny wave, a brilliant blanket. That's a sexy dance. It's hard not to love a spectacle like that. But it's all style, no substance.

Fire isn't even necessary to burn something at all. Hot water will affect skin in much the same way. So will steam, radiation, and even long enough exposure to sunlight. That's why they call it a sun *burn*. Flesh burnt badly enough will literally die while still attached, a patch of blight on an otherwise healthy organ, and become like sun-bleached leather, waxy to the touch. Or it might harden into coal-black scales, otherworldly armor.

Watch. The skin reddens, then blisters. Fatty bubbles begin to appear like soap on the surface of still water. Small at first. Then they grow. They swell, balloon up, ready to bloom like the bulbs of some strange fleshy flower, waiting to burst open in a shocking display of new life. When they do, the freshly revealed skin is the glistening newborn result of that flickering, feverish passion.

Watch the pretty skin. See it change. It will whiten, melt and pool, reassemble into a great and terrible new visage. Striking. Compelling. A human recreated, not in the image of a kindly God, but by the design of heat. Burn wards are Satan's art gallery. The figure in each bed a grotesque new rendition of an alien vision for the human form, an interpretation of the old flesh. Beauty reimagined. Not beholden to the constraints of symmetry, or even function, the new flesh splits through the old, rending violently through to breathe and touch, to be touched, in a dizzying display of a striking new aesthetic.

Losing her face was the best thing that ever happened to Vicki's mother.

Every year, deep fryer accidents are responsible for about five deaths in America. Catherine was almost one of them, but she lived. They didn't think she would and, at first, she wished that she hadn't. Recovery was slow and arduous, indescribably painful. But the best experts in the country were consulted, all of them eager to attach their name to such a sensational case study, and they were able to save one of her eyes, replace her lips—sufficient enough for her to speak—also reconstruct enough of her ears so that she could eventually wear large stylish sunglasses.

The scar tissue, smooth and leathery, enveloped her head like the hood of a wetsuit. Thick crimson tentacles snaked down from her neck in both the front, curving sensuously between her breasts, and also in back, like the seeking appendages of a parasite. The division between the new burned area and the old pale skin was a rough barrier of scale, like the hide of a primordial beast, surrounded by a tender, pinkish outline.

Catherine took to wearing scarves and hats, wigs sometimes, but she loved masks most of all. She had an impressive collection by the time Vicki's father left. He couldn't look at his wife anymore. He couldn't stand the thought of touching her. It was almost funny. Before the accident he never cared if she was in the mood or not.

When he wanted her affection, he took it. She eventually learned not to struggle.

Now Catherine wanted it all the time. She was ready, positively in heat. She strutted around the house in her wigs, her masks, and not much else most of the time. In a carnival disguise or a domino mask and scarf, lace panties peeking out from under a sheer teddy or riding low beneath a bustier, she moaned and writhed yet to no avail. What's the saying? She couldn't get laid in prison with a handful of pardons.

Dad hadn't been around much before the accident, so it wasn't a hard adjustment for the kids when he split. Vicki's older brother Gregory was upset at first, but even he got over it soon enough. Besides, there were plenty of men at the house after that. There were other things for him to be upset about too.

Delivery men were easy. So was the plumber, the handyman and the paper boy. And when Catherine couldn't think up a job to bring a new man over, there was always the internet. The lawsuit settlement with the deep fryer manufacturer paid the doctor's bills and left Catherine with plenty of cash and plenty of time at home to be available for entertaining. Though it hadn't been true for Dad, most men will overlook almost anything in the face of a guaranteed score. If some lonely slut wanted to wear a mask, or a wig and maybe do it only from behind, what did they care? They got off just the same.

Vicki heard her mother often in the bedroom with her men—and in the living room and in the bathroom and in the garage— encouraging them, urging them, commanding them. Harder. Faster. Deeper.

It was as if along with her face the boiling oil had relieved Catherine of the person she had been beneath it. Where once she was meek, now she was in control. Where was once she was passive, now she was insatiable; once sad, now gleeful. As her new face had torn free in a violent eruption of steam and blister flowers, so had the person she was meant to be.

And when it got really lonely, when she couldn't get anyone else to tend to her, Mom could always tiptoe down the hall to Gregory's room. He was fifteen by then, after all.

"Such a big boy," Vicki would hear her mother coo from inside her brother's room at night. "Mommy's big, sexy boy."

"No," he said. "Don't. I don't like it!"

"But look here." Mom would giggle. "That means you do, baby. Looks to me like you like it a lot."

He eventually learned not to struggle.

It was Vicki who found her mother dead in the bathtub.

She was naked. Really naked. She hardly ever wore much, but she was not wearing a mask or wig either. Her wrists were severed. She'd been serious, too, cutting up and down, not across. Determined to die. Every mirror in the house was broken, smashed to bits, and she'd used one of the biggest pieces to gouge the deep, moist slits into her skinny forearms. Vicki had heard the glass breaking the night before, lying absolutely still in bed. She had been terrified, but she knew by then to stay out of Mom's way. When Mom was in a mood, it was best to lay low.

Catherine had tried to fuck herself back to life. It didn't make sense to Vicki then, but later on she began to understand. Her mother's plan had worked, for a little while. She'd filled herself with a Naval fleet's worth of cock, and enough jizz to float their ships on, but it hadn't been enough. She could never feel desired enough, be wanted enough, to look at herself for very long. For just a little while though, she had been happy. But Catherine couldn't embrace the change. She got caught up in the surface. All style, no substance. The change is what's really important, and that happens below. It happens within.

Gregory was eighteen and out of the picture by then. So Vicki was alone when she called the police. She was alone as she watched TV and waited. She was alone when they finally arrived to take her mother away forever.

Years passed.

Vicki didn't often think about her mother. Though, in another way, she never really stopped thinking about her. It wasn't so much a case of thinking or not thinking about her, really. The memory of her mother coated every feeling she had, every action and thought, like a layer of dust that she couldn't wipe away.

Tonight, once more, she had her hands full of hair. Beautiful strawberry blond hair, beneath which her roommate Andrea spat and sobbed into the toilet. Devastated by another man, the comely petite girl from Minneapolis had again tried to assuage her feelings with vodka—a lot of vodka—and now she suffered on her knees before the pitiless porcelain goddess.

Sitting on the side of the tub, leaned forward with elbows on her thighs, Vicki gathered up the sad girl's hair into one fist and slid her other hand to her roommate's heaving back. She rubbed small, comforting circles.

"It's OK," Vicki said again. "It's all going to be fine," for the hundredth time. Then she said, "You're better off." Vicki searched for what usually came next in the speech. She came up blank though and went back to rubbing and shushing instead.

Tomorrow would come the hangover, brutal and debilitating but a necessary period in the depressing run on sentence that was Andrea's love life. Then the slow recovery, until her next paramour and the accompanying, almost assured, infidelity, dishonesty and mistreatment.

Andrea was a beautiful girl. The broken ones almost always are. But it did not make her happy. Vicki felt bad for her. She felt a lot of things for her. She'd watched Andrea for the three years they'd lived together, watched her very closely. She'd seen her desperately squeezing herself into the role dictated by the world, killing herself at fitness classes and starving herself to slip into seductive clothes. Still not happy. Andrea wanted to be the girl she thought she should be so badly. So many long, painful hours, so much time standing before mirrors analyzing and adjusting. So many trinkets, tricks, powders, gels and sprays. And she was still not happy.

Vicki had watched Andrea alter herself for every man who came along. Hair, interests, mannerisms, they'd all been changed easier than underwear if the next willing cock in her life had seen fit to encourage, or forbid, something. They were never real changes, though. Just a surface disguise. A mask to hide behind.

"Shh," Vicki said in her friend's ear. It was stretched and punctured by many heavy, twinkly, eye-catching baubles. "It'll be OK. I promise. I love you."

"Thanks," Andrea said, staring down into the toilet, head on her forearm. "I love you too, Vick."

MARANO

Andrea didn't really mean it. Not like Vicki did. It was just one of those things heartbroken girlfriends say to each other. Fueled by sorrow and Smirnoff, it was an easy thing to say. But Vicki could pretend, just for a moment at least, that her friend's words meant more than that. In the darker private places of her mind she always did. But all she said was, "I'll always take care of you."

Moans and whimpers are the crickets of the nighttime burn ward. Occasionally, a lone shriek would pierce the relative quiet the way a wolf's howl might ring out over an otherwise hushful landscape. Vicki moved like a silent specter in her white scrubs among the still aberrations displayed in uniform rows, their mutations thinly veiled beneath hospital blankets and stark patches of alabaster gauze.

Vicki often worked shifts for other nurses. She liked to be at work—especially late at night when there were less people around—and she was qualified to work in many departments. Her primary duties were in the burn ward, though. It was a specialty she had chosen without much conscious thought. It just felt right.

Regardless, it was an excellent fit for her, and a position that not many others could handle. The doctors were all impressed with her unflinching coolness in the face of the horrors effected on humans by heat and her attentive hands-on approach to each newly warped victim. Vicki had advanced quickly, and she enjoyed her position at the hospital. It was where she had first met Andrea.

She paused at the foot of the bed of a man who had earned his new countenance in a car accident. Third degree burns are more serious, more often fatal. But second degree burns are more painful because the nerves survive. This man was covered in the latter variety, and he cried in his semiconscious, drug-induced haze. As she slipped the thin sheet down to reveal his wrecked body, Vicki absently wondered if he even knew he was crying.

Dangling tubes descended from high on metal arms to penetrate his tumescent skin and deliver medications and liquid food. The man had become swollen, saturated with the dripping sustenance like waterlogged driftwood. His insides strained against the confinement of his own skin, like something left in the microwave too long. Rips had begun to show, and crimson fat split through the growing fissures.

Vicki ran a finger along those lines and remembered her mother's husky pleas—the soundtrack to her own budding sexuality. The man's scrotum had ballooned up to cartoonish proportions, and Vicki lightly prodded him there too. He made a pathetic little mewling sound—*I don't like that! I don't like it!*—and she imagined the strong calloused hands of working men caressing perfumed scabs. The man's eyelids were bulgy, like rotten fruit. Vicki poked them gently, imagining they might pop.

Tomorrow, she knew, they would cut him. As the pressure choked off blood vessels, the man's skin would suffocate and die. He would rot from the outside in. So the surgeons would cut him free by slicing vents in his constrictive skin casing.

She'd seen it done many times, including the long gashes sliced into her mother's neck and shoulders. Like tiger stripes, she'd thought at the time. Or gills, like the kind a mermaid might have.

Vicki rested a hand on his plump tummy, guts tightly corseted in overcooked leather wrapping. His entire body lay engorged beneath her touch, pulsing and warm. Like he might burst at any second.

She reached into her pocket, took out a tiny digital camera and began to photograph the extraordinary specimen before her, all fevered tension and mounting pressure. The man made a babyish keening noise. It leaked out from between his bloated lips like air escaping from a balloon.

Vicki crouched lower for a close-up. She wondered what the man had been like before his accident, and what he was becoming beneath his hardened cocoon.

Days later, Vicki returned home from a double shift at the hospital to the sound of Stevie Nicks. Today, she'd been subbing in pediatrics. It had been tedious and boring. She had no interest in children and it was Andrea's day off, so Vicki could not even look forward to catching a glimpse of her roommate while making the rounds or sharing a meal break.

Inside the apartment, she found Andrea bopping near the stereo, drink in hand, wearing tiny gray shorts and an old Metallica t-shirt that was too big for her, a comfy relic of a long-gone boyfriend. She was devastatingly sexy. From the doorway, Vicki watched her dance for a moment that seemed to last forever.

"Vick!" Andrea cried, turning to face the entrance as Stevie Nicks sang. "Vick, Vick-ay! How was your day, slut?"

Vicki groaned, playing her established part in their domestic act. She dropped her bag near the couch and kicked off her white sneakers.

"Yeah." Andrea made a pouty duck face, nodded sharply and turned back to the stereo. "Fuck work. Slip out of them scrubs. There's margaritas in the kitchen and pizza on the way. Fingers crossed we get the blond delivery guy with the neck tattoo."

"You seem to be feeling better." Vicki headed to the kitchen, dragging her eyes away from Andrea's legs and reaching for a glass.

"I'm fucking great," Andrea said, sauntering in behind her for a refill. "Come on, shed the work clothes and get with the party. You're off tomorrow and I know you got nothing planned."

It didn't matter if she did or didn't have plans. Vicki knew she could never disappoint Andrea. She never would. She poured herself a glass of the frozen booze concoction, topped off Andrea's and headed off down the hall toward her bedroom.

Alone, Vicki stripped and tossed her clothes into the hamper by the closet. She saw herself in the mirror above her dresser. She eyed herself dispassionately with a professional, clinical gaze, then opened the bottom left drawer and took out a mismatched pair of fluffy socks. One was bedecked in dolphins, the other a pattern of cherries. She rubbed them between her fingers and ran them up and down her bare legs. Goosebumps broke out over her entire body. They were Andrea's socks. She had taken them from the laundry, one at a time, over the course of the winter. Slob that she was, Andrea hadn't even noticed. Vicki held them both to her face, inhaled deeply.

She set the socks on her bed and, from the same drawer, took out some red lace boy shorts, also pilfered from the laundry. She ran them likewise over her legs, then caressed her stomach, gliding them up to her breasts, tickling herself. She held them close to her face and licked them daintily.

BURNT

From the living room, Andrea called, "Pizza's here." There was a lot of giggling; she must have gotten the blond guy after all. Stevie Nicks played on.

Vicki pulled the underwear away from her mouth. "Coming."

She stepped into her roommate's panties, grabbed some sweats off the back of her door and dressed. Stevie Nicks now sang "Talk To Me."

You can set your secrets free, baby

Andrea caterwauled along with Stevie. With her blond hair, and having retrieved a black wide-brimmed hat and scarf from her room a few drinks ago, she looked the part more and more. An obsession with the gypsy rocker was one of the things that Vicki loved about Andrea. It was an unapologetically corny thing they shared. Vicki sipped from her glass. It was only water now and had been for a while. She let Andrea drag her off the couch, gave in and danced along. She couldn't let Andrea down, even if she wanted to. And she never did.

Dusty words, lying under carpets
Seldom heard, well, must you keep your secrets
Locked inside, hidden safe from view?

Vicki felt, as she always felt when she heard this song, like Stevie was talking to her, like the lyrics were written for her. She watched Andrea sway and stumble near the record player, sloshing more margarita than she was drinking, with a smoldering American Spirit stuck between her flawless lips and her hat tilted way back. Buzzed enough to be brave, Vicki came up close behind Andrea and danced a little slower.

Well is it all that hard?
Is it all that tough?
I've shown you all my cards, now isn't that enough?

Andrea suddenly fell away from Vicki's grasp and caught herself against the entertainment center, the record skipping and scratching over Stevie's haunting voice.

"You okay?"

"Sorry," Andrea slurred. She shuffled over to the couch on unstable legs. Vicki followed and kept her hands on Andrea's toned obliques, helping to guide her.

"It's OK."

"Just need a rest." Andrea sunk into the couch, her limp arm hanging over the edge, smoldering filter inches above the carpet. She was instantly asleep.

Andrea could be happy. She just needed some help. She needed freeing from her cycle of disappointment.

Vicki thought about this while sitting at her computer an hour or so after Andrea passed out. She was angry, frustrated and disappointed. She was also excited.

She scrolled through the photos in a desktop folder labeled "Research." Some she'd taken herself at the hospital, others she'd been sent in trade. Most came from a man who claimed to be a paramedic in Nevada, including the ones in front of her now. Her favorites.

The blackened, twisted form of a woman in a number of lewd poses bared itself for her. A life-sized sex doll the man said he'd found in the remains of an adult shop that burned down. He liked to send Vicki pictures of the things he did to her. The poses he put her in, the clothes he made her wear. She sent him back suggestions.

The aberration is the attraction.

That's what he'd written. She'd never put it into words before, the slippery thing that coiled deep inside her, but it was true. Pouty lips blistered just right. A coquettish smile stretched and smeared into a novel, unreproducible expression. The world's full of pretty girls. But real carnage? That's rare. Before the fire, this doll had been like any other. Just one more on the shelf. Ignored. Not special. Licked by flame, assaulted by the inferno, though, she was divine. Special. She was saved.

She and Andrea could both be happy. They deserved to be happy. It had almost worked for her mother. It would have worked, if she hadn't been so alone. Vicki was older now. She finally understood. She would be there for Andrea, and she would make sure it *worked*.

She would comfort and care for Andrea. She would sate her. She wouldn't leave like Dad had. Like Gregory.

Vicki crushed sleeping pills into a glass of water and managed to wake Andrea long enough to gulp it down. "You'll feel better tomorrow if you drink this now," she said.

"Thanks, slut," Andrea mumbled. Then she was out again, slumped on the couch and sleeping more soundly than ever.

Vicki gathered her tools, then waited.

An hour passed. The harsh blinking digits on the microwave clock told her it was almost three in the morning. She splashed the face of her comatose love, her very own sad sleeping beauty, with the last of the tequila and tucked the soaked scarf securely around Andrea's face. Vicki lit a cigarette from Andrea's nearby pack and pressed it to the sodden silk.

Watch her pretty skin. See it change from pink to crimson, then darken still further. See it crack and rupture. Fatty bubbles begin to appear. Small dots. Then they grow. They swell and bloom like the bulbs of a fleshy flower, a bloody bouquet.

Vicki gazed down with wide, unblinking eyes as it happened, a great secret show, just for her. She knew that Andrea's once smooth skin would melt and pool, and reassemble itself. A beautiful new flesh would eventually burst free, split through the old. She would be changed, permanently this time, and for the better.

Andrea woke, a guttural scream swallowed by the fire. She pawed at the molten cloth sticking to her face. She tried to roll off the couch, but Vicki was there. She wore thick rubber gloves pulled up to her elbows and grabbed hold of Andrea's flailing wrists and held them tight in her determined, sober grip. She pounced on Andrea's stomach, pinning her to the couch, and held her hands far away from her burning face.

Vicki watched, tears running over her smiling face as she listened to the wails, as Andrea's lips pulled back so far the budding blisters tore open. Her skin ripped and curled, peeling back like worn paint, and she bucked wildly between Vicki's legs like a live wire.

Finally, Vicki let go and leapt onto the floor. She grabbed the fire extinguisher—the one she would tell the police she ran to get from the kitchen—and let loose the cool white foam.

Later, from the chair beside her love's hospital bed, Vicki stared longingly at the bandaged figure lying silently before her. She stroked Andrea's arm above one of her gauze mittens. The doctors were confident they could save her hands. They had not been so badly burned as her face. Her eyes too, they thought, would probably be all right. Though the scarring would be severe.

Thank God, they'd said, that Andrea had the good fortune to have another nurse for a roommate—a burn specialist, no less—who was on hand when she passed out drunk with her lit cigarette. She must have spilled tequila on herself after Vicki went to bed. It happens. It happens every day. This could have been worse, they all agreed. She could have died.

Vicki nodded, but of course she had known that wouldn't happen. She would never allow her friend to die. Andrea would probably not remember Vicki's part in her accident. She had been very drunk, and mixing alcohol with sleeping pills . . . The trauma of seeing her new face would be devastating to her memory too.

Vicki moved a hand under the bleach-smelling covers and ran her fingers up Andrea's bare leg. Yes, she knew that Andrea would need to feel encouraged and supported. She would need to feel loved. Her fingertips moved up over Andrea's knee to her thigh. Unlike with her mother, Vicki knew what to do now. She knew how to help. Her hand moved under Andrea's paper gown and found its way between her legs. Beneath the bandages, Andrea moaned. It was an ambiguous sound, painful arousal.

"I know," Vicki whispered. "First it will only hurt. But it will get better. Soon, you won't even remember why you were so afraid."

Vicki worked her fingers. Andrea stirred and moaned louder. She squirmed and tried to pull away. Vicki grabbed her arm, dug her nails in hard and shushed her.

"I'm right here," she said. "I'll never leave you alone."

It was true. That was another way that Andrea would not be like Catherine. She couldn't kill herself even if she wanted to. Vicki would see to that. She would be around all the time and she would give Andrea what all those men, what even her own brother, could never give Catherine: affection without end. Idolatry.

She leaned close, put her lips to the thick gauze covering what was left of Andrea's ear and sang softly.

BURNT

I can see we're thinking 'bout the same things
And I can see your expression when the phone rings
We both know there's something happening here

She playfully licked the fabric cocoon covering her love's mouth, exploring her own damaged doll. Vicki felt herself getting wet inside Andrea's stolen, red panties.

"I'll help you change," Vicki whispered. "I'll take care of you."

Luciano Marano is a newspaper reporter, photojournalist and author. His award-winning reporting, both written and photographic, has appeared in numerous national and regional publications. Burnt is his first published work of fiction. A U.S. Navy veteran, he enjoys reading, jogging, craft beer, oldies music, traveling to new places, and would choose Wolverine-style healing abilities if he could have any superpower—or maybe just the ability to grow Wolverine-style sideburns. His favorite movie is Point Break *and his favorite book is* Something Wicked This Way Comes. *Originally from rural, western Pennsylvania, he now resides near Seattle, Washington.*

Get to know him better at www.luciano-marano.com or citmyway101.wordpress.com.

JUNK

RYAN HARDING

NICK DIDN'T KNOW where the impulse came from, but he followed it with vigor. It seemed to have been there as long as he could remember, like a post-hypnotic suggestion. Those moments were the only ones that mattered in his life. All the rest was simply preamble and postscript to the thrill.

The website was called InterphaZ. Nick thought of it as some kind of glory hole for casual conversation, a way to meet new people from all walks of life and forge some kind of friendship or perhaps even a relationship. A complete waste of time, in other words, but it hadn't taken him long to realize its potential for his own needs. That's when the fun began. And it hadn't let up in the past four months.

Virgins were the conquest—the ones who just signed up on InterphaZ and were more likely not to have had the random chat experience spoiled for them. New arrival HelKat84 looked promising, an attractive blond with hair tied up in two twists on her avatar. Like horns, he thought at first, but then realized they were supposed to affect cat ears. She must have liked what she saw from his avatar and profile (expertly crafted to present a charming and unthreatening persona after weeks of trial and error), because she accepted the chat request. Her webcam feed sprang up in the left corner of his screen.

He had it down to a science. As soon she accepted his request, he bolted up from his ergonomic chair and hit his mark like a consummate pro. The view of his maroon shirt and plain face—eyes too close together, nose too thin as if compressed by the nearness of his eyes, his fingers curled over his chin to suggest a pensive harmlessness—vanished in a flash, a smash cut leaving HelKat84 with a window to the bearded thatch of his scrotum. He lifted his shirt to allow her the unhindered view. And of course he was rock hard; how could he not be? This was the pinnacle. He could have run dick-first into a brick wall and crashed through like the Kool-Aid Man.

"Ugh!" HelKat84 grunted over the computer speakers. She recoiled from the image, eyes squinched shut like he'd proffered a photo of children blown to pieces in a drone strike rather than a pulsing boner. The resolution on webcams always left much to be desired, so it wasn't like she could see Rand McNally tributaries of veins spreading the good word about his arousal through the length of his girth, but if she wanted to act like it was the first time Cinderella went to ball, Nick was all for it. This was the kind of reaction he relished best.

HelKat84 finally realized she had the power to disconnect this live feed to genital horror, and she groped for her mouse with one hand. The other she kept in front of her eyes to block him, like he could glaze her face through the computer screen. E-facial, the next stage of human evolution.

"Sick bastard!" she shouted.

HelKat84 has disconnected this chat.

Nick sat down again, grinning ear to ear. Would she report him? It wouldn't be the first time. Nick changed his ISP address like some people changed their Facebook status. There were always ways around banishment.

He went ahead and blocked her. The prospect of a sequel down the line was amusing in theory—*just when you thought it was safe to InterphaZ . . .* —but it gave them time to process the encounter and reflect on what they should have said for maximum damage, a tirade against him and his ilk. They could run these little mental fire drills and assure his surprise reappearance (with a new name and profile) displayed the law of diminishing returns. Better to hit and run.

"Cock and awe, bitch."

This had been a good night with consistently satisfying reactions—disgust, horror, anger. Some nights were less fulfilling, prompting only indifference, boredom, and sarcasm. *Is that all you've got? My webcam doesn't have a microscope feature, little man.* Not tonight, though. They cringed, they shuddered. One even shrieked. The cross in her avatar suggested big time Christian beliefs. She was probably kneeling in broken glass and flagellating herself. Nick's personal project tomorrow during the misery of the call center would be to craft a more religious-friendly profile. That would be fishing with dynamite, something he should have considered long ago. Few were more predisposed to be forever haunted by the specter of Nick's throbbing gristle.

It was funny to think he would never have done something like this in different circumstances. On a crowded bus or in line at Starbucks, never. There were real world penalties for that, jail time from the cops, pepper spray, and sharp fingernails from the civilians. Doing it online in the privacy of his own apartment, though, it may have been unwanted, but it was tolerated, the same as someone texting at a movie. You go to a theater, you expect to see the glowing screen of a smartphone during the feature presentation. You go online, someone's throwing a dick in your face. That was just the way of the world now.

He hadn't been thinking of doing it when he bought his webcam. He just expected to chat with different bitches who would get naked on their own cams every week if not every night (law of averages), but it hadn't worked out that way. When the familiar disappointment shadowed his latest attempt to escape his incessant boredom in life, he was inspired by a new idea with a different objective. This one was working. He was winning.

A chime played through his speakers. New email alert. He clicked over to the tab. Another InterphaZ notification of his latest expulsion. *Failure to uphold community standard . . . conduct unbecoming . . . violation of membership agreement . . . blah, blah.* It meant about as much as dying in a video game. It was a fine paid with Monopoly money.

He frowned at the subject line of another new email: SAVAGE YOUR PENIS B4 ITS 2 LATE! That was a far cry from the usual promises of genital size enhancement and aphrodisiacs. Maybe it was supposed to pique his curiosity enough to read it (fail). It must work on someone out there, maybe the sort of person who thought they'd been personally selected to play cash mule for the Prince of Nigeria.

Nick marked the junk mail as spam, for all the good it would do, and closed the tab.

His preferred notification of a chat request from InterphaZ—the quaint sound of a ringing phone—brought him back to the mission at hand. This was surprising since Nick was supposed to be locked out again and had expected the need to switch to a new ISP and profile, presto-change-o, before another chat encounter. The notification came from user nerXam83, the avatar a photo of some primo jailbait. She might have handled more dicks than a porn set fluffer or maybe the only cramming she did was for the SATs. (Or as a popular meme once said, why not both?) It was hard to tell these days. The 83 was questionable, but it didn't necessarily mean year of birth. If it was just some creepy guy, he could pull the plug easily enough.

Nick accepted. The window appeared in the same sacred place where so many InterphaZ users of yore found themselves blinded by a wall of his junk.

Nick's eyelids vanished in comical surprise. NerXam83 was definitely a man, a man who had bested the master of Cock and Awe at his own game. There was a twist to his version of surprise scrotal maneuvers, however. NerXam83 was *afflicted*. Like something out of a medical textbook passed around in a macabre parlor game to see who puked first. Pustules spread across the shaft of the dick filling his chat window in a formation like bubble wrap. Perhaps it was the delay from the feed where a second here and there was lost, but Nick would swear the fleshy growths pulsated as he watched. Unfortunately, the resolution of this window to repulsion seemed mysteriously like Blu-ray quality to better disgust him with its palette of moist reds and yellows. Some nodules were blood blister-like, while others oozed with a custard syrup in milky tributaries he could see gradually advancing over and between the protuberances of inflamed skin like time lapse photography. NerXam83's presentation front and center on the world's sharpest webcam opened the coral reef of penile rot currently festering inches away.

In Nick's shock he looked far longer than reason dictated, both grossed out and engrossed by this abomination the same as he would have been by an animal with two heads. Perhaps more so because this was the same species . . . someone who even shared the same pastime.

"Ugh!" Nick finally groaned and disconnected the chat without looking directly at it another second, lest he turn to stone. He needed his own eye wash station.

Some distance from the computer seemed like a good thing, so Nick made his way to bathroom down the hall. An afterimage remained. What could have caused that? Did he bang some leper whore with syphilis near Chernobyl? Nick didn't think he could have shown his face to the world after contracting something so hideous, much less the spoiled genitals that were part and parcel of it.

It had to be fake. Dude could just be some special FX wizard looking to freak people out, that was all.

Sicko.

Mystery solved, he intended to relieve himself and then get back to the business of flashing his junk in the faces of unwary women on InterphaZ.

Another bone strike of Cock and Awe, that's the ticket.

He unzipped his pants, then forgot all about his special FX theory and plans for scrotal domination as the burst of pain ignited at the release of his bladder.

"Ow, fuck!"

He twitched like a frog hooked up to a car battery, the entirety of his world condensed to an inch of blazing fury at the tip of his organ. It was like pissing napalm and he had failed to fireproof his dickhole. His keening wail accompanied this slow eternity of urination, unselfconscious about the thin walls between him and his neighbor. Right now all that mattered, all that existed, was the geyser of molten lava. The last drops singed as well, as if they had claws slashing through membrane on the way out.

Nick had shut his eyes tight against the onslaught and now opened them to a world blurred by tears of pain. His aim was scattershot from the spasms, leaving splashes of red across the seat of the commode, the roll of toilet paper, the floor, the wastebasket.

That's blood, he thought dumbly, cold sweat beading in his scalp. *All of that was blood.*

He tenderly shook off, grimacing at the wetness on his fingers.

He already dreaded a couple of hours when the call of nature forced him through this process of torture again. The first time might have only been a warm-up—

His train of thought derailed.

Wetness on his fingers? He didn't think he'd somehow sprayed himself even with all of his cringing a moment ago, but expected to see the same bloody excretion when he examined his hand. It wasn't, though. It still had traces of blood, but more suggestive of pus. A runny wax not unlike what he saw on the computer a moment ago.

He laughed with barely suppressed hysteria because the cause and effect was so impossible. Even if nerXam83 was one apartment over instead of another state or continent altogether, it was no more logical. Nick only looked at a computer screen.

It went viral, he thought and almost laughed again. It made an ominous sense, however crazy it was, especially when he considered the circumstances. Banned by InterphaZ but still able to receive that one request from the site. Now this.

Nick's guts double and triple knotted as he stood in front of the mirror and examined his penis. Perhaps it was largely psychological, but now that he knew the infection was there, his shaft felt tingly and hot, as if he could sense new pustules forming on a microscopic level. He held his length gingerly by the head, inspecting the column with mounting horror. Several sores had burst already from his tightened grip during the throes of anguish. A cobweb of stringy flesh dangled on the underside, having peeled off from the base. The layer revealed was raw, crustacean red.

Nick met his own stricken gaze in the mirror, mouth agape, his sickly pale reflection commiserating: *Are you seeing this?*

Unfortunately he was, and no reset from a universal do-over restored the integrity of his genitalia.

He had some gauze in one of the bathroom drawers. He didn't know what else to do but wrap himself up. Smear the bandages with some triple antibiotic (assuming quadruple antibiotic didn't exist) and pray for a miraculous return to its pristine state while he went through life in the meantime looking like a stunt dick for Claude Rains.

He reached for the drawer, and that was the point when the corona of his cock seemed to lose solidity and adopt the texture of a sponge. His index finger and thumb pushed trenches into either side instantaneously. He shrieked and withdrew his pincer grip, but the caverns remained. A piece dislodged within the crumpled pillar and dropped to the counter.

Nick looked around frantically, as if a bottle of Acme Dickhead Skin Regrowth Ointment™ would magically appear somewhere. It didn't.

The impulse now was to call for an ambulance, but what would he say? *My dick is rotting before my fucking eyes because of some freak's webcam. Hurry!* When they finally accepted it wasn't a crank call and actually sent someone, what could they do?

SAVAGE YOUR PENIS B4 ITS 2 LATE.

Yes, that was what the strange email said. It seemed no more coincidental than nerXam83's request. He gingerly walked back to the bedroom, stripping off his shirt so it didn't catch his groin and exacerbate the damage. He launched his email again, heedless of the rancid juices left behind on the mouse and keys and the pitter-pattern of droplets on the carpet from his sores, like melting icicles. The nausea in his stomach churned with greater urgency.

At last he found the email in his spam folder and opened it. The sender name contained the word InterphaZ (and "no-reply"). There was no text, only an embedded .GIF file of a man with his sex organs on a flat table surface as he swung a meat cleaver at the scrotal pouch, an unsettling smile on his face. An animated balloon obscured the actual hit, filled with the word **THWACK!**

That was savage, all right. Not exactly the most tempting prospect for a potential cure.

B4 ITS 2 LATE.

2 late for what?

He looked forlornly at the disgusting thing attached to him, which had been perfectly normal not ten minutes ago. The disease progressed like an old school werewolf transformation with superimposed special FX, a process rapidly achieved.

"No," Nick said. "Oh God, no."

The sac of his scrotum showed burgeoning, bloated pearls emerging between the furrows. Hundreds of them, like mutant spider eggs primed to hatch an adipocerous offspring. The burning, tingling sensation erupted in full, with tiny needles prickling every millimeter of skin. The sensation was maddening.

There could be no doubt—it was spreading. Within minutes it had already done this much to him. By the time paramedics arrived, it could be far worse.

B4 ITS 2 LATE.

Nick hurried to the kitchen, the droplets now more poignant against linoleum. As he reached for the electric carving knife, he assuaged himself with the countless miracles of modern medicine. People lost body parts all the time and had them sewn back, although Nick of course didn't want his "gangroin" reattached. But with practical advances in technology, they could basically spin straw into dick, couldn't they? He wasn't out of options, as long as he survived this. The solidity of the carving knife handle reassured him. It featured a slide button rather than a trigger, so it would keep cutting if he passed out.

He called 9-1-1 first for an ambulance, reporting massive blood loss from a carving knife mishap. He claimed it was his fingers since they probably wouldn't get here any faster anyway. They assured him someone was coming and he hung up, his eyes blurry again.

He revved the carving knife as he took hold of everything in his other hand, cupping beneath his testicles with the palm, his fingers and thumb forming a C-shape. Any doubts about the necessity of his course of action were neutralized in short order with one last humiliation of the flesh. The patchwork of pustules slipped beneath his fingers like some kind of revolving cylinder, both on his dick and the sac beneath. Skin barely adhered to the organ now. It pulled loose from the stalk with ease, lasagna-colored meat beneath. The loose rope of dangling flesh slid away, abracadabra. It sloughed as a shed snakeskin, popping and bursting in the few places still attached, liquid tendrils stretching like taffy to reveal shimmering tissue. The underside tore with it in a burst as if something had detonated beneath. The sac detached in tandem like a wet rubber glove in his palm. The testicles and cords dropped like dead jellyfish, oysters in a Jell-O mold upon his quivering hand. The emptied pouch hung limp like a flap of torn curtain, the penile skin like the empty husk of some insect draped in his palm. It all clumped wetly to the floor. He watched it go like a wounded soldier unable to hold in his own intestines. There was curiously no pain, other than the trauma of the sickening sight, the nerve endings perhaps jellified now. Clinging contents of the pouch sagged like syrup, halfway to the floor. His actual penis was but a strange glistening tendril apart from the head, which still had its skin and something of its shape save the trenches left from his fingers. Otherwise he beheld something virtually skinless, corroding.

On the plus side, he had much less he'd need to cut now.

Nick engaged the carving knife again. Whatever whimpers he made were drowned out by the whirring blades. He locked in on his target, a miraculous sliver of pale flesh at the base of his organ. There was pain at the root where the true skin remained, but far less than he expected. Perhaps that was the silver lining to an impromptu session of unlicensed surgery to rid yourself of your liquefying fuckmeat. He screamed anyway, for this insanity that had dethroned the natural order of his life. The blades shredded through the tissue effortlessly, an explosion of crimson giblets blown across the kitchen counter and sink, the refrigerator, his stomach, thighs, and feet. He held his other hand up to block the blowback before he gave new meaning to "facial tissue." In seconds it was over—barely longer than his webcam session with HelKat84.

Nick left the carving knife grinding, the circuit breaker in his mind so overloaded he couldn't remember how to turn it off at that moment. He looked at it as if he'd never seen such a thing before and didn't know how it wound up in his hand, but finally connected enough dots to see the slide button and remember its function as "on/off." Simple, sane. He was placing his thumb over the button when the awful tingling suddenly lit up across all the fingers of his right hand—the one with which he'd held himself in the bathroom. Even within the spatters from his operation, he saw the blisters forming like islands in a bloody ocean, felt them shifting beneath like tectonic plates.

B4 ITS 2 LATE.

His 9-1-1 call would be truthful after all.

Unsure if he heard an approaching siren or it was just the grinding serenade of the blades, Nick withdrew his thumb and guided the carving knife over to his fingers, trying not to think about all the places now covered in his fluids.

Ryan Harding is the author of Genital Grinder *and co-author of* Reincarnage *with Jason Taverner, both from Deadite Press, and co-author of* Header 3 *with Edward Lee. He was a contributor to the multi-author collaboration*

JUNK

Sixty-Five Stirrup Iron Road. *His stories have appeared in the anthologies* Into Painfreak, In Laymon's Terms, *and* Excitable Boys, *the chapbooks* Partners in Chyme *(with Edward Lee),* A Darker Dawning *and* A Darker Dawning 2: Reign in Black, *and the magazines* Splatterpunk *and* The Magazine of Bizarro Fiction. *He also contributed a chapter to Matt Shaw's* The Devil's Guests. *Upcoming projects include a contribution to* Torso Spasmo *with Jordan Krall and Philip LoPresti, a novel with Bryan Smith, and the sequel to* Reincarnage *with Jason Taverner.*
Amazon author page: www.amazon.com/-/e/B01N1HSDZ5
Facebook: www.facebook.com/ryanhardmorbid

THE PACKAGE

KRISTOPHER RUFTY

KNOWING HER PACKAGE was waiting there for her, Meredith couldn't get to the post office fast enough. Her shift at the restaurant had dragged by, being a slow Tuesday night. She didn't think closing time would ever come.

Meredith slowed her Nissan when the post office came into view—a small building to her right, painted in shadows. Keeping her speed at a crawl, she angled the car into the parking lot. A sodium light pole in the far corner washed the tiny area in a dim glow.

Only one other car was in the lot: an older sedan, missing its wheel covers, parked in the handicap space near the front.

As she drove behind the sedan, she noticed its red taillight covers were busted, leaving only jagged plastic teeth around the bulbs. The bumper was a rusted bar of metal, and she couldn't read the license number through the black muck smeared across the plate.

Meredith drove up two more spaces and parked. She looked out the passenger window. The sedan's driver's side door was pressed in with dents. The window was down and she could see the shape of someone sitting inside.

Looked like a man.

She felt a pinch of alarm.

Why's he just sitting there?

Meredith remembered watching the news in the breakroom a couple weeks ago. A young woman from two towns over had disappeared. Last place she'd been seen was at the post office earlier that day.

Meredith stared at the sedan, detecting no movement inside, but clearly saw the contours of a man behind the slanted steering wheel. Maybe he was waiting for someone to come out. His wife could have gone in to check the mail.

That made sense to Meredith . . . though a good husband wouldn't let his wife go inside on her own, especially after that other woman's disappearance.

Didn't they find the inside of her car covered in blood?

Maybe this guy's wife was one of those women who fussed whenever the husband tried to do anything for her. He'd let her go in, but not by choice.

Feeling better, she killed the engine, pulled out the key, and climbed out of the car.

Meredith stepped up onto the sidewalk, where the light didn't quite reach.

Somebody could be hiding right in front of me and I wouldn't even know it until I bumped into them.

There was nothing around, either. The school was one road over on the other side of the woods. This time of the night it would be deserted. No houses were close by. Meredith could be jumped right here on the sidewalk and nobody would know.

The guy in the car would be able to see.

She checked. Dark filled the inside of the car except for a small patch by the window where she could see the white of his t-shirt.

He could get me and nobody would know it.

Meredith felt a cold chill as she suddenly remembered what she had on. Looking down, she saw the pale stems of her legs sticking out from under the frayed bottom of her denim skirt. They looked very bare and smooth in the shadows, like two gleaming towers.

Of all nights to wear a skirt.

Short, the skirt didn't even reach the middle of her thighs. She'd chosen to wear it because on a slow night, she needed all the tips she could get. Her shirt was also short, just covering her navel. And *tight*. There was no hiding her large breasts from how they jutted up like two firm, glossy hills behind the thin fabric. Another reason why she'd selected it for this evening's shift.

Meredith didn't care what she had on. She should be able to check her mail without worrying about such matters. As she reached the end of the sidewalk, where the ramp started toward the front door, the sedan's horn gave a single quick *honk*.

Crying out, Meredith snatched back her foot as if she were about to step down on fire. Her hands flew to her chest, fingers brushing her chin.

Huffing, Meredith slowly turned to look at the long, dark car.

An arm reached out the window.

Though it wasn't quite lanky, there hardly seemed to be any muscle on it. The pale hand faced her, fingers curled inward to motion her over. Dark spots that she assumed were scabs dotted the insipid flesh.

Meredith felt a brief jolt of fear that was quickly replaced by anger. Shaking her head, she muttered, "Don't think so, pal."

The nerve of this asshole scaring her like that. If he did have a wife inside, she was going to hear about this.

If he thinks I'm going to walk over there, he's an idiot.

She started to turn, putting her back to the sedan and the ugly arm.

"Excuse me, Miss . . . ?"

A voice so weak and raspy, Meredith hardly heard it. Pausing, she turned her head to peer over her shoulder.

The arm was now patting the air, as if trying to get her to stop.

"Miss . . . ?"

The voice sounded as if it was coming from a very old man.

Meredith frowned. What if he was in trouble? Maybe he'd had a heart attack and she was the first person to come along all night.

Or he's some kind of vampire.

Little taps of ice traveled up her spine, making her rigid.

Stop. There's no damn vampire in that car.

But it was the kind of car that looked like it might belong to one. Long and creepy, beaten up and in bad shape.

"Yes?" she heard herself say. Her voice sounded much softer than it had moments ago.

"Could you help me?"

Uh-oh . . .

Something *was* wrong.

I'm such a bitch.

Thinking he was some kind of pervert or something.

THE PACKAGE

Or vampire.

Meredith started toward the car, feeling embarrassed and a bit ashamed of herself. She was halfway down the ramp, when she slowed her stride.

What if this is his act? Lures women to his car by pretending to be hurt? Maybe that's how the other girl got it.

"What's the matter?" she asked from the ramp.

"Can you check my box for me?"

"Box?"

There was a long phlegmy inhale before he added, "Inside."

"Oh, your mailbox?"

"Yes." The arm went back into the car. It returned a moment later, a long key pinched between two fingers. A faded tag dangled from the back of it.

Keeping her guard up, Meredith slowly walked to the bottom of the ramp. She titled her head, trying to see inside the car. Blackness seemed to cut off the man's head. She could see a shoulder, a short white sleeve, and the extended arm. This close to him, she realized the dots on his skin weren't scabs, but infected sores.

And I'm thinking about taking the key from him?

It would have his *germs* on it.

But she couldn't tell him no. She still had to go inside and get her mail. He'd still be here when she came back out.

Tell him you can't and just come back in the morning.

He already knew she was going inside. If she didn't, he would know it was because of him. That would embarrass him. Besides, she simply couldn't wait another night to get her package.

I've got hand sanitizer in the glovebox . . .

Meredith stepped up to the car, keeping a good distance from the open window.

"Sure," she said. "I can check your box."

"Thank . . . you. I've been here . . . a while, waiting for somebody to come along. It's too hard for me to walk these days."

Stepping up to the window, she held out her hand. She noticed clear tubes inside that seemed to be rising from the darkness of the passenger seat. More light glinted off a dark metal surface that Meredith thought might be an oxygen tank.

RUFTY

This guy isn't a vampire, he's sick.

Meredith reached out her hand, palm up. The key dropped into it. It looked just like hers, but on the paper tag *263* was written in a shaky scrawl. She tried to get a look at his face, but the shadows were like a curtain blocking his features.

"Be right back," she said.

"Thank you," he wheezed.

Meredith hurried up the ramp and entered the post office. The light made her squint. The air-conditioning must have been turned off, since it was warm and stuffy inside the building. And it was awfully quiet. The clacking her sandals made as she walked down the corridor of mailboxes reverberated around her.

Her box was 319, and she looked at the metal door as she walked past, knowing there was a key inside to a parcel locker that was temporarily housing her package.

Check his box first, then get mine on the way out.

She stopped in the section where his box should be and scanned the numbers on the plates. She spotted 263. She raised his key to the lock and slipped it in. She didn't turn it.

What if something's in there?

Like mail? What a shock!

Smirking, Meredith shook her head at her silliness. Still, she hesitated another moment before forcing her hand to twist the key. The gate opened a bit.

She realized she'd stepped to the side as if preparing to dodge something that might leap out.

Knock it off!

Taking a deep breath and holding it, she pulled the gate all the way open.

She couldn't see anything and realized she'd closed her eyes.

Opening them, she looked inside the mailbox.

It was empty.

She released her breath, puffing out her cheeks. Then she closed the box, locked it, and moved on to hers. Opening it, she saw a couple of envelopes leaning against the side. In the small cubby between the mail and the wall was a tiny key with a plastic tab dangling from it.

Smiling, Meredith pulled everything out of her box. She locked it and carried the parcel key to the stack of lockers. Keys protruded from some of the locks where other packages had already been retrieved. She matched the number to the key and opened it.

A small brown box sat inside, a thin slit along the top.

Finally.

Leaving the key dangling in the lock, she carefully slid the package out. It was heavier than she'd expected, but still easy to hold. She needed to get home as soon as possible and get the box open.

Meredith carried her package and envelopes with her outside. The night air was cooler than it had been inside. A breeze blew against her back, breathing on her legs as she walked down the ramp.

The sedan was still there. Its grille looked like the mouth of an ancient metal beast. It seemed to be smiling in anticipation of Meredith's return. She felt some of her good mood slip away as she neared the car.

The arm reached out from the dark, palm up, as if expecting something large to be set on it.

Meredith put the key ring on his hand. "Box was empty," she said. "No mail today."

"Empty?" he asked in a gravelly voice. "But I was expecting mail today."

"Sorry. Have a good night."

Meredith started to turn around.

"I was expecting a package." His hand folded into a fist, finger extended. "That size."

Meredith looked down at her box. "This?" She held it up. "No. This one's mine. Sorry."

"Is that my package?" he asked. "I'm expecting one."

"No. This one's *mine*." She spoke slowly, as if she were talking to a child.

"Then let me see it." He coughed. "Prove you're not a . . . thief."

"I am *not* a thief!" She stepped closer. "Were you expecting a package from Australia? Huh?" She flashed him the shipping label, keeping her finger over her name and box number. "See? Australia. Not for you."

His hand swiped through the air, making a grab for the package. Meredith easily avoided it.

"Stop it," she said. "Just because you're expecting a package doesn't mean I'm going to *give* you mine."

"That's mine! You can't take my package!"

"I'm not going to argue with you," she said.

Meredith turned around and started for her car.

"I'm going to get my package!"

"Of course you are! When you find somebody else kind enough to check your mail for you. *Tomorrow*. I'm sure it'll be there then. You're welcome, by the way."

Meredith got into her car and pushed the button for the auto-lock. Her doors thumped when the locks engaged. She had trouble getting the key in the ignition because of her shaky hand. She needed a moment to calm down, but knew she couldn't take the time to do so. Not with the wheezing bastard parked over there.

Checking to see what he was doing, she saw he hadn't moved. The windows were dark, no headlights on. He wasn't getting out, wasn't shouting at her. Didn't look as if he'd even cranked the car. Meredith wasn't going to hang around for him to do any of the aforementioned actions. She started the car and backed out of the space without putting on her seatbelt. She drove past the sedan, bracing for it to launch backward and slam into her.

It didn't.

She kept glancing at the rearview mirror to make sure he wasn't going to follow her. When she turned out of the parking lot, she could no longer see the post office behind her.

Meredith reached the road she lived on a few minutes later. Every so often, she checked the rearview mirror. Nobody was trailing her.

Asshole.

That was what she got for doing something nice for somebody.

Calls me a thief!

Meredith couldn't believe his nerve. Sure, she could understand the disappointment of not getting a package you've been waiting on, but to claim she had taken it was out of line.

She remembered how she'd acted when he'd accused her. She'd gotten defensive.

So what if I did? He deserved it.

But as she pulled into the driveway of her small, two-bedroom house, something her mother used to say kept repeating in her mind.

Usually when someone's guilty, they're quick to show anger.

And Meredith had *definitely* shown anger. No wonder he hadn't believed she was innocent.

She should have just shown him her name on the shipping label. That would have put an end to the old man's accusations.

Oh, well. Too late now.

Hopefully, she'd never see him again.

Tonight had been her first time running into him and she'd been getting her mail there for a year. Packages had started to disappear from her residential mailbox, so she'd opened up a PO box.

I know what it's like to have packages stolen. That asshole has no idea!

Meredith's anger was causing her to sweat as she climbed out of the car with her purse slung over her shoulder and her package against her chest, the mail on top. She walked up her sidewalk. Cheap solar lights imbedded in the ground threw a barely existent glow on the concrete trail that led to her small back porch.

Under the stoop, she fumbled with her keys. She could hear Sprinkles on the other side, rubbing against the glass of her patio doors, his meows growing impatient. Though he had a litterbox inside, he only used it for peeing. Since she'd been gone for six hours, he was ready to visit the yard.

"Hang on," she said, slipping the key into the lock.

When Sprinkles heard this, his meow increased in loudness and persistence. Now he was using his claws to scratch the door.

Meredith hurried with the deadbolt and opened the door. She saw the brown and white blur and felt the fuzzy tips of his fur on her calves as he dashed out between her legs. Sprinkles stopped long enough to rub against the furniture on the porch, then leaped into the grass. She watched him dart to the back of the yard, vanishing behind the sheets that hung on the clothesline.

Shit.

She'd forgotten to bring the clothes in. Since it was supposed to be such a hot day, she wanted the sun to dry her laundry. Save a little money on her power bill. Plus, the smell of breeze-dried sheets was the best.

Then she'd forgotten about them.

They're probably drenched in dew.

She'd have to throw them in the dryer for a while.

Shaking her head, Meredith entered and bumped the door shut with her hip. She reached behind her and twisted the lock on the knob.

First thing she did after turning on the lights was put her junk on the coffee table in her small living room, making sure the package was in the center of the table so it wouldn't fall off. She then went to the small laundry nook, grabbed the clothes basket, and headed for the backdoor.

She passed by her package on the coffee table. That initial excitement she'd had about it had dwindled. The old man had ruined so much. She'd been eager to get the package home, tear it open, and finally behold what was inside. She'd seen plenty of pictures online while researching, but it wasn't the same as seeing it in person.

Just wait a bit longer. Let that excitement build back up.

First, she had to retrieve the clothes. Though there wasn't much on the line, going outside and taking them down felt like too much of an exhausting chore. But if she left them out there all night, she'd just have to rewash them, then rehang them, then take them down again. Might as well do it tonight, and be done with it.

Then she could open the package. There'd be nothing left to distract her from the total enjoyment.

With a groan, Meredith headed to the patio doors, the clothes basket tucked under her arm. She pulled it open and realized she'd forgotten to turn on the outside light. Though the moon seemed to swath the yard in silver light, it wasn't enough to see by.

As she was about to turn back to switch on the outside light, a path of light suddenly raked across the house.

And she heard a loud, grumbling engine.

Gasping, Meredith stepped back, slamming the door. She reached for the wall plate and shut off the inside light. Darkness fell over her, but the blinds glowed from the light outside glaring against the glass. The rumble of the idling engine vibrated the door.

Meredith tossed the basket aside, then pulled down one of the blind slats far enough to peer out. She saw that only one headlight had cut a funnel through the darkness, highlighting a path across her grass. The other headlight was an empty socket that reminded her of a hollowed eye. She recognized the long, narrow shape of the sedan parked beside her car as belonging to the man from the post office.

Thick clouds of exhaust puttered from the back of the car, floating over the sedan like an ocean fog. The swirling grey began to blanket the backyard.

A deep groan resounded from outside, followed by a long creaking sound.

She saw the driver side door slowly swinging open.

Oh shit!

She knew she shouldn't be standing here. Instead, she should be on the phone with the police, reporting an intruder. She had no idea why she hadn't already handled that phone call. The very least she could do was open the door and tell the creepy old shit to leave.

But she felt as if she'd lost control over her physical and vocal abilities. Only her eyes worked and they remained locked on the sedan that was nearly concealed by the exhaust that looked ethereal from the shimmering headlight. She began to make out a portly shape clambering out from the inside of the car amongst the gray swirls—hunched over, stooped shoulders tipping the top of a rotund figure. Where his head should be looked like jagged tongues of fire, but she quickly realized that was the light underlining his wild, frizzy hair.

He seemed to be leaning against the car, using it for support. Very faintly, she heard the soft clanks of something metallic being dropped on the gravel of her driveway.

"I want my package!"

Meredith let out a frightful cry as she jumped back, her fingers sliding out from the blinds. The slat remained opened, though, and she could see the light between the pale bars of the blinds.

His voice!

Though it had held that same raspy tenor, it no longer sounded weak and hoarse. There was a deep booming quality to it that she'd felt inside of her.

Why's he doing this? I don't have his package! I don't!

Spinning on her heels, she faced the living room. She felt as if she were in a cartoon as her legs pumped but she didn't move, her feet slapping the floor over and over until finally finding purchase and sent her dashing toward the coffee table.

Though she knew where everything was in her house and could usually maneuver around with her eyes closed, she bumped and bounced off everything on her way. Her shins bashed the edge of the coffee table, knocking it forward. The hard wood felt like a baseball bat against her legs.

Crying out, she stumbled. Her knee whammed the top of the coffee table. It slid on the mail, which caused her to twirl sideways and fall on top. Her hip hit the table first, the rest of her body folding over it.

The box started to slide over the edge, but Meredith caught it before it could fall. She heard a thump as what was inside smacked against the cardboard wall.

"Sorry," she muttered through a moan.

Meredith was hurting, but she didn't let it slow her down. She rolled over, throwing mail and old magazines and sales papers out of her way. She realized she'd shoved her cell phone aside a moment too late, but didn't stop to find it again.

All that mattered was putting the package back on the table, which she did with careful precision. She felt like Indiana Jones trying to switch the sandbag for the old artifact. When the package was settled, she carefully peeled off the shipping label. It had her name, box number, and the return address vividly displayed in typed font.

She let loose a shrill discharge of air.

With the light from outside in front of her now, she could see the obstacles much clearer and didn't collide with anything on her way back to the door. If she could show him the shipping label, it would prove that she hadn't stolen the package from him.

Meredith didn't hesitate when she reached the door. She fumbled with the locks, managing to get them disengaged after several tries. Then she flung the door open, not moving out of the way fast enough and bashed her shoulder as she darted out.

The muggy air clung to her already sweaty skin. The usual sweet scent of summer was being choked by the pollution pumping from the sedan's tailpipe. With each heavy breath she pulled in, she tasted burnt oil.

"Mister . . . " she said in a winded voice. "Just look at this . . . it shows that I . . . " Meredith stopped talking when she realized the old man was nowhere around. The car was still there, the engine sounding like a chugging train about to depart. The headlight was still on. The driver's side door still hung open as tendrils of exhaust slithered over like gray water.

"Hello?" she said. Meredith looked around, but couldn't find him. He had to be somewhere close. As she walked, she kept her guard up, expecting him to reveal himself any moment. He never did. She ambled down the steps, her footfalls turning crackly when she reached the gravel.

"Sir?"

Maybe he got back in the car.

Meredith walked slow and stilted to the open door. The interior of the cab was filled with heavy gloom. She reached the edge of the door and peered inside. The front seat, threadbare and worn with exposed patches of stuffing, was empty.

Where the hell is he?

Meredith started to stand upright, but her eyes caught something in the backseat.

"What the hell?" she muttered.

After another quick look around for the old man and not finding him, Meredith stepped closer to the car. She crumpled the label in her fist as she leaned over, sticking her head through the open door.

I can't believe I'm doing this.

Meredith's skin felt as if it were too small for her body. She put a knee on the seat. The material felt like dehydrated fruit against her skin. An odor like cigarette smoke combined with rotted meat seemed to cling to the upholstery. The windows were dark with streaks of filth.

But all of this was ignored as she gazed into the backseat.

"My God . . . "

There was no backseat, at least not one that could be spotted underneath the pool of manila-colored cargo that filled the back of the car. She saw boxes of innumerable sizes poking up from a deep mound of bubble mailers, cardboard sleeves, and paper shipping bags. The packages on top looked fresher, the multiple shades of brown a tad crisper. The mass underneath was faded and worn, the tape holding the packaging paper together peeling and yellow from time.

One thing all the packages had in common were the dark stains scattered across their fronts. The shipping labels she could vaguely read were addressed to different people.

"What . . . is this?"

She spotted a crumpled mailer near the front. It seemed to call out to her for rescue.

This can't be happening.

But when she grabbed the mailer and read the addressee's name, she couldn't deny that it was. In her head, she heard the reporter's account, detailing the sparse facts of the missing woman. The name resounded over and over as she read the label.

The names matched.

This is her mail.

And that meant that these others packages belonged to other . . .

She dropped the package. It landed on top of the myriad others.

She wanted far away from this car.

Meredith started scooting backward, making her way out. As she turned to leave, she spotted the mounted rack on the dashboard that reminded her of what hung on the wall inside a locksmith's shop. *Keys.* Hanging from the pegs were multiple keys. Each of them twinkled dully in the darkness.

And attached to each of them was a faded, paper tag.

Everything came together with such clarity that it seemed to sap all of Meredith's energy.

"Get away from my packages!"

The old man's growl was the shot of adrenaline she needed. She scrambled out of the car, turned around, and spotted the old man coming toward her from the side of the house. It looked as if he'd gone to the front door and was making his way back. She heard the soft squealy sounds of wheels with rusted hinges moving with him.

"You took their packages," she said in a shaky voice. "All of those keys—you have PO boxes all over the place. That's how you do it. You find somebody willing to check your box . . . and if they have a package, you kill them."

"They have *my* packages!" he growled.

As he neared, the squeaks became louder. She realized that he was pulling a cart beside him. The oxygen tank was strapped to it, a clear tube trailing from the top was attached to his nose. He wore thick glasses that reflected the headlight's radiance in the lenses, making it look as if his eyes were smoldering.

"And now, *you* have my package," he said. "You're just like all the others! And I'm going to punish you just like them!"

He charged at her, the cart bouncing beside him with each wild step, clanging and rocking from side to side. His speed surprised Meredith and she barely dodged him when he lunged. As she reached the bottom step of her porch, she heard the bang of his body colliding with the open car door. He cursed, then she heard him start running again.

Without looking behind her, Meredith screamed. She ran up the steps and was just crossing the porch when she heard him start up the steps behind her.

Another scream tore through Meredith as she bolted for the door.

The cart clanged and squeaked, growing louder as he closed in on her. His asthmatic breathing sounded as if it were right next to her ear. She could feel the putters of each breath stirring her hair. She reached her backdoor and shoved it open. Turning around, she started to swing it shut.

The old man was inches from her.

Meredith let out another scream, then the door banged shut. She barely had time to take a breath before the glass exploded and the blinds were knocked loose as the oxygen cart busted through. Shards slit her skin. The blinds whacked her head, folding around her like a stiff, vinyl netting that knocked her to the floor.

On her back, her head and arms poking through the blinds in different sections, she gazed at the door. The old man stepped through the jagged maw of broken glass. She could hear the faint hiss of his oxygen tank pumping air through the nostril tube.

Meredith tried to work the blinds off her, but the more she struggled the further entwined she became. Trying to pull them all the way down her body was no help and seemed to make it worse. She could do nothing but lay there. Nor did she really have the energy to move.

"My package?" he said, shambling forward. The cart squeaked as it rolled beside him.

"Coffee table . . . " she said.

"Much obliged."

When she heard him let out an anxious sigh, she figured he'd found it. He reappeared, carrying the package. "You're riding with me," he said to Meredith.

"That's my package . . . " she said. "I paid for it."

"They're all my packages. And you are too."

Meredith resisted the tears that wanted to come. She was going to be on the news in a few days, that same reporter talking about Meredith's disappearance. Maybe somebody would link her to the other girl. Maybe not.

She looked at the old man again and saw he was no longer watching her. He held the package close to his face. It looked as if was trying to strain hard enough to see through the cardboard.

"What the hell's *in* here?" he asked.

"Don't open it."

"It's my package," he said.

"Then you should know what's in it."

"Smart-mouthed bitch . . . " he grumbled under his breath. He shook the box, hard. It made muffled thumps as his hand jerked back and forth.

"Please!"

The old man laughed. "Sounds like . . . a belt."

"It's not. Just stop shaking it."

Finally, he did. He started picking at the tape that kept the corners down. She warned him again not to open it, but again he didn't listen.

"What's this?" he said. "A sack? You got some jewelry in here? I know how you ladies like your fancy trinkets."

"No," she said. "It's for . . . "

He untethered the rope that held the top shut. As he was about to stick his hand inside, the sack suddenly shot open and a dark, slithering stripe sprang out. The old man didn't get to scream before it attached to his throat.

" . . . my snake," Meredith finished.

Now the old man screamed as he stumbled forward, stepping into the puddle of light that filtered in from outside. The snake dangled from his neck like a twitching, living tie. It plopped off, leaving behind two holes that were already swelling into dunes.

Hand pressed to his neck, the man dropped to his knees. The venom seemed to be working even faster than what her research had led her to think. His face was beginning to swell, lumps appearing under his eyes that forced them shut.

He fell onto his side as his screams began to thin out from his expanding throat.

Meredith tore at the blinds trapping her. After she finally managed to free herself, she ran into the spare bedroom, flipping the light switch. Blue light filled the room in a cool glow, igniting the enclosures alongside her wall in UVA rays. As if sensing her presence, the snakes began to stir, slithering up the glass, heads bobbing from side to side.

Hisses came from all directions, sounding like speakers filled with static.

She ran over to the table where she kept her supplies, grabbed her thick rubber gloves, and pulled them on. When she ran back into the living room, she saw the old man had managed to drag himself closer to the door but was now no longer moving. Though it looked labored, he still appeared to be breathing.

She spotted the snake, slithering near the prone man, gnashing and biting at the air.

"Whoa, buddy," she said in a sweet voice.

The snake spun around, coiled up, and acted as if it was about to strike. Reaching down, Meredith gently scooped the reptile into her hands. Just like her other babies, it didn't attempt to bite her. But she still planned to keep on the gloves. This baby had gotten pretty riled up from being bounced around inside his box.

"H . . . help meeeee . . . " the old man moaned.

"What am I supposed to do?" she asked. "Call the police? You want them to come over and see what you've done? I don't. They'll find the snakebite on you. Then they'll find my babies. They're illegal, you know. Can't own them in the U.S. That's why I had to send out to Australia for this baby." She held the snake to her face, sneaking a quick kiss on the top of his head.

Again, he didn't try to lash out.

"*Pleaseee* . . . " the old man said in a raspy whisper.

"Shut up. I'm not calling for help. I told you not to open the box, so it's your own fault. This little guy can kill a hundred men with the venom from one bite. Isn't that impressive? He's a baby, so his venom is pure, which makes him the deadliest snake in the world. Usually takes a healthy, large man about half an hour to die from a bite like yours. But you? I bet you'll be dead in ten minutes."

The old man let out a strained groan, then went quiet. He'd bloated to nearly three times his normal size. He managed to lift his arm, only for it to drop back to the floor with a limp thud.

He was dead.

"Well," she said, "more like seven minutes."

Smirking, Meredith kissed her snake again, then carried him to the room. She put him in his enclosure that had arrived last week. She had a UVA bulb in the tank and plenty of dirt and faux vegetation for him to slither around in. She watched him investigating his new home for a few minutes, then left the room. She made sure she shut the door. The snakes didn't mind Meredith, but they seemed to not care very much for her cats. Sprinkles was the only one left out of the four she used to have.

Meredith returned to the living room. The old man was leaking puss from where his bloated skin had cracked open. It was forming a murky puddle around his body.

"Gross."

Keeping her gloves on, she grabbed him under the arms and pulled him outside. Then she returned for his air tank. It took her a while, but she managed to get both the old man and his oxygen loaded in the sedan's spacious trunk.

She mopped up the mess the old man had left on the floor. Then she drove his car to the state park and parked in a secluded camping spot. Nobody seemed to be using it. She searched around the car, making sure she wasn't leaving any evidence behind.

My DNA's all over the place.

She doubted it mattered, though. She wasn't on file anywhere.

While searching, she found an old scrapbook under the passenger seat. Glued to the pages were newspaper clippings from Tennessee, dating back to the early eighties with such garish headlines as:

THE PACKAGE

THE PACKAGE KILLER STRIKES AGAIN!
STILL NO LEADS!
PACKAGE KILLER CLAIMS ANOTHER ONE!

Paying attention to the headlines, Meredith skimmed the articles for information. She knew enough to piece together most of the details.

TEENAGE GIRL MURDERED! PACKAGE MISSING!

After flipping past several clippings about the Package Killer and the women he'd attacked, Meredith closed the book.

He's changed up his act a bit since coming to North Carolina.

Meredith had almost become a headline herself. And her package, with her sweet serpent inside, would have been taken as a twisted memento. Tossed in the backseat with the others, where her little guy would have starved.

Meredith felt even less remorse about leaving him to rot in his trunk.

She left the scrapbook out, so the authorities would quickly see it.

Then she started the long walk back home. She was ready to call it a night and eager to spend some time with her babies.

Kristopher Rufty lives in North Carolina with his wife, three children, and the zoo they call their pets. He's written various books, including The Vampire of Plainfield, Jagger, The Lurkers, The Skin Show, Pillowface, *and more, plus a slew of horror screenplays. If he goes more than two days without writing, he becomes very irritable and hard to be around, which is why he's sent to his desk without supper often. For more about Kristopher Rufty, please visit his website: www.lastkristontheleft.blogspot.com*

RED

RICHARD CHRISTIAN MATHESON

HE KEPT WALKING.

The day was hot and miserable and he wiped his forehead. Up another twenty feet, he could make out more. Thank God. Maybe he'd find it all. He picked up the pace and his breathing got thick. He struggled on, remembering his vow to himself to go through with this, not stopping until he was done. Maybe it had been a mistake to ask this favor. But it was the only way he could think of to work it out. Still, maybe it had been a mistake.

He felt an edge in his stomach as he stopped and leaned down to what was at his feet. He grimaced, lifted it into the large canvas bag he carried, wiped his hands, and moved on. The added weight in the bag promised of more, and he somehow felt better. He had found most of what he was looking for in the first mile. Only a half more to go, to convince himself; to be sure.

To not go insane.

It was a nightmare for him to realize how far he'd gone this morning with no suspicion, no clue. He held the bag more tightly and walked on. Ahead, the forms who waited got bigger; closer. They stood with arms crossed, people gathered, complaining behind them. They would have to wait.

He saw something a few yards up, swallowed, and walked closer. It was everywhere and he shut his eyes, trying not to see how it must have been. But he saw it all. Heard it in his head. The sounds were horrible and he couldn't make them go away. Nothing would go away, until he had everything, he was certain of that. Then, his mind would at last have some chance to find a place of comfort. To go on.

RED

He bent down and picked up what he could, then walked on, scanning ahead. The sun was beating down and he felt his shirt soaking with sweat under the arms and on his back. He was nearing the forms who waited when he stopped, seeing something halfway between himself and them. It had lost its shape, but he knew what it was and couldn't step any closer. He placed the bag down and slowly sat cross-legged on the baking ground, staring. His body began to shake.

A somber-looking man walked to him and carefully picked up the object, placing it in the canvas bag and cinching the top. He gently coaxed the weeping man to stand and the man nodded through tears. Together, they walked toward the others who were glancing at watches and losing patience.

"But I'm not finished," the man cried. His voice broke and his eyes grew hot and puffy. "Please . . . I'll go crazy . . . just a little longer?"

The somber-looking man hated what was happening and made the decision. "I'm sorry, sir. Headquarters said I could only give you the half-hour you asked for. That's all I can do. It's a very busy road."

The man tried to struggle away but was held more tightly. He began to scream and plead and two middle-aged women who were waiting watched uncomfortably.

"Whoever allowed this should be reported," said one, shaking her head critically. "The poor man is ready to have a nervous breakdown. It's cruel."

The other said she'd heard they felt awful for the man, whose little girl had grabbed onto the back bumper of his car when he'd left for work that morning. She had gotten caught and he'd never known.

They watched the officer approaching with the crying man he helped into the hot squad car. Then, the officer grabbed the canvas bag, and as it began to drip red onto the blacktop, he gently placed it into the trunk beside the mangled tricycle.

The backed-up cars began to honk, and traffic was waved on as the man was driven away.

RC Matheson is a #1 bestselling author and screenwriter/producer for television and film who has worked with Steven Spielberg, Stephen King, Dean Koontz, Brian Singer, Roger Corman and many others. He has been

MATHESON

head writer and executive producer for countless dramatic and comedy TV series, written hundreds of episodes, pilots and mini-series and had 15 feature films produced including cult favorite Three O'clock High. *His one-hour adaptation of Stephen King's* Battleground *which has no dialogue won two Emmys. Matheson's dark, psychological stories have appeared in 150 major anthologies, including many "Year's Best" volumes. His critically acclaimed novels and collections include* Created By, The Ritual of Illusion, Scars and Other Distinguishing Marks, Dystopia, *and* Zoopraxis. *Matheson has worked as a UCLA parapsychologist and is a professional drummer who studied with CREAM's Ginger Baker. He is president of MATHESON ENTERTAINMENT.*

8 OUT OF 10

DANIEL I. RUSSELL

JOHN OFTEN CALLED his mother stubborn, but *she'd show him.*

Her son was the dogged one; not her. He'd been that way since he was a toddler, refusing to eat his greens and shitting all over the floor. Over the years it brought a refusal to clean his room and failing to get his sorry arse in before ten. Now he insisted she move out and come and live in his backroom, where he could *keep an eye on her.* Jean wasn't stubborn; she just refused to do as he said. Still, he insisted on calling her every night; checking on her since the operation, prying if she'd changed her mind yet.

She gazed at dishwater clouds through droplets streaming down the glass. Closing the window, she shut out the drone of rain. Behind her, curled up on the back of the sofa, George released a pathetic meow of protest.

"Not like you were going out there," grumbled Jean. She hobbled back to the worn out cushions and gingerly laid her wide frame back onto the thinned fabric. A pause during the painful descent allowed her a quick tickle under the cat's chin. Gritting her teeth, Jean leaned back, raising her bandaged right foot onto the arm of the sofa.

It had been more ammo for John, the controlling little sod. She'd been getting along just fine by herself all these years. It took more than a minor operation to change that. Though not according to her son. The phone never stopped ringing. *You could've died* or *You shouldn't have been carrying that kind of weight.* A large tin of cat food. How silly to nearly croak from dropping a tin of cat food on your foot. Still, blood clots don't play around.

RUSSELL

John could talk. Jean had been to the supermarket with him and seen the size of those sacks of dry mix dogs need. That *and* tinned meat? His mutt ate better than her. Drop one of those sacks on your foot and you might be trapped for days.

Jean wiggled her toes and grimaced. She had a clear view of her propped up foot. A crazy itch had driven her to ignore the doctor, and she'd pulled the bandage down just an inch to get a knitting needle in there for a good old scratch. The deep gash, where the surgeon had done all manner of poking around, lay dark and crusty, running down between her big toe and its neighbour. The flimsy butterfly stitches seemed to barely hold it together. Don't they use needle and thread anymore? That's the problem with people today: too afraid of a little pain.

"Pussies," said Jean. "Pussies? Ah, there you are."

Cara, her only female, snuck around the skirting board of the kitchen doorway. With continents of tortoiseshell on white, her furry body was the map of a distant world, with a country shaped like India between the eyes, lending the gentle lady a permanent frown. Cara stopped as something caught her eye, but after deeming it unworthy of enquiry, continued on, settling under the heater.

How could anyone want a dog? Beasts. All drooling and shedding. John's dog smelled like a damp mop with a coat to match. It always tried to jump up at her, pushing with those dirty great paws. *He likes you*, John always said. Rubbish. It would rip out her throat given the chance, like all those poor children you see on the news killed by Pit Bulls. Cats on the other hand never jumped on her without invitation. A tentative pad to test your permission before gently sliding into your lap for dozy purring. Such polite creatures. Who would want a dog? Who would want an overeager shaggy child when such elegance was on offer?

To think! John wanted her to give him a key. A key to her *home*. Letting that dog walk around, shedding hair on the carpet.

"There's your sister," said Jean to George, playfully pinching the cranium of her small, grey male. His tail curled in response, yet from his perch high on the sofa back, he watched Cara with little interest.

Her bigger male, Samson, a beautifully pale Devon Rex, had stayed in the kitchen.

Jean strained to hear over the television, but knew the familiar sound of the slender feline nosing the food dish across the linoleum. She sighed. Jean had certainly not developed a phobia of cat food after her little mishap; she'd just forgotten to fill their dish again.

"Shit."

She peered across the room to the phone on the bookcase, expecting it to ring. *How can you look after three cats if you can't look after yourself?* she heard John say. She looked after her cats just fine. That was another reason she refused to move into his home; her babies would have to go. Can't share a house with that canine monster.

"Just wait," she called, settling back on the sofa. "Mummy just has to rest her foot." Using the remote tucked between the cushions she turned the television up just enough to drown out Samson's impatient game of dish hockey. "I'll do it after this show."

A sudden blare snatched Jean from her dreams, and her eye popped open, groggy regard seeking out the horrendous din.

A young man on the television, the sleeves of his t-shirt crudely cut to show off thick, tattooed arms like slabs of far rotten meat covered in dark moss. In contrast, the guitar that he thrashed was clean and white.

She felt along the sofa for the remote to turn the racket down, but failed to see it in the darkness. While the rain had continued, the hazy grey light from the window had slipped away. Only the harsh, twitching glare from the screen lit the room.

Fell asleep, she realised, finally finding the remote. *God help my power bill . . .*

Her fingers tightened around the remote, threatening to snap the plastic casing. Something had pounced on her chest and smashed the side of her head. Jean released a single hacking cough, dropping the remote to the floor as it slipped from her convulsing fingers. Her back arching, she stared at the dark ceiling, the television projection distorted across it to the cutting, ragged din of the guitar, the endless pound of drums, wailing, screaming . . .

Jeans eyes rolled up. Her bladder let go, soaking her body in warmth. Her injured foot, still managing to retain its place on the arm of the sofa, shuddered, the bandage slipping.

Emerald eyes watched from beneath the heater, and seeing nothing of interest, slowly closed back into the darkness.

Drunk.

The word slurred through Jean's mind as the cold steel light of an unforgiving morning dragged her consciousness back, kicking and screaming.

I'm drunk. Must be.

One eye fluttered open against the invading sun. The other stayed closed and content, hidden and dozing in its bed. The light burned through her eye and into her head, her brain seeming to swell, squeezing against the inside of her skull. Jean groaned and closed her eye from the attack.

She remembered a time before John's father: twenty-two, early sixties. Her elder sister, rest her soul, and a few of her friends had taken her dancing. Some of the local boys had a crate of cheap wine stashed behind the town hall, which, of course, had been readily shared. While she often reminisced over the remainder of that night, her psyche had buried the following morning deep. It came crashing back. Everyone remembers the first time they got rip-roaring drunk.

But I haven't had a drop, Jean strained to think, recalling something about a shining white guitar in the dead of night.

Her tongue probed the back of her teeth, both feeling as furry as the backs of her babies.

Jean fought the sensation of her brain leaking out of an opened tin and forced herself up from the sofa.

Nothing happened. Her body refused to move an inch.

She opened her eye, inviting another solar blast to the retina. She winced . . . yet her face stayed slack, the flesh numb, like she'd been beaten to a pulp and only the few untouched patches stayed receptive. She blinked several times. Her right eye obeyed. Her left stayed dark.

No, she tried to say. Her lips quivered, and she released a subdued grunt. Spittle gathered at the corner of her mouth.

Jean released a long slow breath.

On the television a cartoon cat chased a mischievous mouse, attacking it with a frying pan and missing every time. The room had filled with the sound of raucous crashing and banging, all set to a swinging, merry orchestra. The cat promptly ran into the fist of an upright bulldog; its elastic skull expanding back as the lithe body continued on.

Jean attempted to reach for the remote again, hoping that a little quiet might help her think straight. Her hand defied, fingers barely trembling. Nor could she lift her head for a better view.

I think we're in a spot of bother, old girl.

Her body didn't feel weighted or tied down; it simply didn't feel *at all*. Her right eye remained under her control, and she still had sensation in her lips, jaw, and cheek despite the muscles ticking against her will. She concentrated on moving each individual limb, rewarded only with a slight tingle in her right arm down to the fingertips. It had slipped off the sofa in the night and hung out at an angle over the carpet.

Movement under the radiator caught Jean's eye.

Cara slid out from the narrow gap as if her spine was liquid and idly stood before the heater. The cat yawned, stretched, and sauntered across the carpet to the sofa. Fixing Jean in her amber eyes, like tiny, slashed pumpkins, she hopped up on the cushion.

"Maargh," Jean gurgled, meeting the cat with her one working eye.

Cara mewed and gave Jean's side a gentle poke with a front paw.

Drool seeped from the corner of Jean's mouth as her lips flapped like a fish trying to find water. "Maaamaarg." She swallowed with some difficulty to avoid choking.

"Mew," answered Cara and turned away, watching as George too leapt up onto the sofa, nestled between Jean's motionless legs, and curled into a ball.

RUSSELL

With her left arm lying palm up, and only the black leather band of her watch exposed, the passing of shows on the television and failing light from the window proved Jean's only indication of time.

She coughed: a weak rattling sound from deep within her chest. After just a day, the parts that hadn't abandoned betrayed her with pain. Her lips had dried to thin, shrivelled husks that split with every gabbled sound. Her throat seemed narrow as a pencil and filled with dust.

You have to move. She'd stopped listening.

Cara and George had settled in for the duration of the day, and Samson remained out of sight. Little use they were. Even their usual company provided no comfort.

Speaking of company, where the hell is John?

How many times had he dropped by without so much as a phone call first to spoil her afternoon? If he knocked down the door holding a glass of ice-cold water, Jean considered she might take him up on his offer . . .

He'd love that; being right all along. *This wouldn't have happened if you'd been home with me. I told you to take it easy after your operation. I told you to give me a spare key.* So stubborn.

She imagined a stroke: some blood clot that idiot surgeon had missed floating all the way from her foot up to her brain, blasting through her grey matter like a ricocheting bullet.

I can't call for help, but I can use the television. Turn it up loud enough. Someone's bound to complain; all the old busy-bodies around here . . .

She licked her cracked lips with a fluttering, useless tongue and gazed down the side of the sofa to the threadbare rug. With one eye and unable to lift her head, she focussed on her hand dangling over the side. Faint electrical sparks of feeling still fired in the extreme of her digits. Jean concentrated, picturing a rubber ball lying in her palm. How many times had she squeezed fruit in the supermarket, testing the freshness?

Her fingers barely moved.

Come on . . .

A twitch: her forefinger brushing her thumb.

Jean gave up and gasped in deep breaths. Her body did very little but lie rigid, eye staring thoughtfully at her outstretched hand like some homely Renaissance painting.

George stretched both front legs before lazily climbing to his paws. He surveyed the room for a moment, shot Cara a challenging glare, and ambled down from between Jean's legs, heading for the arm of the sofa. After a short jump, the cat sat proud on the thin stuffing, watching Jean. He gave the loose bandage an inquisitive sniff.

Get away from there. Silly cat.

The drool had really started to flow from the corner of her mouth and slid down her skin like slime. Her thirsty lips quivered, desperate to soak in the balm.

George placed a front paw on the bandage, glanced back at Jean, and mewed.

Leave that alone!

The rough fabric caught in the feline's claws. He yanked, and failing to get free, swatted Jean's foot.

She tried to flinch, expecting a sting from the tender wound beneath. Nothing registered; her foot lost in the void, the connection severed by plundered neurons.

George's tugging had worked the surgical tape free, and with one final swipe, he liberated his claw. The end of the bandage swept down, unravelling from the foot. George snuffled the pale skin, placing his paw against the deadened flesh. His nose explored the crispy scar of her incision.

Jean tried to prod the cat with her big toe, to cause him to leap from the sofa and slink into the kitchen. Nothing happened, and unhindered, the cat continued to poke and probe.

Stop it. George, stop it.

The cat repositioned to plunge its small face in between her toes. His paw pressed against the discoloured butterfly stitches. He licked the thin strips of binding fabric.

George!

His tiny pink tongue rubbed against the patches of dry, brown blood and one particularly nasty spot where Jean had seeped an off-yellow ooze. He lifted his head and began to chat: a series of short, frustrated cries, jaws trembling.

Jean also released her own sound of aggravation: a deep

gurgling from the back of her parched throat. The slightest
movement would send the cat scurrying; she'd done it enough
times when one of her pets had grown too keen. Samson had
always been the worst for that. The boisterous big male would turn
innocent play into a battle, eager with tooth and claw. A firm swat
would send him on his way.

She took a deep breath, hoping to make enough noise to at least
distract the cat. Her dangling fingers convulsed, and her mouth
opened and closed, thirsty lips squeezing against each other over
and over. Her eventual noise, distorted by her slapping lips, was the
cry of a baby.

"Mamamamama . . . "

George struck the bridge of her foot, caught a stitch in a hooked
claw, and tugged it away from the operation site. The adhesive clung
for a second, creating a tent of skin that in turn pulled at her barely-
healed wound. Yet no pain blasted through her sliced tissue; nerve
endings were switched off to the fresh ripping of the laceration. Blood
gathered slowly in the small reservoir formed by the opened gash.

"Mew." George, having ditched the scrap of medi-strip from the
stitching, spied the glistening ruby within the desiccated folds and
promptly began a steady lapping with his quick tongue.

Jean's eye widened. "Mamamama!"

The cat tilted his head for a better angle and reaffirmed his grip,
tearing yet more of the stitching away. The strips hung from his claw
like shreds of flayed skin. Disturbed further, the deep laceration gave
up more of its crimson nectar, encouraging George to delve further
still. A trickle of blood escaped the zealous notice of the cat to
meander down Jean's foot, soaking into the remains of the week-
old bandage.

"Mew?" came another quizzical call from the floor.

Jean looked to the side.

Cara stared up from the base of the sofa, appearing disgruntled
with George's actions due to the scowl created by the pattern on her
face. Eager for attention, she turned on the spot beneath Jean's
outstretched hand; fur tickling the tips of the old woman's fingers.

The phone blared.

Without so much as a glance, George bolted from the sofa and
across the carpet, out of sight.

8 OUT OF 10

Jean's phone, a beige unit on the bookcase, continued with its harsh chirp. John was the only person who ever called; for his nightly check in on how she was coping, to ask how her foot was healing.

Jean's mind cried out. She reached out and grabbed the phone with a phantom hand and screamed into the receiver. That pesky plastic handset; the times she'd raged at filthy Indian callers trying to sell her internet and phone plans. She'd take it, take it all. Spare a moment. Be interested to hear more. Agree to terms and conditions.

Just send someone!

She'd lost count of the shrill calls of the phone. How long did John usually wait? She had no answer machine or voicemail or whatever they call it now. She *always* answered, just to break up her evening with discussing John's dismal love life or that goddamn stupid dog she always heard barking in the background. He'd realise, surely? The one time she didn't answer. Certainly, he'd follow that. He'd jump on a chance to prove his point.

She listened to the rings until they stopped.

A dysfunctional mind worked much like a computer. No matter how many wires were severed, that tiny battery-powered component kept track of the time and made appropriate changes when it logged on.

Having been left alone by the cats, Jean's endless pursuits to grab the TV remote had grown monotonous. The descending darkness and comforting chatter from the television had lulled her back into a fretful sleep, eventually disturbed by the gentle persistence of dawn from the window. She opened her eyes, blinking away the grime. Another day, this one smelling more like old piss than ever.

Staring at the ceiling, she tested her functions. Her fingers twitched and curled; better than yesterday. If her arm would obey, she believed her chances of actually clasping the TV remote had greatly improved. Now she tried her voice, hoping some audible cry may have come available. Her lips flapped, and a weak gargle escaped from her withered throat.

Why hasn't he come?

This was all John ever wanted, and not answering the phone was like a gold-leafed invitation.

The volume of sensation had been turned down a notch. Jean feared the stroke had been but an initial attack from her rebelling nervous system. Had further pops and severance taken what little she had left?

No. This is ... this ...

Hunger? Dehydration?

Probably both.

She drew a laboured, papery breath. Her eyelid felt like a razor blade, but beggars couldn't be choosers. At least she could still half-see.

Cara and George sat hunched on the arm of the sofa, their glossy backs to her. Her bare ankle sat between them, vanishing among their curling tails and bobbing coats. Jean breathed deep and unleashed an almighty groan to try and shift them from their roost. The resulting pathetic gargle did little to stir the felines.

Cara licked her paw and swept it back over her head, smoothing down an ear, which sprang straight back up.

Jean squinted at the top of the cat's nodding head. Cara seemed to have smeared something over her ear: a dark, wet substance slicking the fur.

A fibre of entrenched muscle in her foot twinged. With nothing but a numbed ocean from the neck down, this insignificant, tiny hook had still snagged in the depths and somehow made its presence known. Yet still no pain, just an indistinct tug.

Jean feebly cried out once more to shoo them away. Her dangling fingers twitched and coiled in useless animation. Her wretched gargle drew the attention of George, who lazily looked back over his shoulder, surveying her with cold, green opalescent eyes.

Between her pets, Jean's foot remained propped up on the worn fabric of the sofa arm. She started at it for a moment, unsure what to make of the destroyed flesh that still stood upright on the thin cushion. Her first thought was that of a chicken carcass. After a hearty roast, Jean would take great pleasure in peeling thin scraps of meat from the spread leftovers, plucking shreds from the narrow, greasy bones. This carnage, which George now returned to, had a more vibrant palette: from the black tissue deep within the gaping wound, stark against the shiny clean bone, to the rich cherry blood that dribbled down her pale skin, escaping the cat's attention in places and drying to patches of rust.

Jean released a long croak; one eye staring, the other still closed.

George and Cara had worked through the site of her operation, obliterating the stitching and tearing into the succulent meat within. Tooth and claw had snipped through tendon and nerve with a precision to make her surgeon jealous. With the pets having eaten most of what lay between, her big toe had been separated from its neighbours, leaning a good few inches away from the cluster of grimy digits. It stood like a gnawed cocktail sausage on an ivory skewer; the cats had reduced it to nothing more than bone and a few tenacious scraps.

Jean listened to her breaths snap in and out and gazed at the ceiling.

Another ghostly tug pulled from the darkness. How a sinew must scream with pain when chewed through. Jean just felt another slight twang and an odd release: bones sliding further apart perhaps, free from their sallow moorings.

The phone started to ring.

Please, Jean begged, turning her gaze to that taunting beige handset. It had to be John. *Please!*

Close to her left ear, drowning out the trill of the phone, came a low, throbbing purr.

"Murgh?" cried Jean, trying to turn her head to the direction of the noise. Her working eye swept back and forth, her fingers twitched and scratched.

A slender paw with neat, short grey hair landed daintily on her chest, just below her throat; claws like ivory splinters nestled within the fur. Azure eyes peered at Jean, set within a wrinkled face under gremlin ears. Samson, the Devon Rex, sat upon her like a night hag, reminding her of the stories her grandmother had told her as a child: dream demons crushing your chest while you slept.

Cara and George continued to feed, digging into the widening bloody chasm before the larger male inevitably chased them aside.

Samson dipped his head, staring at Jean. The tip of a single fang protruded from under his lip.

Jean closed her eye, her mind reaching out for the blaring phone with a telepathic hand, yanking it from the cradle and screaming into the receiver.

She cried out from a warm touch to her lips, snatching her back to reality.

Samson had pressed his paw against her mouth; the soft skin of his pad surrounded by tickling fur. Jean met his eyes, whimpering. The cat pushed further, like he tried to quiet her.

Sssshhhh.

The phone obliged. The television played on, the banal chatter from the women on screen drowning out the satisfied lapping from George and Cara.

How long? If John decides to leave right now . . . how long would it take him?

"Mew?"

Jean looked back to her pride and joy: the beautiful short-haired Samson. Now his eyes seemed cold, the triangular face and large ears more like a goblin than a sleek feline.

The first pinch of his claws stabbed at her lower lip, a slight hook catching on her flaked skin.

Jean grimaced, pulling back her trembling lips, brandishing her teeth.

Samson looked down and, not one to be denied, struck once more. His claws poked through her dry skin, fastening into the flesh.

After the lack of sensation over the last few days, the pain exploded through her face, knocking her dizzy. Blood pattered from the tiny incisions as Samson, leaning forwards and toying with her lip, pulled it back and forth, opening the gashes further. Jean issued a long, garbled cry between her clenched teeth and tried to pull back from the cat's hold. Samson clung on, stretching the parched lip further still. The skin cracked, feeling like a sheet of paper had been swept across her mouth, cutting the corners.

"Gargh!" cried Jean, failing to think through the sparks of agony flaring through her head, and snapping her teeth at the cat.

Samson leaned in to delicately lap at the blood spilled across her chin.

8 OUT OF 10

During Jean's slumbers, the sofa had started to bob on gentle waves, the currents turning her around while she floated. Sounds drifted across the dark ocean: voices, gunfire, music. Cats fighting, their alien cries and yowls piercing her skull. Claws scurried across the carpet. Fur brushed her cheek.

Jean wailed through the hurt. A ring burned around her mouth; a clown smile of hot coals. Her throat threatened to collapse in a cloud of ash and flakes at the slightest touch. She fought to open her one good eye.

Cara and George both lay scattered on the carpet on their sides, basking in the warmth from the still burning heater. Samson sat perched on the arm of the sofa, a living gargoyle, next to her mangled foot.

Jean stuck out her tongue, seeking the source of the excruciating pain around her mouth. Samson had sliced her up pretty bad before she'd passed out, but surely a few cuts . . .

At the end of the sofa, the male cat began to groom himself, licking his paw and dragging it across his wet, sticky fur.

Jean tried to find the withered husks of her lips. Her tongue probed over exposed teeth, arriving at the ragged, pulpy mess past her gums.

Anything loose. Anything readily available. That's how the cats worked. Why take on the main body of work when you could nibble away at toes, devour lips? Next would be her fingers. Eyes didn't take much digging out. Jean also remembered a story of a man cutting out his own nose with a pair of blunt scissors. If he could do that, it would be no problem for her team of master surgeons. A slow operation. A banquet served over many, many courses.

She closed her eyes and concentrated, not on her twitching fingers that still hovered over the remote, clutching to her fragile plan, but her darkest, deepest recesses. That little cluster of cells that had shot through her brain, punching holes through her grey matter and popping her circuitry; it still had to be lodged in there somewhere. She willed it to continue on, to jar loose and press ever onwards, ripping neurons, plundering cortex.

Worse ways to depart this world existed. She'd learned that.

A heavy knock at her front door caused her eye to spring open. Three solid strikes against the wood sounded over the television.

RUSSELL

Cara and George sprang up from their relaxation and slunk underneath the heater. Sampson watched them, dipping his narrow head slightly, before staring back at Jean, licking his lips.

Jean tried to call out, but even her pathetic gibberish had become too much of a demand. She wheezed, fixated on the door beside the television, praying for it to open.

"Mum?" came the distant voice from the hallway outside.

John! My John! I knew he'd come. My sweet, sweet John!

The woman on screen was talking about dietary supplements. Jean wished the trollop would shut up just for one moment.

He knocked again, really giving it some, desperate to be heard over the television. She could hear him! *It's on too loud, son. Something's wrong. Come inside! Come inside!*

"He . . . " she managed, tears streaming down her cheek. "He . . . jo . . . "

The brass handle of the front door rattled as he tried to force the door. He had no key.

"Mum? Are you in there? I can hear the television. I called, but . . . "

Open the fucking door!

Samson, still preening the short fur on his blood-soaked cheeks, flicked his tail and began a careful decent from Jean's split foot, padding between her legs and onto her stinking groin.

Even with her tongue hanging out, Jean gnashed her teeth together, straining to deter her pet.

Samson continued his slow progress, his head low, wide ears curled forward and playful.

With her worn incisors chomping on her quickly bloodied tongue, Jean relished the burst of moisture and fed from it, the coppery taste giving her more incentive to snap her teeth together and drive the cat back.

One more hard fist slammed against the front door. "Fine! Suit yourself Mum, you stubborn old bird. Call me when you come to your senses."

No!

Jean took a long pause, panting and struggling to hear over the television.

John?

The silly woman onscreen continued to prattle, undisturbed by any more knocks or shouts. Jean even glanced pleadingly at the telephone.

Samson ventured farther across her chest, reaching her throat and lifting his face into her view. Jean gazed into his cool orbs, her eye unblinking. Such a lithe, hungry little beast.

"Mew?"

Worse ways. At least the cats would be fed for the rest of the week.

Daniel I. Russell has been featured in publications such as The Zombie Feed, Pseudopod *and* Andromeda Spaceways Inflight Magazine. *Author of* Samhane, Come Into Darkness, Critique, Mother's Boys, The Collector, Retard, *and* Tricks, Mischief and Mayhem, *Daniel is also the former vice-president of the Australian Horror Writers' Association and was a special guest editor of* Midnight Echo. *His latest novel,* Entertaining Demons, *is due for release in 2017 with Apex Publications. Daniel lives in Western Australia with his partner and four children, and is currently completing a BA in psychology and counselling.*

THE MACHINE

BENTLEY LITTLE

"YOUR GARAGE IS so cool," Matt said, looking around. "You have all this *stuff* in it. We don't have *anything* in ours. My dad always says we have to leave room for the car, even though he parks it in the driveway instead of the garage."

It was kind of cool, Derek had to admit. He'd never really thought about it before, but his dad did have some pretty bitchin things stored in here. On the wall above the rake, broom and lawnmower was a green street sign from Anderson Lane that his dad had stolen from a country road on a trip to Cleveland. Anderson was their last name. In the corner next to his dad's workbench was a plaster moose with a broken leg that his dad had found at the dump. The only reason the moose was able to stand was because the top half of the leg rested on a log that had been chainsawed to look like a bear. Around the garage were various orange and yellow traffic cones, as well as empty wooden cable spools the size of tables, on which were various pieces of broken machinery that his dad had salvaged and at some point planned to fix. The center of the crowded space was taken up with boxes, trunks, racks and bookcases filled with spillover stuff from the house that couldn't fit and needed to be stored out here. From the open-beam ceiling hung a kite, several fishing poles and a kayak.

On a shelf, they found a bunch of old primitive video games, small handheld devices that had yard lines, goal posts, baseball diamonds and tennis nets painted onto tiny screens. Most of the games were dead, but one still had batteries and worked, and they both laughed as Derek turned it on and it made electronic beeping noises as small red dots moved fitfully across a football field in approximation of the players.

"This is what my dad used to play with?" Derek said wonderingly. "It sucks!"

They'd come in looking for an air pump in order to fill up the half-flat basketball that was still lying out on the driveway, but, distracted by everything they found in the packed garage, they ended up searching through the bewildering array of objects until it was time for Matt to go home.

After his friend left, Derek continued his exploration. Inside an old trunk, he discovered baby toys that he'd forgotten about but that jogged his memory the instant he saw them. Within a cardboard box were videotapes of old movies from the 1980s. Opening up a cabinet located behind a life-sized cardboard cutout of Princess Leia, he found three tin shelves, empty save for a dirty, peculiar-looking device that sat in the exact center of the cupboard. It was a machine of some kind. Slightly bigger than a shoebox, it was made of a dull once-gold metal and had a button and toggle switch flanking a dusty domed light. Next to the light was a jiggly little valve, and flush with the casing top was a single gear enmeshed within a spoked wheel. There was no power cord nor could he find a spot where batteries might fit. On the side of the machine, in its center, was a hole.

What did the machine do? Or what was it *supposed* to do? Because it was clearly broken. He turned it over in his hands but could think of no possible purpose for the device. Was it some type of old-time radio receiver? That was the best he could come up with, although just by looking at it he knew that was wrong. He flipped the toggle switch, pressed the button, used his finger to turn the wheel and gear, but nothing happened.

It was the hole that really intrigued him. He was afraid to put his finger in there, afraid the machine might suddenly come to life and chop it off or mangle it beyond recognition, but he did hold up the device so that the hole was at eye-level and he could peek inside. Even with the light on, the garage was dark, however, and the hole was completely black; nothing could be seen within it.

He and Matt had come across a flashlight earlier, and Derek went back to get it. The beam was bright when he turned it on, but when he shone the light into the hole, the blackness seemed to absorb the illumination, leaving the interior of the machine as dark as ever. Taking a screwdriver from his dad's workbench, Derek held tightly to the plastic handle, inserting the tapered metal rod into the opening, but nothing happened. The machine did not turn on, there were no sparks or noises, the screwdriver did not vibrate in his hand. Strangely, however, the tip of the screwdriver did not hit the back of the object, although it should have since the tool was almost as long as the machine was wide.

Weird.

"Derek!"

He heard his mom calling and put down both the machine and the screwdriver, turning off the flashlight and leaving it on the cement next to the device, before hurrying out of the garage. "Coming!" he called.

It was time for dinner, and when he emerged the sun was almost down. He was surprised to discover it was so late. Taking a last look behind him, he dashed across the lawn, through the back patio and into the house.

That night in bed, he replayed in his mind the events in the garage, and thinking of the machine, recalling the round black hole in its side, he felt a strange tingling, an excited shivery sensation that encompassed his entire body but seemed centered between his legs. His penis was hard and sticking out, pressing against his pajama bottoms the way it sometimes did, and he found himself wondering what it would be like to slide it into the hole of the machine. The idea was completely crazy and made no sense at all, although he couldn't help reflecting that the opening was just the right size for that.

In the morning, he awoke well before his parents, as he did every weekend, only this time he didn't wake up his mom so she could make him breakfast. No, this time he carefully put on his slippers, then made his way down the hallway to the laundry room, where he quietly turned the lock and opened the door to the back yard. He paused for a moment to make sure neither of his parents had been awakened, then tiptoed through the patio and hurried soundlessly across the grass to the garage.

He had dreamed about the garage last night. More specifically, about the machine, though he was still unsure whether or not the dream was a nightmare. In it, he had been kneeling naked on the cement floor, holding the machine in both hands as he slid his organ inside the hole. The sensation was amazing, and when he'd awoken, his penis had been sticking up, quivering, and so hard that it hurt.

It was still hard, which was why he was sneaking out to the garage.

He wanted to put it in the machine.

Derek knew how stupid the idea was and how dangerous such an action might be. He had no clue what would happen once he inserted his penis into the hole. But the impulse was strong, and, driven by his experience in the dream—

nightmare

—he opened the small garage door and made his way through the gloom to where he'd left the machine on the cement. The screwdriver was still there, as was the flashlight, and he flipped on the flashlight, pointing the beam at the side with the hole.

If anything, his penis had gotten harder, and, just as he had in his dream, he pulled down his pants, knelt on the cold hard floor, put down the flashlight, picked up the device, positioned the opening in front of his crotch and slowly slid his penis in.

The sensation was amazing, unlike anything he had ever experienced, far better than even his sleeping brain had imagined. The hole felt soft around him, smooth, as though it was lined with silk, and there was a slight hint of pressure that intensified the feeling in his member. Acting on instinct, he held the machine firmly in place and began to move his penis in and out with slow even strokes. It felt better and better by the second, growing more and more intense, and he quickened the movement of his pelvis, becoming harder and more excited, until finally, at the end, a jolt of ecstasy shot through him, causing his entire body to shudder. On the top of the device, a green light flashed and a little valve moved up and down, emitting a low pleasant whistle.

Then the machine was still and silent again.

His penis was soft now, and Derek was suddenly filled with an overwhelming sadness, feeling both guilty and let down, exhausted and empty.

He drew out, standing and pulling up his pants. He could hardly bear to look at the machine now. The very thought of it disgusted him, and he picked it up gingerly, holding it at arm's length as he returned it to the cabinet in which he had found it. Using the flashlight, he put away the screwdriver and returned to the house, where, thankfully, his parents had not yet awakened.

He went into the living room, turning on the TV and his Wii, playing a Mario game until his mom got up and asked him what he wanted to eat.

At breakfast, his parents didn't speak to each other, although they both spoke to him. How long had this been going on? He tried to think of a time when they had talked to each other at breakfast and realized that maybe they never had. He could not recall them ever having a mealtime conversation, and he wondered why that was and why he had not noticed it until today.

He felt different than he had before using the machine. Something had changed, although he did not know what it was.

Derek looked from his mom to his dad. There was no animosity between them, but there was nothing else either, and his mom asked him what he planned to do today and his dad asked him if his jump shot was getting any better, and both of them smiled supportively at his answers.

Matt came over mid-morning. Derek wanted to show him the machine, ask his friend what *he* thought it was, but at the same time he wanted to keep it a secret, and instead of taking Matt into the garage, the two of them played basketball in the alley.

His mom invited Matt to stay for lunch, but they were having leftovers and Matt hated leftovers, so he pretended as though his parents were making him go home for lunch. Derek promised to come over after he finished eating, and Matt said they could play with a new game he'd gotten for his Xbox.

After lunch, however, Derek found himself sneaking into the garage. He *told* his mom he was going over to Matt's, and he fully intended to do so—eventually—but first he wanted to see the machine again.

It was exactly where he had left it, in the cupboard, although, in the split second before pulling open the wooden cabinet door, he was filled with the certainty that it had moved, that it had hidden itself from him in another part of the garage. The machine was there, though, resting calmly alone on the middle shelf, its metal as dull as ever, its design as inscrutably old-fashioned.

Its hole as warmly beckoning.

Had he placed it in that position, with the hole facing outward? For some reason, he thought he had not, though he could not be certain that was the case. The doubt disturbed him, and it kept him from reaching out and picking up the device, which was what he wanted to do.

What was the point of the machine? he wondered. What did it do? Who had made it and why? He had no answers for any of those questions. He was not even sure he wanted answers, and he closed the cupboard door, left the garage and hurried over to Matt's house.

Usually, an afternoon at Matt's would have sped by, but even the Xbox couldn't distract his mind from thoughts of the machine and the sense memory of what he had done with it this morning, and the afternoon dragged on and on. He wanted more than anything else to go back home to the garage, but he forced himself to stay at Matt's even longer than he would have ordinarily.

It was nearly dinnertime when he returned home. His mom was in the kitchen cooking, his dad was in the living room watching the news, and after getting a drink of water and announcing to both of them that he had returned, Derek snuck outside, into the back yard and the garage. He had decided to bring the machine into his bedroom and hide it in his closet, although he was not sure when that resolve had occurred to him. He was committed to it, though, and he picked up the object and carried it to the open door of the garage, checking to make sure his mom wasn't looking out the kitchen window before hurrying over to the house.

He carried the machine in front of him, holding it with both hands, and its position was nearly the same as when he'd *used* it. The hole was at crotch level, and as he hurried across the grass, it bumped against him, and he was aware of the fact that if he were naked, he would be able to stick his penis into the machine as he ran. The thought made him hard.

Inside the house, he slipped out of the laundry room in the hallway, and then into his bedroom, where he slid the machine underneath his bed. Just in time, too, because seconds later his mom called out, "Time to eat!" He washed his hands in the bathroom sink and went out to the dining room, where his mom was bringing out plates of spaghetti, and both of his parents ignored each other and asked him if he'd had fun at Matt's.

Tomorrow was a school day, so he had to take a bath and go to bed early. He wasn't sure he'd be able to sleep, knowing that the machine was under his bed, and he wondered what had made him bring it into the house in the first place. But he dozed off almost immediately and did not wake up until his dad came in at six the next morning and told him it was time to get ready for school.

The day was long, and he wished it was summer. His mind kept going back to the machine, and one time when he thought about it at recess, his penis popped up, and he had to hide in the bathroom until it went down so he wouldn't be embarrassed.

His mom was waiting for him on the couch when he got home that afternoon.

The machine was sitting on the coffee table in front of her.

Seeing it, Derek was filled with a mixture of fear and dread. He should have known that she might find it. Monday was the day she did laundry, and she always checked on the floor of his room and under his bed to make sure he hadn't left shirts or socks there instead of putting them in the hamper. His mouth was dry, and he watched her carefully. She didn't look mad, but he still said nothing, waiting for her to speak first.

His mom pointed to the machine, smiling. "So where did you find *this*?"

He squirmed uncomfortably. "In the garage."

"It's a family heirloom. Did you know it used to be your grandpa's? He told me that it used to be *his* grandpa's. So it's really old."

Apparently, he was not in trouble, and he managed to relax a little. "What's it for?" Derek asked. Maybe his mom knew. "What's it do?"

She picked up the device and turned it around. "See this hole here? You stick your dick in it."

Derek felt cold. He had never heard his mom say such a word before. He was shocked to learn that she even *knew* that word. And she certainly shouldn't be using it in front of him. What would his dad think if he heard her talking this way?

It's the machine, he thought. *It's making her say this.*

THE MACHINE

She offered him the device. "Why don't you pull your pants down and try it?"

"No!" he shouted and ran out of the room. His heart was pounding a mile a minute, and he sped out of the house the way he'd come in, stopping next to the car in the driveway, breathing deeply. He looked back toward the living room window, glad it appeared dark from this angle, glad he could not see his mom. He wasn't sure why he'd overreacted like that, why her suggestion had triggered such a violently immediate response in him, but he knew that he did *not* want her to find out that he already used the machine.

What he didn't want to admit to himself—and what he would *never* admit to his mom—was that he wanted to do it again. That first time, in the garage, he had felt horrible afterward, lower than he ever had in his life, but the high before the low was so amazing that it was worth suffering the letdown, and the truth was that his brain had had little room for any other thoughts since. It was why he had smuggled the device into his bedroom, why he'd had to hide in the bathroom at recess. Even now, his penis was hard.

What was going to happen after this? Was his mom going to keep the machine? Put it back in his bedroom where she'd found it? Return it to the garage? Tell his dad about it? He didn't know, and the uncertainty made him feel anxious.

Not knowing what to do, afraid of returning to the house, he went into the back yard, found his basketball, and shot hoops in the alley until his mom sent his dad out two hours later to tell him to come in, it was time for dinner.

The machine was no longer on the coffee table, and his mom said nothing to him about it before, during or after dinner. When he went to bed later, after doing his homework and watching TV with his dad, he found the device back under his bed.

Unable to sleep, he lay there thinking, planning, closing his eyes when his parents came to check on him. Later, much later, when he was sure they were asleep, he brought out the machine, placed it on the edge of his mattress with the hole facing outward, pulled down his pajama bottoms and underwear, stuck his already hard penis into the opening and started thrusting.

He exploded.

The green light went on, the valve fluttered and whistled.

LITTLE

Again: after the elation and ecstasy, depression, sadness, regret.

He began using it every night—and thinking about it when he was not using it. More than once, he returned from school to find that the machine had been moved, and he chose to believe it moved itself, because the alternative, that his mom went into his bedroom while he was gone and inspected the machine to see what he was doing with it, made him feel repulsed and sickened.

He grew braver. On Saturday morning, he used the machine while his dad was mowing the lawn and his mom was pulling weeds in her flowerbed. One weeknight, he brought it with him into the bathroom in the middle of dinner, excusing himself from the table and quickly using it while his parents ate. It was a compulsion, and increased frequency did not lessen his craving but boosted it.

On the following Friday, he aced a math test, and Derek decided to reward himself after school by using the machine, a thought he titillated himself with all afternoon. He hurried directly home, speeding ahead of Matt and their friend Nick, holding a textbook in front of the obvious bulge in the front of his pants. Shrugging off his backpack and throwing his book on the coffee table, he rushed back to his bedroom, hoping to finish before his mom even knew he was back.

She was sitting on his bed, waiting for him.

Derek started, almost crying out he was so startled.

"Looking for your little toy?" There was something accusatory in her tone.

"No," he lied.

"Your dad's using it."

Derek was filled with a sense of disgust. Just the thought of his dad sticking his . . . *thing* . . . into the hole of the machine made his stomach feel queasy, made him want to run out of the house and never come back. But there was another feeling beneath the disgust. Jealousy? Not exactly, although that was close. It was more a sense of having his space invaded, having been robbed. The machine was *his*, and how dare his dad take it for himself? The device had been sitting in the garage for years. Why hadn't his dad used it before now? Why had he waited until *Derek* had found it to . . . do what he was doing?

"He's in the bedroom right now," she said. "Putting his dick inside there."

THE MACHINE

Isn't that what he's supposed to do to you? Derek thought, and it was as if his mom could read his mind because she gave him a sad smile and said, "Sometimes things can't be undone."

What did that mean? He suddenly felt that he was seeing his mom—and his dad—in a new light, but he didn't know what light that was. He felt confused and frightened and wished he'd never snooped around in the garage and found the stupid thing.

At the same time, he felt its pull.

Not wanting to be there when his father finished, Derek left his mom on the bed, and went outside, going into the garage and stopping before the open door of the cabinet where he'd found the machine, breathing heavily. Fear, confusion and anxiety were all balled up in one heavy knot of collective dread inside him as he stared at the empty shelves.

What was he going to do now?

He didn't know. But it was a school night, and, on a practical level, he had homework due tomorrow. He would like to be able to stay out here all night, would like to be able to run away and never have to face his parents again, but neither of those things were going to happen. He wandered restlessly around the inside of the garage, knocking over some of his dad's tools, kicking a hole in a cardboard box, trying to calm down, before he finally forced himself to go back into the house.

He was thirsty, and the first thing he did was get a drink of water. As he was filling his cup in the sink, his dad walked in, all smiles. "How goes it, Sport?"

Derek nodded, mumbled and got away before any questions could be asked by either side.

In his bedroom, his mom was still seated on the bed. She was holding the machine in her lap. He looked at it, revolted. The fact that his dad had used it was just gross, and acting on impulse, he grabbed the object, lifted it above his head and smashed it down on the floor. Pieces of metal broke off, but the machine was still basically intact, so he grabbed his baseball bat, leaning against the side of his dresser, and began furiously pounding on the device, using all of his strength to demolish it, stopping only when the machine was no longer recognizable but was merely a collection of metal fragments strewn about the floor. He could not even differentiate the parts that had once created the hole.

He expected the noise to draw in his dad, but from the front of the house he heard the sound of the television and CNN, and he knew that his dad wasn't coming.

Derek put the bat back in place. Staring at the broken pieces of the machine, he had the sudden urge to drop to his knees, gather up the pieces and put the whole thing back together. He wanted to use the hole again, wanted to feel that wonderful building sensation and the ecstatic release and even the sadness afterward. He wanted to see the light go on, wanted the valve to pop up and whistle.

At the same time, he knew he'd done the right thing, and he looked over at his mom for confirmation. But she only said, "You think that will make a difference?" She shook her head and gave him the same sad smile as before. "Sometimes things can't be undone," she said again.

Who *were* his parents? he wondered. What did he really know about them? He had never felt more distant from anyone, and he wondered if they felt the same way about him, if they were all just strangers living in the same house.

His mom stood up from the bed and walked out of the room, saying nothing.

Maybe he *could* put the machine back together, Derek thought. Or maybe he could build another one. Maybe he could build two: one for himself, one for his dad.

Maybe.

Sometimes things can't be undone

Maybe.

The world's third so-called "test tube baby" and the first to become a horror writer, Bentley Little is hated and feared in equal measure. Woe to those who try to cross him.

POSTHUMOUS

LLOYD KAUFMAN &
LILY HAYES KAUFMAN

This story is dedicated to the memory of Karen Black

A SUNDAY AFTERNOON, quiet except for a faint squeaking. A fragile mouse's face twitches in the frame of a computer screen. The image zooms out and we see the skinny rodent suffers, starving on a sticky-trap. Desperate to free himself, he pulls one leg at a time. Confusion, fear, and pain are etched into his beady eyes.

Across the expensively decorated home office, Geoff is glued to a jumbo screen. I hope you got that spelling down; Geoff hates when people spell his name "Jeff." The plebeian spelling his parents gave him at birth disgusts him. Geoff is a modern day "Master of the Universe." He's one of the smug guys out of *Bonfires of the Vanities* meets the creep from *American Psycho*. He's clean cut and wears nice suits. He's got the right haircut. "You can take him anywhere," your mother would probably say.

Geoff's apartment is a typical *nouveau riche* bachelor pad. A full-size pool table stands where a dining room table might otherwise go. Although the apartment has four bedrooms, Geoff converted one to his home office. Another is a wall-to-wall temperature controlled wine storage room, the third he turned into his gym, and the fourth bedroom, where he sleeps, hosts a stripper pole. Sharp angled furniture and cream suede walls scream "I am built to be harmed by, or harm, little kids who come in contact with me." Geoff happens to have two kids. But it's not like he lets them visit his man palace.

Geoff turns a second webcam towards his own face. He clicks

UPLOAD LIVE TO YOUTUBE on his computer and *voilá*, his webcast *House of Worth* is streaming. A split-screen pops up on the monitor: suffering mouse on one side, Geoff's sweaty face on the other.

The idea occurred to Geoff yesterday that the mouse might help him tap into a new market, so het set up his camera to film the suffering. Geoff checks his account statistics—250,000 people have tuned in to the webcast this afternoon. He clicks to the "Trending" tab and scans the list of the internet's most popular webcasts: *How To Straighten A Pig's Tail, Weird Things Couples Do With Their Dogs, Extra Body Parts You Won't Believe!* Nope, Geoff's webcast, *House of Worth,* is not trending.

"What the fuck." Geoff slams his fist on the table. He is determined to get 1 million subscribers. He's tried all the dirty tricks—paying a sleazy online service for the first 150,000 subscribers, and then forking over another $200k to advertise his channel. The next 100,000 sheep subscribed on their own for 6-11 hours a night of live Geoff. Now he's got a quarter of a million subscribers, but no, he isn't fucking trending yet. Even after torturing a mouse!

With *House of Worth* running as smoothly as it can without trending, Geoff settles back in his Herman Miller desk chair and bites into his lunch of spare ribs. The mouse activity is heating up—in a last ditch measure to free himself, the mouse chews through his own leg to escape. He is bleeding and defecating, fluids are coming out of all orifices. Mouse juice is about to spill off the trap and onto Geoff's pristine white marble floor.

Geoff heads over and stands above the mouse's sticky torture pad. "You goddamn incompetent mouse trap. Can't you do your job without making a mess on my floor!"

The mouse breathes faster, his little heart races. He rips one leg free. Geoff jolts back, startled. Angered, he steps on the trap to crush the mouse. The trap sticks to the sole of his Gucci loafer. Geoff slaps his foot on the floor to free himself. He uses his other foot to step on the edge of the trap and frees his right foot, only to find his left foot is stuck.

"Oh good one, stick to my foot, you bastard." Geoff kicks his foot angrily to free himself. "Goddamn sticky trap. Get off my foot." The sticky pad has trapped him like flypaper. Geoff is no different than the mouse. "How dare you?" Geoff yells at the sticky trap. "Get off my foot! What are you stupid or something? Do I look like a mouse to you? You dumb piece of sticky shit."

Geoff hops around on the other foot and tries to pull off the trap. He doesn't want to touch it with his hand so he tries to remove the sticky trap with his other shoe...again. He passes the trap from one shoe to the other and back again, hopping side to side. With the right dramatic lighting and minimal music, if you were just channel surfing the internet and landed on Geoff's webcast, you might think he was performing an interpretive dance. *Is this the Martha Graham channel?* A YouTube channel surfer asks herself, clicking on the webcast. *A traditional Riverdance performance?* Geoff's subscriber base ticks up to 275,000 viewers.

The choreography comes to the grand finale as Geoff bends over into a *port-de-bras*. He sweeps his hand down to his foot and with one final swing of the arm he frees the sticky trap and mouse carcass from his shoe and tosses it into the garbage.

Geoff looks at the stove clock. It's flashing 12:00. Not again! The clock is always resetting on him. Geoff checks his Rolex. "Great! Thanks a lot. I'm twenty minutes late." He has to prepare for his next show this evening.

Washed, shaved and perfumed, Geoff directs a beautiful redhead. He doesn't remember the woman's name, but he made sure to spell his when they met. He's sitting on the love seat while the redhead is now dancing with her back to him, leaning forward on a stripper pole. The pole fits perfectly in Geoff's bachelor pad.

"You like that," the woman says.

"Mmmhmm," Geoff says, though he's more interested in adjusting the camera angle. He has to make sure he gets shots that are perfect for his channel, but he can't get it tilted just right. "Fucking camera," he mumbles. "You are just as worthless as the stove clock."

"Just relax, baby." She coos. Geoff figures she's probably too stoned to know or care about his filming or that Geoff cares more about getting a good angle on himself than her anyway. He has to look good for his viewers.

When they're done, the woman asks for water.

"You've got legs, don't you?" Geoff sneers from his office where's he's already back at the computer again.

She leaves the love seat and makes her way to the kitchen.

"The fridge light's burned out," she says when she returns. She takes a sip of water. "Just thought I should tell you."

Geoff ignores her. He's done with her. And besides, it's not important. He can buy new fridges and clocks for that matter. What he needs is more subscribers. He is addicted to collecting followers, obsessed with making people appreciate his worth. Now if only she would leave him alone to work.

"I guess I'm gonna leave," the redhead says. Geoff is relieved she's gotten the hint. He adjusts the camera until he's pleased that in the background you can see pictures of him on a yacht. More bonuses from his marriage.

"You don't have to be so angry all the time. It's not like it's going to help anything," she adds.

"Get the fuck out!" Geoff snaps.

Ding! 290,000 subscribers. Geoff smiles. His cruelty to her is better ratings than her striptease.

THE NEXT DAY

Park Avenue: the epicenter of the Upper East Side Elite. A jam-packed Christmas Caroling session is in full swing. Mink and Manolo Blahniks crush against one another for a glimpse of the excessively cheerful children's choir singing on the steps of an excessively charming church. Even the toy pedigree dogs are wrapped in pashminas.

But fashion isn't the point; these rosy-cheeked carolers are here to celebrate Christmas, the holiday of family, giving and love. The annual event is always three weeks before Jesus's Birthday. And for that one sacred hour, dads put away iPhones, stay-at-home moms tune out of Facebook, kids turn off their Xboxes, all for an hour of quality time together.

Geoff is here with his family, but only at his wife Isabella's insistence. It's part of the deal they have: Isabella refills his bank account each month, Geoff makes appearances at family events and charity benefits a couple times a year. He charges extra for photo opportunities. That was the agreement they came to when Geoff tried to cash in his marriage.

Marrying Isabella was the best investment Geoff ever made. A doyenne of New York Society, Isabella's family roots go back centuries. The family bank accounts, trusts, properties, businesses, jets and yachts generate an endless stream of wealth which will ensure a billionaire legacy for future generations to come.

Geoff charmed his way into her family. He proposed to Isabella with an heirloom diamond Isabella's grandmother provided (at no cost to Geoff of course). He wisely refused to sign the prenup and less than two years later, when Isabelle was eight months pregnant with twins, Geoff announced over a filet mignon that he was ready to split.

Isabella refused to divorce him; whether she loved him or not was irrelevant, it was just about the money. The two were able to agree on a comfortable monthly stipend Isabella would continue to put into his account after Geoff moved out. For the benefit of the kids, and to maintain her own pride, Isabella insisted Geoff agree to show up at a couple family events.

So here Geoff is, making his appearance. He doesn't hoist his daughter onto his shoulders. Even if he were to put his arm around Isabella, she would surely shrug it off and step away from him. Unlike the joyful carolers singing around him, Geoff instead is deep in conversation talking business with Monty, another Park Avenue Dad.

The choir leads the carolers into an elaborate round of everyone's favorite holiday classic "Jingle Bells". Over the singing, Geoff is trying to tell Monty about a new deal. It won't be public info for another week or so. The damn singing is so loud though that Monty can't quite hear him.

Geoff repeats himself: "Uniforms, for the military." Monty leans in; he still didn't get it. "Uniforms!" Geoff sees nothing obscene about combining war profiteering and this touching holiday gathering to celebrate peace and love. After all, a deal involving 3 million uniforms, plus accessories, is one hell of a sale.

Now hundreds of carolers dig deep into their pockets and pull out sets of keys attached to silver Tiffany & Co. key chains. They shake the keys to the chorus of "Jingle Bells".

Monty leans in closer to hear Geoff, but it's a losing battle against the tinkling baubles. "Soldiers!" Geoff repeats, screaming. No use, Monty can't hear. "You stupid keys! Why do you have to be so damn loud?" Geoff yells at the sea of keys around him. "Damn you all, I'm trying to have an important conversation here."

Geoff indiscriminately reaches into the crowd of hands and keys. Before anyone sees him, Geoff snatches a set of keys out of a random child's hand unobserved by the victim, and hurls them. Forget it, he'll talk to Monty some other time.

Later That Night

Back at his immaculate apartment, Geoff closes the front door behind him and tosses his own keys onto a silver tray. He breathes in, relieved to be alone. The cleaning lady has left and the marble floor glistens with no trace of the dead mouse. Geoff loves the wealth that is expressed throughout this apartment. It makes him so happy every time he walks in the door to know that he lives here—without his kids.

In his bedroom, Geoff unwinds and takes his shirt off to get comfortable for the evening. He switches on the computer and camera to record the next installment of *House of Worth*, allowing his followers to enjoy every moment of his godlike existence. He catches his reflection in a big mirror that hangs by his bed and flexes his pecks. A notification beeps on Geoff's iPhone and alerts him to the number of viewers who are watching at this moment: 270,000 subscribers.

Evaluating his tan hairless chest in the mirror, Geoff uses his iPhone home automation app to dim the overhead lights. The lights lower and flicker, casting eerie shadows around the apartment. Geoff thinks the dimmed lights make him look even more attractive. He can't take his eyes off the reflection off his tan hairless chest. He slowly dances for his viewers. The iPhone beeps notifying Geoff: 295,000 subscribers.

Encouraged, Geoff dances across the bedroom to his stripper pole. His iPhone beeps again—297,000 subscribers. Geoff turns to look into the camera while he swings himself around the stripper pole. A monitor just next to the camera shows Geoff the scene his viewers are enjoying. Geoff is entirely absorbed in watching his own dance on the monitor. He becomes aroused by his own appeal.

DINNER TIME

In the Kitchen, Geoff hangs a collection of expensive Japanese knives on a magnet over the stove. He selects a banana from a bowl of fruit. Nearby, a screen on his kitchen counter keeps track of the number of followers currently tuned into his webcast.

The viewers have dropped down to 250,000. Distracted by the disappointment, Geoff reaches for a knife. Somehow the knife slips from his hand; it's almost as if it intentionally jumped *from* him. The blade flies past the counter and falls, slicing through his limited edition Nike shoe. The knife stands straight up. Holy shit.

Geoff panics and reaches for his cell phone typing in 9-1-1. "Sir, what's your emergency?"

"I've been stabbed. The knife just stabbed—"

But he realizes there's no blood. Geoff retracts the knife from his foot and pulls off the sneaker. Miraculously, he's unscathed. Not even the skin is broken. The knife fell directly between his big toe and second toe. Had the knife fallen just a fraction of a degree differently, he would have lost a digit. He hangs up on the operator. The iPhone beeps: 350,000 subscribers.

The spike in subscribers encourages Geoff. He collects himself, holds the knife close to his face. "What the fuck was that?" he yells at the blade. "You coward, you don't even have the courage to break my skin." Geoff laughs and hurls the knife across the room at the wall.

"And you . . . " He turns to the banana. "Don't think you're getting off easy. Guess what? I'm not going to eat you. So who's sorry now?" He throws the banana. It splatters and drips down the wall landing in a messy heap on the floor. For a moment, the walls seem to darken. Geoff rubs his eyes. "Screw this kitchen." He looks around the kitchen and his eye lands on a magnetized menu hanging on the fridge. "I'm ordering out."

Twenty minutes later, an elderly man delivers Geoff's dinner. The poor guy is dripping from the rain, his hands shake, he's a little hunch-backed. He might be in his 70s; certainly way too old to be running around late at night in the rain delivering heavy bags of food.

Geoff grunts and grabs the bag. He hates old people. Even his parents. They're out of touch with the times, technology, and they never understand what he says. "What?" "Huh, I didn't catch that?" Disgusted, Geoff only tips the sad old man a dollar.

Geoff tosses aside the cheap disposable wood chopsticks. He takes out a pair of silver chopsticks someone gave him and Isabella for their wedding. He holds them up to the webcam. Behind him, the noodles dangling from his mouth cast monstrous shadows against the back wall of his office. If you squint, the shadows almost look like mutated octopus tentacles swarming around Geoff's head, ready to attack at any moment.

The iPhone beeps alerting Geoff that his subscribers have fallen to 300,000. The internet has spoken, and watching Geoff eat dinner is boring. Geoff scowls.

The noodles slip between Geoff's smoothly polished chopsticks. "Are you fucking kidding me?" Geoff stabs at his noodles with his chopsticks. "All for show? I hope you are embarrassed. You are a failure as chopsticks." The chopsticks roll off the table and onto the floor, as if their feelings have been hurt. "Boo hoo, I'm so sorry, did I upset you, chopsticks?"

THE DAY IT ALL CHANGED

The next morning, Geoff wakes up and takes his time getting out of bed. Still lying down, he checks his YouTube stream status from his iPhone. He's smugly pleased to see he's gained 2,700 subscribers. Geoff turns his head to a webcam positioned above his bed and addresses his followers: "Good morning, you lucky people."

Geoff downs a couple extra Five-Hour Energy bottles to rev himself up for the big day. He tries on one newly pressed Anderson & Shephard custom tailored shirt after another. He can't find one that is exactly right. He drops each discarded shirt on the floor in a heap for his maid to throw out later.

In between shirts, Geoff admires his naked chest in the mirror. He looks into the camera: "I'm building up my body, ladies; come back next week when it's bigger and better. When I break a million subscribers, I'll show you my perfect ass." It takes a couple wardrobe changes before Geoff is satisfied. He double checks his handsome reflection in the mirror, cat calls himself, and walks to the front door.

POSTHUMOUS

Geoff reaches for his keys. But they aren't in the sterling silver engraved dish by the door where he left them. "What the fuck." Geoff turns the lid of a decorative jar over looking for the keys. "I don't have time for this!" He looks inside a drawer. Nothing. Geoff pats down his pockets. Nothing. Frustration mounts. Then Geoff spots the keys peeking out from beneath a Chinese menu, just inches from the silver dish.

"You low class, rough cut pieces of base metal!" He wants to scream more, but he is a little concerned that the keys were out of place. He wonders if someone is fucking with him. Did Isabella have a way to get into his apartment? Would she pay someone to come in and mess with his stuff while he slept? It would explain a lot, but he doesn't have time to worry about it now.

Geoff swipes the keys. For a second, he thinks he hears the faint sound of laughter. He pauses to listen and looks around him, skeptical. The indistinct laughter stops; it must be the keys jingling. He storms out.

GEOFF'S BIG DAY IN THE OFFICE

Geoff puts the finishing touches on the uniforms deal contract. This is the last step before he prints and messengers the document to the bank to seal the deal. But before he hits print, the computer freezes. All his cursing, banging on the keyboard, rolling around the mouse, pounding the restart button are for naught. The pinwheel of doom spins in front of him at the center of the screen.

Eventually the document goes through to the printer. "Finally!" Geoff storms from his desk, and heads for the door. *BANG!* Geoff is on the floor. Stunned, it takes Geoff a minute to figure out what happened. He tripped on something, but what? He looks down, and the horse bit buckle of his Gucci shoes has gotten tangled up in the wire spaghetti mess under his desk.

In the workroom, Geoff kicks the printer when he finds his pages have not finished printing. "Why are you so goddamn slow? I could hand write each memo faster than you piece of shit machine." The printer chugs along, one line of text at a time, slowly inching out a single page at a time. Geoff doesn't have the patience. He bangs the printer's side. This achieves nothing, of course. He bangs the printer

LLOYD & LILY HAYES KAUFMAN

harder. Suddenly the printer clicks, it's as if it's shifting gears. With a whirr, it speeds up!

"I'm brilliant! I'm a genius! I fixed you!" Geoff triumphs. The printer whirls harder, spits out paper faster and faster and faster! It's literally spitting out paper, and it's flying out of the copy machine with such speed and force that it is slicing Geoff. He can hardly swat it away. Geoff screams; no one pays attention. A new associate hears the screams from his cubicle. He figures it's just Geoff, pissed again and being destructive in the copy room. The associate puts his earbuds in to block out the noise and returns to a NSFW but hilarious video his buddy just sent him.

Geoff struggles to stop the sharp papers flying at his face and body; he is literally covered in paper cuts. He bats his arms furiously, and tumbles out the door into the hallway.

Freaked out and shaken up, Geoff leaves the office and heads for home. He catches a glimpse of himself in the reflection of the revolving glass door as he leaves his office building. His face is cut up and a bruise is starting to swell over his left eye from when he fell down in his office. Geoff pushes through the revolving doors. But *SLAM!* He falls again. His suit jacket has gotten caught in the door, and as it rotates, it's pulling Geoff with it. He yells for the person exiting the building to stop pushing, but the lady is deep in Instagram, checking how many likes she's received. Head down, focused on her iPhone, the lady doesn't see Geoff stuck. He tries to bang on the glass but his suit, sucked into the revolving door, has become a straitjacket, and now it's sucking his entire body closer and closer to the blade-like revolving doors.

Geoff is inches from being squashed in the revolving door. He drops to the floor and tears his suit in two, freeing himself. Just barely. Jesus, he could have died. He lies on the ground. Inches away, the revolving door whooshes by and spits out the woman. She looks at Geoff, disgusted. "Get a job, you drunk," she mutters at Geoff as she steps over his body. "The homeless in this city have no shame."

Later at Home

In the hallway outside his apartment, Geoff puts on a brave face for his webcam. Everything is going to be okay. He's home now. His castle. He puts his stuff down and walks into the kitchen. Geoff takes another step and his foot lands on the discarded banana peel. *WHOOSH* his feet swing up. His head slams down. Were it not for the hollow *CRACK* his skull makes as it slams onto the marble floor, this slapstick moment would offer his webcast viewers some comic relief. But there is nothing funny about a concussion of this severity. Geoff is knocked out for a moment and totally winded. On the bright side, his subscribers pop up to 500,000, an all-time high.

When Geoff comes to, he stares at the ceiling stunned. What just happened? He slowly stands up and staggers forward, dizzy. He needs some water; he is parched and weak. Geoff stumbles toward the fridge and opens the door. Inside he looks for a bottle of water; he pushes aside last night's leftover Chinese noodles and knocks over a set of chopsticks. The chopsticks roll out of the bag from the fridge, then another pair of chopsticks roll out, and another.

Geoff can feel energy in the room. Something electric, tingly, and dark. He senses the darkness though all the lights are on. The chopsticks pick themselves off the ground. They appear to be levitating. In the front of the pack are his polished silver sticks.

Woozy, Geoff steps back; he's hallucinating, has to be. The chopsticks distribute themselves in mid-air, from six inches above ground to about six feet above ground. Two speed toward Geoff and plunge themselves into his nostrils. The chopsticks dive deep into his sinus cavity, spewing fluid out of his eyes.

Geoff reels back and turns toward a nearby webcam. To his audience, he looks like a walrus with chopsticks for fangs. *FLACK FLACK FLACK FLACK;* the rest of the pack impale Geoff like a voodoo doll. Totally caught off guard, and still unsure if this is the concussion speaking or if it's real, Geoff struggles to remove the chopsticks. They are deep. He pulls one or two out. Blood drips down where his skin has been pierced. The iPhone beeps: 550,000 subscribers.

The walls of his apartment seem to be alive. They breathe in and out, seething with a vengeance, with worth. Geoff stumbles—he's got to get out of the kitchen. As he reaches the door, his eyes land on the magnetic knife holder above the stove. The magnet is empty. But instead of worrying about that, his attention hones in on a noise humming in the air. Vibrations from somewhere in the house? The noise intensifies, louder; he holds his hands to his head to make it stop, but it strengthens and becomes a loud jingling, louder, louder louder LOUDER. *SWOSH!* Geoff is blindsided by a set of objects flying towards his head.

Geoff's keys have freed themselves from the ring in order to launch the offensive. One sharp metal key burrows deep into each of Geoff's ear canals and twists through the wax as if opening a lock. The pain alone is acute, but what makes it truly unbearable is the grinding noise so loud and so close to Geoff's inner ear. Geoff gags as the keys swivel into the eustachian tubes that connect his ear with the back of his nose and throat and unlock a stream of mucus. The keys pierce the eardrum membrane and blood explodes from his ears.

Word is spreading on the internet about the Tromatic scene unfolding on Geoff's webcast. Viewers are tuning in and sharing with their friends, setting off a viral chain of new subscribers. *House of Worth* is climbing the charts as more than 700,000 people tune in. If only Geoff weren't distracted by the torture.

A Japanese knife flies in and pierces Geoff's arm, cutting deep through veins and bone. Hoarsely he calls for help. Geoff looks for his iPhone. It's fallen a few feet from him when he fell. Geoff crawls his remaining free hand along the floor reaching for his cell phone, but his wrist is stuck. It won't budge. In fact, the more Geoff's tries to pry his wrist up off the ground, more of his arm becomes stuck to the floor. The entire floor has become an enormous glue trap.

Geoff opens his mouth to scream, but before he can get a word out, the fridge door opens, and from the dark interior a banana cream pie is catapulted out. It splatters onto Geoff's face, silencing him with the thick cream filling.

Geoff's final breaths are near; he is past the ability of calling for help. He isn't even strong enough to wonder who will find him in this position. How long will it be? Surely he will be dead; will the stench of his rotting carcass be what drives a local neighbor to discover him? Geoff fades in and out of consciousness, still stuck to the floor.

Across the room, the webcast camera records Geoff's final moments. His eyes flutter and close for the last time.

On the computer screen, a YouTube window flashes. Geoff's

grand finale webcast is trending. He has made it to 1,000,000 subscribers. Posthumously.

Lloyd Kaufman is co-founder, with Yale friend Michael Herz, of the 41-year-old legendary Troma Entertainment, which is arguably the longest running independent movie studio in North America. He directed many of their feature films, including the world famous The Toxic Avenger, Class of Nuke 'Em High, Sgt. Kabukiman NYPD, Tromeo & Juliet, *and* Poultrygeist: Night of the Chicken Dead. *Kaufman has written six books on filmmaking and has presented his "Make Your Own Damn Movie" master classes globally from Oxford University to Singapore. His latest film,* Return to Nuke 'Em High Vol. 1, *produced in association with STARZ, premiered in* The Contenders *series at New York's Museum of Modern Art along with movies by the Coen Brothers, Martin Scorsese, and Woody Allen. Kaufman is currently editing* Return to Nuke 'Em High Vol. 2 *and preparing* The Toxic Avenger Part 5: Grime & Punishment. *In 2008,* The Toxic Avenger *was turned into a musical by Joe DiePietro and David Bryant of Bon Jovi, which ran in NYC for a year and won the Outer Critics Circle Award for Best Off-Broadway Musical.* The Toxic Avenger' Musical *is currently available for licensing through Music Theatre International (MTI). To thank Troma fans for over 40 years of support, Kaufman and Michael Herz offer over 250 free feature length movies, cartoons, and new daily content on The Troma Movies YouTube Channel:*
https://www.youtube.com/Tromamovies

Lily Hayes Kaufman writes, directs and produces original content and documentaries for Pitchslap.tv, a video production company she founded with her sister. Lily Hayes wrote and directed a web series Rare Birds of Fashion *which she sold to NBC Comedy. She has worked on a range of film & TV productions including* Weinstein's St. Vincent, Dreamworks/NBC's SMASH *and the relaunch of Troma Entertainment's YouTube Channel. She has written for Forbes.com, womensworldbanking.org and worldpolicy.org. In a past life, Lily Hayes developed commodity investment strategies for institutional investors to pay her way through the Harvard Business School.*

BURY THEM DEEPER

DAVID SANDNER

I HATE TALKING about the bodies in the basement, but Ray-Ray wouldn't let up. I had to pound him so hard, I'm not sure I ever stopped.

"They smell rotten," he said, "like old eggs."

"Shut up," I told him.

"Why didn't he bury them deeper? They smell like stale pee."

I hit him so he doubled over, gasping for breath. I'm sure he saw stars. His pale little face turned red, then a sort of purple. After a while he straightened up, not even looking at me, just staring ahead, tears in the corner of his eyes, with the strangest expression on his stupid face. Like he'd done what he needed to do, all he could. Then we walked quietly to school after that without any more talking. Every day it was the same thing.

I always hit him the second time he said something about the bodies. I would tell him "shut up" the first time and hit him the second time. He never stopped after the first time. I had learned to hit him in the stomach, or slap him hard across the face with the flat of my hand. No marks. When he first started in on the bodies in the basement, and I had gotten sick of it, I had hit him in the face, giving him a black eye. My mom had hit me across the back of the legs with a switch, which smarted for two days. The black eye lasted five, though, which made it almost worth it. But going for the stomach was better, since I had to hit him every day we walked to school, five days a week. His mom wouldn't know. And my mom wouldn't know and punish me.

Our moms were friends. They played Scrabble together and cried about how their husbands didn't talk to them. After awhile, my dad had left. Ray-Ray's mom said it was better to have a man gone than hitting you. Our moms snuck cigarettes together and laughed about how they should be crying.

I was eleven, starting sixth grade. Ray-Ray was the same and lived next door to me at the butt end of a cul-de-sac, the only two houses on the round turnabout at the end. All the other houses were stacked neat in a row way away from us, up against each other, but we each had huge, misshaped yards, mostly choked with weeds, that backed up against a dried-up streambed that took up runoff in the rainiest part of the year. With the deep fall-off, we had no need for back fences.

Ray-Ray's dad had a chicken coop on their property; on ours sat the rusty innards of a car my dad had always intended to fix up when he didn't have to be hustling up work. Ray-Ray's dad odd-jobbed it in a seasonal way that repeated, selling in the pumpkin patches in the fall, tree farms in the winter, and mostly taking night shifts at some of the hotels along the coast down the highway other times, or else he was too tired to do anything but sit in front of the TV or tend to the chickens. Sometimes he dug up areas out back, said he would start his own pumpkin patch, but nothing ever grew there. Except tough weeds, rust colored as if with blood.

He spent hours with the chickens. He used to call us out to watch him kill the chickens when it was killing time. Ray-Ray and I both had to watch. He used to give us the heads in bag and motion out to the weed-choked yard.

"Bury them," he'd say. "Bury them deeper than you did last time."

We had to use broken-handled shovels. Ray-Ray's dad had a lot of shovels, from all the digging he did for the pumpkins. The ground was hard clay. Ray-Ray always threw up halfway through and I'd finish up alone. Ray-Ray's dad seemed to think it was funny.

Little Ray-Ray wasn't brown-stained-underwear-sticking-out-above-his-baggy-pants weird like some of the occasional deep woods kids they bused down to school that no one talked to or anything like that. Those kids' families just moved away deeper into the woods after the authorities found them, and pretty soon the kid wouldn't come back so no one worried about them. He was his own weird. Ray-Ray walked stiff—like a machine, a robot—with a straight stare that made me mad. He'd tilt his head back and forth like a bird. And his face was lean, with cheekbones sticking out, which looked robotish too.

Mostly, the thing was, he wouldn't let things be. He was always coming up to me at recess and trying to talk to me about stupid stuff. My friends laughed at him, but he still stayed until they just got bored and irritated and then they didn't want to be around me. I'd pinch him and kick him when the lunch ladies weren't looking, but it was like having lice in your hair—nothing short of cutting things off completely would do.

My family had known their family for near five years, back to just a couple of years before my dad left. Ray-Ray hadn't gone to my school until he reached fifth. He had been home schooled, but now his mom said it was time for him to socialize, meet girls. The moms would laugh at us when they said the last. They always added that to embarrass us.

"You have any little girlfriends?" Mrs. LaRouche would ask.

"No, Ma'am," I'd say, trying to keep it short. That always made them ask more questions until we squirmed.

"You had your first kiss?" Noises behind hands to each other and laughing.

"You keep it in you pants, hear?" My mom would hit Ray-Ray's mom lightly on the arm when she said something like that and say, "Now, come on now," which meant it was about to all end this time, but didn't really mean she should stop saying it ever.

"Denny will watch Little Ray-Ray, won't you, baby," my mother said when Mrs. LaRouche said Ray-Ray would be in school with me in our first through eighth building tucked into the hills off the highway, only about half a mile from our dead-end houses. "You walk him to school and watch out for him," she said. "That's kindness."

She hissed out of earshot of her friend when I protested. "You watch that boy or there'll be trouble. His family is like family to us."

My mom always repeated these warnings to me in the morning, when she had her hair tied up so it wouldn't blow wild in the winds off the ocean. A handkerchief, blue, usually, or green, tied at the back. She wore jeans with the cuffs rolled and plaid shirts hanging out. I thought she looked beautiful, but cold, like the sea.

"Yes, mom," I'd say, defeated.

I'd trudge out to the street and off toward school, hoping Ray-Ray wouldn't appear. But I would hear his door slam before I got anywhere, and he always came running up behind me. And then, only then and at no other time during the day, he would start in on the bodies buried in the basement. It was so damn weird, and felt so cut off from everything else I never considered telling about it—my mom didn't want to hear it, and it was done in a secret way, too hard to even explain how it came up. I figured Ray-Ray had finally figured out how to get a rise out of me. Making me hit him was better than having no friends at all, is the thing.

"Do human bodies run around like chickens after the head's cut off?" he asked.

"Shut up," I said, already balling my fist like a dog trained to eat by a bell.

"Does the head still try to talk?" And I hit him so he bent in half. I'd seen that, a headless chicken, with Ray-Ray, of course, out by the coop under the bare electric bulb sticking out the side of the building.

"They're prepping a chicken over there," my mom had said one day. "Go watch."

That's how it started—my having to go over there and see, and bury the heads. When I said that was gross, she said to get my ass over there—I didn't have a daddy anymore, so it was good to spend time around Mr. LaRouche. It was man stuff, she meant, "prepping" the chickens, something my dad would have shown me.

Ray-Ray's dad never let us in the coop. Not that I wanted to go in, though it was usually cold outside of an evening. It smelled in there, and a sort of sticky rust coated the wooden walls while the chickens clucked. I saw that much. He had unclean tools and a table in there, too, beyond the chickens. He was always building stuff in there, but must have taken it apart again, unsatisfied. He didn't want to show us any of that. We waited, close together, by the side of the coop. Trying not to wrinkle our noses and make him mad, just keeping our faces blank.

Ray-Ray's father had chosen his chicken carefully, handled it casually, lifting it with one hand round its neck. He knocked it against the cutting stump, dazing it, then struck fast with the axe, making me flinch. Ray-Ray didn't flinch. His dad held the head in his hand, constricting the blood. The chicken had run one way, then another, almost as if it still had eyes, seeking escape, almost as if anything mattered anymore. Then it seemed to get tired of thinking without a head and just lay down and twitched. Mr. LaRouche laughed but it didn't seem to be because it was funny.

After a while, a dark look came into his face and he told me to stop crying and go home. I didn't even realize I was crying. I had thought I was just standing there, like Ray-Ray. I didn't cry after that first time, so he came up with putting the heads in a bag and getting us to bury them, even deeper than last time, finding places in the yard not already piled with dirt. He hadn't really dug up the yard, I learned. It was more like he piled up dirt from somewhere else. But at the time, I just knew to stay away from the piles, however they came to be there. I just needed a new place to bury the chicken heads.

Again and again, as I trudged to school, Ray-Ray would run up behind me, then start speaking about the bodies.

"It ain't pink," Ray-Ray would say, "the hair of the dead. But it is sticky like cotton candy—brittle, sticky—maybe from blood?"

"Shut up," I said.

"They whisper to me about things they did when they was alive."

I hit him in the stomach. He doubled over for a while, but soon he had caught up to me. We walked on in silence until we reached the school.

Ray-Ray had brown eyes, wide set, and a large nose. He was lanky and awkward, but that was hardly anything to set him apart. It was more how he stood too close when he talked to you. How he stared at you like an adult does, judging you, not like a kid who doesn't care. How he grinned wrong, or stood swaying in one spot, or picked some sort of red thing growing on his eyelid until it just got bigger and bigger, though his mom said it was harmless.

"The bodies smell like old socks and vomit."

"Shut up."

"Why didn't he bury them deeper? They tell me to stop touching myself."

I slapped him so his head snapped to the left, his neck cracking. It scared me but exulted me when he just came along quietly after—

and that feeling of joy then scared me in a different way. Not the face, I reminded myself . . . not the face.

I tried sometimes to reason with him to make him stop talking to me about dead bodies in his basement.

"So you're telling me your father killed people?" I said one day. "That's who you mean must have done it, isn't it? He killed them and buried them in the basement?"

He didn't answer, just grinned wrong at me. His eyes would almost cross when he did that. We were the same age, but I was bigger than Ray-Ray.

"I've been in your house. Nothing smells funny. I've been in the kitchen where the door to the basement is—nothing there."

"There're scratching like rats in the floor," he said.

"Shut up, you fucking freak," I yelled.

"There's a dry smacking when they move—like old people's lips when they're hungry."

I hit him into uneasy silence, a break from his madness. The next day he would always be back to tell me more.

"They moan in the wind for lost things."

"Shut up," I said, defeated.

"They cry like waves rolling."

I punched him and stood there for a while with my fist in his stomach, wanting to crawl into the grave myself. My friends wouldn't talk to me anymore. Ray-Ray always came up to me in the playground and we stood there together, numbly and dumbly, waiting for the day to be over.

"The dead miss me when I'm at school," he said.

"Shut up."

"They think if I would come down, turn them a bit, they'd rest more easy."

I gave him a quick punch to get it over. No malice, just a duty and then a hurried march to school and a waiting for the day to turn 'round to the next one when Ray-Ray would come up behind me as I set out for school again, his feet dogging my steps until his thin voice would break the silence and give me purpose again—to strike him.

"Their skin is stretchy to touch, like old rubber gloves my dad uses when he preps the chickens."

"Shut up."

"The dead taste rancid, like—"

He didn't get farther then that—it was the line crossed. The point of breaking, the last straw. Why that day? It was gross, the tasting them, but he had been gross before; it was the end, was all. That was the day, a late November day when the pumpkin work has given way to the tree farms, when I hit him again in the face, like the first time I hit him. When I would hit him for the last time, eventually. How many hits were in between . . . I can't count them. I can't remember how many I piled on him that day—as many as I could until my arm grew sore.

"Deeper," I shouted, "bury them deeper."

Lips balloon faster then you might think when you split them against teeth with your fist. Blood splatters like paint on a canvas of skin. A tooth chip lodged in my hand but I didn't stop. Bruises marked his eyes and cheeks. An eye gets loose in its socket when you break the thin bone along the outer corner. Finally, his eyes uncrossed, even as he grinned at me wrongly. The skin begins to be like a softened steak—tender in its welting, soft and pliable. The blood streaks the face but also runs along inside the eyes with bursting vessels, while streaked spit smears red around the mouth.

I couldn't feel my hands, I hit him so much. I blubbered until tears fogged my vision and wet snot and spit dripped from my chin. I didn't know at the time who took me off him—some older kid from the high school, Tom something, who wouldn't have normally thought twice about us kids fighting, but my determination to hit Ray-Ray until the dead stayed dead had moved him to drag me off my unconscious doppelganger.

In the time before I was taken away from that place, that town, Tom told me about it once, but he seemed shaken. He had weak blue eyes and a dusting of freckles; telling me the story of the fight made him so pale he looked ill. "You just kept repeating as you hit him over and over, 'Bury them deeper, bury them deeper.'" He shook his head and took a long drag on his cigarette, trying to exorcize things. "'Bury them deeper.'" He exhaled a long stream of smoke into the fog.

When Tom had finally stopped holding me back after the beating, I had run into the woods, back past my house, past the rusty car and the chicken coop, over the drop off and away. I shivered at night but no one found me, huddled under a tree, far away from everything. I sat and stared at the dark . . . and the dark stared back.

I had dreams after that—peaceful dreams of postcard scenes that filled me with anxiety because I felt something had been forgotten; maybe just out of frame, or below the ground, or behind the trees, or behind me looking on, they waited, the restless, unseen, pushing into the frame at just the next moment. A hand from the earth. A touch at the nape of neck. An eye staring from deep cover. It waited only a moment before it struck.

"Bury them deeper!" I would awake shouting, striking out.

There were no bodies in the basement. No. They were below the chicken coop. No one found them until after we had moved away. Mom read the newspaper reports and I read them over her shoulder, trying not to tremble with memories of terrible walks to school with an imp poking me until I beat him senseless. For a while I worried that cops or reporters would track us down and ask me, the neighbor kid, if I suspected anything. I would answer with the truth: I knew nothing. I can't even truthfully quite describe Mr. LaRouche to you. I never really looked at him—just at the chickens running without heads. Mr. LaRouche had never dropped any dark hints. I had seen no mysterious goings on—no body bags hastily buried at midnight hours, no "missing" reports piling up, no serial killer trophies in a pile like on TV. But I knew another truth: I had been told every day for months on end about the bodies. I had been told and refused to listen, with violence.

But what I really feared was when I heard Mr. LaRouche had buried seven young women under the coop and along the dry creek bed—women he had met in his job as night clerk at hotels along the coast, or picked up hitchhiking along the beautiful highway—all I wanted to do was beat Ray-Ray in the face.

Somehow I knew that was the thing to make everything all right. Strike until they stopped. Until the dead stayed dead. I wanted to bury them deeper.

I wanted to beat Ray-Ray until he was in the hospital again with all the tubes in his face and arms. And I would tell him "sorry" again, like I did the last time I saw him, with his mom glaring at me and my mom shaking my arm. Ray-Ray never returned to school, and I left by the end of the year, friendless and alone, and my mom and I moved down to Oakland by the Bay. And I wasn't sorry about it at all. Like the beating had gotten me out of that place, and away from his nagging. I wanted to beat him until he stopped bugging me, until he shut up, until death stopped dogging me. I wanted to beat his face from my dreams, to stop his broken, bloodshot eyes from looking at me and to wipe his all-wrong smile from his busted, bloated lips.

I wanted to beat him so I never had to know about men like Mr. LaRouche—a man acting just like a chicken with its head cut off, running just to run, no thought, just mindless action; I didn't want to know about the women; I didn't want to cry; I wanted to beat Ray-Ray until I didn't have to remember that all I wanted, more than anything, was to beat him until my heart, pounding against my chest like a fist to the face, finally burst and I could stop wanting anything and could rest without remembering. I wanted nowhere to walk to, no one behind me about to speak about the bodies and what they wanted, or what they were doing now: I wanted nothing. I wanted to hit and hit.

I wanted to stop thinking about hitting him. I would ask someone, I don't know who, someone: bury me deep, and bury me deeper. Because I don't want to know, bury me deeper still. Dirt over my head—bury me deeper than everything—and maybe everything would finally make sense.

But even there, in the grave, I would hear, behind me . . . a voice, calling: *I hear them,* the voice would whisper, *the bodies. And I know what they want.* And I would struggle, against myself, my death, even in the confines of my coffin, to turn and strike and make it stop. But, no.

I will hear them, all those bodies. And they will smell like sulfur and sweat. And they smell like bile and urine. Like fear.

I bury them deeper in the basement, the bodies. But I don't want to talk about them. I bury them where they can't be heard. I bury them deeper. I bury them deeper still.

David Sandner is a member of the HWA and SFWA. His work has appeared in leading magazines, anthologies, journals, websites, podcasts, and radical zines. He is a Professor of English at Cal State Fullerton. He has written and edited books on the history and origins of the fantastic and its genres, including Mythopoeic Award Finalist Critical Discourses of the Fantastic,

1712-1831. *He recently Chaired the 2016 Philip K. Dick Conference and curated the Philip K. Dick in Orange County website. He is working on a novel, on a scholarly collection,* Philip K. Dick, Here and Now, *and on a site called* The Frankenstein Meme, *exploring the influence of Mary Shelley's novel. He can be found at davidsandner.com.*

THESE BEAUTIFUL BONES

BETTY ROCKSTEADY

THE CRACK ZIG-ZAGGED across the basement, ripping it nearly in two. That was definitely where the draft was coming from. Rather than fixing the fucking thing, the landlord had covered it with boxes stuffed with junk, cutting corners wherever he could. Suzanne was sick of this dingy place already, but it was the only thing she could afford. Well, the only thing her mother could afford, and that cash was running out quick.

How did the landlord even get insurance on this place? The dirty floor smelled awful. Musty, but in a very human way. If she was being honest, it smelled like an unwashed cunt. The opening ran deep into the earth. It was probably full of bugs and rats. The piles of boxes concealed it at a glance, but there was no hiding it once you got down here. There was no hiding anything down here. Tacked up posters peeled away to reveal walls covered in graffiti or drawings or something.

Suzanne sighed, shoved boxes back in place. They must be creating at least a little bit of insulation. The stack of cardboard wobbled, spilled out a mess of torn clothing and dirty magazines. Suzanne grabbed a handful of clothing and dropped it again. Bits of lace and pliant leather, combined with nudie magazines . . . gross. She stood up and brushed her hands on her jeans, frowned at the mess. This was disgusting. She tried to shove the pile aside with her foot and just made things worse; more boxes tumbled and spilled— a stack of photos that she didn't even want to look at, stained paintbrushes, a dagger. She paused.

It was dangerous looking, even in this pile of junk. She reached for it, but drew her hand back when she noticed the handle—it was intricately carved, and right where she would wrap her hand around it, it was shaped like a gigantic, exaggerated penis. Her cheeks went hot. She kicked it back into the pile with the rest of the stuff. What the hell was wrong with him, renting the place out like this?

She yanked out her phone. Anger churned in her stomach, but what good would calling him do? He must know about the crack and all this shit already. He was the one who hid it. Who else could she call to complain? Her mom was already worried enough, and Eric . . .

The phone rang in her hand and she nearly dropped it into that disgusting hole. God, how would she ever get it out? She couldn't imagine reaching her hand down into that gap, moist and earthy and unknown.

The phone rang again.

It was Eric.

She didn't want to answer it, but it rang again and again and finally she did. She had to. Who the fuck was she to resist? She peeled a bit of a Coke poster off the wall, revealed a sliver of whatever was painted beneath. She didn't say anything.

"Suzy?"

The sound of his voice was familiar and awful. It wound into her ears, clutched at her heart.

"Suzy, don't hang up. I'm so glad you answered. I've been so worried about you."

She trudged up the crooked basement stairs. "Oh, poor you. So worried." She found her purse, rummaged out a pack of smokes.

"What have you been doing? Where are you? When are you coming home?"

"I'm fine. It doesn't matter where I am. And when I'm coming home is up to you." She sat on the back steps, stared into the forest. The leaves were starting to fall, the branches bare and cold without them.

"I'll come get you anytime. You have to come back. I know you will. We belong together, you and me. You've been gone long enough already."

"Did you fire her?" She lit a cigarette and tried not to cough.

"Suzy, are you smoking again?"

"Who cares?" She blew smoky O's, an old trick she was happy to

ROCKSTEADY

see she could still do. Through the haze, she realized there was a little hut or . . . something that she hadn't noticed before, out in the woods. A shed. It must be a shed.

"I care. You know that."

"Did you fire her?" Her voice was sharp. "Did you?"

She could hear him breathing on the line. He was trying to think of a way to make it sound better. "I can't do that, honey. She needs the job. Besides, what would my boss say? She's a good worker. How would I explain it?"

"How will you explain it to me?"

He didn't answer. He always had an answer for everything, but he didn't have an answer for that one.

She should hang up, end on a powerful note, but she couldn't help herself. "Are you still fucking her?"

He hesitated again. She could picture the look on his face. Eyebrows folded into concern, a smile tugging on his lips, urging her to forgive him. Before he could say anything else, she cut him off. "Forget it. Call me when she's gone." She hung up. Again.

She rubbed her eyes. She was so fucking sick of crying. He didn't deserve her tears. He didn't deserve anything from her. So why did she keep answering his calls, and why did she keep checking her phone when they didn't come?

Fuck it. She stubbed her smoke out. Her phone rang again and she tossed it on the step. She should check out that shed. Maybe she could find some wood or something to board up the hole in the basement. Maybe she could distract herself for at least a couple of minutes.

She hopped off the step and into the trees, where branches snatched at her hair and mud sloshed onto her slippers. The woods yawned open to reveal piles of rock and dirt. The overgrown grass abruptly gave way to bare earth. There was no shed, just a huge slab of stone, balanced atop a jagged staircase that reached nearly to her bust. What the fuck *was* this? It must have been used for something at one point in time, but now it was broken and disused like everything else around here.

Something else to complain to the landlord about.

She climbed the stairs. The top was stained with rust. She ran her hand over the surface, smooth and warm. It must have been baking in the sun all afternoon. She sat down, dangled her legs over the edge, lit another smoke. From this angle, she could see a pile of disturbed earth, nestled beneath a tree. Some attempt at gardening?

The tree was hideous, dead, coated with black rot. Maybe they had been trying to dig it up by the roots and just gave up. Her eyes lazily traced the curves and angles that jutted out every which way. A hammer laid atop the pile of earth, from the same set of tools as that dagger—its handle was shaped into a massive phallus. Someone had carved something into it once, but she couldn't make out the letters, they were all jumbled together. It reminded her of something. Something wordless. She felt it, deep in her gut.

The rock seemed to move, pressing up against the seat of her jeans. The warmth and firmness felt good. She shifted and the seam of her pants rubbed against her crotch. The breeze was warm for fall, but her nipples stood to attention. She pressed against the rock, felt a wetness grow between her thighs.

The carving on the hammer was so detailed.

Jesus Christ, she was getting horny. Pathetic. It had been ages since she had gotten laid. Even the last few times she had fucked Eric, she could tell his mind just wasn't in it.

Maybe she should go to the bar downtown and pick someone up, bring them back to this shitty rented house and fuck them. But it would be just her luck to run into someone Eric knew. Then she would have to explain herself and honestly, it was far more likely she would bring someone back here and end up crying because they weren't Eric. It was his familiar body she wanted in her bed.

What the fuck was she doing out here anyway?

The rock pulsed beneath her cunt. She tore her eyes away from the hammer, tossed her cigarette and went back to the house, feeling even worse than before.

"Have you heard from Eric?"

"Only every day."

She heard the *click click click* as Mom snapped her tongue against the roof of her mouth, sending shivers of annoyance up Suzanne's spine. "Why don't you just come home?"

ROCKSTEADY

Why didn't she? "I can't, Mom." Eric could still turn things around. But she was so tired of being stubborn, of waiting for him to make the right choice. What was there for her back home? Move back into the room she had spent her childhood in, get a shitty fucking job, try to figure out who she was without Eric. She blinked tears away.

"I'd love to keep helping you, honey, but I can't afford to wire you any more money. If you want a plane ticket home, that's one thing, but I can't just keep sending you money every week. You need to figure out what you're doing."

What the fuck *was* she doing? She couldn't go crying back to Eric just because she had nowhere else to go.

"I have to say, Suzy, as sorry as I am for you, I'm not surprised this happened."

"Is that so?" The words tasted bitter on her tongue.

"You know how you two got together in the first place. He's too old for you, anyway."

It was true. Everyone told her it would happen. A man who leaves his wife for a younger woman is the type of man who will leave the younger woman for his secretary. And now here she was, all alone, with ten lousy years of memories to keep her warm at night.

"He might fire her. He misses me." He wouldn't fire her. He would keep fucking her and whatever Suzanne did, she couldn't change that. "Never mind. Can we talk about something else? Anything else?"

"Sure, honey. What have you been up to lately? Are you looking for a job?"

"I'm fucking miserable, Mom. I have not been looking for a job."

"Are you getting out of the house at least?"

"I've been walking," she lied.

"That's good. It's important to get some exercise. That's bound to get you feeling better. What are you up to tonight?"

"I don't know, I might tidy up or something. Read. Watch TV."

"Oh, your father's home. I better get going. Remember, call me anytime. There's always money for a ticket home."

She hung up the phone, listened to the silent house. She flopped back on the couch and flipped through channels. The colors and shapes blurred, made her eyes heavy. Another exciting evening.

THESE BEAUTIFUL BONES

The moon glared through the window bright and angry, and Suzanne woke up confused. Springs from the couch dug into her side, and the TV droned some bullshit infomercial. How long had she been asleep? She fumbled for her phone, couldn't find it. Her head felt light, strange, and a dream danced through her consciousness, just out of reach. Something red and wet and ripe. She could smell that scent from the basement.

Something about the basement.

Something about the walls.

Had she seen something behind the posters earlier? Or had that been part of the dream? Her mouth tasted sour. The solution to something dangled just out of her reach.

Moonlight dribbled down the walls, surreal waves that made her feel dizzy.

She stumbled into the kitchen for a glass of water. For something to clear her head. The basement door loomed open, and the smell was so strong. She was halfway down the stairs before she knew what she was doing. She yanked the chain for the light, and it swayed, revealing thick tears in the haphazardly hung posters. A faded strip peeled away as she watched.

Weird that they had covered this up. There was a mural on the wall, and it looked clean and fresh, much nicer than the shitty posters it had been covered with. Fresh, but old fashioned. People, dozens of people, faces . . . and so much skin. They were all naked. Something religious?

No, not religious. She yanked more posters down, and wondered if she was dreaming again.

The landlord was a pervert, or whoever lived here before her was a pervert. It was a giant orgy. Maybe he would be pissed she was ripping these posters down, but they were so fragile they practically flaked away in her hands. Hell, just since this afternoon they had started falling apart.

The smell got stronger. It was so familiar, the way it wormed into her brain. Damp and musty, a sex smell. It made her think of Eric. Her gut twisted painfully.

It must have taken forever to paint. Complex configurations of men and women, cocks and pussies and assholes and tongues, licking and sucking and fucking, wet and sweaty and frantic. Every position you could imagine was displayed. Who would go to the trouble to paint this?

She tried to swallow. Her throat felt tight and sore. She had torn the paper down in a frenzy, and now she regretted it.

One character repeated itself throughout the mural. He was beautiful. Tall and blonde and smiling, his body as hard and glistening as his enormous dick. The rest of the figures were a little more stylized, their faces indistinct, but he was rendered in loving realism—especially his throbbing cock. Much bigger than Eric's. Despite herself, she was getting wet. She had always wondered what it would be like to take a huge dick. The figures in the painting seemed to enjoy it. His grin nearly split his face in two as he shoved it into every available hole. The artist had captured a certain charisma in that smile, one that fluttered butterflies in Suzanne's belly.

She had never been one for pornography. Eric had wanted to watch it with her once. He had even suggested they make their own. She hadn't done it, but maybe if she had, maybe if she had been a little more experimental . . .

Maybe if he had made her feel a little more comfortable.

Maybe there was more to her than that vanilla side.

Her eyes scanned the painting. Men with men and women with women and women with men and everywhere she looked, that beautiful man with the huge penis, everything hard and firm and beautiful.

Her hand slipped inside her blouse.

Two women bent in front of a line of men, their sweet faces surrounded by massive erections. Wet, glimmering parts spread out. Legs scissored across each other. Huge hands on buttocks, leaving behind imprints. Crooked smiles. Heavy breasts and small breasts and dainty little tongues licking swollen clits. Faces buried between thick thighs. Faces blurred, indistinguishable in their pleasure. Swollen cocks ready to burst, mouths twisted in pleasured screams, pubic hair lush and shining.

Suzanne slipped a hand between her legs. So much naked skin, so many hands and legs and nipples and pussies. Asses laid across altars, pointed in the air, inviting. Her vision swirled, coalesced on an altar and that beautiful man, penetrating women in turn, one after the other, sliding his cock in and out, in and out. Suzanne thumbed her clit, slowly at first, then faster.

His huge cock throbbed and gleamed and he was ready to come, and so was she.

No.

Something was wrong.

The scent let up, a breath of fresh air, and her head cleared and all that wet pleasure became something else. Suzanne whimpered, and her vision sharpened suddenly to pick out details she hadn't noticed before.

The smiles were more sinister than she thought. Some of the women held knives, gleaming with redness so wet she felt like she could reach out and touch it. Pussies spread open, ripped too far, gaping puzzles of flesh torn all the way to their assholes. Their faces were contracted with pain, not pleasure, but still they writhed against each other.

It was horrid, grotesque. They pulled out knives, made new holes to fuck and tore each other apart. Men smiled around wet mouthfuls of flesh. Women impaled themselves on wicked branches from trees, and that beautiful man in the centre of it all, atop the altar—and fucking Christ, was that the stone and tree from the backyard?

This was some kind of joke. What kind of person would paint this? How had she not seen this? Sick guilt churned her stomach. Suzanne pulled her sticky hand out of her panties and heaved herself up the stairs, slammed the heavy basement door behind her. She didn't stop until she was outside, cigarette in hand, blinking back tears.

Even she deserved better than this.

A dozen donut holes and an extra-large café mocha. Not a great use of her last five bucks, but honestly, how far would that five bucks have taken her anyway? A mouthful of chocolate and she was pawing at her phone again, making sure she didn't somehow miss a call in the thirty seconds she managed to tear her eyes away.

ROCKSTEADY

She *should* call the landlord. She *wanted* to call Eric. Why couldn't she just go back in time and not read the emails? Suspecting but not knowing. Christ. Couldn't she just have ignored it a while longer, at least gotten a better plan in place? Suzanne dabbed at her eyes with a napkin, refused to meet the eyes of the older couple sitting next to her. Their sympathetic smiles made her want to puke.

Okay. Deep breath. Call the landlord. The place was a dump, and if she complained, if she threatened to take her complaints further . . . maybe she could stay in the dump for a while longer while she figured out what the hell she was going to do with her life.

She fucking hated confrontation. Her chest clenched while the phone rang. And rang. Fuck it. She hung up, groaned, ran a hand through greasy hair. The couple next to her got up and left and she dabbed her eyes again.

Now what?

Call mom and give up, get a ticket and try to imagine a new life for herself, or call Eric? Either way she was accepting defeat. She tapped chewed fingernails against the table, brain tugging in one direction and then the other.

She had a few more days to think about it. Put off the inevitable a day longer. She tossed the rest of the donut holes into the trash.

She kept her phone in her hand as she walked home. Maybe he would call tonight. Maybe their last conversation was the push he needed.

The night was still warm, but the moment she stepped into the house, she was freezing. The air was cold and damp, and the basement door was wide open. Suzanne's stomach clenched. There was no way she had left it open. The landlord?

"Hello?" Her voice cracked, and she hated the sound of it. She peered down the stairs, into the darkness. The air was moist against her cheeks. She could almost taste it, salty and thick. "Hey, is someone down there?" There was no answer, of course. God, with her luck, there was probably some crazy person down there. Whoever lived here before, whoever painted that weird fucking mural. Maybe she should call the police.

She held her breath, listened. She didn't hear anything. She couldn't call the police. She wouldn't be the hysterical woman all alone, getting paranoid every time something creaked.

There was no one down there. But she had to make sure. She groaned, grabbed a knife from the kitchen. Like that would do anything. Like she knew how to use it.

Maybe the psycho would kill her and do her a favor.

"Hey, I'm coming down there now. If anyone's down there . . . I have a knife."

The light played shadows across the walls, and the walls were covered with paint, and there was nothing obscuring it anymore. Just brilliant, lurid color, covering every inch of space. And that *smell*. Spicy, thick, musty, *sexy*. Her head wobbled. Her thoughts felt far away. The pictures swam out at her and her eyes couldn't keep up.

God, she had never imagined being fucked in so many ways before. Thick cocks crammed into tight holes everywhere. Her own hole pulsed, grew wet. But it wasn't just cocks going into those holes. It was knives, it was spikes, and she had never been interested in any of this shit before, had never even thought . . .

She slid a finger in her mouth, wet her lips.

No matter where she looked, there was more to see, and He kept smiling at her. *At her.*

She reached out to the wall, stroked it, and the faces seemed to look at her. Some of this looked so familiar—that twisted tree out back, and those women, with their knives, thrusting, thrusting into a man, and he loved it, *he loved it* and his cock spurted cum and the phallic hammer swung and blood rained over the altar.

Suzanne's phone buzzed. She shook and yanked her hand from her pants with disgust. What was she doing? Eric was on the phone and she couldn't answer it, not now, the colors were too bright and something was not right in her head.

She slammed the basement door behind her. It was sure as hell shut this time, and it was going to stay that way.

Blood and sex swam in her head. There was still a bottle of wine in the fridge. She curled up on the couch with it, and every time she closed her eyes she could see them writhing.

Hands groped their way up her thighs, oily wet, smooth against her skin, someone moaned—was it her? Firm hands on her tits, squeezing her nipples, too hard, and it *was* her that moaned this time. Her cunt was wet and slick, someone was licking and chewing and it was *so good.*

She stirred awake, and so many sets of painted eyes were on her.

She was in the fucking basement. How did she get in the fucking basement? Her pussy pulsed, begging, and she scrambled to her feet, and there was a sound of something tearing, a great groaning, and that wet cunt smell overtook her. She stumbled back, heart pounding, thighs shaking. She had to run, but she couldn't tear her eyes away from the mural.

The figures had turned away from each other. They were looking at Suzanne, smiling, all those teeth, all that red. Static blared from everywhere, from nowhere, from inside Suzanne's head. Her clit was wet and huge and throbbing. The wall warped, turned liquid, and there were so many eyes, looking at her, *wanting* her, there were hands all over her body, touching her, prodding her, needing her. Something huge was ripping through the floor and she was ready to bend over and take it, every inch of it, she was filled with red hot pulsing need and she was coming, she was coming, oh god, she was coming.

She was on the floor, ass in the air, thighs trembling. She couldn't catch her breath. The moon had gone dark, and in the shadows, the painting moved.

Her stomach churned, she felt like she was going to throw up. She lowered her head to her hands, closed her eyes, tried to remember how to breathe.

That was fucked up. She was fucked up. There was something wrong with her. She was an emotional fucking wreck and she was half asleep and she let this stupid fucking house get the better of her. It was just the work of some pervert. It was nothing. She wouldn't look at it.

Suzanne's legs shook. She looked out the window, to the trees.

That mound outside. The mural. The dreams.

She had to know for sure.

She pulled on sneakers, but didn't bother to change. The landlord had left a shovel in the porch, and she grabbed it before she stepped outside. Wind tickled through her nightgown. The moon was bright enough to lead her.

She shouldn't be doing this, she *knew* that, but there was an insistent nagging in her brain that wouldn't let her stop until she felt the dirt beneath her fingernails.

The trees were still, the stone structure loomed between them. The dirt next to it was loose and light. Grass had never dared to grow back in.

She dug.

She was grateful for the breeze that broke her sweat as she shoveled. She was grateful for the trees that kept her out of sight of the neighbors.

She caught the scent of herself in the air, musty, un-showered, insane. Her back ached. There was nothing out here. She was cracking up. It was time to go back inside.

But her shovel struck something, and she crouched down to push dirt aside, revealing a sliver of something hard and yellowed. She clawed deeper, snagging a nail, and was rewarded with the gentle curve of clavicle. The wind raised gooseflesh on her arms, tickled her thighs.

She had to call the police.

Blood pounded through her ears. She needed to see the whole thing. She shouldn't. She should be terrified. She should be upset. She should be running back to the house *right now*. She kept digging, gently, unearthing it bit by bit.

Muck had picked the flesh from the bones, leaving the skeleton filthy but whole. The top of the skull was shattered and splintered where it had been caved in by the hammer. She cradled it, feeling strangely tender toward this man she had never known. He had been discarded too. Fucked and left for dead, and wasn't that kind of the same as her? Fucked and used and thrown aside.

The eyes of the skull were dark and beautiful. She slid her hand down, caressing his cheek. The bone was rough and dirty beneath her fingers. Hard. It was so intimate to touch this part of a stranger, the deepest insides, the last piece that remained. Her nipples were so erect it was painful.

The man had been beautiful once. She knew it. Even in death you could see that. These beautiful bones laid out before her, strong and whole but for that wicked head wound. Shining beetles crawled through his ribcage. She slid her hand down his arm, took his chalky hand in her own. The bones creaked as she led the hand to her cheek, turned her face to kiss the cold death of his palm.

There was a pulsing in her groin.

Something wasn't right.

She dropped the hand, disgusted with herself, but it fell so gently, caressing her, brushing against her nipple on its way down, making her sigh.

She had never been with anyone but Eric before. Had never even thought of it, really.

She crouched in front of the bones. She was lost. Her hand slid down the bumps of his vertebrae and across the cage of his ribs, where his heart had once pounded in fear.

She took his hand again, licked the tips of the fingers. They tasted like dirt. She slid the hand down, across her breast. Bumpy phalanges tore her thin nightie apart. The bones were cold and rough, their caress pinching, teasing, as they slid down her bare belly.

She sat astride the pelvic bone, grinding down, gasping as the curve of hip jutted into her wet panties. She slid back and forth, took fingers deep into her mouth, stared into empty eyes. Blood pulsed in her ears, along with the pulse of something else, deeper, but she was so fucking horny, she couldn't concentrate, she could only buck and writhe and gasp.

It wasn't enough.

Hard fingertips scraped her breast, rough and jagged, releasing bright trails of blood. The pressure it released felt good. She leaned forward, pressed her forehead against the cool, rough skull. Her tongue glided across his teeth. They tasted dirty. She felt dirty.

She slid her hands over herself, smearing blood and dirt across pale skin. She yanked her panties off. Her pussy was hot and wet, throbbing, and she straddled the hipbone again. This time it rubbed against sweet bare flesh. Bits of dirt flaked, sandy against her clit. It still wasn't enough. Her head swam. She could barely breathe. This wasn't her, but she needed more. She needed to be closer. She needed it inside her.

She pulled the bones from the mud, dragged them atop the huge stone altar. She could move freely now. The femur pulled away from the hip bone with a snap and she stroked it, let fibula and phalanges dangle into her lap. The head of the bone bulged obscenely. She sucked it into her mouth, greedy, swirling her tongue around. She groaned. It was so hard.

She slid it between her legs.

It was too big, and she bucked her hips in frustration. She wanted it, she wanted all of it. Everything in her body was screaming with want and need and desire and she thrust her hips down, hard, and her pussy ripped and it felt so fucking good.

Blood soaked her hands as she thrust the bone in, again and again, forcing her cunt to accept it. Tender skin tore, warm wetness flooded her thighs. Her hand was covered in hot wet blood and she rubbed her clit and fucked herself harder and harder until her eyes rolled back in her head and everything shivered and quaked.

She came painfully. In those seconds of black stillness, she saw something, she saw *him*, his body exquisitely sculpted, beautiful, his face a blur of black sketchiness, the mask thrown aside, his cock massive and throbbing and perfect, ready to rip everything apart with its strength, ready to fuck great fissures into the earth, tear it apart from the inside out.

And then she was sitting amid trees in her backyard, astride a skeleton, bleeding and cold and stuck, her insides screaming with pain. She tore the bone from her pussy. Hunks of flesh and hair came with it and gore soaked the stone.

Blood splattered the kitchen tile. She was woozy. She needed to call 9-1-1, but, god, she just couldn't help herself.

"Hello?" Eric's voice was sleepy. Was the bed next to him empty, or occupied?

"It's me. Can . . . Can you come? I hurt myself." Her legs trembled.

"Suzy? What's wrong?"

"I can't talk about it. I just need you to come. Please?" Her forehead was soaked in sweat. Everything she touched was smeared in blood. She needed a doctor. She needed stitches. She needed mental help. First, she needed Eric.

"I'm so glad you called. It's time to come home. "

"No, Eric, I just need you to come here. Please." She choked off a sob. "Something weird is happening. I'm at a place on Baker's Lane. The last house on the left. Just come here, please."

She turned the phone off so he wouldn't call back. She didn't want to talk. She just wanted him to come.

Suzanne was dressed and soaking through a pad when the car pulled up. Even in this bizarre situation, she felt nervous. What could she even say to him after all this time? How could she explain this?

She opened the door and he smiled, blue eyes shining. How had she never noticed they were dead inside? He took her into his arms and the smell of his cologne teased her nose. She should have showered. She must smell awful.

"Suzy, what the hell is going on here? You look like shit." His eyes softened, "I'm happy to see you, but you don't look well. God, I'm so happy to see you. Look at you. You need me. You haven't been taking care of yourself."

"I've been doing fine." She pulled away from him. It hurt to walk. "This is all going to sound insane. I need to show you something in the basement."

"I'd rather talk at home. I'd like to get you in the bath first. Jesus, what have you been doing out here?"

"Please, I think it would be better to show you first."

He shrugged, "Have it your way, but let's make it quick. This place is disgusting."

"You don't know the half of it." She gestured toward the kitchen, led him to the basement door.

"Can we just get to what's going on here? Are you limping?" His brows furrowed with concern, a robot imitating human emotion.

"Really soon, yes, we'll talk. I just want you to see this so you can understand. Please?"

He followed her down the stairs, into the darkness. "What is that smell?"

"Just . . . " She gestured a limp arm at the wall. At the painting. "Look. Just look. I'll explain."

But she didn't. She couldn't tear herself away. All that wetness.

The blood and the sex and the guts and the cum. Eric frowned. "Did . . . did you paint this? What the fuck is this?"

"It was here when I got here. Does it look right to you?"

"I'm not gonna sit here all night looking at some old porno painting. What is going on with you? Have you been drinking?" He reached for her, but she swatted his hand away.

"It's not what you think . . . just . . . look at it a little longer. It's the only way for you to understand what's going on here."

"And then you'll come home?"

"Just look."

"What am I looking for?" He turned back to the wall. She reached down. The hammer was heavy. Need was growing in her chest, in her gut. She would know when the moment was right.

Red spurted from the wall and Eric turned to Suzanne, confusion in his eyes, and Suzanne swung and the sound the hammer made when it connected with his skull was music.

Flesh split from skull, bone crunched beneath hammer. Eric swayed, grimaced, his mouth an O of surprise. She wasn't strong enough. She had to hit him again. He fell from the couch, his eyes squinting beneath the waterfall of blood. The dent in his head was the size of a baseball. "K . . . Karen . . . " he muttered.

"Who the fuck is Karen?" She swung again, hit the opposite side. His eyeball turned to liquid, squelched against the floor. Something rasped deep in his throat and he collapsed.

He didn't even look human anymore. He looked like art. Thick fluid pumped from his shattered face. His remaining eye flickered. She thought he was still breathing. She swung again and a spray of brain matter misted her face. She licked her lips, tasted salt. She swung again and again and chips of bone and meat sprayed new blood on the walls as his skull finally shattered.

She yanked off her sweater and her jeans. There was no time for teasing. She wanted him *now*.

The knife was dull. She hadn't had much time to prepare. It was a lot of work to open him up. Grunting with effort, she slid through his flesh. Fat and muscle slipped away from her hands, and she opened him wide, like a present. He smelled like meat, like blood, like sex. She could hear laughing, somewhere far away. Was it her own? Her face hurt from smiling. She slipped her hands into the opening. He was so warm and wet inside. Rib bones scraped against her hands, sending a chill through her body.

His heart came out with a wet squelch.

It was hers, finally.

Blood spurted over her teeth. It was thick and bitter, but it tasted delicious. Juices leaked onto her face, her breasts, made her wet and warm and slippery. She slid her hands over her breasts and, god, she had never been so fucking horny in all her life.

It had been wrong to fuck the skeleton. She knew that now. She belonged to Eric. She would make it up to him. And all the eyes in the painting could watch.

She cracked his rib bones with a snap, shoved their jagged ends into her own smooth skin. She wanted everything of him to enter her, everywhere. Her flesh was unwilling but yielded. She stabbed broken bones into her stomach and a beautiful arc of bone jutted out beneath her sternum, like a crown.

She wasn't patient enough to slice through tendon and meat to get to the bone. She needed it all *now*. She tried to carve his arm off, but the thick muscle and bone was too much for her knife. She groaned in frustration. She would have it anyway. He still wore their wedding ring, but her pussy was ripped too far open to feel it when she shoved his fist inside.

"God, that feels good." She moaned and leaned forward to kiss him. She slipped her tongue inside what was left of his mouth, tasted blood, swallowed shattered teeth.

There was so much of him; bones and muscles and tendon and meat. She wanted it all.

The knife was sharp enough for her own soft skin. The ruin of his head gaped at her as she slid a blade between her tits. Exquisite pain jolted through her body. She slid a finger inside the cut, teasing, coy, and carved a muscular ribbon from his thigh. It curled around her fingers, and she slipped it inside the wound, greedy fingers shoving, until his flesh was hers.

She could stuff every bit of him inside herself if she just made enough holes.

She cut and screamed and fucked and came. Painted figures screamed in ecstasy. The floor turned red beneath her, and blood dribbled into the hungry mouth that tore the basement in two.

THESE BEAUTIFUL BONES

Betty Rocksteady is your everyday Canadian weirdo with a leaning towards the macabre and grotesque. Besides writing violent and sexual and just plain weird fiction, she does black and white horror illustration. Her debut novella, Arachnophile, *was part of Eraserhead Press' 2015 New Bizarro Authors Series. If you've been dying to read about a man who falls in love with a giant spider, this is probably the book for you. Her short fiction has been published in* Eternal Frankenstein, Lost Signals, *and* Turn to Ash. *In 2017, her second novella will be released by Perpetual Motion Machine Publishing. Find out more at www.bettyrocksteady.com or connect on twitter @bettyrocksteady.*

SUBJECT #270374

C.M. SAUNDERS

DAY: -1

They call it 'Day Minus One' because the actual testing doesn't start until tomorrow. That'll be an eleven-day trial, but today is all administration stuff. I was admitted to the research facility a little before midday on February 11th, 2016. I gave the required blood and urine samples—they test for recreational drugs—and had my height, weight and vital signs recorded. I signed consent forms, was given a wristband with my name, age, photo, and strings of numbers on that I don't understand (Trial: G5HY787, Code: 49864000948, Group: 327, Subject: #270374) and told to wear it at all times. I am no longer a man, I am a "subject."

After the formalities, I was shown around. There is a common room with newspapers and a pool table, which doubles as a dining room, two TV rooms, one with bookshelves and the other with an Xbox, and three other wards. Then I was shown to my bed. The place looks like your average hospital ward, eight beds, all full of people like me. Male, 21-45 years old. Mostly white. There's a token black guy and a couple of the others speak in foreign accents. Polish, Romanian, something. Lots of people in white coats mill around looking busy. Most of the staff are Asian. Not Indian or Pakistani like you would expect. But Vietnamese, Chinese, Thai. I guess they work for lower salaries. My bed is against the far wall, under a big window with tinted glass and security bars. Apart from the plastic sheets, it isn't really that bad. Comfortable. The guy in the bed next to me, Dwayne from Manchester, farts a lot.

There are strict rules here. No smoking or drug use—beyond

what they give us—no sugar or caffeine, controlled diet. Lights out at eleven. The curtains around the beds have to be drawn closed, which I don't mind one bit. At least you get some privacy and don't feel like you are being watched all the time. Even if you are.

Dinner was avocado with beans and a fruit cup.

DAY: 1

And so it begins. Me and the other new arrivals, four in total (the other four on the ward are already a few days in), are awoken at 7 am and taken to what they called the "sleep study room" to be hooked up to an ECG machine which reads our brainwaves. Fucking electrodes took forty-five minutes to put on. Then I had to endure three twenty-minute tests with wires and suction cups glued to my head and face. The first test consisted of sitting in a darkened room, alone with my thoughts. That was easy. The hardest part was staying awake. For the second test, I had to wear a set of headphones and count some high-pitched beeps. If I am more than two off we have to do the test again. I count thirty-nine. I am exactly right on the first try. Problem is I felt nauseous afterwards and it gave me a headache.

The third test was the truly weird one. A doctor came in with a file. At least, he looked like a doctor because he was wearing different color coveralls to distinguish himself from the other workers and wore a stethoscope hung around his neck. Inside the file were pictures. Computer print-offs and some polaroids. Awful, terrible pictures. Body parts. Pools of blood. Car crashes, industrial accidents, a few shots that looked like they were taken in the aftermath of an explosion in a war zone. It was all pretty harrowing stuff and wasn't what I would expect in testing a new anti-depressant drug. Or any kind of drug trial, come to that. I'll admit I was a bit disturbed by it all. My stomach did a mini-flip at one image in particular. Even after all that's happened since, I can still see it when I close my eyes. It was a close-up of a man's naked torso, the face blacked out. He had been flayed. At least, that's how it looked. Strips of mottled skin hung from his body, exposing tiny slivers of something white and glistening buried beneath the meat. His ribs.

Spent the next hour in the shower washing glue out of my hair with baby shampoo. The only thing that does the job, apparently.

After the tests I was given breakfast (toast and cereal) and my first dose of meds. Two nurses came in white coats with red armbands (means they are doing something important and can't be disturbed) and gave me a capsule to take with a cup of water. After I took the capsule they looked in my mouth to make sure I had really swallowed it and told me to stay in bed for thirty minutes. I imagine that's so I can't throw up the capsule. After that they took more blood, and would continue to do so another five or six times, the last being taken at 2 am. There can be nothing scarier than waking up in the middle of the night to a stranger standing over your bed with a syringe saying, "I want your blood."

DAY: 2

Nobody plans a life like this. I suppose I should briefly explain what I'm doing here. I need cash, and fast. I know, doesn't everybody? Before I was a "subject" I was a writer on a national magazine. I got head-hunted by another publishing company planning a new launch. Promotion, pay rise. I was ambitious, so I took the gamble. It didn't pay off. I didn't see eye-to-eye with my new editor from the start. Guy called Ted Readham. Great name for an editor, right?

Ted was full of unreasonable demands. Looking back, I'm convinced he made things deliberately hard for me. It didn't matter how long or hard I worked. Twelve, fourteen hours a day. Weekends. Every piece of writing I submitted came back with jagged red lines through it. It turned into an impossible job. I started cracking under the pressure, and missed a few days' work. That was the excuse Ted Readham needed to terminate my contract with immediate effect. No second chance, no reprieve. No severance pay. The ruthless cunt. It was a Friday afternoon. I spent the rest of the day walking around the city in a daze.

No ECG today. No print-outs or polaroids. Just a blood sample, and dosing. Felt a little woozy afterwards, though I don't know if that's because of the drugs or all the blood I am losing. One of every four subjects is given a placebo. Double blind, they call it, which means neither the staff nor the subject knows who's actually getting it. Placebos work. It's been scientifically proven. Isn't that weird?

I stayed in bed all day, reading and watching TV on my laptop. I tried to write something. The next great novel, perhaps. But the words won't come. I never believed in writer's block. I always thought of it as a myth, an excuse. I told people that when writing is your bread and butter, your only source of income, writer's block is a luxury you can't afford. Whoever heard of a bricklayer getting bricklayer's block? Or a bus driver getting bus driver's block?

I'm not afraid of boredom. Only boring people get bored. I have a million things to do. Websites to surf, job boards to check. This is pretty much what I do on a daily basis anyway. It doesn't matter where I am as long as I'm logged on. Being active helps keep my mind away from slipping into the Dark Place. The place where all hope is lost, where I've fucked up my life and things will never be the same again. The place from where you can never really come back. I know it's there. It always is. The Dark Place isn't too far away from any of us.

We go for meals individually, at staggered times. Not sure why, but I like it that way. Saves me having to socialise and answer awkward questions like, "So, what do you do for a living?" I guess most of the other people here are in a similar position to me. Or else they'd be at work.

DAY: 3

There are seven on the ward now. Not eight. Last night someone must have walked out, or been kicked off the trial after being caught smoking in the toilet or something. I can't place who it is. It's someone on the other group I never talked to. All I know is that now, there's an empty bed.

Blood sample, vitals, dosing.

Same routine. Like a ritual.

Another ECG day. Same room as before, same routine with the electrodes stuck to my head and face. Test one, silence. Test two, I count forty-four high-pitched bleeps this time, and I'm right again. Still giving me a headache though. Then more of the pictures. Some looked the same. Dismembered bodies, flayed skin, gaping wounds. I saw someone's brain for the first time through a skull that looked like it had been shattered with a hammer. It was white and mushy.

This time, the doctor, a fifty-something with a big hairy mole on his cheek, asked me a load of questions and took notes. How do the pictures make you feel? Do they upset you? Have you ever actively sought out anything like this before? Do you think this person suffered before they died? What would you say was the ultimate cause of death?

Apparently this drug is supposed to override certain receptors in the brain, or so I am led to believe. What that has to do with pictures of corpses in car wrecks and war zones I don't know. I suspect it might have something to do with stimulating emotions. And while I have to admit the whole thing made me a bit uncomfortable, I didn't feel depressed. If anything, there was a sense of relief that I was the one looking at photos of them, and not vice versa. Perhaps the drug is working.

When I signed the consent forms I basically agreed to let these fuckers do whatever they wanted to me. I am not even a subject; I am a Guinea pig. A lab rat. I left my identity at the front door. I just have to ride it out. Just doing my bit, you understand. And earning a few quid in the process. Another week or so and I'll be out of here, and over three grand richer. That will keep the wolves at bay. For a while at least.

Had a brief conversation with Farting Dwayne in the next bed. I don't think he's the type to talk a lot. Which is cool, because neither am I. He's a self-employed plumber by trade. This is his thirteenth drug trial. He says it's like a holiday. The easiest money he earns.

Dinner was pork chops with potatoes and carrots.

DAY: 4

After I got fired, I freelanced for a few months. Got a few gigs here and there. But then the work dried up. Maybe it was just bad luck, or maybe Ted Readham had more influence than I thought. I wouldn't put it past him, the manipulating bastard.

My savings didn't last long, and the bills didn't stop coming. Rent, utilities, loan repayments. The car was repossessed. I applied for jobs everywhere. Most potential employers told me I didn't have the right skill set. I'm a good writer. But that's all I can do. Print journalism is dying a slow death, thanks to the Internet. Websites don't pay enough. The meagre advertising revenue they pull in doesn't allow them to.

So I applied for manual labour jobs. Then, potential employers started telling me I was overqualified. I mean, what kind of assessment is that? You are too smart to do the job? What if I wanted to do something that didn't require much in the way of thinking? That's when the depression really settled over me like a dark cloud. It came as a relief when Susan took the kids and left me.

I'm having a bit of trouble sleeping. I guess I managed two hours. It sounds like such an easy thing to do, doesn't it? Just switch off and drift away. But for some reason, sleep wouldn't come. Maybe it's worry, nerves, apprehension.

At 7:30 I was called for breakfast. Toast and cereal. No coffee. Well, they have decaf. But that's not real coffee, is it? It's like smoking a nicotine-free cigarette. Fucking pointless. Do they have nicotine-free cigarettes yet? If not, why not?

After breakfast it was blood sample, vitals, dosing. The ritual.

After that, I did nothing. I don't have any AEs, as they call them. Adverse Effects. Apart from not being able to poop. I don't know if that counts. We're supposed to tell the staff about every little detail, but I don't think they need to know that. They'll only give me a laxative that has me shitting through the eye of a needle.

Get this: one of the nurses is a tranny. I mean, a full-on man with tits. Looks Southeast Asian. His/her name tag says his/her name is Libby. Libby was given away by his/her thick, hairy arms, black stubble, square jaw and Adam's apple. I'm not homophobic or anything. Live and let live is my motto. But meeting Libby added an extra layer of surrealism to the whole experience.

DAY: 5

Someone else has disappeared off the ward. This time, I knew him. We were admitted at the same time. He was in the bed at the end of my row. Young guy. Sean, Sam, Steve. Something with an S. When the nurse came around at 7 am to open all the curtains, he was gone, along with all his stuff, and his bed was stripped. I guess he couldn't handle it.

Didn't sleep well again. An hour? Probably less. Developed a headache. Thought I should mention this one, in case the drugs they have me on cause a brain bleed or something. A doctor came and logged everything then gave me some painkillers. After that it was the usual blood sample, vitals, and dosing. Worryingly, I am beginning to enjoy the little stab of the needle. It makes me feel alive.

Then another ECG test. First, silence. Second, fifty-seven high-pitched bleeps. Is it me, or is this bit getting progressively harder?

More images. And more questions. Except this time, they were different. The guy in a white coat asked if I was getting sexually aroused. Just came out and said it. I mean, what the fuck? Who in this world could or would get turned on by pictures of mutilated bodies and severed limbs? After he said that, I realized for the first time that there was a sexual undertone to many of the photos. I was just so fixated on all the blood and gore, it hadn't registered. There was a guy (or a girl?) hanging upside down in a rubber gimp suit. A hole had been made in the ass, and something protruded rudely from the victim's rectum. On closer inspection, I saw it was a rolled-up newspaper. And a very substantial one at that. Obviously one of the Sundays.

Another sequence started with two men kissing. In the next photo, one was sucking the other's cock. Then he was biting the end off and chewing it while the ruined member squirted a stream of blood into his face.

These photos have to be fake, right? Prosthetics.

The strange thing is, I was getting aroused. I didn't even realise until he asked. After that, fucking was all I could think about. Maybe it had something to do with being shut away with no . . . home comforts. Not that I had much comfort at home. Our sex life disintegrated long before mine and Susan's marriage did. Not like we ever experimented with anything like I was shown in the polaroids. I mean the gimp costume, not the dick chewing.

Though things hadn't been right between us since I found out she'd slept with her manager two years ago.

Dinner was pork chops with potatoes and carrots again. As I ate, I couldn't stop thinking about the images they kept showing me. And other stuff. Human flesh. Don't they say it tastes like pork?

DAY: 6

Couldn't sleep last night. Not a wink. And I still can't poop. I can feel it inside me, like a compressed ball.

Blood sample, vitals, dosing. The ritual. This time, when the needle was buried in my arm, Libby the transsexual Asian nurse did something wrong. Not sure what. But a little jet of blood spurted out, hitting him/her in the face. It reminded me of the cock biting photos. Libby just smiled and wiped it off. He/she must get that a lot. What a trooper.

Even stranger is the fact that I like it, too. The sight of my own gushing blood? The thrill that often accompanies the unexpected? I don't know what it was exactly, but something gave me a rush.

Another ECG test. The silence, then the bleeps. This time, I get the answer wrong and had to do the whole fucking test again. Twice. Got it right at the third attempt. Sixty-seven bleeps. Sixty-seven! Then came the images. They are getting steadily worse. Or better, depending on your point of view. This time, the one that stood out portrayed a woman, sitting on a white leather couch, naked from the waist down. Her legs were wide open, and she appeared to be masturbating with a severed arm. That took fisting to a whole new level, but I must be getting desensitized, because they didn't make me feel sick any more. I even kind of enjoyed answering the ridiculous questions. It felt good to talk about it. Stimulating. Exciting, even. I started to get the strangest feeling that I'd always wanted to talk about this stuff, and see images like this. I just didn't know it before. I knew something was missing from my life, but I didn't know what.

Now, I know.

There was one photo in particular. A decapitation. It was a dude. I could tell because he was wearing a smart suit. Looked designer. Expensive. When you see a dead rich person, it makes you realise that in the eyes of the Reaper, everyone is equal. It doesn't matter how rich and powerful you are, how many people you manipulated to get there. When your card is marked, it's marked. The end.

I don't know how it happened, but the rich guy's head had come away clean, like it had been sliced off with a sword or something. You could make out white flecks of vertebrae in amongst the gore and actually see down his windpipe. To me, it looked like a vulva. A big gaping cunt. Wide open, glistening, and ready to receive a cock. I could feel myself stiffening. Weirdly, the fact that I was getting hard for a guy felt more unusual than the fact I was getting hard for something that wasn't meant to be fucked. When I told the guy in the white coat this, he didn't seem surprised. He didn't even flinch. Just scribbled it down in his notebook.

I imagine he's heard much worse.

SAUNDERS

Woke up during the night needing a piss. I say I "woke up," but I'm not sure I was really asleep. Probably not. Sleep is a stranger to me now. Instead, I have these weird fugues where I surrender to my thoughts and let them take me where they want. They usually want to take me back to the images I get shown in the sleep room. In particular the headless guy in the suit. So I let them. Why not? Nothing else to do here. I don't think you'd want to know exactly what I was thinking about. At times, I even shock myself.

I went to the toilet to find some guy having a wank. He wasn't even in the shower, or a cubicle. He was just standing over a sink, looking at himself in the mirror and tugging himself off furiously. That isn't even the strange part. He'd cut himself. On the chest, I think. Or arms. There was a broken disposable razor in the sink and he'd rubbed the blood all over his cock and balls. When I walked in, he didn't even stop. Just looked at me and grinned. There was a look in his eyes. Manic, unhinged, gleeful. I hope I don't look like that when I'm cumming. So I'm not the only guy in here having uncontrollable sexual urges, but at least I was keeping mine in check. For now.

I had a piss and went back to my bed without a word. I didn't want to disturb the guy. He looked disturbed enough as it was.

When I went back to brush my teeth a couple of hours later, just as sunlight was beginning to stream through the bars on the window, the guy was gone. Along with any trace of him ever being there. No blood, no tell-tale globs of semen hanging off the sink. I began to wonder if I'd dreamed the whole thing. Maybe I'd been asleep after all.

Two more disappeared off the ward last night. Now there are only four of us left. That means we've shed half our original number. Where are they all going? Nobody seems too concerned, and nobody talks about them after they leave. While she was doing the ritual, I asked one of the nurses, and she just said something about not being able to discuss it because of a confidentiality agreement. All the secrecy in this place is enough to make a man paranoid.

Pork again for dinner. I must have eaten half a pig by now.

DAY: 8

Stayed awake all night wondering if Libby still had a cock and balls or if he/she'd had them chopped off. Not that it makes much difference to me either way. I still wouldn't fuck it. Or let it fuck me.

Would I?

Slightly awkward when he/she came to do the ritual. Blood, vitals, dosing. When he/she was taking my blood pressure he/she leaned right over and pressed his/her fat tits against my chest. It felt good. Really good. After being starved of attention for so long, my cock sprang to attention right away, despite the hairy man arms and prominent Adam's apple. He/she didn't need to lean over me like that. I mean, it could easily have been avoided. Makes me wonder if he/she wants to fuck me. Is that weird?

Then I started wondering . . . do I find it weird that someone wants to fuck me? Or do I find it weird that someone of a questionable gender wants to fuck me? I mean, a fuck's a fuck, right? Every hole's a goal and all that. And who looks at the mantelpiece when they're poking the fire?

Saw the guy I caught having a blood wank. He was in the TV room. I only popped in to catch the lunch time news. He was in there alone watching that French film *Irreversible* on DVD. I remember it well. That film fucking traumatised me as a teenager. The part where the guy gets his head smashed in with a fire extinguisher. Wanking guy was watching the rape scene. Frame-by-frame. I left before he got his cock out and started tossing off again. On my way out he tipped me a wink, like he was letting me know that he remembered me from the night before. Should I be worried?

Pork. Again. I don't know what their cooks are doing to it, but it tastes fucking delicious.

I am reminded of an internet meme I once saw. Someone making a chicken omelette. The caption said: I WILL COOK YOU IN YOUR CHILDREN.

Genius.

DAY: 9

I am awake. I am always awake. I can't remember the last time I slept. Usually, I'm thinking about fucking. I moved on from fucking glamorous movie stars and lingerie models a long time ago. Boring.

I even stopped thinking about Libby's equipment. Or lack of. Now I just think about fucking body parts. Obviously, the windpipe that looks like a cunt ranks highly on my "to do" list. But I also think about making incisions in a plump belly and sliding my cock in good and slow. Then I would fuck the hole gently. Like a teenage virgin. Until I get to that point of no return. Then I would bang that thing like a raging madman, the cut becoming bigger and more accepting with every thrust, warm blood running over my balls and down the insides of my thighs, gathering in a pool at my feet.

Under the covers, I push my cock down between my legs to stifle my erection. I'm waiting for the ritual. Blood sample, vitals, dosing. The needle. That's the best part.

When Libby comes he/she tells me this is the last of them. I feel a little strange. Disappointed? I don't know. Despite all the weirdness, I'm getting used to being here. I think I'm starting to get institutionalized. Like a prisoner who doesn't want to leave the sanctity of jail. Here, I get fed, I have a bed, I can think a lot and for the most part, I'm left alone. There are no outside pressures.

Plus, I'm going to miss those tits.

The needle goes in, I savour the sensation, and even let out a sigh as it pricks my vein. I normally avert my eyes. This time, I watched.

Fish for dinner. Fish? What the fuck. I couldn't eat it. Couldn't even be around it. I wanted pork.

DAY: 10
So, no dosing today. No ritual. No nothing, in fact. It says in the paperwork that after the last dosing you are kept under observation for thirty-six hours. Sort of a come-down period, I imagine. What am I supposed to do for thirty-six hours? I don't feel any different. Still can't sleep. Don't even want to.

Still having . . . urges. If anything, they are getting stronger. More depraved. My thoughts keep being dragged back to the windpipe. How glorious it must feel to slip my stiff penis into that warm, wet hole. I also find myself fantasising about eating human flesh. Slicing chunks of someone's arms or legs, frying it, and eating it. Maybe that's the ultimate act of dominance. You fuck someone, maybe in the windpipe, then feed off them. Consume them.

In the afternoon I go to the toilet, drop my trousers, and sit on the seat. I don't feel the need to go, but my stomach is cramping. I am literally full of shit. Unfortunately, that's normal for most journalists. I need to get all this waste out of me somehow. I sit there for twenty, thirty, forty minutes. Fifty. I strain periodically, but not too hard in case I rupture something and shit out my intestines. Something slithers and stirs in my bowels, like a snake, but still nothing comes out. I poke my fingers up my ass to see if there's a blockage. At least, that's what I told myself I was doing.

Eventually, I give up and go back to bed. I look out of the window at the grey skies and rain, and I realise I don't want to go out. Ever. In here it's a controlled environment. Outside it's a fucking zoo, where crooks prosper at the expense of others and working slobs like me get used and discarded. What am I going to do out there? I have no job, no family, no prospects. My old life, where I had everything I wanted, doesn't even exist anymore. It was snatched away. Right now, if someone asked me to do the whole trial again from scratch, I would bite their hand off. Literally. But nobody does. So I lie still, covers pulled up to my chin, pondering what to do next.

Suddenly, it comes to me.

DAY: 11

I lay awake all night. Thinking. Then, at 9 am I pack my things, fill in some more forms, say goodbye to Libby, flash him/her my best smile, and walk calmly and confidently out of the door. I'm not going home. Nothing to go home for. What I need is to find a hardware store. I'm going to buy a kitchen knife. Or even better, a machete. The biggest, sharpest one they have. Then, I'm going back to the office.

I don't know if my security pass still works. Security in the media world got a whole lot tighter after the Charlie Hebdo massacre in Paris. But I'm not bothered if the pass doesn't work anymore. I'm on good terms with both Laura in reception and Dan, the security guard who sometimes fills in for her when she goes on her breaks. I scored him some coke once at a party. He owes me one. I'm sure I won't have any problems getting inside the building. I'll just say I've come to finish clearing my desk or to pick something up from HR.

When I'm inside I'll head straight for the fourth floor where Ted Readham, my old editor, works. No doubt he'll be at his desk, sitting on his throne. Arrogant fuck. But a stupid fuck. Trusting fuck. He seats with his back to the elevator. That's good. I'll be fast. I can sneak up behind him, hack off his head, and stick my cock right down his windpipe. To the hilt. I reckon I'll be able to get a good few thrusts in before the police arrive. Who in the office is going to stop me? They'll all be too horrified. I can see it now. The carnage. The blood. If I give it to him good, I might even have time to cum. I'm already hard.

My only regret is that there won't be enough time for me to cook any of his meat. I guess I'll just have to eat him raw.

The dark fiction of C.M. Saunders has appeared in over 30 magazines, ezines and anthologies, including Raw Nerve, Fantastic Horror, Trigger Warning, Liquid Imagination, *and the* Literary Hatchet. *He is a hybrid author with nine long-from releases under his belt, the most recent being the novel* Sker House *and the charity novella* No Man's Land: Horror in the Trenches, *available through Deviant Dolls Publications. He is represented by Media Bitch literary agency. He welcomes stalkers to contact him via his website:* cmsaunders.wordpress.com

BEER BATTERED

K. TRAP JONES

WE STARTED OUT early in the canoe and the lake was calm as could be. I was two sheets to the wind; caught five keepers and drained an ungodly amount of *Natural Light* when I heard it.

"You hear that?" Denton said, pissing off the side of the boat.

"Yeah, I hear it."

The sun was in full effect, making it difficult to see anything from the direction of the noise. It sounded off again as my feet shifted within the piles of empty beer cans. Denton pinched off his piss current every time only to start back up a few seconds later.

"Could be vultures. Do they make noise like that?" Denton said, shaking himself off.

"Birds don't howl. At least I don't think they do." I finished off another beer.

"Those vultures are nasty pieces of shit. Did you know they don't have a single feather on their heads? Makes it easier to burrow their beaks into the rotting corpses," he continued, packing a can of Skoal.

It made perfect sense, but I wasn't sure whether he was making it up or not. I had good reason to doubt. I'd known Denton for as long as I could remember and he wasn't the sharpest pencil in the desk. Not his fault though; he just fell out of too many trees when we were young.

We tried to be quiet, but two southern boys in a canoe, well, it wasn't the easiest thing to do. Between the spitting and drinking, it was almost impossible to find any type of silence. However, every time we heard the noise, we did our best to freeze like we were playing Red Light, Green Light.

"Could be Bigfoot," Denton said.

"I doubt Bigfoot would be down here in the South. It's too fucking hot. Nah, his hairy ass is somewhere cold, like Canada," I answered, putting in a fresh dip.

"Probably right. I bet he pounds some sweet Eskimo poontang. Sneaking into an igloo on a cold night." Denton moved his hips back and forth, humping the air.

"Stop that shit, you're gonna tip us. Bigfoot ain't banging humans. His dick's probably as big as my leg. I mean, he's got a *big fucking foot*; therefore he has a *big fucking dick*. He would be splitting Eskimos in half. Damn thing would skewer them before he even busted a nut."

"I bet when he cums it's like one of them Roman candle fireworks going off. Just *bam, bam, bam*," Denton said, rocking the boat again. "Hey, does that shit freeze? Up there in Canada, if you toss water in the air, the shit turns to snow. Let's say you unload on some chick's ass, would it freeze to her skin?"

"How the fuck should I know? I'm not Canadian. If people are fucking outside in the winter, they got bigger problems to deal with. I can't even take a cold shower without my dick becoming a second belly button."

"Maybe that's why everything's white up there. Maybe the big guy is fucking Mother Nature bareback every night and unloading on her perky mountains."

"Exactly, that's why we live down here." I popped another beer.

"With blizzards, he must be getting one of those good nuts which makes your spine tremble."

The noise echoed from the trees again.

"It's coming from over there," Denton said, raising his beer.

"Shit, might as well check it out. Fish ain't biting anyways." I reeled in the lure.

Shifting around the dip in my lip, I kept my eyes on the shoreline for any movement. The fog from the morning was still swarming within the dense trees. I ain't gonna lie. I was nervous; real nervous. Damn Bigfoot could be anywhere and I couldn't see shit with all the lingering shadows, plus I'm not exactly sure as to how many beers I had. After carving the boat into the dirt, we crept up the shoreline.

"You think Bigfoot gets fleas?" Denton stated.

"What?"

"With all of that fur . . . or is it hair?"

"Shut up for a second, I hear something. Give me the machete."

"I don't have it."

"You didn't bring it?"

"You told me to go back and get the bait. When I did, I put it on the table."

"Sweet fucking Jesus, man. You're killing me, you know that?"

"The best I got is this bait knife."

"If this is Bigfoot, we're done for. He's gonna log stomp our skulls into mulch. And we better hope he ain't horny. No matter how tight you squeeze those cheeks, if he comes a knocking, no backdoor is gonna stop him."

"That's not funny. If I get raped by Bigfoot, I won't be happy," Denton said, tightening his belt.

Peeking through a bush, I could see it. Fucking thing was brutal looking from what I could make out. Definitely wasn't Bigfoot; it was too small. More like a pig with a thick brown hide and blackened hair which stood on end. Its ass was facing me while it had some guy pinned against a tree. The horns atop the head were burrowed deep into the torso of the man. He was one of those fancy runner types wearing matching sweatbands and shit. Blood was seeping from his mouth, coating his fluorescent orange shirt. I kind of felt bad for him being torn to bits and all, but not enough to break cover. To make matters worse, the guy lifted his head.

"Help," he mouthed, staring at me.

Pulling back from the bush, I sat in front of Denton.

"Is it Bigfoot?" he said with an eager grin.

"No, not Bigfoot, but it's definitely fucked up. There's an angry damn boar gutting a dude."

"Serious?" Denton said, trying to pass me.

"The thing is covered with intestines, I think."

"Damn. So, that's what the smell is. I thought it was rotten potato salad."

"The guy's still alive."

"No shit? I wanna see."

"Hold on a second. Let him bleed out first. It's all kinds of fucked up with him looking over here. It's awkward, like the time you wanted to watch Becky and me in the back seat."

"We had a rule," Denton said. "When one of us gets some, the other could watch."

"Let me see if he's dead," I said, sticking my head back through the bush.

The man was trying to drag his dangling organs back into his torso even as the beast was gnawing. His throat convulsed with an ungodly sound and he puked atop the creature's head. The sight of the man holding his own stomach outside of the body broke my threshold of tolerance. Beer-battered bile spewed down my chin as the slightest cough leaked from my mouth.

Shit.

My eyes never left the beast as it turned and looked. With an elongated snout and tusks like a sabre-tooth tiger, I damn near lost it. Bloody entrails were dangling from the set of cracked horns. Falling backward, I scurried within the dead leaves.

"Run!"

"What?" Denton said, trying to pick me up.

"We gotta get out of here!"

We ran as fast as our jean shorts and drunken vision would allow. Denton jumped into the canoe, turned around and froze. Noticing he wasn't moving, I stopped with my hands on the edge of the boat.

"Hold up," Denton whispered.

I remained still. Our eyes were about a foot away from one another. He was speaking through the smallest crack in the side of his mouth.

"Don't move," he said. "It's right behind you."

"What's it doing?" I whispered back.

"It's staring at you. The dude—it's wearing him as a hat."

"I need to get in the boat."

"No, stay still."

"Help me," the man moaned from behind, draining my courage.

"How in the hell is he still alive?" Denton whispered. "He looks like a meat puppet."

"Fuck you, I'm getting in."

"No, no," Denton said.

"Why not?"

"It will swallow your ass if you move. I don't think it cares about me. Its red eyes are only looking at you. Push me off first, there's no reason for three of us to be eaten."

"If I live through this, I will kill you."

"It doesn't like your anger. It's got horns, man. Oh shit, I think it's slurping on the guy's heart."

"Get a beer. On the count of three, I will push off and jump in as you throw the can at it."

"I don't know; there are a lot of teeth showing. It really looks pissed. It wants to fuck you up something bad."

"One."

"Okay, okay, hold on," Denton said, reaching for a beer.

"Two."

"Do I open it or just throw it? Should I shake it up first? Can you shake up beer like soda?"

"Three!"

At first, I didn't know how the beer can did this, but the loudest explosion sounded off. I landed face first in the canoe with ears ringing uncontrollably. My head hurt instantly and my vision blurred, but I didn't give a shit as I felt my ass was still intact.

"What the hell?" I said, rubbing my head to relieve the pain.

"I shouldn't have shaken it up," Denton said, pushing beer cans away from him.

"Hey, you in the boat!" a voice said from the shore.

We both peered over the canoe's edge as it spun in the water. Some guy dressed in combat fatigues was waving at us.

"Tagged a big one!" he said, adjusting a large weapon on his shoulder. "It's all right, come on back."

With our brains pounding against our skulls, we reluctantly paddled to shore.

"Name's Stan. Sorry about that there. Ole Betsy here has quite the kick back." He patted the long smoking barrel. "This here is a M1 Bazooka; anti-tank rocket launcher. She's a beauty, ain't she?"

Denton and I just stared at the guy. It was as if we were blasted out of reality. He was completely decked out in army gear from the helmet all the way down to the boots. He even had dog tags.

"I'm a WWII collector. I have everything, even got me one of those German Lugers. Greatest generation of our time, if you ask me. Looks like you fellas found a good one here." He knelt down next to what was left of the beast.

"What is that thing?" I said.

"That right there is a hell hog," he replied without an ounce of sarcasm.

All I wanted to do was fish. I was perfectly happy on the lake. I had more beer and dip than I could handle. Instead, I had to deal with potential Bigfoot, a gutted jogger, a man from WWII, and a hell hog. Needless to say, the day took a turn for the worse.

"These dirty bastards burrow up from the Devil's asshole and wreak some demented havoc. I've been seeing a lot more of them lately," Stan said, holding the shattered remains of the skull. "They use the horns to skewer their prey. The tusks tear through the ribs where they feast on the innards. Nasty little shitheads; I saw one devour a full buck in under a minute. Damnedest thing I ever saw."

"There's more?" Denton said, looking around.

"This one here is a scout. They creep around a lot. I first caught the things trespassing on my land eating rabbits and whatnot. Normally, when you see a lone one, it ain't too bad to get a kill shot on them, but they've been increasing in numbers. You were lucky; this one didn't get too pissed off. When they get real mad, they burst into flames. It's kind of like armor. Real tough to kill after that. I've never seen one with two heads though," Stan said, holding up the dead guy's mutilated skull.

"It was eating someone when we found it," I stated.

"Ah, well, that makes more sense. What a shame," Stan replied, tossing the human head aside without care.

"Smells like bacon," Denton added.

"Yeah, they cook up real nice, but the meat is a little tough. Makes for some good jerky though."

Right about then was when we heard several howls echoing across the lake. All our eyes shifted toward the opposite shoreline where smoke was funneling up through the trees.

"Well, that's new," Stan said.

"This one had some weird markings on his chest," I said.

"The Devil's brand; certified hellish meat from the contaminated bowels of the planet."

The howling intensified.

"Looks like we have a situation brewing."

"I knew we shouldn't have gone fishing today," Denton mumbled.

"Best you boys come with me. I got plenty of guns and ammo back home. We don't have much time before they reach this side of the lake." Stan lit up a cigar.

After loading up our cooler, we grinded through the dirt on his Willys MB jeep with a pair of mounted Gatling guns. He had a knack for explaining every piece of WWII memorabilia he had. While driving, he could control both by the elongated handles with customized triggers. The dirt road twisted through an endless amount of trees. Once we passed through a large gate, Stan pressed a button on the dash. Looking back I saw not only the gate close, but large spikes erecting from the dirt road.

"Best to mind your footing. I got traps everywhere. One misstep and you'll be hating life. Those doomsday preppers were right the whole time: *Hellageddon* has arrived," Stan said, shifting into park. "Follow my steps and don't be prancing anywhere on your own. I don't want to have to pick you up in pieces."

We waited for him to come around to our side of the jeep. We traced his every movement and stopped the instant he did.

"Shit, wrong way. Ha, that could've been messy," Stan said, changing directions.

We walked up to a large barn door. There was some high-tech shit happening, but I didn't understand any of it. He placed his whole palm on a screen and the damn door just opened like in the movies.

"Now, some of this stuff is pretty unreliable, but most will get the job done," Stan said.

The lights automatically turned on as we walked inside, kind of like those freezer lights at Walmart. Rows of tables held every single known weapon from the WWII era; a flea market of antique firepower.

"Over here, you got your handguns: Berettas and Colts. On that table, we got the more automatic ones. I'm still missing a few, but if rapid fire is your specialty, you can't go wrong with the Thompson or the M2 Carbine. I've done my best to restore them, but the aging process is a bitch sometimes. Always carry a backup in case they jam on ya. Of course, if one jams up, it will most likely blow your face off. Best to check first. For a more intimate kill, I got a few Garands. Over here, we got the big boys. The M2 Flamethrower ain't gonna do shit against these fire bastards, but the M7 Grenade Launcher will cause some skid marks if needed. All the rifles have been customized for the bayonet attachment. You'd be foolish not to grab one of those as well. You both up to date with your tetanus shots? If not, I'd leave the rusty ones alone."

"How many we talking?" I said, checking the scope alignment of a Carbine.

"Depends."

"On what?"

"How pissed off the Devil is. If his molten panties are in a twist, he could send everything he's got. It could be a few or the earth could decide to open up, coating us with a whole batch of evil diarrhea. If that happens, we might as well spend our last few minutes in a circle jerk so we can at least leave this world satisfied," Stan said.

"On the bright side, the Devil is probably the last person we haven't pissed off yet," Denton said.

"There are trenches all around. Use those for starters, but don't go beyond them. I've lost count on the traps I've set over the years. Some are duds no doubt, but the live ones will gut you good. I felt real bad for the pizza delivery guy last year. Poor bastard triggered a mine I forgot about. Blew his right leg clean off, tossing it into a tree. If you squint, you can see the femur bone." Stan pointed upward.

"Did he live?" Denton said.

"For a bit. I tried my best to seal the wound, but once the pack of wolves caught wind, he didn't have a chance. Dragged him right off into the night. The pizza was good, though," Stan said, a wistful look in his eyes. "Listen, we hit them with mortars first, rifles next, then autos."

"Then what?" Denton asked.

"Hopefully it doesn't go beyond that. If it does—hand to hoof combat."

"How do they get up here?" I said, holstering a Beretta.

"I'm betting there's a death pit somewhere in the northern woods. I've been scouting a few times but have yet to find it. If I ever do, I figure I'll give it a go trying to implode it; seal it off for good."

The howling intensified as the wind shook the barn door.

"We best be getting ready. Grab what you want and head to the trenches. I'll fire up the tank," Stan said.

"Tank?" I replied. Even asking the question sounded odd.

"Like I said, I'm a collector. Also, we're going to need these to communicate." Stan handed me a large metal case. "There's some static, but these field walkie-talkies will work just fine."

"This old man's crazy," Denton said, putting on a helmet with the word *Ace* scratched into the front.

"We survive the night and I promise we'll never fish here again," I said, spit shining a frag grenade.

When the barn door opened, I swear I was looking at the largest bonfire ever created. The horizon of trees was ablaze, splitting the darkness. Even the full moon had a red glow to it. We jumped into the nearest trench where a mortar was already set up with about five rounds. After turning on the walkie-talkie, I rotated the dial until I heard a voice.

"This is the Iron Maiden, can you read me, over!"

"Yes, yes, we hear you, over!" I replied.

"Get those mortars ready, soldiers."

"Give me one of those," I said, pointing to the shells.

Denton quickly grabbed one and fumbled it just like he did on the high school football team. Everything slowed to a creeping pace as the mortar fell, clanking against a pile of grenades. I squinted in preparation of being blown to bits, but nothing happened. Instead of asking for another, I got it myself.

"I've seen this on TV. You just slide it in and cover your ears," Denton explained.

I dropped it in and sure enough the damn thing fired, but it almost went straight up. We scattered from the trench like roaches in the light. The explosion created a new trench near ours.

"I forgot: make sure to adjust the angle before firing the mortars!"

As the howls got closer, I was able to shift the hot base of the mortar. The old thing could've used a little WD-40, but there was no time for that. Looking through a cracked pair of binoculars, Denton was playing the part of soldier.

"We got two brigades of hogs approaching from the north. A combat unit heading east . . . possibly flanking us, over!" he explained.

"Roger that soldier, you should have eyes on me soon!"

The tank came barreling around the barn. The grinding of the tread caused all kinds of chaos chewing up the dirt. As it rolled forward, it produced a sound of shifting rust and decay. The tank came to a stop a few feet away as the barrel shifted upward.

"Cover your ears boys, she's about to moan in ecstasy."

We buried our heads so deep within the trench and stayed there waiting for the blast.

"Come on baby, you know you want to. Don't stop now. Is it stuck? I don't want to put another one inside. I don't think you can handle two. You want me to jiggle it? Here, I'll use more oil. Ah, I think I'm getting it. I can feel friction now."

When she let loose, the earth shook and damn near buried us alive. I could barely hear anything as the sky illuminated with bits of red glowing hog pieces. Stan popped the hatch and came out smoking his cigar.

"Best lay in town, boys," he stated, straddling and stroking the long barrel.

His attitude quickly changed as he manned the Gatling gun attached to the top of the tank.

"Bogies at 12 o'clock!"

Peering over the edge of the trench, I about shit myself. A mass of fiery hogs was galloping our way. I had no time to think; I grabbed the Carbine and started shooting. The grenades Denton was throwing were doing some good damage. Bits of flaming hog flesh were soaring through the air like fireworks. On the plus side, the chunks provided light, but when they landed, small new fires ignited.

"Would you boys like some lemonade?" a female voice said.

The sight of a frail old lady holding a tray of glasses confused the shit out of me. Between the bullets and angry hell hogs pouncing around, she was either deaf or blind or just plain stupid.

BEER BATTERED

"Stan didn't tell me he was having visitors," she said in the calmest of tones as a severed hog head on fire barely missed hitting her shoulder. "The lemons are nice and plump this time of year."

I obliterated a hell hog that was about to attack her as she lowered the tray. I could barely hear her with the amount of firepower Stan was laying down.

"Don't be shy, boys. There's plenty to go around."

I didn't want to be rude, so I reached for a glass.

"Thank you, ma'am," I replied, splitting the skull of a hog with a bullet.

"I have a batch of cookies. They're about to come out of the ov—" A chunk of flesh slammed against the tray causing the pitcher to fall.

"Oh my, that was certainly rude," she said, wiping excess lemonade from her face.

The Carbine seized up, so I opted for the Thompson. It felt real good in my hands, but the discharges were a bitch. Due to the closeness, the shells kept hitting Denton in the head. Stan jumped into the trench with Betsy on his shoulder.

"Well done, soldiers! We've definitely provided some hurt to the enemy. When life gives you a sack, you go balls deep," he announced, readjusting Betsy on his shoulder.

Without warning, he fired her. The explosion ripped through a small horde as well as toppling some trees. As the frontline of the beasts kept coming, several of them were disappearing beneath the ground.

"Sure glad I fired those up," Stan said.

The crazy old man had buried tree chippers. The hogs were falling into the grinders, but that's where the coolness ended. The output shoots stuck out of the ground like a chimney and were pointed in our direction. A wave of molten hog innards drenched us with a warm, thickened sludge. I saw the red rain approaching and ducked, but Denton wasn't that lucky. He got pimp slapped across the face with a hefty portion of the Devil's stew. The aroma of bacon filtered through the trench.

"Fuck me," he said, trying to spit out the excess.

"They're coming hard, soldiers. Switching to semi," Stan announced.

We pounded the shit out of another approaching horde. I was in the zone until I heard the sound of a guzzling chainsaw. To our left, the old lady had returned and was carving up a hog. Her frail arms quivering as the blades grinded through the skull. With the hog dead, she planted her pink slipper on the snout and pushed the carcass, dislodging the weapon.

"Ma, I told you to stay inside!" Stan yelled.

"I fight on the side of Jesus," she calmly said. Revving the chainsaw and wearing a blood-coated flowered apron, I was pretty sure she cared less about the blood splattering her face.

"Stan didn't tell me he was having visitors," she repeated herself while Stan helped her down into the trench. She kept sporadically firing up the chainsaw while waving it around. Denton and I were nervous as we had to duck on several occasions.

"Easy, Ma. With your arthritis, don't hold on the gas while idling," Stan said, trying to control the swaying weapon.

The horde kept advancing, leaping over the chippers as they became clogged with bone and meat. We riddled the front line with a swarm of bullets until I heard the most chaotic scream. Denton was yelling like a fat man being cut off at a buffet bar. Sparks from the chainsaw carving into the back of his helmet illuminated the trench.

"Ma! He's on our side," Stan said, pulling back her arms.

"Did I get one?" she said, adjusting her blood splattered spectacles.

"When's the last time you had your eyes checked?" Stan asked.

"What's that? I already watered the tomatoes on the deck," she replied with a smile. Her white hair was saturated red.

"Sorry about that, soldier. Her depth perception is not what it used to be." Stan smiled, patting a stunned Denton on the helmet.

"Time to call in some support, boys. It's go time for the napalm. I know it's not from the same era, but I'm trying to expand the collection." Stan pulled out a small remote control device.

"I thought you said fire won't do shit," I said.

"Exactly, that's why I customized the napalm to be frost instead. Pressurized dry ice is the weaponry of the future, boys. You are about to witness greatness in modern warfare. Here, put these on." He handed us goggles before putting a pair on Ma.

After he pushed a button, two launchers extended from the roof of the barn.

BEER BATTERED

"There's a chance this could work. Worst case scenario, we turn into popsicles and die a painful death while waiting for our lungs to freeze," Stan said, rotating the knob for alignment.

The whistling of two flying bombs was mesmerizing. I didn't even care they were coming from behind us, soaring over our heads. The metal casings glistened against the backdrop of the moon and starry night sky. I blinked when the explosion occurred. Twisting my head slightly and wiping the frost from the goggles, I looked to Denton. His long scraggly hair was blown backward and frozen. Excess dip drool was encased in ice on his cheeks.

"T-t-t-target nullified," Stan said with a shuddering voice.

"Is it winter already? I need to cover the plants," Ma said with frosty lips.

Apparently my mouth had been open because everything in it was frozen. I couldn't even close my jaw. My bones ached as I tried to follow Stan out of the trench.

"Switching to secondary," he announced.

Exiting the trench, we entered a wasteland of ice. It was snowing during August in the South. If it weren't for all the hogs in blocks of ice, it was actually peaceful; a winter wonderland with demented yard decorations. A bullet from Stan's Colt shattered one of the ice blocks, obliterating a hog in the process.

"We gotta hurry before they thaw," Stan explained, speeding up his rounds.

Denton and I wasted no time chipping away at the horde. Ma fired up the chainsaw and carved through the ice with ease. All of us stood over the last one with three barrels pointing at the head. That's when we heard it: a lone howl stretching through the smoldering trees.

"A scout," Stan said.

"Sounds like it," I said.

"Another horde behind it," Denton added.

"What are you boys doing tomorrow?" Stan said with a grin, lighting up a cigar.

"Stan didn't tell me he was having visitors," Ma repeated herself again. "Would you boys like some lemonade?"

K. Trap Jones is an author of horror novels and a ton of short stories appearing in numerous anthologies. Specializing in narrative splatterpunk horror, he draws inspiration from Dante Alighieri and Edgar Allan Poe along with his appreciation towards narrative folklore, classic literary works and obscure segments within society. His novel The Sinner *won the 2010 Royal Palm Literary Award. As a product of the '80s, he likes his movies bloody and his music heavy. He can be found lurking around Tampa, Florida. His novels include* The Big Bad, The Charm Hunter, The Drunken Exorcist, The Harvester, The Sinner, The King's Ox *and* One Bad Fur Day.

L'AMUSE BOUCHE

HAL BODNER

EACH TIME JOEL caught a glimpse of himself in the mirror behind the bar, he was freshly astounded that any guy could resist him. His Hotness Factor, while not quite a Ten, was a solid Nine-Point-Five that strained upwards. At thirty-three, he figured he had a few more years before it would begin dropping. Barring a disfiguring accident or a freakish quirk of his metabolism or genetics, he doubted that he'd ever fall below Eight-and-a-Half, at least not before it was time for him to start collecting social security.

He was living proof of the old adage that circulated in the Gay community that there's no such thing as an unattractive bartender. Consequently, he had his choice of men. Yet, almost inevitably, no matter how good looking his conquest, Joel was surfeited by a single night of carnal pleasure—or an afternoon, or a morning for that matter. He was strictly a "Wham! Bam! Thank-you Man!" kind of guy. On rare occasions, and only if the man was both exceptionally skilled and unspeakably handsome, his desire might not fade until after the second date. Even then, he'd never wanted a chance at the trifecta.

Joel's admirers were legion. Any weekend saw his serving station jammed by a dozen young men clamoring for him to pay attention to things that had nothing to do with Joel mixing their drinks. Any of his erstwhile suitors could have easily appeared in an international advertising campaign for men's cologne or designer briefs, stripped almost nude with genitalia artfully hidden from the camera by a strategically positioned limb or angle of the body, exquisite torso glistening with a sheen of oil to highlight a physique that was already close to godlike perfection.

Though he had his pick of the crème de la crème, Joel sometimes indulged moderately sadistic impulses and condescended to have sex with less desirable guys, mere Seven-Pluses or Eights. He got a kick out of the expectations he raised with those one-night stands. He thrilled at the trick's crestfallen expression of misery and rejection when he later pretended to have no memory of the interlude or when he pretended to be confused at how anyone could have possibly interpreted his whispered words of undying love as anything other than casual pillow talk.

"It's not you," he would say, while gazing into the man's eyes and holding tightly to his hand with feigned regret, "it's me. I'm just not wired that way. If I could commit to anyone, it would be you. You know that, don't you?" How he loved twisting the proverbial knife, especially when he came across as so sincere and innocent that no one could possibly accuse him of deliberate cruelty.

Joel never rebuffed anyone overtly, never mocked him nor risked subjecting him to public ridicule; he earned his living with tips after all. At worst, he would assume a friendly and polite but detached attitude when mixing their cocktails. He acted as if the night they'd spent together was so meaningless to him that he barely remembered it. The resulting self doubt as his target wondered what they could have possibly done differently to make a better impression was as delicious to Joel as sipping a fine liqueur.

Perhaps that was why, when he met the rare young man who seemed uninterested in him, or who could rebuff and ignore the subtle overtures of interest that so many other men craved, a blinding curtain of raw and scarlet fury descended. With a charming smile, a devil-may-care insouciance, and a generous dollop of panache, he always masked his anger. Inside, he seethed at the insult and he always, *always* avenged it.

Figuratively, his bedposts were notched with slightly more than a dozen disinterested young men who had dared to reject *him* at first. But he always got them in the end, one way or another.

For some time, he was oddly unaware of the young man sitting alone at the far end of the bar. The boy was at a prime age, mid-twenties, thirty at the most. Dark, intelligent eyes surveyed the crowd while the stranger idly sipped his drink, alternately amused or bored by the antics of the bar's more effusively drunken customers. A stylishly unruly mop of hair hung low on his forehead, neither brunette nor blond but some indiscriminate shade in between. Even when a hank of it fell across his eyes that surely obscured his vision, he never raised a hand to brush it back.

His physique—what Joel could see of it—was certainly worthy of interest. Taut chest muscles strained against his shirt and parted the open collar enough to display more than a glimpse of tawny smooth skin, hinting that the release of each successive button would expose a fit, athletic body. Trapped behind the bar, Joel had trouble getting a full-length view. But when the youth vacated his stool and headed toward the rest rooms, Joel noted that he had a bubble butt, so perfectly formed that the dimples in the muscles of his ass cheeks were discernable through the denim.

As well-built and as good looking as the customer was, Joel was nevertheless baffled by the power of the attraction he felt. In a city where model handsome guys were a dime a dozen, this young man was far from extraordinary.

What he *was*, though, was irresistible. He oozed a raw and nebulous sensuality, more penetrating than the most intoxicating pheromones. Joel had to fight the urge to reach inside his own pants and rearrange himself more comfortably. Distracted, he even screwed up an order, so rapt was he in the fantasy of bending the guy over the bar and forcibly taking him in full view of the other bartenders and the rest of the crowd.

His longing for the stranger grew painful, as if he'd had blue balls for days. Normally, by this time, Joel would have expected to have seen some interest on a customer's part, mild flirting or an attempt to engage him in conversation at least. But the newcomer had barely acknowledged Joel's existence. He seemed disinclined to do anything other than to watch the crowd.

To get things rolling, Joel pushed a drink across the bar, accompanied by a seductive wink and a pointed, "It's on me." The customer smiled, raised the glass in a small salute of gratitude and replied with a simple, "Thanks." Two drinks later, Joel's frustration was hovering on the edge, about to topple over and ignite. While the youth's responses had been polite and congenial, they'd been cursory; there was still no evidence whatsoever of reciprocal interest.

Joel had rarely been so openly or completely taken for granted.

Clearly, the youth was aware of his presence; he simply appeared not to care unless he needed Joel to serve another drink. Joel's rage began to simmer.

With unaccustomed generosity, he decided to give the lad a second chance. It would be a shame to waste the sexual opportunity simply because he'd failed to realize that the young man's rebuff was rooted in nothing more than shyness.

Joel waited for several hours, watching the boy watch the crowd with a slightly superior air that would have seemed smug had it not been clear that he was genuinely amused by the goings-on as the evening progressed and some of the men had one too many. Finally, just after midnight, there was a lull and Joel seized the opportunity it offered.

"So, how's your night going?" He extended his hand across the bar. "I'm Joel."

"Adam."

The boy's smile touched his features at the exact instant their fingers made contact. Joel gasped at the transformation. Adam was still good looking but now, Joel ached with the deep, unrequited yearning of a freshman's desire for the varsity quarterback. It was lust, pure and simple, possibly the most powerful he'd ever felt.

He was abundantly conscious of their palms touching; the commonplace gesture of shaking hands had somehow become so much more. A tingle from Adam's hand ran up Joel's forearm and split into two separate streams of arousal; one infused his chest with lustful heat while the other made a beeline for his swollen dick and aching balls.

"I never saw you here before." The comment was contrived to be casual, but it held a deeper meaning.

Clearly, Adam understood what Joel meant. Nevertheless, his attention remained focused on the crowd with a sense of anticipation, as if he was waiting for someone specific to make an appearance. A long time passed before Adam seemed to register that the bartender was trying to strike up a full-fledged conversation.

A little shame-faced, he grinned. "I have a confession to make."

"Yes?" Joel could not take his eyes off the way Adam's lips moved when he spoke. He had to physically brace himself to keep from leaning across the bar and kissing them.

"Tonight, I'm breaking almost three months of sobriety."

"AA?"

For an instant, Adam's brow furrowed with confusion. Then, his features evened out and he smiled. "Not exactly," he replied. "I'm fighting the urges but . . . " He shrugged.

With four drinks in him already, Joel concluded that it wouldn't be long before the alcohol triumphed over whatever restraint Adam could muster.

"It's not easy."

Joel nodded sympathetically. "It can be . . . hard." The innuendo was obvious but, when Adam failed to notice it, Joel pressed his point. "And if it is . . . hard, I'd love to help you with that. I'd like to see . . . more of you."

Adam looked startled for a moment, surprised. His attention shifted away from the crowd and settled on Joel. The wall that Joel had sensed between them came down, and suddenly it seemed that Adam was seeing him anew as an actual person, not just as a faceless bartender. Adam's gaze was penetrating, measuring. Under such scrutiny, Joel involuntarily flexed his biceps and chest. He had no idea why this young man attracted him so but if preening like the proverbial peacock was what it took to get him into bed, Joel was more than willing.

The silent inspection continued. Joel felt an unfamiliar but no less horrid sense of inadequacy and impending disappointment, a feeling that was confirmed when Adam finally said, "I'm sorry but I don't think so."

Joel maintained his devilish grin, but his eyes grew cold and hard and his rage threatened to blossom into full flower.

"I'm sorry?" He pretended to misunderstand.

Adam leaned over the bar and in a soft and strangely intimate tone, he said, "I don't mean to be ungrateful for the drinks but . . . do those lines really work?"

"Huh?" Joel was flabbergasted. Never before had a prospective pick-up confronted him so directly.

"Don't get me wrong." Adam wasn't being deliberately cruel. He projected the ambiance of a grade school teacher who was trying to avoid hurt feelings by assuring a tragically untalented child that his finger-painting was indeed the best in the class.

"You're very hot. I mean that. I really do. I've rarely seen a better body and your face . . . " He held up both hands as if in surrender. "You're definitely Top Ten. Best in Show. Drop Dead Gorgeous. But here's the thing . . . "

Transfixed by Adam's every word, Joel drew closer as if it would somehow help him understand how his advances could possibly be rebuffed.

"I'm not interested."

Joel blinked, recognizing a tone of finality. He instinctively knew that no amount of wheedling, manipulation, seduction, coercion or plying Adam with drinks would change his mind.

The burn, when it came, was searing as it had never been before. It was as red hot as the instruments that would shortly cause Adam to regret his hasty and unfeeling rejection.

"Don't take it the wrong way. It's not you," he said, inadvertently voicing Joel's own frequently uttered and manifestly insincere excuse. "It's me." Then, Adam added brightly and with what appeared to be genuine hope, "But maybe we could be friends?"

Seething, Joel didn't trust himself to speak; he merely nodded.

"Most excellent!" Adam enthused. "Just because I think it would be a mistake to fuck you . . . " He blushed scarlet when he realized what he'd said. "I didn't mean that to come out as crass or brutal as it sounded."

"No problem." Joel forced a smile. Though the rejection might sting, it would only be for a little while. Joel was perfectly willing to concede if, in the end, he got what he wanted.

"What I mean is . . . I think we really could be friends."

"Of course." Joel kept his tone noncommittal.

"I'm serious," Adam replied, showing a little pique now that Joel was the one who was acting distant. "I get the strangest feeling there's a lot about you I'd like, just not in that way. I don't want to get all touchy-feely and New Age about it, but don't you sense we might even be kindred spirits? At least on some level?"

Kindred spirits.

The phrase took Joel aback and he examined it for hidden meaning. Was there a subtext to the words? Was Adam hinting at something darker lurking unrevealed below the surface? Joel's self protective instincts shifted into high alert in case there was something he'd overlooked. Was it possible that Adam had heard rumors about him? Joel was always very careful about his conquests but, as a bartender with much of his time on public display, it wasn't uncommon for him to be the target for the most vicious gossip and innuendo, though generally, it was because *he* was the one who'd rebuffed a customer's advance.

In the end, he could find no signs that Adam was anything other than he appeared to be: a moderately good looking fellow with a somewhat bland personality. He was passably charming, maybe a little awkward and perhaps not particularly bright. In short, he was fairly normal except for the inexplicable way Joel was drawn to him sexually.

Chalking it up to that nebulous phenomenon he knew of as "chemistry", Joel shrugged off his lingering doubts and his anger began to fester. Some not insignificant part of his bruised ego began plotting its plots and planning its plans.

"D'you know?" Joel feigned astonishment. "I felt the same way! The minute you sat down, I thought I sensed this . . . " He moved his hands back and forth in the air between them. "Connection."

"Me too!"

Every shred of aloofness had vanished. No longer was Adam surveying the other bar patrons with that detached and superior interest. He seemed to have abandoned waiting for whoever-it-was to show up. Now that Adam's entire focus was on him, Joel felt tingles of anticipation.

"Are you doing anything after the bar closes?" Joel asked.

"That's kind of late, isn't it? Unless we were planning . . . which we're not, right?"

"I meant for a quick bite of something. Why?" Joel batted his eyelashes outrageously. "Did you think I was going to try to seduce you?" Playfully, he made another show of flexing his chest, his pectoral muscles strained the fabric of his t-shirt. "No worries. I'm not exactly desperate."

Adam laughed with delight and applauded with good natured mockery.

"Or are you meeting someone? From the way you kept looking out there before, I thought . . . "

"No, no," Adam hastened to reassure him. He added, not without some embarrassment: "It's the sobriety thing. It might be embarrassing if anyone knew I was here."

How convenient! Joel clamped down on the predatory smile before it touched his lips.

"Coffee or a sandwich sounds great," Adam continued, eagerly.

It dawned on Joel that, in spite of his good looks, Adam might not have very many friends. He'd leaped at Joel's suggestion as if he were starved for company.

"When do you get off?"

Joel repressed a smirk at the unconscious innuendo.

"Closing out the register takes twenty minutes. I could meet you in the alley behind the bar at, say, 2:45?" By then, any stragglers should have stumbled off elsewhere. "One thing though . . . "

"Yeah?"

Joel nodded toward a gaggle of overbuilt thirty-somethings with tattoos overflowing their skin-tight t-shirts and drifting across their partly exposed pectorals and onto their throats before flowing down their arms. The ink provided an incongruous contrast to their pretty-boy mannerisms and model handsome faces.

"See those guys? The one in the red muscle tee and the shorter one, the blond wearing the baseball cap?" Joel did his best to look sheepish and slightly uneasy. "I maybe wasn't too tactful when I turned down their friend earlier tonight."

"Who's that?"

Again, Joel inclined his chin. "The thin guy holding the beer has a thing for me and . . . well . . . he's kind of pushy. Tonight . . . " He sighed as if mildly ashamed of himself. "I finally told him off. His friends weren't happy about it. They think I've been leading him on."

"Were you?" Adam seemed to legitimately want to know.

Joel did his best to look shocked at the suggestion and shook his head. "But the thing is, if any of his pals see me leaving with someone else . . . they might take it personally and . . . well, just *look* at them!"

"Say no more," Adam said. From his shudder, he'd found the quintet of bodybuilders as intimidating as Joel had hoped. "It's between us. I'd rather have coffee than spend the night at the ER anyway." He chuckled.

You'll wish *for an ER once I get started on you,* Joel thought, and he tried not to leer.

L'AMUSE BOUCHE

Until Last Call, he kept a discreet but steady stream of free drinks flowing in Adam's direction. From time to time, when things slowed down, he paused to share a clever quip or flashed him a special smile while he was waiting on someone else.

He beat his prey to the 24-hour café by a healthy margin and parked at the far end of the lot under the dimmest streetlights. He struck quickly, not even giving his target time to get out of the car. The hypodermic went in smoothly and, before Adam could so much as gasp at the sting, he was unconscious. When he awoke, the lingering effects would be mild: a slight dizziness and heightened nerve sensitivity. The latter condition suited Joel just fine.

Once back at his apartment, with the ease of practice, Joel cut away Adam's clothing. He secured the shackles around the young man's wrists and ankles and hauled him into position. Held tightly spread-eagled by chains attached to tall, sturdy bedposts, Adam's body was on full display and gave Joel easy access to all of his most tender and most vulnerable parts. Joel was so powerfully attracted by the sight of such beautiful helplessness, it was an effort to refrain from masturbating even before he made the first slice.

Adam's ass was indeed everything he had hoped and more: two perfectly rounded globes covered with the finest down, begging to be probed. The boy's chest was beautifully sculpted, two hard slabs of muscle, mostly smooth but for the tiniest patch of hair in the center of his pectorals and a thin ring of short silky strands around each plump raisin of a nipple. A slim treasure trail led down his stomach, the ridges cut like the plates of a turtle shell, until it reached his groin. Though his penis dangled flaccid, Joel suspected that when engorged, it was a respectable girth and length. His genitals were large and full, covered with a dark fuzz of hair.

A guttural groan came from deep within Adam's chest when Joel slapped him fully awake. His eyelids fluttered open and, to Joel's surprise, his gaze was clear and alert, not at all milky or confused from the lingering vestiges of the drugs. So much the better.

Joel allowed his captive to gradually register his predicament. Adam's eyes darted around the large studio, taking in the thickly draped windows and the sound proof tiles that lined the walls and ceiling. He mumbled something into the gag, perhaps a question, perhaps a protest, but it was unintelligible. It was far easier for Joel to interpret the widening of the young man's eyes when he spied the merrily boiling kettle, the screwdrivers and metal skewers heating in the flame of the camping stove, and the power drill on its charger.

"And now, Mister Bond," Joel said with a preposterously phony accent, "I expect you to die."

Joel giggled at his own cleverness. But from Adam's look of confusion, he saw his joke had fallen flat. It was just one more thing about Adam that frustrated the hell out of him.

"You know, if you weren't such a stuck-up prick, we could have had a lot of fun together. But now," he shrugged and then giggled again, "at least *I'll* be having fun."

Adam tugged at the heavy leather cuffs; chains rattled against the wooden posts. There was a flash of panic when the youth realized how vulnerable his nudity made him and how thoroughly he was restrained. Or maybe it was because the meaning of the plastic sheeting on the floor beneath his feet became clear. The captive struggled and strained, writhing in his bonds and putting on a nice show long before Joel ever touched him.

When he realized his gyrations were futile he slumped, his chest heaving and his body already damp with fear sweat. Joel tugged his bowed head by the hair to better examine Adam's face, expecting silent and desperate pleas for pity. He was surprised, but not entirely disappointed, to find grim defiance instead. Oh, this was going to be good!

First, Joel fucked him. It was rape pure and simple, perfunctory and intended only to highlight his victim's powerlessness. Once he'd taken the edge off with his first climax, Joel decided to begin the evening's main event with a light warm up. Adam shook his head violently when Joel wheeled the utility cart displaying the various whips into view. Joel grinned, knowing that Adam's first glimpse of the various modifications and additions to the leather flails must have terrified him as he cringed in anticipation of how they'd feel.

Joel started simply with a plain leather whip. Each time the lash cracked, the impact made Adam's entire body jerk. Drops of sweat flew from his brow and spattered onto the plastic sheet. Joel gave Adam no respite until the skin of his back and shoulders was scarlet and stretched tightly over incipient bruises. The ruptured capillaries should make the surface of Adam's skin exquisitely tender. Lightly,

Joel ran his fingertips across the inflamed flesh to test the sensitivity; even a gentle touch made Adam writhe.

Adam screamed shrilly through the gag when Joel showed him the strands of barbed wire woven into the flails of the second whip. His screams mounted when the sharp points ripped into his swollen flesh, leaving a pattern of ragged starbursts of blood with each stroke. Again and again, Joel swung the flail and, soon Adam's back was a curtain of torn strips of skin that caught in the tines of the wire with every swing, only to be ripped away when Joel tugged them free after each stroke. Joel stopped only when he could no longer see more than an inch of unblemished skin.

His chest was heaving, and he was sweating heavily himself from the effort of swinging the whip. But his cock was rock hard and he was eagerly anticipating what came next. Using only Adam's mingled sweat and blood as lubricant, he thrust his dick into the boy's ass a second time. The noises he made as he pumped in and out were animalistic; he grunted and gasped, relishing the hot stickiness every time his bare chest slammed into the thick blood oozing from the wounds, and thrilling to the moist sucking sound when their bodies separated between strokes.

The second orgasm was even more intense than the first.

Unmindful of the gore that covered his torso, Joel stood in front of his victim, idly fingering his still tumescent dick and considering what he wanted to do next. Though tears streaked Adam's cheeks and his eyes were filled with pain, he still met Joel's gaze evenly, as if daring him to continue. Joel happily accepted the challenge.

Some men's nipples were surprisingly vulnerable to torture, most likely because of all the tiny nerve endings concentrated in such a small area. To test whether Adam was one of them, he brushed the backs of his hands across the boy's heaving chest and smiled evilly when the young man's cock stirred.

Adam shrieked anew when Joel brought out two pairs of needle-nosed pliers. Taking his time to fully savor Adam's aborted struggles to retreat of reach, Joel carefully positioned the jaws around each perky bud. He clamped the tips lightly, an ominous portent of what was to come.

He paused to appreciate the way the steel jaws bit into the sensitive nubs. Adam's pectorals fluttered as his muscles involuntarily blenched. Joel waited until Adam looked at him, silently pleading, before he began to squeeze the handles.

The boy's eyes bulged and a deep guttural whine came from the back of his throat. Joel increased the pressure, and Adam's body stiffened, as if by holding still he could somehow alleviate the agony. Joel increased the pressure until he was squeezing as hard as he could. Adam's shriek came clearly through the gag as his right nipple popped; a thin jet of blood spurted like puss squeezed from a pimple. The left one remained intact, offending Joel's sense of symmetry. To even things out, he adjusted his grip on the pliers and twisted sharply, ripping the entire nipple, areola and all, from the boy's chest.

Adam's eyes rolled back into his head and he lost consciousness. Though delighted at the effect he'd produced, Joel was unwilling to allow his captive any respite so he thrust a bottle of ammonia under his nose. Adam's groans seemed to travel from his ears directly to his groin and, though it had been scarcely ten minutes since his last orgasm, Joel's dick tingled and stiffened, aroused by the twin streams of blood running down the boy's chest.

Again, he jerked off. Joel had often before cum twice in a single night, sometimes even thrice. But he'd had to work at it. Tonight though, Joel was effortlessly erect again almost immediately after shooting his third load. His ego preened at the evidence of his own erotic stamina.

To stem the blood, Joel used an electric paint stripper to cauterize the wounds. The air filled with the sweet stench of burnt pork when he pressed the heating element into Adam's chest, blackening the skin and searing new faux nipples of char where the fleshy ones had been pulped or ripped away. He amused himself by moving the gun across the boy's torso, letting him feel the searing heat, but not allowing the muzzle to make direct contact. The skin reddened and took on a shiny, plastic appearance. Blisters bubbled and burst, weeping a clear fluid that the heat gun effectively boiled away.

Adam's once attractive physique was ruined and Joel could not understand why he was still turned on by it. There should be nothing scintillating about the scorched chest nor the bloody tatters of his scourged back. Yet Joel saw a sensuality in the angle of the boy's arms, an artistic quality in the way they were spread-eagled to form the top half of a giant X. When Adam screamed, the muscles and tendons of his throat stood out in bas-relief as if sculpted from marble, as gorgeous as a Renaissance painting of a martyred saint.

Before he knew what he was doing, Joel buried his face in one of Adam's exposed armpits. He filled his nostrils with the scent of the young man's sweat, tangy and acrid, tinged with the sweetness of cooked flesh. Seized by an odd compulsion, Joel lapped up the salty moisture, taking in a measure of blood along with the perspiration. The intoxicating coppery taste lingered after he swallowed; the musky, sharp essence of his victim's body odor overwhelmed him and set his head spinning. Transfixed by the unexpected sensations, Joel's hands roved lightly across Adam's torso, stroking and gently kneading the muscles, teasing with soft flicks of his fingertips . . .

Joel's eyes snapped open and heat flushed his cheeks. What the hell was he doing? He didn't want to arouse Adam's passion; tenderness was the farthest thing from his mind. He wanted the boy screaming as he'd never screamed before, gibbering with terror and despair, knowing that the pain would only increase until he begged, *begged* Joel to kill him if only it meant that the agony would cease.

Furious at his weakness, Joel seized a pair of clothes irons and viciously jammed them into his captive's armpits and held them in place while the hairs crisped and Adam's skin fried in his own sweat. He pressed the searing plates even harder, determined to incinerate any trace of the evocative smells and tastes that had ensorcelled him.

The young man's body went rigid and the muscles of his chest and shoulders clenched in a rictus of agony. He rose up onto his toes as if lifted by the hot irons under his arms. Adam squealed, high pitched, like an animal being butchered. The keening rose in pitch and intensity until, abruptly, it cut off. Adam had passed out a second time and hung, sagging in the chains.

Blood trickled from under the gag; Joel figured the boy had bitten through his tongue. He was miffed that his plaything had fled into unconsciousness again. The irons peeled away from the melted flesh of Adam's armpits with a sucking sound. Joel made the mistake of looking before he replaced them on the utility cart; even his hardened gorge rose at the sight of what was fused to the stainless steel plates.

BODNER

For variety, Joel splashed a bottle of rubbing alcohol across his captive's torso to rouse him. A deep, guttural scream emerged from the depths of Adam's ravaged chest. When it faded, Joel grabbed him by the hair and pulled his head back, forcing their eyes to meet.

Though he searched the boy's ravaged visage, he did not find what he expected. True, there was agony. But Joel was accustomed to also finding confusion as his captives wondered, *Why me? Why are you doing this?*, and a sense of disbelief as their minds fought to come to terms with the reality of what was happening to them.

Adam's implacability mocked him. Unlike previous victims, he grimly and stalwartly endured. Though he screamed, Joel would have expected gibbering by now, begging, or a retreat into madness. Something about Adam wasn't quite right.

Joel grinned to hide his confusion.

Playfully, he held a vegetable peeler up to the light, turning it so that it glinted like a knife wielded by a matinee serial killer. With precise attention to the curves of muscle, he peeled away a thin layer of flesh from Adam's stomach, leaving an aesthetically pleasing and bloody outline of his washboard abs behind.

Though Adam was lean, a thin layer of subcutaneous fat still clogged the blade. At first, Joel carefully wiped the instrument clean between strokes, but eventually the task grew tedious. He resorted to flicking his wrist to fling away the worst of the gore and, though he'd started by carefully and artistically gouging out the spaces between Adam's abdominal muscles, the areas closest to the youth's groin were sloppily carved with bits of white gristle peering through the glistening and pulsating tissue.

Another few splashes of rubbing alcohol got Adam writhing nicely. But when Joel checked again, there was only a fiery will smoldering in the boy's eyes in spite of his having been half skinned alive. Something figuratively buried inside him gave the young man strength; Joel was eager to dig, quite literally, as deep as necessary to get at it. The thought of breaking Adam's spirit was titillating and Joel's hand moved to his own penis once again.

He winced. The double rape and jerking off had rubbed the skin of his shaft a little raw. Spitting into his hand eased the friction, but it still stung. Inspired, he pressed his hand into the wounds on Adam's stomach, liberally greasing it with blood and other fluids.

L'AMUSE BOUCHE

The congealed muck was sticky, but moist. Thinned with some more spit, it worked just fine as lube.

Unfortunately, though he was stiff as a board and wanted to cum, his penis refused to cooperate. Frustrated, Joel quickened the rhythm of his strokes, gritting his teeth against the sting that felt as if he was jerking off with a handful of sandpaper. His climax was unimpressive, a weak ooze of semen. Mildly disgusted by his body's betrayal, he shook off the meager droplets. They plopped to the floor, tiny white pearls swimming in a scarlet sea, and Joel realized there was a *lot* of blood covering the plastic tarp.

Adam's back still bled, but sluggishly, and Joel had cauterized his chest. Naturally, where he'd been flayed, blood welled and dripped, matting the hair of his groin and trickling down his thighs with tendrils of scarlet. Even so, it seemed to Joel that the floor was bloodier than it should have been, so awash that the footing was treacherous.

Closer examination revealed a steady flow of dark, fecal-tainted blood from Adam's ass. The rapes had been as brutal as Joel could make them; apparently, he'd torn something inside Adam's rectum. Stanching the blood was a priority if Joel didn't want his plaything bleeding to death before he was ready. With a malicious grin, Joel had a delicious inspiration on how to solve the problem.

Adam's weary eyes looked puzzled when he first saw the curling iron. But when his torturer told him, in loving and graphic detail, how he planned to use it, the youth began to struggle against the steel restraints anew. A tiny stream of blood welled from underneath the shackles; it trickled down his arms to drip from his scalded armpits, crimson rubies of perspiration.

Joel positioned the curling iron at the crack of the boy's ass, deliciously prolonging the moment when it would begin to scorch the delicate flesh. Blood dripped from Adam's ass onto the bare metal heating element, hissing and popping as it burned away. With a sizzle and crackle of singeing meat, he firmly inserted the iron into Adam's ass, easily overcoming the boy's feeble attempts to clench his butt cheeks closed. Adam's back arched like a drawn bow, and every muscle of his ruined upper chest stood out in stark relief while he shrieked in agony.

Adam shit himself. A raw and fetid odor filled the air, a fecund and metallic scent of blood and semi-liquid feces heated to boiling. Joel's eyes watered and he fought not to gag. Some of his previous guests had also lost control of their bowels, but since this particular trick with the curling iron was a new one, Joel had never had to contend with this particular stench before. Annoyed by the stink, he viciously shoved the curling iron all the way in.

Adam came close to dislocating his shoulders, wildly thrashing against the chains that held him in place. Joel took his time, twisting and turning the tool to make sure the hot metal made contact with as much of Adam's insides as possible. He removed it only after he was fairly certain he'd stopped the bleeding by cauterizing every inch of the youth's anal canal.

Though Joel knew he should be sickened by the mélange of par-cooked diarrhea dripping in a half-clotted bloody stream down the inside of Adam's thighs, the sweetly fetid smell was oddly arousing. His dick stiffened yet again, weirdly stimulated by the foul odors and the sensual way the agglutinated blood and charred feces oozed between his toes. Uneasy at his response, Joel fought the feelings. Normally, it was the power and not the torture that turned him on the most. Once his victim was no longer pretty, Joel was usually mildly repulsed by the gaping wounds and the oozing burns. Eroticism fled, allowing him enough objectivity to concentrate entirely on punishment and revenge.

Though he would be the first to admit that he got an erotic kick out of sadism, it had never risen to the level of a fetish. Except for these rare times when he needed retribution, Joel was perfectly fine with plain old sucking and fucking.

Tonight though, something was askew. Joel's attraction to his subject continued to increase, contrary to all of his experience and expectations. Even Joel's warped psyche sensed how unhealthy it was for him not to be repelled by the damage he'd inflicted. Yet he wanted more from Adam; he *needed* more. Even now, even as he thought it would take hours for his body to generate more spuge, his dick was dripping pre-cum.

Nor was the unsettling miracle one-sided. Unbelievably, Adam had not succumbed to shock while his insides were roasted. Pushing his concerns aside, partly for fear of what they might reveal, Joel instead distracted himself by kicking things up a notch.

L'AMUSE BOUCHE

He had a theory about men that he enjoyed testing. Joel believed that no matter how brutally the rest of a man's body was abused, it all paled in comparison to an attack on his genitals. Aside from the physical torment, there was the added mental anguish that accompanied the torture of a guy's junk that made the experience ever more agonizing and terrifying.

He cupped the boy's balls in one hand. God, the kid was well hung! His testicles were heavy and full, with decent heft. Joel squeezed, once, as hard as he could, and even in spite of everything he'd endured so far, Adam emitted a strangled scream with a fresh, new intensity.

"I like my men clean shaven," he whispered, tugging the hairs on Adam's balls.

The boy's eyes bugged when Joel lit the candles. Though the crisping hair stank, it was nothing compared to what he'd smelled already. Patiently and deliberately, rarely taking his eyes from Adam's face, Joel slowly roasted his balls in the flames. Adam writhed in his bindings, squealing and twitching while the juices inside boiled and seethed until, after an excruciating eternity, each testicle burst through the blackened skin like an overcooked grape.

Something—perhaps melted fat—dripped onto the flames, squelching them. Impatiently, Joel tossed the candle aside in favor of a small blow torch. Adam's ravaged testicles crackled and popped; at one point, the skin actually ignited. Joel hummed to himself, enjoying the slow castration by fire, never letting up until the testicles were steaming lumps of blackened flesh.

When he was done, his own balls were tight, clamoring again to release their juices. Joel wanted to taunt the newly-made eunuch with his own priapic erection, but the minute he touched his dick he winced. He retreated to the bathroom where he used a warm, damp washcloth to tenderly wiped the last of the bloody lubrication from his dick. It was no wonder that the organ was hypersensitive. He'd rubbed himself raw; tiny friction abrasions all along the staff leaked a clear fluid. Using even the slightest bit of hand soap to clean it stung enough to make him yelp.

He grabbed a bottle of baby oil anyway and returned to the bedroom. Unbelievably, the fresh sight of Adam's ruined body turned him on even more powerfully than if he was seeing the boy for the first time, pristine and whole, quivering in fear at what he only imagined was in store for him.

Joel's libido betrayed him. Though he knew it would hurt, he could no more refrain from another wank than he could have ignored the original offense to his ego. He squirted some oil into his palm and, with exquisite care, he began to polish the smooth head– the only part of his penis that he could still touch without flinching.

When he ejaculated, some time later, his body shuddered with the effort and the few meager drops were downright pitiful. A deep ache settled into his balls, as if someone had been slapping them too roughly; his urethra burned like he had a urinary infection. He was annoyed to discover the limits of his own body; limits he'd never approached before. Perhaps his body's failure to produce was a sign that he'd *finally* taken the edge off of his lust. Joel took a brief reprieve from his torturous game, but the anticipation of inflicting further indignities on Adam's ruined body only made Joel ache to touch himself again. Even though he knew his balls were completely drained, he was unspeakably horny and mild uneasiness at his inexplicable arousal morphed into an ominous sense of foreboding.

But he closed his mind to any fear. He replaced it with anger for which Adam was a convenient target. Throughout the remainder of the night and into the next day, he played with his human toy. Despite every atrocity he inflicted—and Joel taxed his sadistic creativity further than he ever had before—his eldritch sexual arousal continued to build.

By noon, he'd cum five more times, each climax more painful than the last. Now it was Joel who begged. He pleaded with his victim to apologize, to grovel, to ask for Joel's forgiveness and spare himself further torment. But though Adam shrieked and blubbered, he refused to utter a sensible word.

Joel's dick could no longer tolerate any friction at all, yet still it remained rock hard. His libido had taken control of his body, flooding it with sexual impulses he could not fight and warping his release into something twisted and unwholesome. In desperation, he donned an old pair of boxing gloves from college out of his bedroom closet and found, to his horror, that he no longer needed to touch himself to cum. His body was nonetheless wracked with desiccated orgasms that were beyond his control. A deep, primal pain originated in his balls and quickly extended into his torso where it settled in the pit of his stomach, making him dizzy and nauseous as his body desperately strove to expel *something* from the end of his dick even though all his reserves were drained.

He howled aloud now. At the first sign of an erection, he gibbered and even prayed. He burst into tears without ever realizing that he was crying. One more ejaculation and he feared he would die.

Midnight came around again and the thing hanging in chains hardly looked human any more. All thoughts of vengeance, of retribution, of restoring dignity to his offended ego were gone. He stumbled around the room, searching for a knife so he could end things, though if he found it, he wouldn't have been able to say whether the throat he intended to slit was Adam's—or his own.

Sometime close to the following dawn, the fog over his mind lifted and Joel realized that, for the past several hours, he'd been clutching the bedpost to keep himself upright while his free hand listlessly poked at Adam's flesh with a barbeque skewer without paying attention to what he was doing. His cock, of course, had stayed rock hard throughout, pulsating with need. He seized those few moments of mental clarity to plunge beneath a frigid shower, not to clean himself, but in a fruitless attempt to cool the sexual fire that consumed him. A freezing jet of water from the shower wand made his balls shrivel, but Joel's relief was palpable: the tumescence *finally* eased.

Unfortunately, the respite lasted barely moments. When he stepped out of the bathroom and caught sight of Adam's ravaged figure once again, his penis surged to full attention as if it yearned to detach from his groin. To his horror, he felt yet another involuntary orgasm building. Shudders racked his body when he came, shooting complete blanks with pain as razor sharp as if he'd plunged the barbeque skewer into his own urethra. His knees gave way and he sank to the floor.

He barely managed to crawl across the room, there to cringe on the befouled plastic sheeting at Adam's feet. He wrapped his arms around his knees in a fetal position and slowly rocked back and forth. His mind was no longer capable of focusing on the pool of congealed blood, the clots of ichor, or the puddles of piss and shit in which he huddled.

He wept openly now, and without pause. He could no longer control the spasms in his fingers, now incapable of wielding a hammer or holding a pair of garden shears. Atrophy seemed to have attacked his forearms and biceps. Far too weak to rise and inspect himself in the mirror, it wouldn't have mattered if he could. His robust tan had faded to an unhealthy yellow. Even as he watched, he saw the jaundice on his arms replaced by patches of sickly, deathly grey pallor.

He moaned and the sound grated in his throat. Joel was parched but it was not water he craved. His agonized balls contracted and pumped uselessly. His staff bobbed and twitched, mocking his pain with its friskiness. Joel prayed for release; anything, *anything* to relieve the torment.

His entire body felt strange, lighter somehow. He fancied he'd lost as much weight as a starvation victim. But the impression was fleeting against the pulsing demand from his groin. With his strength ebbing, he could not stop himself from gripping his penis for the umpteenth time, even though he dreaded his own touch.

The skin along the shaft was unusually dry and Joel was too exhausted by his ordeal even to gape in horror when a bloodless fissure opened from foreskin to groin. Horrified, he watched desiccated flakes slough away, dancing upon the sweat and exertion-heated air of his apartment. From Joel's lips came a brief rattle, then a sigh and then . . . nothing.

Joel need never again fear being rebuffed.

The apartment was silent for a very long time.

Eventually, the chains rattled and Adam coughed. His cheeks were flushed as if he had a fever, and his eyes were glassy. This time, when he moaned, it was a sound of surfeit, not of pain, as if he'd just pushed back from a table after a feast. Though his spread-eagled body was still streaked with blood and pus and even a little char, his skin was miraculously unblemished; he was filthy but whole.

The chains clanked against the wood again. He grimaced and tugged anew.

"Shit," he said.

The word was slurred, as if he had been drinking heavily. His smile held self-deprecating humor and he said aloud, with wry chagrin, "Well, this is certainly inconvenient."

He hung limply and rested for awhile; he might even have dozed off. When he raised his head several hours later, the irises of his eyes burned a deep scarlet. With a shrug of his shoulders and a muttered word, the chains fell from his wrists and ankles; a faint trail of sulfurous smoke drifted upwards from the opened clasps.

"You," he addressed the rapidly cooling corpse, "were great. Seriously. One of the best fucks I've ever had. And that's saying something."

Gracefully, he sank into a lotus position on the floor next to Joel's body.

"I understand if you don't want to see me again," he said, with mock sorrow. "I don't know why but I can never seem to keep a guy interested past the first date."

He grinned, impressed with his own humor.

"A kiss goodbye then?"

Adam lifted Joel's head and kissed the cracked, dead lips.

"Aww," he whined and pretended disappointment. "No tongue?"

He shrugged and climbed to his feet. Humming to himself, he made a beeline for the bathroom and, turning on the water as hot as it would go, he took a quick shower to rid himself of the accumulated filth. When he finished toweling dry his hair, he stood in front of the mirror, nude, admiring himself.

In the bar, Adam had been attractive; now, he was painfully handsome. Ethereally stunning. He oozed an irresistible and raw sensuality that was almost palpable. Anyone who saw him would be astounded by the discovery that such a paragon of male beauty could exist. Naked, he could have modeled for Praxiteles, been a muse to Michelangelo, or first inspired Bianchi or Weber to pick up a camera.

And he knew it.

He posed and flexed, blew kisses at the glass, and licked his lips with a sultry gaze that would have put many of history's most famous harlots, both male and female, to shame. When he was finished posturing, he sensuously licked his lips again and addressed his reflection.

"So much for abstinence, eh? What a meal! Blew my diet all to hell, didn't I? I should be stuffed to the tits. And yet . . . "

Adam assumed a pensive, serious expression as if he was pondering some weighty matter. Slowly, it gave way to a devilish grin.

BODNER

"And yet," he repeated with a wink at his mirrored image, "I can't help wondering . . . what about dessert?"

Hal Bodner is a Bram Stoker Award nominated author. While best known for his gay satire/comedies, he often writes in the horror genre. His freshman vampire novel, Bite Club, *made him one of the top-selling LGBT authors in the country at the time of its publication. Thereafter, he spent several years writing erotic paranormal romances, which he jokingly refers to as "supernatural smut." He is currently working on a series of thrillers which paint classic "noir" with a decidedly lavender glaze. Hal is married to a wonderful man, half his age, who never knew that Liza Minnelli was Judy Garland's daughter.*

PROUD PAPA

ADRIAN LUDENS

JAKE LOOKED ON in breathless wonder, watching his newborn son grow. He found an undercurrent of tragic beauty in the realization that his offspring would be dead within minutes. But that was how the magick worked.

The sun hung low in the sky, casting soft reddish light into the bedroom of the snuggling couple.

Hannah favored Jake with an impish grin. "How was work today, love?"

Jake kissed Hannah's neck and earlobe. His warm breath induced goose bumps on her skin. "You were all I could think about at work. I'm so glad you could make it over tonight." His hands cupped her breasts through the fabric of her satin blouse.

"Me too." Hannah's face crinkled into an enchanting mosaic of eyelashes, dimples, and cheekbone curves as she smiled. "Between you working doubles at the hospital and me finishing school we never get to see each other. That drives me crazy."

"Same here. I care about you, Hannah—more than I've ever cared about anyone." Jake waited a beat and then asked: "Condom again, right?"

"Yes, please." She sat up, slid off her blouse, then unhooked her bra and cast it aside with a flourish.

Jake rolled over and slid open the night stand drawer. Amid the scalpel, washcloths, and latex gloves, he found a condom. "You ever think about children?"

She scrunched her nose. "I know you get on this baby kick every once and a while, but now?"

"I think you'd be a good mom."

"Someday, maybe. But not anytime soon. We're seven months strong, but I'm not falling into the trap of being an unwed mother—besides, I think I'd rather be a cool aunt than a mom."

"Of course." Jake peeled off his t-shirt. "Taking a kid for a few hours, having fun, enjoying the moment, spoiling them, and then dropping them back off with their folks sounds great to me too."

Hannah giggled. "Exactly. But smelly diapers, temper tantrums, homework . . . it's like, 'no thanks.'"

Jake smiled. His hands roved, caressing her skin, and she moaned in delight as he worked his way down to her jeans. Over the unzipping metal he asked, "Did you ever read that story about the planet where they had only one day of sunny weather in a year? And the girl who appreciated it the most missed it because they locked her in a closet?"

Hannah gazed at him, looking bemused. Her blond curls nearly hid the pillow under her head. "What does that have to do with anything?"

"When everything finally goes right, I won't have to answer that." Jake slid off her jeans and panties, and then reached up and gently tweaked her nipples the way she liked.

"What in the world are you talking about?"

"Nothing. Everything." Jake shifted and lay down beside her. "I'm thinking about the cycle of life. The most beautiful thing in the world. A couple has a child. They get busy with work, paying the bills, keeping house. They get caught up in the monotony of day-to-day existence and then one day look around only to find the child has grown, moved away, and they've missed it all. It's ugly and tragic. Don't you think? But what if—"

"You're quite a deep thinker, love, but as hot as that is, let's not get carried away. I just wanna have fun tonight." Hannah rolled into him and began nuzzling his neck, playfully biting.

Jake didn't respond, instead, he asked, "Have you heard this riddle? What has four legs in the morning, two legs in the afternoon, and three legs in the evening?"

Hannah pulled back from his neck; her facial expression told him she wasn't going to respond.

"Sorry, maybe now's not the time." Jake reached down to trace a horizontal infinity symbol around his partner's clit. "It's just that lovemaking, birth, death—it's all so incredible to me. And watching as a boy grows up to become a man, or as a girl grows into a woman, feels miraculous and beautiful and tragic all at the same time."

Hannah fell silent and closed her eyes. Jake was sure she was trying to focus on his hand massaging her vulva. He knew he was killing the mood, but how could he not speak what was on his mind?

"Yes, it's all very beautiful and tragic at the same time," she finally said. "But deep discussions later. Right now, just keeping doing that." She rocked her hips against his fingers until he was cupping her pussy.

Jake smiled. Yes, tonight was going to be the night. And now at least he knew for sure that she would understand the magical gift he had spent years perfecting. He planted kisses between her breasts then down to her pelvis. Hannah squirmed with pleasure and Jake knew that each pulsating twist brought her back into the moment. He reached under the pillow on his side of the bed and his fingers found the pink fuzzy handcuffs he'd stashed there. He dangled the cuffs over Hannah and met her gaze.

"I'd like you to wear these."

Hannah's eyes gleamed. She reached up until each hand grasped one of the metal bed frame's vertical bars. "Yes, sir," she cooed.

He clicked a gaudy fabric-covered metal loop around one wrist, strung the short chain behind one of the bars, and then cuffed her other wrist. He knelt and withdrew two ten-foot lengths of nylon rope he'd secreted beneath the bed.

"Oh my God!" Hannah said. "When you decide to get kinky, you go all out."

Jake grinned. "Well, the last few times you did say you wanted to experiment more."

"Fuck yeah," she said, her voice husky. "I know I'm safe with you."

He secured her ankles to the legs of the bed frame with a few well-practiced motions.

"I bet you didn't learn that in Boy Scouts."

He caught her eye, winked, and then studied her pussy. The cleft between her waxed labia glistened and Jake felt pleased seeing her wetness. Jake watched her wriggle her hips in anticipation. She seemed to enjoy being bound. *All the better*, he thought. He made a show of rolling a condom onto his erection and climbed onto the bed.

Jake crouched between Hannah's legs and probed the folds of her slit with his tongue.

With one hand, he slid the condom back off and dropped it off the edge of the bed. Hannah didn't appear to notice. He rose and entered her with a single thrust.

Hannah's eyes widened and she gasped. "Oh god, yes."

Jake thrust into her bound body, rocking the entire bed, but ignoring her cries of passion, focusing instead on the task at hand. *Just get this part done*, he thought. *Everything will work out fine this time.* He kept his mind focused on the moment of conception, willing the magick that would follow.

"Don't stop, baby." Hannah gritted her teeth and met his thrusts the best she could against her bondage, continuing to offer unabashed encouragement. He pushed aside his irritation. This was far more than just a few minutes of pleasure to him.

He saw bittersweet magnificence in everything, felt emotions more keenly, and was uniquely-equipped to fully appreciate life in all its stages. He once again found himself in an exceptional position, on the cusp of unrealized potential. He'd been close before, but something had always gone wrong. This time it would work. Hannah was the one.

Jake had no desire to make Hannah suffer, but some measure of pain couldn't be avoided. He'd considered offering her painkillers, but had decided against it. He felt sure she'd want to be conscious, aware of and invested in what came next. If he experienced the miracle of life and she did not, he would have cheated her. Besides, many women opted for natural childbirth every day.

Envisioning those babies emerging from their mothers overwhelmed him and he ejaculated inside his partner. Jake grunted his way through the so-called little death that he knew would lead to the creation of life. Afterward, he withdrew and slipped back into his boxers, his mind racing. He mentally went over the next few steps. When he glanced down at Hannah, he'd hoped for understanding but saw only confusion.

"Could you unlock these before you finish getting dressed?" Her features betrayed irritation, but Jake knew the feeling wouldn't last. Soon she'd bear the fruits of their labors—and be amazed.

"The restraints need to stay on for a few minutes longer," Jake said. "It's for your own safety." He grabbed a towel from the drawer and slid it under her buttocks. Then he pulled on a pair of latex gloves and glanced at the clock on the wall above the dresser.

Hannah tried to smile but it faltered and fell away. "Jake, what the hell are you doing?"

"If you've conceived you'll start to show in about fifteen seconds."

Hannah gaped at him in disbelief. "What the fuck! You were supposed to wear a condom! And I'm not pregnant already." She grimaced and twisted against her bonds. "I can't be . . . "

Jake noted her increased respiration. The telltale yellow liquid soaking into the towel he'd placed beneath her was all the proof he needed that her expanding uterus was putting undue pressure on her bladder. Something challenging enough to accommodate in the span of nine months was forced upon her body in less than three minutes. Hannah loosed an agonized cry as her abdominal muscles stretched until they tore.

"It's coming to term, just like I knew it would!" Jake said, jubilant. "Listen, I realize you're in a great deal of pain and I'm sorry, but it can't be helped. You're not dilated yet so I'm going to help you with that."

He grabbed the scalpel from the dresser drawer and knelt on the edge of the bed. Hannah saw what he held and began to scream so loud it made Jake's ears ring.

"Calm down!" he shouted. "It's just an episiotomy. Women get them all the time. You gotta trust me; I know what I'm doing."

Hannah continued to writhe on the bed. Knowing the timing was crucial, Jake drove his knees into her quadriceps and pinned her to the mattress. He plunged the blade through her flesh at a downward angle, careful not to get too close to the rapidly-developing baby. Rivulets of burgundy followed the blade's path. Hannah fell silent— or perhaps she'd fainted.

Jake spoke to her anyway. He wanted to keep the lines of

communication open. "I'm going to reach in and pull the baby out, okay? It's going to be painful but he—or she—is growing too fast to wait for your body to try to start contractions. Neither of you would make it."

Hannah roused and cried out again, but she seemed to have lost the will to fight. Jake focused on the essential task facing him. Timing was imperative. Already her belly looked alarmingly distended and he wasn't sure he had enough experience using a scalpel to perform an emergency C-section.

Jake pushed both hands inside the birth canal, exerting more force than he had expected necessary, and tearing her open further. Hannah, he saw, glared at the ceiling, eyes bloodshot, face tear-stained. Her hands, still shackled, clenched together behind the bar as if praying for an end to her suffering. Her breathing came hard and fast. Jake admired her fortitude but felt a pang of guilt. "This will all be over soon," he said. "And you'll see it'll all be worth it."

Hannah let loose another agonized scream followed by a hoarse question: "What the fuck did you do to me, you goddamned freak?"

Jake scowled but ignored the insult. She didn't get it. Not yet. He felt the baby's head down low in her pelvis. That was good. Blood pooled beneath her, seeping through the sheets, no doubt. He chided himself for forgetting to put down plastic painters tarp. Too late for that now; time was short. The baby's head was crowning, its rapid development apparent in the full head of hair it exhibited. A dark, wet cowlick protruded from her engorged and hairless labia. Jake had a moment to associate it with a giraffe's tongue, and then tensed his muscles and pulled the baby free.

"We have a son," Jake announced. He cut and clamped the cord and stood cradling his slimy but healthy baby boy in front of the tall mirror attached to his bedroom door. "He's the most beautiful human being I've ever seen!"

Behind him, Hannah only moaned in reply. The placenta and membranes from the boy were pushed from Hannah's uterus and out of her vagina onto the towel. Transfixed by his newborn son, Jake missed this development.

Jake could not take his eyes away from the miracle he saw reflected in the mirror. His son cried and grew. Jake forgot about Hannah for the moment, lost in the spectacle of new life unfolding in his arms. It had worked. *Finally!* His past failures with other women had all led to this. Hannah didn't want to be a mother, nor did he truly want to be a father, but he craved the experience and now they could share it.

The child howled, announcing his arrival, and continued to grow. Jake watched in rapt fascination as hair sprang from his son's scalp. Baby teeth sprouted from his gums in two ivory horseshoes. Fingernails and toenails lengthened at a rapid pace; Jake had already decided trimming them would be a wasted endeavor.

He hummed a lullaby but stopped after one stanza; the age for lullabies had already passed.

The child's bones extended and muscle fibers weaved as the body of a toddler altered to that of a lanky boy. His limbs slid through Jake's clasping arms so he readjusted his grip. He had not expected the child to scream so! And behind him, Hannah cried out as if in response. Jake pressed his lips together. He would not give in to her attempts at distraction. Right now his son deserved his undivided attention.

The boy grew heavier in his arms. Jake looked down and noticed his permanent teeth had begun pushing their way out. He knelt and turned his son facedown. Jake bit the wrist end of one glove and pulled his hand free. He spat the glove aside and used his free hand to pluck the baby teeth out of his son's mouth. To have him choke on a stray tooth would be horrible.

The boy's terrified, uncomprehending eyes had turned brown. His hair had darkened and grown well past his shoulders. The boy alternately jabbered and shrieked.

Jake laid his son on the floor and stood. He removed the other latex glove and let it fall. Jake gazed down, monitoring his son's growth, and reflecting. He found the old adage to be true; life was not always perfect, but it certainly was a beautiful journey to behold. Jake wiped away a tear; he only had minutes with his son before the circle of life drew to a close.

"The time we share together is exceedingly concentrated," father whispered to son.

The newborn man-child babbled and tried to stand. Jake leapt forward and caught him before he fell. Jake stood behind his son, bracing him. He kept him close, feeling the figure between him and the mirror grow. Pubic hair sprouted, then chest hair. His son's eyes rolled in their sockets, weak and unfocused. Jake whispered reassurances and proclamations of fatherly love in his son's ear. He focused all his efforts on keeping his son on his feet; the second stage of man in the famous riddle did not feature him flat on his back, after all.

Jake watched his offspring mature in the mirror. Now he wished for the power to slow time down so that he could cherish this experience longer. Time spent together as a family was fleeting indeed. The sum of the days somehow took away instead of adding. A person was left with a graying spouse, a recliner, a television, and the knowledge that the world will move on when you're gone, oblivious to your exit.

His son, for a time taller and larger in stature than Jake, now had begun to wither. A beard that had been brown became frostlike with white strands. He slouched, his skin showing lines and wear. The man's hair began to gray at the temples. It thinned and fell from his scalp as he gibbered and drooled. Muscles atrophied, skin sagged, and bones became brittle. His son gave a goat-like bleat, cantankerous yet frightened. Jake lowered him into a sitting position and knelt behind him to prop him up. He told his son he loved him.

The figure, elderly in appearance, but still less than one hour old, sat on the floor and shivered. Tears of pain and incomprehension trickled down his cheeks. Jake felt for and grabbed another towel from the top of the dresser, covering his aged son. The old man seemed to nod off, only to jerk his head back up, startled. He coughed. It was a wet, phlegm-filled cough.

This went on for two glorious minutes. Glorious, Jake thought, because even in sickness there is the splendor of the battle being fought within the body. And how many fathers remained in control of their health and faculties while observing their children's twilight years? Precious few, Jake decided.

Then the old man wheezed, shuddered, and slumped forward. Jake's knees popped as he stood and stretched. Beneath him lay the shriveled and sunken frame of his son. A white beard curled over an immobile chest. Ribs showed through the graying flesh. Finger and toenails had curled into yellowed seashell shapes. Long strands of snarled white hair trailed from the back of his head. The old man's bald pate reminded Jake of when the baby had crowned. That had been a lifetime ago, and yet the sun held nearly the same place in the sky, now just grazing the horizon.

The old man's bladder and bowels relaxed, messing the floor, and filling the room with an earthy aroma. Jake took note of his son's first—and last—defecation and, smiling proudly, wiped away another tear.

Jake felt for the edge of the bed, sat, and watched the gruesome splendor unfolding before him. Gasses built up and escaped. He saw his son's limbs stiffen and then relax in the span of a few seconds. The flesh started to putrefy. Jake vowed to watch until only bones remained.

"What a treasure, what a blessing, to be able to see our son's entire life cycle play out in front of us like this. We didn't miss any of it! I'll treasure this for as long as I live. And, Hannah, thank you for sharing this with me. Now do you understand? It was all worth it, wasn't it?"

Hannah made no reply. Perhaps she was still angry with him. Or maybe she still ached from the trauma of the baby coming so quickly to term, and his violent birth. Jake turned, intending to unlock the handcuffs—forgotten in the thrill of the spectacle until now—and froze.

"Hannah?" At first Jake couldn't understand what his eyes were showing him. It took several seconds for his brain to process and catalog the information.

He noted the crimson-drenched tangle of limbs. His lover's internal organs had been rearranged like a child's jumbled toy-box. An extra set of legs reposed on the bloody sheets between Hannah's, in contrasting shades of peach and gray. And to whom did the emaciated, skeletal head bursting from beneath Hannah's ribcage belong? It drooped like a dying mushroom, mouth thrown open in a silent shriek. Above this, Hannah's eyes were bulging, bloodshot, and glassy, reflecting his silhouetted frame leaning in for a closer look.

And then he understood. A vinegar-dipped stone filled his throat. Tears welled, brimmed, and fell. Jake shook as violent sobs overtook him. He'd been cheated. He'd been so absorbed in witnessing the birth, life, and death of his son that he'd completely missed the equally transcendent phenomenon unfolding behind him.

He reached out a shaky hand to stroke Hannah's cheek. The room grayed as his emotions threatened to physically overwhelm him. He bent to kiss Hannah's blood-smeared lips. His heart ached with sorrow and yet pumped the drum beat of happiness. He treasured her gift, and regretted her sacrifice. Life and death, as always, proved so beautiful and heartbreaking in equal measure.

Jake perched on the edge of the mattress and marveled. On their first try, Hannah had blessed him with twins.

Adrian Ludens is the author of the story collection When Bedbugs Bite. *Recent publication appearances include* The 4th Spectral Book of Horror Stories *(Tickety Boo Press),* Dark Horizons *(Elder Signs Press), and the weird western novelette* Bottled Spirits *(Grinning Skull Press). Adrian is no stranger to Blood Bound Books, having published stories in* Blood Rites, Unspeakable, *and the original volume of* D.O.A., *among others. Adrian is a fan of hockey, music, reading, and exploring abandoned buildings. He is a member of the Horror Writers Association with Active status. Visit him at www.adrianludens.com.*

CRY THE BANSHEE

C. CAMERON ROSSI

GRANNY WENT BANSHEE again last nite, screaming like she was being torn limb to limb. Pa told me just to ignore her, but it's getting impossible to sleep with all that noise. I mentioned it to Honey-gurl when she came over this morning to tend to Moma's boils, cause I knew that she was sorta sweet on me and that Pa is sweet on her. I figured that maybe she would put the thought into Pa to do something about Granny and her wailing. It's gettin reel hard for me to work our fields, do my work for the Bullough's, and then come home to read and write in my diary without no sleep. Course, I guess it could be a lot worse—instead of just having the sores or the boils, they all could be full banshee.

Boy oh boy things are sure getting strange around here. If it weren't for Moma needing me around to help with everything, I'd head off for the Dakotas at next sun-up. I heard frum Honey-gurl they still have clean water out there, and don't have to worry about boars eatting all their crops and killing and eating little babies, what few are left. But I just can't leave Moma, not at least until she gets better or dies. She's the only Moma I got.

I need to start focusin on the main points if I want to sharpen my writing skills so that when I get to the Dakotas I can be a writer and not stay a poor farm hand. Two nights ago, after Honey-gurl was over, Granny started in on her hollerin again just as me and Pa and Moma finished dinner. Moma got up to clean the dishes; usually Pa won't let her because her arms are full of boils that open in the water and the dishes come out brown and smellin like ass that hasn't been washed for days. But this time he just sat back and gave me mean sideways glances.

Moma finally finished the dishes then shuffled slowly to the basement to sleep. Down there you could close the big storm doors and not hear Granny screaming so loud. When Pa was sure Moma was all the way down, he limped into the smokin den and called me in with him. I sat down on the hard wooden floor while Pa put his bony ass in his favorite rocking chair, got out his big pipe and stuffed it full of dreamy-weed. I don't like dreamy-weed much cause it makes me sick to my stomach and feel like I'm floating around and dreamin even though I'm awake, but I took a few puffs anyway cause Pa always offers and tells it's rude not to take something that's offered to you.

We sat for a while and my head started gettin all funny-feeling like it was floating off my shoulders. I put my hands on top of it to stop it from drifting away and Pa started laughing, showin his mouthful of brown teeth. Even though I wasn't happy I started laughing too, and we sat and laughed until I thought I was gonna puke. It set Pa to coffin' and he did puke but he didn't care, just sat on the chair and played with the green and red chunky puddle on the floor with his bare feet until we both got quiet.

"Not a real pretty sight is it, a grown old man playin with his own juices," he finally said. I shrugged my shoulders and stayed quiet.

"I used be a strong young buck when I was fifteen, sure as hell stronger then you," he continued on, his voice shaky but defiant, "but that was a long fucking time ago, back when me and your Ma were just startin together, thinking maybe we could make something better for ourselves then our Ma and Pa . . . thinkin that maybe we all was over the time of the banshees."

He grew quiet again and I tried to get the thick fog out of my head from the dreamy-weed, when Granny started her screams upstairs. Me and Pa both jumped, and then he started giggling. But it wasn't a happy sort of sound; it was one like when you're upset and it made me nervous to hear him do it. I tried to get up and leave but his eyes got real wide and he stood up real fast.

"Did I say you could leave, boy?" he said, his voice low and mean. I shook my head and sat back down, making sure I didn't sit in Pa's puke.

"I know what you're thinkin, that maybe your Pa is getting weak in the head, that maybe he's cracking just like this ol' crazy world," he said, his scarecrow-thin figure towering over me. "Well, maybe I am and maybe I ain't, but it don't matter cause sometimes, a man just can takes so much and then he can't take no more." He then did something I never thought I'd see my Pa do. He broke down and cried. Four what seemed like forever he cried like a little child and that made me even more nervous than his gigglin.

"I'm okay," he said after a couple more minutes, his eyes all red and puffy. "It's not an easy thing, this here life. Hearin your granny scream all day and night, watching your Ma fall apart, not havin a wife to couple with when the urge comes over me." He stopped for a second and looked at me hard. "You been gettin those urges yet, boy?"

I thought of Honey-gurl and how good it felt to have my pecker-head in her mouth, even with all the oozing sores on her tongue, and I was thinking how I would do just about anything to have her do it again. But then I remembered how I caught Pa and her in Granny's bedroom one day when they was supposed to be changin her bedding. Instead, Honey-gurl was sittin at the head of the bed, combing what was left of Granny's hair in one hand and pulling mightily on Pa's little pecker with the other until he dripped his mustard-colored seed all over the floor. I didn't think they seen me peekin, but Pa always looked at me funny from that day on.

"No, sir," I said, keeping my eyes down so he couldn't see the lie in them. "I ain't been havin those urges."

"You will soon enough," he said, more quiet like now. "Soon enough to make you realize why God brought all the bad that he did on us, soon enough to make you realize that sometimes, a man has to do things that eats up his soul." Suddenly, like she was agreein with him, Granny let out another powerful banshee wail, enough to shake the foundations of the house and make my ears hurt.

"I can't fuckin stand it!" Pa yelled, real loud and angry like while shaking his fist at the dirty ceiling. "What more do you want, you fucker? Didn't we sacrifice enough for you? Didn't enough blood spill for you? What the fuck more do you want?"

ROSSI

He broke down and started crying again, and I didn't know if he was yelling at Granny or God. I hoped it was Granny, cause we sure didn't need any more wrath of God coming down on us. When I got up to leave, Pa just stood there and didn't say anything, so I went into my corner room and wrapped myself up tight in my blankets, hoping I could drown out Granny's screamin and finally get some sleep.

I sure hope I can remember all that has happened today, cause when I finally get to the Dakotas I know these here writings will make me a lot of money if people know the whole story. I shoulda known that some mighty weird things would be happening as soon as I opened my eyes in the morning and saw brite sunlight beaming through the cracks in the ceiling. Seein as how Pa always gets me up at least an hour before sunrise I knew something was up, and it wasn't long before I realized something else was different: Granny wasn't screaming anymore.

Now, I knew that meant one of two things, that either Granny had died or she had gone somewhere, and that if she had gone somewhere it meant somebody had took her. It had been weeks since she had been able to walk, her legs all puffed up and covered in sores that leaked red and black pus and smelled like rotten meat sittin in the summer sun.

Thinking this made me feel bad, since I could remember how Granny was nice to me when I was smaller and would give me food from her plate even though she was skinnier then me back then. And I was damn skinny.

I looked for Pa but he wasn't around, so I went up the rickity stairs, and halfway up noticed Granny's door was open. I just knew she wouldn't be up there but I had to look anyway, so I went the rest of the way up and sure enough, no Granny, just some piles of soiled clothes on the floor along with some puddles of dark, putrid-smellin oily-looking stuff on the bed. I wundered what it was, but I knew enough to let it be, so I closed the door so the bad smells wouldn't come downstairs. I figured that maybe Ma would know where Granny had gone cause I had already figured that it was probably Pa who had took her somewhere.

I usually don't go down in the basement. Ma doesn't scream like a banshee yet but has at least a hundred boils from her head to toes that pop in the sun, causin Pa to board everything up so it's real dark down there even in the day. I lit a lantern, then walked real slow and careful like down the stairs and stood at the bottom for a couple minutes to let my eyes adjust to what little light there was.

Ma was in bed, illuminated by another sputtering lantern on her nightstand. She wasn't moving at all, and I thought that maybe she was dying or even maybe dead, but then she let out a loud, wet fart and I was happy cause that meant she was still alive. I was gonna go over and try and wake her up to find out where Pa and Granny were when I felt a hand go under my legs and grab my balls. I damn near soiled my pants and screamed even though I didn't want to. Ma just turned over and kept on sleeping. I jumped back to the foot of the stairs and put up one fist even though at first I thought it was a devil come to take Ma away and would get me instead.

"Did I scare ya?" Honey-gurl giggled, holding her hand over her mouth, her eyes buggin out even more then usual.

"What the hell are you doin down here?" I said, my voice cracking and full of scared.

She took two steps closer to me. "I'm taking care of your Moma." Even though she wasn't very pretty with her long nose, bushy eyebrows and crooked teeth, I didn't really mind her getting closer cause then I could see her tities better and the way they poked out from underneath her shirt.

"Maybe I should be the one askin what you're doing down here," she said, putting her hands on her skinny hips, covered in a short, ratty-lookin skirt.

"I live here and I'm entitled to go where I please," I said, a little more loud since my heart didn't feel like it was gonna jump out of my chest anymore.

She moved even closer to me and started rubbing her hands up and down my chest. "I was thinking maybe you knew I was down here and wanted to do some playin. Is that what you were thinkin?"

I really hadn't been thinking that at first, but when she was that close and rubbin on me I really couldn't think of anything else. I grabbed her shoulders but she pulled away and walked over near Ma's bed. Giggling, she took off her skirt and even in the dim light I could see her big patch of dark curly hair. I went damn near half crazy as she began to rub herself right there next to Ma.

"What's the matter?" she said. "Don't you want to learn how to do me like your Pa does me?"

By that point I was gettin wild, half of me wanting to do whatever she wanted, and the other half full of fear that Ma would wake up and see us.

"Why don't we go upstairs?" I said. "We can go up there and I can lock all the doors."

"I don't wanna go upstairs," she said real loud, and I was afraid that Ma would wake up but I was gettin excited watching Honey-gurl work on herself. I didn't know what to do.

"C'mon," Honey-gurl said, "you come over here and after you do me I'll do you."

As crazy as I knew it was, I was ready to get down on my knees and start kissin on her honey-pie, but then I heard the upstairs door open and realized that Pa was home. I stood there like a stone, scared and crazy as Pa started to bellow for me. Honey-gurl didn't do a thing except continue rubbing herself and let out little moans now and then. It was only when I heard Pa's footsteps on the top stairs that I made myself move, and the only place I could figure on going was underneath Moma's bed.

I guess one day I might write a whole lot more on how I felt that afternoon, laying in the dust and filth underneath Moma's bed. How it was that Pa came down to see Honey-gurl gettin herself all wet and excited. How he started licking on her like a thursty dog lapping up water, all the while standing next to the bed with Moma snoring away before she kneeled down and worked on him, the open sores on her tongue leaving a trail of pus and blood on his quivering pecker. How, after Pa gave a great grunt before a weak stream of his seed dribbled onto her face and chest, they both started gigglin like two naughty kids and walked upstairs. Yeah, maybe one day I'll write a whole lot more on all the hurt and shame and hate I felt, but right now I think if I started in on it I would never write anything else again.

I don't know how long I lay under the bed, but I knew it was a long time, as long as it took for Honey-gurl's musky smell to leave the air. I finally crawled from under the bed, pain all over from being so still. My pecker and balls hurt from stayin hard so long watching Pa and Honey-gurl, and guess all of that made me mad off enough so that I went right up them stairs and into the living room, not caring if Pa was there or not.

He was up there all right, sleeping on the floor buck naked, a half-filled pipe of dreamy-weed next to him. Honey-gurl was nowhere to be seen, which was probably good cause I don't know if I could have held back my hate if I would have seen them couplin. At first I didn't even try to wake him, but then I just went and kicked him hard in the ribs. I felt a lil crack when I did it, and it set Pa to coffin' again.

"Where's Granny?" I asked, feeling tingly and hot as he looked up at me with bloodshot eyes. I knew that he knew it really wasn't all my worry about Granny that made me kick him, but my hate from having watched him and Honey-gurl.

"No, boy," he said, shaking his head slow. I kicked him again harder, and I felt good and bad at the same time, almost like when Honey-gurl kissed and sucked my pecker-head.

Pa didn't even try to get up and fight me. He just lay there with that horrible coff bringin up red snot lookin stuff out his mouth, with a look in his eyes that scared me and gave me strength at the same time.

"All right," he finally said, his voice raspy and low, "I'll tell ya all the things," and suddenly I didn't want to hear any of it. I just wanted to run out of the house, but I knew I had to stay cause it was my time to know.

"It's kinda funny, you and me talkin here," Pa started out, "just like me and my Pa talking a long time ago. Course, I was younger than you and had more respect for the commandments so I didn't go and kick the shit out of him." He stopped for a minute, maybe waiting for me to apologize or something, but when he seen I wasn't, he kept on talkin.

"I never told you this before, boy, but your great-grandaddy was there when it first all came down on us. He was just a youngin, but he remembered, back when men still could fly through the skies in air machines. He told me sometimes he thought that's maybe why God sent the sickness down, cause man was getting too close to God's own house. I used to think about them words and spent many a hour on my knees prayin about it. But I don't anymore, cause I think God is just watchin us now to see if we learned our lesson, and now and then he still gives women the banshees to remind us it could all come back, every terrible bit of it."

He took a deep breath and his closed his eyes, and I thought he was falling asleep, but then he started talking. "Cry the Banshee, hear her scream; Cry the Banshee, deep in your dreams . . ."

Pa finally opened his eyes. "I don't remember anymore of that sayin, but me and what few kids were left in those days used to sing it until our folks beat the shit out of us to make us stop. See, we weren't around in your great-grandaddy's day. Back then it was a million times worse, cause back then there was a million times more people, and damn near most of the women were banshees. He said in the cities it sounded like a thousand screaming tornadoes, and if you didn't die of the banshees your head would explode from the sounds. Then the men started goin crazy when they realized there weren't nuthin they could do for their women. They killed each other to protect their own . . . and course to lay stake to any healthy ones left.

"That's why we've always been country folk; your great-granddaddy and my Pa thought that by bein in the country, the banshees wouldn't get to us. But he was wrong." Pa pushed himself into a sitting position, grabbed his pipe, tried to light it, then gave up as he continued with his story.

"But all that remembering don't mean a thing. Most all of the people are dead and we live like the old times and that's that. Cept of course when it comes back into your own home like it has to us, like to your Granny, and maybe soon to your ma, and I don't know—" He stopped suddenly and coffed, and I could see more globs of dark red in his spit. When he was done coffin' he looked up at me.

"So you really wanna go see what anger God still has in him? All right then, boy," he said, his eyes never changin their hard stare, "go see her. Go see yer Granny and see what God does to show us who's the real boss."

Pa stood up real slow, holding his side where I kicked him. He walked over to the old cabinet that stood in the other corner of the house and pulled a dusty, brown piece of paper out of the bottom drawer.

"This here's a map of the Bullough's land," he said, handin me the paper. "The red circle in the corner of the wheat field is where there are three old oak trees, probably older then the time of the banshees. The middle tree of them is the one where your Granny is." I took the map from him and looked it over. Although I had never been anywhere far away from the Bullough's house, I reckoned I could figure out where the tree was without too much problem.

"Hey, boy," I heard my Pa say. I looked up and damned if he hadn't come up with the tree-splittin axe in his hands, and I figured that he was gonna pay me back for kicking him, but he just handed it to me nice and easy.

"Boars might be out tonight," he said quietly. "No need for you to give 'em an easy meal."

"Thanks, Pa," I said, and I wanted to say more, and part of me even wanted me to say that I loved him, but as soon as he gave me the axe he turned around and lit up his pipe.

Since it was near dark I decided to get my diary and a bedroll in case I had to stay out overnite. Then I headed on out the door, prayin that I wasn't gonna make an easy meal for the boars.

The sun was already below the horizon as I crossed our last field of rye and moved onto the Bullough's land. Pa told me once that the Bullough family had kept this land for six generations. During the time of the banshees they had even formed their own army to keep the land, spilling a lot of blood so it could be theirs forever. This made me feel kinda funny, thinking that maybe I was walkin on somebodies blood or maybe even their bones, but I tried to put it out of my mind as I kept on movin.

I'm not proud to say it, but I was gettin scared bout then, and even having second thoughts about what I was doing. The winds had picked up, and when I had crossed our creek I had found a pretty fresh pile of boar shit on the banks. It was gettin dark fast, with storm clouds hiding any sign of the moon or stars.

Now, I don't think that I'm a coward, but as I was crestin the next hill I was just about ready to turn around. I dropped to my knees and started praying for strength like I used to when I was a child, and all of a sudden the sky got lit up as bright as daylight by a lightning bolt bigger then I had ever saw before.

I think it was a sign from God, cause right after that lightning bolt I heard it, from a long ways off. I heard my Granny hollerin. The only thing I didn't truly know if the sign from God was for me to go to Granny or to stay away, but I figured I had come pretty far and so I might as well finish. I got up and went toward the sound and pretty soon I could see a group of three trees in the distance. I knew that it was on one of them that Granny was tied.

The moon was shining through the clouds by the time I got near enough to see her. She looked like something out of my worst nitemares I got after smoking dreamy-weed. She was colored yellow and green, not pretty colors like sunshine and fresh grass but sick, dull shades like rancid meat. Even as far away as I was, maybe fifty or even sixty feet, I could smell her, and it was a hundred times worse smell then even fresh piles of boar shit sittin in the hot sun.

The worst part for me was the way she was all swelled up. She was swolled from head to foot, making it hard to tell where just one part of her stopped and another started. She was just sorta one big mess of stinking and quivering goo which moaned that crazy-sounding moan. The more I looked and smelt, the more scared and sick I got. I felt so bad that I had to see her like that and how there was nuthin I could do, and then all of a sudden she started to talk.

I'll never figure how she could see or talk to me since I couldn't tell if she really had any eyes or mouth left. Sometimes I try to tell myself that she really wasn't talking to me, that maybe she was just talking crazy stuff to herself, but, well, the stuff she said sure sounded like she was talkin to me.

"Hep mah," it sounded like she said.

"Granny?" I said. "Granny, it's me, tell me how I can—"

"Ah Gah pleaz hep mah!" she said, louder and with more hurt in her voice. I started cryin, not cause I'm a baby or nuthin but because I couldn't help her.

"Just tell me how I can help you Granny, just tell me how," I pleaded. She mumbled something that I couldn't understand, so I plugged my nose and moved even closer and that's when it all happened.

"Oh God Oh God just help just help just help!" she hollered in a voice so loud and clear that it sounded like it was coming from God Almighty himself. I realized what she meant or at least what I thought she meant, so I swung the axe meaning to cut the ropes which where holding her, but instead I sorta hit her and that's when she exploded.

I don't know how long I was passed out, only that when I came to the moon was already halfway down in the sky. I just layed on the ground for a few minutes, my body pretty much hurtin all over. I finally sat up and noticed I was covered with green and yellow sticky goo all over, which I guess was stuff that used to be Granny. I looked over at the oak tree where Granny used to be, but there was only a few strands of rope.

Maybe it's wrong, but after I rolled around in the grass to get what was left of Granny off me and got ready to leave, I didn't feel bad about what I did. I figured at least she wouldn't be in anymore horrible suffering like she was. These thoughts made me feel a little better as I went lookin for my axe, and it was when I found it that I got my second sign from God.

Next to the axe was Granny's little finger. Not all swollen and yellow, but just a regular finger. Maybe that doesn't sound like a sign from God, but it was on that finger that she wore a ring, a ring with a small piece of gold in the center, and I remembered Granny tellin me more then once that the gold was from a mine in the Dakotas.

Right then and there I decided it was time for me to make my move. I wrapped up Granny's finger real careful like in a piece of shirt I tore off and placed it in my pants pocket, then gathered my gear and headed off to the West. I know the Dakotas are a long ways off, maybe even a hundred miles, and I know that I'm gonna miss my Ma and Pa and even Honey-gurl, but I realized that in his own way my Pa was right about God just watching us, seein what we will do and if we will make the same mistakes. I figured my Pa made a mistake by not leaving with Ma when they was younger, leaving and finding their own place. Maybe God won't send down the banshees anymore, least not on us or me. I sure hope so, and I also hope deep down if he does send the banshees on me that one of my kin will do the same for me as I did for Granny.

C. Cameron Rossi is an author living in the urban wilds of Detroit, Michigan with his two Leonbergers. Rossi has published a number of speculative fiction pieces appearing in tomes and anthologies including Pulphouse, Deathgrip, *and* DOA Volume I. *He counts Joe Lansdale, Kathe Koja, and Richard Laymon among his many favorite authors and literary influences.*

TERRORSLUTS FOR ETERNITY VERSUS THE UNGODHEADS OF THE INTERDIMENSIONALS

ALISTAIR RENNIE

MY DISEASE-RIDDEN SPIT handled the sex toy with great care and appraised its thought-provoking characteristics with a frown on her face, as if she was handling a very dangerous wild animal.

"It is the finest quality." The retailer spoke through gaps in his teeth. "Workmanship is very good."

My Disease-Ridden Spit ignored the retailer as she concentrated on examining the intentionally contorted ruts in the phallus, the serrations of the penile ridge, the exaggerated contours of its elongated ruck-shaft. The pleasure effects of the design gave it a strangely reptilian aspect, which she could identify with quite readily. Its bulbous head protruded with a malicious intent, which further justified her metaphorical appreciation of its serpentine attributes. It had been well-configured for its use—in more ways than one.

"Don't get it wet," said the retailer, chuckling like a nervous idiot. "That's how it makes its very bad function work very good."

My Disease-Ridden Spit grunted. She placed the sex toy back in its protective sleeve and tied it shut. The sleeve was decorated with elaborate swirls that reminded My Disease-Ridden Spit of a psychological disorder. She slipped it into the waterproof insets of her trench coat and would leave it there until she delivered it into the hands of the Prostitute of Death.

"I will say nothing," said the retailer. "You will say nothing. That is the deal. We will say nothing to no one. You understand."

My Disease-Ridden Spit looked at him, her eyes like small vacuums. All the light of the world seemed to get sucked into them, almost to a point of impossible blackness, sucked inward into some hidden depth where the illuminations were piled high and bright like magic towers, sparkling with the genius of her cruelty, her adeptness at planning, and the intellectual basis for her sensuous appeal which, in physical terms, was as clear to anyone as a kick in the face.

That was the core of it, she thought. *Where the chemicals were thought into action—from which they alighted like micro-chemical trinkets. Thought-purposes of spit, manufactured for fatal offload. Once deposited, they would erupt on a subatomic level like emotional cluster bombs—not in any way affecting the nervous system, but homing in on the brain and causing death by madness through prolonged episodes of self-mutilation.*

"In my country," said My Disease-Ridden Spit, who really didn't have one, "we seal the deal with a kiss."

The retailer's eyes grew wide with initial shock. *From one so beautiful as she?* His eyes twinkled with the realisation of great opportunities for fondling breasts, squeezing buttocks, for ravaging other parts of her body with his strong grips and manly petting.

"In my country," he said, "it is impolite to refuse such an offer."

He was already angling his head towards her, with his lips pursing like some hideous sea creature striving after a passing fish. It was the daftest looking man-pout My Disease-Ridden Spit had ever seen in a lifetime of seeing many.

She lay her hands upon the sides of his head, palms pushing into his cheeks. She planted her lips on his man-pout and spat through it with much more force than she'd intended.

The retailer recoiled. She had taken him by more surprise than he'd been subjected to already.

He looked like he was going to start saying something, but then the actions of the psycho-venom took hold. The micro-chemical impacts were acting fast, as they normally did with people of limited intelligence. Cleverer ones would suffer much more in the long term. But a buffoon like this was much luckier than he'd ever know.

When she left him, he was on his knees, hands furiously ripping into the tops of his pantaloons, looking to rip off his testicles and massacre his cock, which some of them did in the initial stages of the inducements of the venom's impact.

She didn't hang around to enjoy the spectacle. She was already emerging from the stairwell of the vault, raising the latch of the door and pulling it open. She slipped into the dark streets of Gothvraggon, the door shutting behind her with a light click of its latch re-locking, just as she hoped it would.

My Disease-Ridden Spit took two or three steps and disappeared into the night, as if she'd stepped into a crack in the darkness.

But there was no crack there. My Disease-Ridden Spit *had* disappeared into the night.

Quite literally.

Two thousand years ago, a teenage boy was being hideously (and possibly) murdered in a manner which was of great interest to Mertens, who now prepared himself to watch it via Exo-anima Tech-attainted retroscopic film footage which, said Leopold Firth, "you may find a little disturbing."

Firth also said: "It's probably best if you watch it through the virtual overdrive, just to get a sense of what's really going on." He handed Mertens a psycho-fluid mix of virtualizer. "It's traumatic. More especially for you."

Mertens gave Firth a comprehensive look. "Go on," he said.

Firth raised a hand and made a series of gestures that threw up an electro-static sheen quickly resolving into a montage of film. Mertens drank the virtualizer and waited for the overdrive to kick in. When it did, he lapsed into the viewpoint of the teenage boy, with no sense whatsoever of what preceded the scene he now entered into . . .

Warren stands shaking in a renovated farmhouse kitchen and gestures as if indicating the corpse of an adored family pet he doesn't want to look upon for more than he has to.

"Get away from me," he says.

But, in truth, there's no one there.

Not yet.

Warren lets his body slouch like he can't hold it up.

"Get away," he says. "I know you're watching me."

He is bewildered. He is scared. But the things he's seen, they are real—coming in and out of the gloom, like flickering elements of old-style cinema—faint traces of shape, odd and grotesque; not like ghosts, but *alive*.

"Get the fuck away from me."

He takes a step backwards . . .

It's impossible to understand what's going on. The kitchen begins to grow dimmer, as if thick clouds are passing overhead, blocking the light from the windows with a mouldering gloom. The walls begin to change colour. The wallpaper darkens. It becomes stained. The kitchen is different—now semi-derelict and more like a steading.

Warren's mouth falls open. He lets out a startled cry that catches in his throat. He tries to take hold of the kitchen unit where the fridge should be. It's gone. The kitchen has become utterly transformed. No longer renovated. It is old and decrepit and smelling of something that might be rotten meat. Dead meat. The remnants of slaughter. There is a heavy tang of fish, too. Rotten fish. All of it rotten. The meat, the fish. The smell was as thick as a substance.

Warren feels himself starting to retch.

A loud, heavy squawk—a rasping, grating, piercing sound—causes him to jump and turn 'round sharply. He staggers back in stunned amazement. He bangs into something. It might have been a table. He wouldn't have known. He's staring at the thing before him, as if his eyes had been drawn to a magnetic impulse.

A tall thing with a man's body, wearing a black suit, stands before him. It has thin wiry arms that start to waver and sprawl like branches on a tree that lean towards him. The hands unfurl. But they are not hands. They're claws. Like twigs. With black hooks on the ends of them. Not fingers. Just knobbly black hooks on the ends of arms that waver like pieces of coral.

But that isn't the worst thing. It's the head. The head, above all. The head of a gigantic seagull propped on a man's distorted, lanky body. Its black eye squinting like a pith of ruin, intense with curiosity . . . and something else.

RENNIE

The head leans back. The huge beak opens up. A stink comes out of it. It squawks—an obscene rasping that ratchets the ear and sets the teeth on edge.

Warren is pinned against the table. If it is a table. Seagull Head is squinting at him. Then it starts to move towards him with shuffling, pathetic, discordant steps. It turns its head at an angle, cocks it from side to side with inelegant, jerky movements. Its beak is angling towards Warren's face. The beak is hard and sharp. Jagged. It stinks. It is the stink of fish and rotten meat— the stink of oceans and the shit that litters them.

Warren turns to run. The urge comes to him like an electric shock. But there's something beside him blocking his path. Something he hadn't noticed before. Something small. With horns. A small boy with the head of a goat.

Warren screams. The Goat Thing grabs a hold of his leg, wraps itself around his thigh, like it was trying to mate with him, the way that dogs do.

Warren starts to struggle. He tries to hit the Goat Thing around the head, batter it with his weak fists. But Seagull Head is upon him and starts pecking at his face. Its claws start to rake into his body. The beak digs into his face with the force of a bludgeon, dunting against his forehead and cheeks, hitting him in the teeth and shattering them with its blunt force.

Warren is grabbed by Seagull Head's hooks. He is thrown onto the table. It was a table. The Goat Thing now has a hold of Warren's hair, trying to pin his head down on the table top. The table stinks of the same stench as Seagull Head's beak—stinking meat and rotten fish; the shit of oceans. The table top is covered in a layer of slime. But it isn't slime. It is blood and gristle. Of animals. Of fish. Of people. Warren knows that it was people.

He knows that it was people because whatever had happened to them was happening to him now.

Seagull Head thrusts its beak and hooks into his chest and belly and begins to rake and peck like some crazed, malfunctioning automaton. Warren tries to react against it. But Seagull Head is all over him, and the Goat Thing is pawing at his face, trying to gouge out his eyes. It isn't clear if the Goat Thing is using human hands with cartilaginous fingers or some kind of mutated variation of hoofs.

When the beak of Seagull Head starts to rip into his unprotected genitals, Warren's eyes burst open like new moons. And then the Goat Thing is able to gouge into them with slow, pawing movements with the hand-hoofs of a small boy. Small enough to enter into the eye sockets, mangle the fleshy orbs and reduce them to a bitty liquid pulp. The destruction of the eyes triggers the negation of the virtual overdrive and positions Mertens on the spatial proximity of egressed voyeur mode.

The Goat Thing pulls itself onto the table and lays on top of Warren's chest. It passes its snout over his face. Sniffing him. Savouring. Warren is convulsing but conscious of it all. Then the Goat Thing unfurls its long, wet tongue, slips it into one of Warren's pulped eye sockets and begins to lick.

The Goat Thing sucks up the mashed fluids of the eye socket, then proceeds to lick out the other one. By then, Warren has gone well beyond the threshold of pain and has entered a new era of sensations.

With his eyes licked out, he can't see anything of the device that the Goat Thing is inserting into his empty sockets.

But Mertens can.

The kid is about to undergo an extraction procedure. The soul particles located in the genetic interior of his brain cells are about to be harvested. The eye sockets have been cleared out for a reason—to allow better access for the soul machine to do its work.

But then, before the grotesques are able to apply the extraction force, something happens.

Two figures appear out of the gloom. They transpire like images through a paper lantern.

Mertens stiffens.

He stiffens because he recognises them.

Waves crashed like the end of the world on the rocks of Sarnath. Stone buildings rose out of the shoreline like exoskeletal extensions to its crooked geology—symmetry rising out of chaos, decrepit and stiff against the backdrop of the Dismal Cliffs of Raaw. Ships lay offshore, precarious against the headwinds, sails folded with their anchors straining against the incessant swell and the boom of the surfs.

The Prostitute of Death pulls her coat around her throat and shivers.

Where oh where is the cobra girl?

She backs into a doorway where the damp shadows offer minimal resistance against the cold. She is nervous. Her mission is extremely dangerous. Her target is a NewGov assassin who's been coalesced with the soul particle of a praying mantis.

"Therefore—" Mertens had stressed the point with an unshakable lack of subtlety—"you know what happens in the aftermath of love-making."

The Prostitute of Death had said, quietly, "I know my insects."

Which is why there wouldn't be any aftermath.

"Here I am!"

My Disease-Ridden Spit emerged from the darkness with the suddenness of a bang on the head.

"Cobra. Must you?" The Prostitute of Death grew flush with anger.

My Disease-Ridden Spit smirked and retrieved the sex toy from the inlets of her trench coat. She slipped it into the hand the Prostitute of Death, who duly deposited it into some secret part of her stylish ankle-length windbreaker.

"So how the fuck do you intend to get personal with this mantis bitch?" said My Disease-Ridden Spit. "Not everyone wants to fuck you, you know."

The Prostitute of Death gave a light shrug.

"I know my insects," she said.

"You think this is going to be hard core easy?" said My Disease-Ridden Spit, her voice straining with rage as usual. "I tell you girl, this mantis bitch is monster crazy. She eats people after she fucks them. Are you aware of that?"

"I know my insects," said the Prostitute of Death, adding, "My pheromonal secretions will do the trick."

"Ah, of course," said My Disease-Ridden Spit, dripping wet with irony, "you've been coalesced with an insect yourself, haven't you? What was it again? A moth? A blue-arsed fly?"

"A butterfly," said the Prostitute of Death, her voice as flat as a slab of concrete.

"Oh, my mistake," said My Disease-Ridden Spit, feigning surprise without feigning the fact that she was feigning it. "Well," she added, "I'll leave you to it, flutter-by girl. Good luck with the crazy mantis bi—"

A screed of metabolic energy thrilled through the veins of My Disease-Ridden Spit like a failed orgasm. The Prostitute of Death received the same influx. The eyes of them both widened with an involuntary act of paying attention.

It was a non-audible message alert, sent via Soul Tech impulse meta-channels, coming straight from the horse's mouth of the Intel Core:

Code Absolute. Code Absolute. Code Absolute.

The thrill in their veins subsided. The message lapsed out. A Code Absolute summons was one that had to be obeyed at all costs. Mertens would be waiting for them.

"Seems like some shit has hit the mega-fan." My Disease-Ridden Spit raised her eyebrows. "You're off the hook, butterfly girl." She winked. "For now."

Oddly, the Prostitute of Death wore a look of puzzlement on her impeccable features that made them look even more beautiful than they already were.

"What's up, whore face?" My Disease-Ridden Spit said this with a modicum of sympathetic interest.

The Prostitute of Death sighed.

"It's just," she said, "I was really psyched up for tackling the mantis bitch."

Then she straightened her shoulders, hardened her gorgeous features and said:

"Fuck it, cobra girl. Let's go."

Mertens, Overseer of the Intel Core of the Anarcho-Pact network operations, was doing what he did best: briefing the TerrorSluts on the particulars of their mission.

"NewGov have secretly deployed several teams of sub-agents called Ungodheads who have embarked on a programme of Exo-anima interdimensional seepage between different versions of the same world. They are looking to harvest the soul particles of historic humans to be used as energy ducts for various power projects. Soul particle energy has enormous potential, especially in relation to developing high tech lighting systems, travel systems, and weaponry.

"In this case, we've tracked two Ungodheads who've transversed time and targeted, in the past, an innocent boy on the cusp of manhood—a teenager. The matter is further complicated by the fact that the teenager in question is a direct descendent of one of the most important figures of the underground networks.

"The Ungodheads have to be stopped," said Mertens, his voice loaded with a dry, emotionless candour that made him sound like an electronic malfunction, "and you're going to stop them."

He looked steadily at TerrorSlut Cobra and TerrorSlut Butterfly, possibly waiting for questions. My Disease-Ridden Spit obliged.

"And just who or what the fuck are they, then?"

"The Ungodheads?"

"Yes."

"Hybrid types," said Mertens. "Bio-mechanical mashups. Old school bastardisations. Genetic fuck ups. The kind of shit that existed before the discovery of the soul particle. But they've also undergone a process of reversed coalescence, where human soul particles have been blended with non-human agencies instead of the other way 'round, which is extremely problematic. As well as illegal."

"Fuckers breaking their own fucking laws," hissed My Disease-Ridden Spit.

The Prostitute of Death looked tense with apprehension and innocence in equal measure.

"Why's it problematic?" she asked.

"Because," said Mertens, "reversed coalescence tends to infect non-human entities with intelligence—the wrong kind of intelligence. It makes them more deliberative, more destructive, more wilfully cruel."

A short silence.

"So what the fuck have they been coalesced with?" My Disease-Ridden Spit again.

"One with a seagull and the other with a goat."

"Shit." My Disease-Ridden Spit stared at the floor. "Those are nasty fuckers. Eat fucking anything."

"Quite," said Mertens.

"And what about this thing with the ancestor?"

Mertens coughed and said:

"Aside from attempting to illegally harvest human soul particles from the ancient past, the NewGov have inadvertently or deliberately targeted an antecedent of one of our most important senior members. If they succeed, and the antecedent dies, this will cause the historical cancellation of his descendants, who will cease to exist even before they began to. Our intel confirms that the antecedent— a boy of fifteen years old—is the ancient forefather of . . . of me."

The TerrorSluts exchanged a WTF glance before Mertens went on.

"We need to undertake a mission of interdimensional seepage transference that takes us back to the cross-points in space and time where we can deter the Ungodheads from completing their task. Otherwise—" Mertens clasped his hands behind his back and swivelled slightly from side to side— "I won't be here to greet you when you get back."

My Disease-Ridden Spit frowned and seemed offended. The way she often did.

"But you're here now," she said.

"Yes," said Mertens. "Which means, your forthcoming attempt to save my ancestor has evidently succeeded."

Silence. Then:

"But," said the Prostitute of Death, "doesn't that mean that there's no need for us to go back?"

"Why?" said Mertens.

"Because you're already here."

"But if you don't go back," said Mertens, "I won't be."

"But," said My Disease-Ridden Spit, "if you won't be here, if we don't go back, then why the fuck are you?"

"Because," said Mertens, "you *do* go back."

"But what if we don't?"

Mertens sighed and said, "Because, if you don't, then I won't be here when you get back. Which means there'll be no Intel Core. Because I designed it. Which means there'll be no Anarcho-Pact. Which means there'll be no TerrorSluts for Eternity. Which means, therefore, you *will* go."

RENNIE

My Disease-Ridden Spit knew he was right. The Intel Core was the centre of everything—and without it, the centre cannot hold.

"In that case," she said, cracking her knuckles as she spoke, "when the fuck do we get started?"

Exo juice: a calculated blend of historical and genetic Soul Tech combinations that transports you to another place in space and time. Transference between the meta-dimensions was a bit like being senselessly drunk for a few split seconds.

Then, suddenly, you were there.

In a semi-derelict farmhouse kitchen where the victim is spread-eagled over a stinking table being set upon by the grotesques of the Ungodheads. They have a device they've pushed into the victim's eye sockets. It's a soul machine, and it's actually attached to one of the Goat Thing's hand-hoofs. The grotesques are about to activate the extraction force, which will kill the boy outright, when:

"Fuck me, butterfly girl. Look at these fucking mishaps of nature. And I thought *you* were the ugly one."

Seagull Head and the Goat Thing turn their heads in bewilderment at the interruption. After a brief pause to allow their dull amazement to run its course, they disentangle themselves from their activities on the table. Seagull Head starts stooping and lurching across the floor, a vicious squawking erupting from his saw-edged beak. The Goat Thing rasps through his malformed mouth, slavers dripping from his nostrils, his tongue rollicking like a gigantic slug. He scuttles on his little legs, hand-hoofs raised; he makes directly for the Prostitute of Death who draws a stiletto from her thigh-length boots and prepares to engage.

My Disease-Ridden Spit turns her attentions to Seagull Head, who shambles towards her like an optical illusion. She draws her blade; he is upon her, faster than she thinks, and cracks his beak right against her forehead. She falls back and slams the back of her head on the floorboards; for a time, all is lost.

She comes to. Seagull Head is pecking into her abdomen with skin-splitting force. He's aiming for her vital organs. Branch-like claws rake into her. My Disease-Ridden Spit tries to roll free but is far too fuck-a-doodle-dandied to do anything.

Through terrified eyes, she sees a big penis appear from out of the shadows, its bulbous head angling towards Seagull Head's beak. Seagull Head sees it coming and turns his head and squawks at it.

The Prostitute of Death is holding the sex toy. But it is not a sex toy. It carries a small explosive device in the helmet of its phallic moulds that detonates when it becomes sufficiently wet or subjected to sustained fleshy compressions from the vaginal, anal or oral cavities.

The Prostitute of Death forces it into the beak of Seagull Head and down into his oesophagus. He instinctively reacts, seagull-like, to allow consumption. The explosion is both small and big enough to mangle Seagull Head's throat area, and this causes his head to detach in a burst of viscera and sparking wires. He totters, falls in a branch-like heap. He becomes still; death overcomes him.

My Disease-Ridden Spit turns her head and sees the Goat Thing convulsing with the broken blade of a stiletto sticking out of the crown of its head, right between the stumpy horns.

She looks up at the butterfly girl, mutters something under her breath about taking "fucking ages to find that cock", then falls into an unconscious slumber.

When she woke again, she was in a bed in the emergency unit of the Anarcho Chambers, feeling remarkably shit.

When Mertens came to see her, he brought flowers.

"So," said My Disease-Ridden Spit, "we managed to save your ancestor, I see."

"He was severely brutalised and rendered blind for life. But, yes, you did."

"The seagull fucker messed me up pretty bad, huh?"

Mertens nodded. "You had a fourteen percent chance of survival."

"So how did I?"

"TerrorSlut Butterfly." Mertens always used their formal names. "She administered a vial of Exo fluid by intravenous injection. You were transported back to the Intel Core. I got you here as quick as I could. It was quick enough."

"How long have I been out?"

"Three weeks."

"Holy shit." She stared upwards. Then: "So where's the butterfly girl? I suppose I better thank her."

Mertens looked down at the floor.

"She resumed her mission to eliminate the praying mantis." He looked up again. "The mission failed."

My Disease-Ridden Spit stared up at Mertens. She lay very still. After a few moments she said:

"It's okay. I've been coalesced with a cobra. I'm a cold-blooded son of a bitch. Her death means nothing to me."

She lay her head back on the pillow, staring upwards. Mertens remained silent.

After a while, she said:

"How about you turn this mantis mission over to me when I get better?"

She looked straight at him. Mertens held her gaze.

He looked down at the floor again, breathed long and hard, and said:

"Okay."

Alistair Rennie is author of the sword and debauchery novel, BleakWarrior, *and has published weird fantasy and horror fiction, essays and poetry in* The New Weird anthology, Weird Tales *magazine,* Fabulous Whitby, Electric Velocipede, Mythic Delirium, XB-1, Pevnost, Schlock Magazine, Horror Without Victims, Weird Fiction Review *and* Shadowed Realms.

He was born and grew up in the North of Scotland, has lived for ten years in Italy, and now lives in Edinburgh in the South of Scotland. He holds a first class Honours Degree in Literature from the University of Aberdeen and a PhD in Literature from the University of Edinburgh. He is a time-served Painter and Decorator and a veteran climber of numerous hills and mountains in the Western Highlands, the Cairngorms and the Italian Dolomites.

He also creates retro-futuristic synthwave concept albums inspired by 1980s horror under the alias O S C U R O Z O N E.

WE BELIEVE IN 5B

AIRIKA SNEVE

HADLEY WOULD NEVER have thought it possible, especially not in the elegant AdTech, Inc. lobby with the marble fireplace and the antique gold telescope, and yet there it was: each effeminate sneeze that erupted from the executive conference room—"Ah-*teu!*"—seemed to summon another boner-wielding gent through the lobby doors. If ever there existed a mating call to the wild North American pervert, it seemed to be that sneeze.

"Ah-*teu!*"

This time, the weak nasal fit brought a tiny Mexican man with a huge purple hickey on his neck and a sleeveless t-shirt with "KISS THIS" spelled out in enormous block letters. His name tag declared him "RAYMUNDO." Like the ten men who had traversed the lobby before him, an unmitigated stiffy tented the crotch of his shorts, seeming to lead the way like a lodestar homing pigeon with an ETA four inches prior to its human attachment.

"5B?" he said in a thick Mexican accent. His eyes found her chest and stayed there.

Hadley pulled her blazer closed. "Conference room straight ahead to your left."

He nodded. "Ladies," he said, slowly pumping his hips. "Ladies like meeeeee."

The words were out of Hadley's mouth before she could bite them back. "Well. Chivalry is dead, thank you for murdering it; conference room to your left." She glared.

Raymundo paused and then winked. Flabbergasted, Hadley watched him vanish around the corner where the CEO, Chief

Operations Officer, and Vice President awaited. Hadley had welcomed and directed the procession before Raymundo: two construction workers, a cable guy, a man in a red pizza delivery costume with no pizza, two men in expensive-looking suits, and the rest in smart business casual attire. As different as they all appeared, each shared one trait: an unrepentant boner that could perforate the oculars of anyone within rutting range.

Why erections? Why a pizza-less pizza man? A construction worker? Why . . . Raymundo?

It sounded like the beginning of a bad joke: a construction worker, a pizza man, a cable guy, and some businessmen get together in a boardroom . . .

From the conference room: "*Ah-teu!*"

It was the daintiest man-sneeze she had ever heard, and someone in senior management was responsible for it. She knew this because the sneeze had come before the procession.

Hadley waited. The lobby doors remained closed.

No pervs this time.

She was beginning to convince herself it had all been a bizarre coincidence when another man walked in, this one tall, trim, and in finely tailored business attire. Her gaze found his crotch: he, too, was hellaciously aroused.

So much for mere coincidence.

"Welcome to AdTech, Incorporated," said Hadley in a flat voice.

The man approached the front desk with the kind of toothy, polished grin made for Crest toothpaste commercials—or nightmares.

"Why hello there, Miss. Matthew Train for the 5B meeting."

"Conference room to your immediate left." Hadley avoided his eyes.

She waited for him to leave. Instead, he stood there at the reception desk, beaming at her with that Tony Robbins rictus. The only sound was the squeak of Hadley's ergonomic chair as she squirmed.

"Is there something I can help you with?" she asked, blushing. She could almost feel him pressing his erection into the polished white wood of the front desk.

"I suppose I would be remiss if I neglected to introduce myself.

WE BELIEVE IN 5B

I'm the President of the 5B Committee, and I can't tell you how much it pleases me to be here. Thank you for having us."

She squirmed. "I can't say I'm familiar with your work."

Matthew cracked a smile that was suspiciously close to a leer. "5B helps businesses reach their full potential through innovative though highly unconventional means. That's not the whole enchilada, of course, but it's the main slice. Last year alone, we helped a small tech startup triple their annual sales with our leadership seminar, which your company will get a taste of today." He licked his lips. "Mmmm-mmmm."

Hadley tapped French-manicured nails on her mouse. "Oh. Have a fantastic meeting."

"Bet on it." He tossed her a practiced corporate wink and strolled his erection into the conference room.

She hadn't felt this kind of unease since she'd walked in on Joe from accounts receivable taking a shit in the unisex bathroom. Not even then.

Hadley pulled up the company's digital calendar on her computer monitor. The morning's event was titled "The 5B Committee: A Seminar in Unconventional Leadership." Matthew Train was listed as the host. The meeting was scheduled to run from 9:30 to 10:30 a.m.

Great, Hadley thought. *Another overpaid consultant coming in to fuck up our workflow.*

With a helluva lotta hardons involved.

Hadley leaned back in her chair, aghast. Had someone slipped some LSD into her coffee? What was with all these bonerous pervs marching into corporate? Were they holding the National Erection Convention at AdTech today, or what? None of this made any sense. Hadley could of course understand the businessmen's arrival (minus the boners), but a pizza deliveryman with no pizza? Construction workers? A cable guy?

Why?

Hadley stared glassily into her monitor, too shaken to focus on the spreadsheet awaiting her formulation wizardry.

She Google-chatted Anthony Skalarzza, her buddy in accounts payable.

Hadley thought for a moment. While Skalarzza was indeed her

break room buddy, she didn't know him well enough to open with a line about erections. She had only been with the company for a few months, after all. This matter warranted caution.

Finally, she typed: *"What's the deal with this 5B meeting? Know anything about it?"*

She waited an excruciating two minutes before Anthony replied: *"Not really. Big secret project of the operations guys, that's all I know. It's the new phase of their 'productivity iteration.'"*

She tapped her fingernails on the keyboard, debating what to say and how graphic she should be in saying it.

Finally, she replied with a simple *"OK."*

This was not a conversation for written documentation.

Hadley Googled "5B," but Google wasn't very helpful. The only results pointed to a website labeled "under construction," as well as a few generic business directory listings describing the company as "Independent Business Consulting."

She heard cheers coming from the conference room. A muffled voice—it sounded like Matthew Train's—shouted, "We don't want a single slice! We want the WHOLE ENCHILADA!"

"YEAH!" the voices chorused back.

"Repeat after me! *We believe in 5B!*"

"*We believe in 5B! YEAH!*"

Hadley scratched her head. They were starting to sound like a Southern Baptist church revival in there.

For the next half hour, Hadley sat at her desk, hazily answering phones, listening to muffled cheers, and staring blankly through the spreadsheet on her screen. It wasn't long before another thump erupted, followed by chants of, "This is leadership! THIS is leadership!"

She clicked out of the spreadsheet and stood up.

Fuck Excel. She needed answers.

Hadley crept around the corner toward the conference room. She figured if someone surprised her by popping out, she could always say she was on her way to the stockroom to get a Coke.

The door was slightly ajar. Her heartbeat tripled.

Carefully, she tiptoed over and peered inside.

What she saw nearly caused her to faint.

In the very same conference room she had dusted and organized a hundred times or more, the upper-management businessmen she normally knew as respectable professionals stood with their pants pooled around their ankles, each drilling a woman with an elaborate ballroom hairdo while expensive gala dresses littered the room in silken piles. Pearls jounced on naked breasts; vigorous corporate thrusts frayed apart careful curls; high heels scattered about the neat cut pile carpeting. One guy had forgone the bare beauties and plugged into a hard-bodied hunk. Lee Marchand, COO, reclined in a high-backed office chair jerking off with a serene, almost regal smile on his face.

The guy was even pretentious when he choked the chicken.

Hadley gasped. There was AdTech's CEO Stokely Yams, Fortune 500 businessman and LinkedIn networking guru, plowing a woman from behind while shouting, *"We believe in 5B!"*

Matthew Train lay naked on the floor with one finger in his asshole while a naked woman buffed his broomstick, panting, "I'll give ya the WHOLE enchilada, YEAH! *The whole enchilada!*"

Another group of men jacked off in the conference table chairs laughing, cheering, and clapping as if they were live at the Super Bowl while a male stripper plowed a naked woman on top of the table. The stripper wore a handmade lanyard around his neck with the word "LEADER" scrawled in black Sharpie.

"He's all berries and no twig!" shouted Ed Jasper, AdTech's senior marketing manager. "I'm a bigger leader than *he* is!"

"I AM A LEADER!"

"Yeah, give 'er the business!"

"Let's FUCK him!"

Without warning, a hand snaked through the cracked door and yanked Hadley inside by the collar.

The party clapped and catcalled as a naked goon dragged her in. The cable guy looked her up and down and exclaimed, "Girl, I'd suck a faht outta yo ass!"

"Look at the turd cutter on *that* one!" whistled one of the construction workers.

Two goons held fast to Hadley's arms while she struggled. Lascivious eyes probed every inch of her body. Leery winks went off like flashbulbs.

"An unexpected guest," said Matt Train, pulling out of his prostitute with that frozen grin. His face was red and wild.

One of Hadley's naked captors clamped a sweaty hand over her mouth, stifling a scream. She wrenched away from their wagging hard-ons.

"Welcome to 5B: Big Boners Bring Big Business," said Matthew, panting. "You are witnessing the most innovative leadership strategy of the twenty-first century."

Hadley thrashed and screamed under the naked goon's hand, spitting salty sweat back into his clammy palms.

"5B has shown via clinical research that sexually satisfied employees produce up to nine times more annual revenue than their carnally parched counterparts. Here today are the top workplace perverts in over nine major industries, as determined by sexual harassment lawsuits, self-reports, and supervisor writeups," continued Matthew. "Phase One of AdTech's business development deal is now in session: *Sexual Satisfaction.* Care to join?"

The goon unclamped his hand from Hadley's mouth long enough for her to yell, "FUCK YOU!"

Cries of "BOO!" resounded all around. Ed Jasper banged on the red plastic "Bullshit" button in the middle of the conference room table. Raymundo armpit-farted.

The hand snapped back onto her mouth.

The male stripper gave no sign of even acknowledging Hadley's presence. He was in his own dirty world as he threw his partner off him and twisted into a ridiculous human pretzel in an attempt to fellate himself.

"Shame," said Matthew between breaths. His forehead glistened. He made no effort to smooth his rumpled coif.

Hadley knew then that the man was absolutely batshit insane.

"99% of male AdTech employees are in favor of the 5B initiative. 99% can't be wrong, Hadley!" Matthew cocked his head. "Look at that pioneer right there." He gazed wistfully, almost proudly, at the male stripper, who was now licking his own shaft. "THAT has leadership written all over it. How many men can do that, Hadley? You should be taking notes."

The stripper's nose was parked firmly in his rectum. His tongue snaked closer to his power bar. He had gulped a full inch of his manhood into his mouth when, from his anus, burst a sharp foghorn report.

WE BELIEVE IN 5B

The stripper's eyes popped open. He gasped. Instinctively, his hands clapped onto the overly-tanned butt-loaves sandwiching the offending nucleus.

He penis flopped limply out of his mouth.

Total silence descended in the boardroom. Hadley's panicked gaze darted about the shocked, disgusted expressions on the participants' faces.

The stripper had killed the mood with a single fart.

A titter of revulsion passed among the businessmen. "Well!" scoffed one.

"How could he *do* such a thing?" gasped another.

"Disgusting!"

"FAUX PAS!"

"HE'S no leader!"

"Well," said Matthew. He frowned deeply. "Flatulence happens, folks. Very sorry." Turning to the mortified stripper, he said, "That will be all, Sir. Your inspirational services are no longer needed."

Hadley couldn't believe it. These men were having an orgy in a corporate conference room, yet a fart was too much for them to handle. She redoubled her efforts to free herself, but she was no match for two turnt-up goons. "I'm very displeased with my investment," whispered Stokely as the stripper yanked his silver tearaway pants on. The room rustled with grumbling, dressing men. Skinny hinders parted down the middle as men bent to the floor in search of ties.

Matthew nodded to Stokely. "Men!" he said in a stentorian boom, turning to address all sides. "This seminar isn't over yet!"

The crowd paused with furrowed brows.

"It is well-known in history that conquering armies in medieval times would often eat the flesh of their conquests in celebration of their victories." He turned to the stripper. "It is in the spirit of victory today that we shall celebrate leadership in spite of this—" He gestured disgustedly, "*Snafu.*"

"I'm out," said the stripper, and bolted toward the door. Jasper from the credit department restrained him while another guy stuffed a pair of tighty whities in his mouth, then heaved him onto the table. Hadley too made a break for it but Matthew's cronies grabbed her and held her tight.

Matthew shot a laser-cold smile at the struggling stripper on the table. "Let's get a little less sexual, boys, and a little more *visceral.* How about we EAT this imposter! What do you say?"

The crowd roared in approval.

"*Leadership!*"

"Let's cut his balls!"

Panicked, Hadley glanced toward the door, which was now guarded by three half-dressed men. Matthew turned to her. "I wasn't planning on revealing Phase Two of our leadership journey quite this early, but due to unforeseen events . . . "

He nodded to the goons who restrained her. They tossed her roughly onto the table, where she collapsed on top of the stripper.

Right before Hadley's eyes, Matthew shed his human form and fleshed into a throbbing monument to vasodilation: a six-foot column of fully erect penis. He lumbered forward on an enormous, rolling base of hairy balls, using his gonads like wheels, bending slightly to point a mouth-like gash where the urethra should be. Snapping spikes of teeth filled the gash, and it grinned at her. *It actually grinned.*

The half-naked businessmen "oohed" and "aahed" as if they were at a spectacular fireworks display.

"We BELIEVE in 5B, and soon you will, too," said Matthew. "Repeat after me!"

The room burst into chorus: "WE BELIEVE IN 5B!"

The prostitutes stampeded from the room like a herd of shrieking antelopes.

"We pump our hips at convention and embrace the conqueror within!" The cock screamed, pulling itself up to its full height. "DEVOUR!"

Half-dressed men with snapping jaws closed in on a screaming Hadley and the stripper from all sides.

Suddenly, a noise erupted from nowhere. It sounded again; it was a woman's moan.

The businessmen froze in their tracks. Flaccid penises stirred like gently awakening doves.

"Hey, *putos!*" Raymundo shouted from where he stood next to the door. He held a boxy object up. From her prone position on the table with four men pinning her limbs, Hadley raised her head to make out the sound dock Raymundo held with his cell phone cradled in its port. On the phone's screen, Hadley saw fleshy forms bucking and writhing.

It was a porno. Raymundo had YouTubed a dirty video on his phone and was broadcasting the audio from a portable sound dock.

Another shuddery female moan ululated from the speakers.

Pelvises shot toward the source of the sound. Penises rose mightily to point one-eyed accusations at the fluorescent lights overhead. Grunting, half-dressed businessmen couldn't yank their pantsuits down quickly enough.

The goons held tight to Hadley's limbs, grinding her wrists and ankles painfully onto the table. She dodged a rigid penis swinging dangerously near her hair.

Another moan sounded. A man and a woman engaging in vigorous coitus materialized on Matthew the Dick's purplish-pink shaft. Its toothy gap curled into an O of surprise.

Raymundo had pointed the sound dock—and his phone— straight at Matthew, projecting the porno onto his body.

"Google Projection," said Raymundo. He tipped a wink at Hadley. "My cousin, he's executive. Ees not yet released."

"What are you doing?" Matthew's urethral mouth-maw shouted. "Stop!"

Hairy hands swam over the warm, towering pillar of Matthew-phallus and smoothed his pulsating veins. An account executive began to grind against the rigid midshaft. Matthew bumped him away, shouting. With that motion, Matthew's coarse curlicue pubes snagged in the corporate pile carpet and he fell forward, little bursts of precum spurting as he bounced. He hit the conference table and smacked over onto his side.

Someone else shoved into a table and sent a coffee machine tumbling down right next to Matthew. He screamed as scalding coffee droplets sizzled the velvet tip of his glans. Spare tape rolls and boxes of paperclips showered down onto the carpet.

"Stop this nonsense! It's just a damn video!" cried Matthew. Apparently, however, these men hadn't received the complete sexual satisfaction promised in Phase One of his business plan.

"Booooobs," panted a man craning forward to lick the bouncing breasts still projected on Matthew's midshaft.

Matthew tried to writhe away, but the man grabbed a staple gun and swung it upside Matthew's glans. His fanged jaws gasped open. Blood poured down a yawning gash running like an open stitch on the side of his penile physique.

As the blood rushed out of him, Matthew began to deflate. His balls darkened to pale cobalt.

Another man took a three-hole puncher and smashed it across the parachute of Matthew's nutsack.

Matthew Train screamed and was promptly taken down by a mob of turnt-up businessmen like a lone elk in a pride of lions. He disappeared in a blood-smeared flurry of pumping butts, penises stabbing the open air and fists white-knuckling office supplies.

Hadley heard "*Nooooo!*" wail out of the vortex. It quickly spiraled away into nothing.

She was free. The businessmen were all-in preoccupied with humping the remains of Matthew Train's limp, blue-balled phallic form. Cheap moans continued from Raymundo's device.

He stood holding the sound dock, grinning. "Chivalry," he said. "Ees not dead."

Hadley hesitated. "Thank you."

Raymundo turned to watch the porno he was now being projecting onto the bloody, bucking, biting businessmen. "I'm a leader. A leader is meeee." He chuckled lasciviously.

"I'm going back to school for interior design," Hadley muttered. "Shit on this."

She left 5B behind as fast as her sensible flats would carry her.

Airika Sneve is a writer, musician, and University of MN psychology graduate from Minnesota. She enjoys ham, cats, and the infliction of nightmares upon unsuspecting readers. Her stories have been published by Weirdpunk Books, Crowded Quarantine Publications, Pill Hill Press, Horrified Press, Issue #3 of Nameless Magazine, Strange Musings Press and more.

TAKING ROOT

CHRISTOPH WEBER

I BEND OVER, place my palms on the cold tile wall, and close my eyes.

"You ready?" Dee asks from behind me.

Swallow. Nod. Bend deeper.

She squeezes the inside of my naked leg, slides her hand up my thigh. When her fingers close around the plant growing from my ass, it tickles.

When she pulls, it does not tickle—the roots shred my colon. I arch my back and scream so loud she stops.

"Keep fucking going!" I cry, slamming my forehead against the tiles.

Lightning branches through my guts as the roots tear through my intestinal wall. I vomit. Blood runs into my eyes. I want to pass out, but I can feel the roots, almost free now, coming together and swimming out my colon like a squid. When they finally evacuate, I collapse to the floor and add tears to my own puke and blood and shit.

Dee lifts my head up, wipes my face with a towel. "You did good, Jimmy."

"Did you get it all?"

She says nothing.

"Dee?" I turn to look up at her, gag at the pain.

She bites her lip.

"Show me."

She holds up the tickler. It's a bit like a horsetail plant. Or a pipe cleaner. The joke is not lost on me. A fresh white rip marks where one of the roots broke free. My heart sinks.

"Round two."

"You can't, Jimmy," she says, her eyes welling. "Take some time, recover."

I shake my head, swallow. "They grow too fast. I'll rest when it's all out."

Her chin trembles as she squeezes my slick shoulder, turns, and walks to the kitchen. She comes back wearing elbow-length rubber gloves, a bottle of lube in one hand.

"You know, you look sexy in those," I say, trying to lighten the mood, trying to get my mind off the fact that I'm probably going to die tonight with my wife's arm up my ass.

She laughs. Or sobs. A bit of both, I think.

"Should we light some candles?"

She blinks a tear away. "Shut up, babe."

"Yes, my dominatrix, I will assume the position." I kneel on the floor mat, ass in the air. "Safe word is Rumpelstiltskin."

She kisses my ear, whispers, "I love you."

Then she proves it. One finger. Two. I gasp as she forces her hand in to the knuckles, stretching, sliding deeper, wrist-deep now, fingers probing for the root.

When she's nearly elbow-deep, she finds it. "Here." She reaches around me with her free hand, gives me a fresh hand towel. I bite down on it, and she pulls.

When I was a kid I choked on a piece of prosciutto and when I reached into my mouth I found the long string of fatty meat stuck on a molar, so I just pulled the thing out and I could feel its entire length as it moved up my throat. It was a visceral, almost ticklish feeling that I can only compare to this. Of course, this is a wee bit more painful, as the prosciutto hadn't bored through the wall of my esophagus and rooted itself in my flesh to obtain nutrients from my blood.

Also, I didn't have a fist in my ass.

I arch my back and squirm, thrashing my head from side to side, the hand towel flapping like a dog's chew toy.

The wet *smack* as Dee's lubed hand leaves my ass is the sweetest sound in the world.

I just remain there on my knees, chest like a bellows as I suck in deep heaves, my forehead leaving red streams in the tile grout.

TAKING ROOT

Dee throws her arm around me, pulls me close. "We got it, babe." Her smile is incongruous on her tear-streaked face. "Let's get you in the shower."

"You know what I love most about you?"

"What's that?"

"Your tiny hands."

"How do you think you got it?" Dee asks the next day as I lie in bed, feverish, unable to get up.

"Spores must've gotten into the water cistern somehow."

Dee bites her lip. "You don't think . . . "

I shake my head. "No. We've been so careful. I don't know how I got it, but we have to leave. The water's suspect and I'm going to clean us out of antibiotics. Food's running low, too."

Dee nods, snuggles up to my side, puts her hand on my chest. "Get better. Then we'll find a new home. You were lucky, you know."

"I don't feel very lucky."

"I'm serious. If that spore had germinated higher up, or even at the bottom of your esophagus, you'd be dead."

"I'm not out of the woods yet. And if that spore had just made it a couple more feet, I wouldn't have needed your arm up my ass."

"When you're better, please bring back the old Jimmy—he was an optimist."

"I'll try." Though it's not yet clear that I'm going to get better. "Thank you, Dee, for sticking around through that. For everything."

"I'm with you always." She kisses my cheek and grins. "Unless I find a man with shredded abs. You know I'm a sucker for those."

"Give me five minutes. Then I'll do some sit-ups."

Dee tends to me as I drift in and out of fevered nightmares. After a week I'm able to hobble around a bit. After three we're out of antibiotics and nearly out of bottled water, so we pack some supplies, don our hazmat suits, and say goodbye to our home of the past year. I walk like a cowboy on his horse too long, my legs bowed to ease the ache in my colon. Real pain in the ass.

The first woman we find is more plant than person. Bristly green shoots grow from her rotted eyes, her mouth, and judging from the tail emerging from her skirt, one other place, too.

Women had it the worst. My best guess is something about the Y chromosome gave a handful of men a fighting chance, because the few survivors I've met have all been dudes.

Except for Dee. The possibility that she's the last woman might have played a teensy role in my asking her to marry me, but she really is special. Hot as hell, and crazy as me.

Downtown, we scavenge. At one time it bothered me to loot the dead, but when the world fucks you this hard you can't be squeamish. You have to be like the ticklers. You find a niche, however repulsive it might be, and you do what you must to survive.

I find a pack of gum, which will be a nice treat after I sterilize it, but most everything's already been pilfered.

Dee stares down at a large squishy man with ragged holes in his stomach. A decomposing dog lies atop him, muzzle half-buried in his gnawed belly. I almost make a joke about Dee finding her man with shredded abs, but the sight of his entrails scattering the sidewalk like withered roots sucks the humor from me. Thick green ticklers grow happily from their hosts—out of the man's shredded stomach, out of the dog's mouth and nose. I think of Ollie, my old Labrador, and shudder. "Think it was his dog?"

"I hope not. It's all backward. Man becomes dog food, dog becomes plant food."

"Let's get out of here."

We walk from downtown to a residential area, where weedy, overgrown lawns rise up like they're trying to devour their homes. Just more plants trying to take over.

One lawn is freshly-mowed.

Dee and I just stand there for a moment, blinking. Then we scramble back behind the corner home, my ass flaring up like it's full of magma.

I peek around the bricks, scratch my ass, and eye the home's door. It looks pretty serious. Like a metal blast door. "What do we do, knock?"

"Could be booby-trapped. I say we wait, get a look at them when they come out." She laughs. "They have to mow their lawn, right? If they don't look like they're going to kill us, then we talk to them."

I agree and we loop around to the cover of some overgrown shrubs across the street. I pull a can of beans from my pack, stare at it longingly.

"It's breezy, Jimmy. You can't open your suit here."

I groan. "I'm sick of canned food, anyway."

"I know. But it's better than anal fisting."

When the sun's about to set, a young man in a hazmat suit walks out the blast door, grabs an old-school push mower and starts to tidy up his lawn, whistling so loud I can make out the tune through his suit: the Bee Gees, "Stayin' Alive".

"Are you fucking kidding me?"

Dee laughs. "Nobody who likes disco can be that bad, right?"

"I say we take our chances."

We stand up together and shout, "Oi!"

The man drops the mower, spins around and pulls a pistol, shouting into his radio.

We put our hands in the air and shuffle slowly toward him. Two more heads appear above the edge of the roof, silhouetted against the setting sun. It's hard to make out much except their outlines, but they look like they're aiming things at us. "Things" almost certainly being those tubes that shoot chunks of lead at supersonic speed, but for some reason I think how awesome it would be if they were holding pool noodles.

We get close enough to see the man behind his faceshield. He's twenty, tops, with clear blue eyes and a nice face. When he catches sight of Dee, his mouth drops open. "You're a woman."

Dee nods.

"Didn't know if any of you had survived. And you?"

"Her husband."

"Armed?"

"Yes. But we will gladly check our weapons with you, if you're willing to let us in for a bit. It's been a long time since we talked to anyone."

The boy whispers something into his radio. "Put your packs on the ground. Slowly." He gestures toward the shooters on the roof.

We do as we're told. A second man emerges from the blast door, assault rifle trained on us. Late twenties, maybe, with the same clear blue eyes and even stronger features than the other boy, who appears to be his younger brother.

"Sorry about all the precautions," the newcomer says, glancing at Dee. "It's good to see that humanity might still have a future. But we haven't made it this far by being careless." He rifles through our bags, takes our pistols. "Any other weapons?"

"Well, there is one more," I say, trying to ease the tension, "but you don't want to see it, and it's really only for my wife to handle."

After a moment the boys laugh, flashing bright smiles. The older one pats us down. "Well, now that's out of the way, join us for dinner?"

My mouth waters its opinion.

We go through a sterilization chamber on the first floor, then drop through an airtight floor door, down a set of stairs, and into what looks like a bomb shelter.

"How'd you find this place?" Dee asks.

"I built it," the boys' father says, beaming with pride. He's fit, bearded, and says he's in his fifties, but looks younger. "My father raised me to be prepared, and I raised my sons the same way." He points to the array of pipes and ducts lining the ceiling. "We have a rain collector and solar panels on the roof, which run our air and water purification systems. And we've stocked enough dry food for years. Plus fresh mushrooms growing on the lower level."

"There's another level?"

"Two more, actually."

"This place is incredible," Dee says.

"It's nice to have someone to show my work off to," he says, grinning. "You want to see some more?"

He leads us through another floor door and down to the next level, which has several video screens on the wall. A joystick juts up from a table below them. "Each level serves as a safe room. If anyone's ever stupid enough to storm our castle, we can retreat downward and lock them in the floor above us." He hits a button. The metal door overhead clangs as bolts slide into place.

"And then what, you just wait for them to die?"

"The locks cut them off from our food and water, but I have a few cards up my sleeve to speed things up." He winks at us. "I'm not going to show you *all* my tricks, though. Why don't we eat, then maybe I'll give you more of the tour."

The eggs are powdered, but they're topped with fresh, sautéed mushrooms. It's been so long since I drank anything but water, the orange Tang tastes like fresh-squeezed OJ.

"Why do you mow your lawn?" Dee asks.

The father wipes his mouth. "Just a little gesture to the plants, show them we haven't given up. Plus, we were hoping some survivors might see it. It's been a while since we heard from anyone."

"Where were you before this?" the older son asks. He's tall, muscled, with ringlets of thick dark hair hanging above his blue eyes. Dee, who's about his age, keeps staring at him. I can't blame her—the guy looks like Adonis.

"Another bunker," I say. "Nothing like this, though. Our water supply was compromised, so we left."

"Your bunker?"

Dee shakes her head. "No. A friend's. Ticklers got him."

"I'm sorry," the father says. "Same thing happened to my wife—to their mother—when they first showed up. Happened to every woman we knew." He narrows his eyes at Dee. "Why didn't it happen to you?"

"I was careful."

"So was my wife."

Dee shrugs. "I'm sorry. Truth is, I don't know why I'm less susceptible than other women." She elbows me. "Maybe because I'm the man in our relationship."

The men laugh. I don't. Adonis, whose eyes keep darting to my wife's breasts, finds it particularly funny.

Dee slaps my leg. "Lighten up, Jimmy. Just a joke."

Adonis looks to his father. "Can we celebrate with a bit of wine?"

"Fine idea. Get the 2009 Zin."

Dee chuckles. "Seriously, wine? What else do you have, steak and caviar?"

"Lobster, too," Adonis says. "Freeze-dried, of course, but still excellent when rehydrated." He turns to his father. "Can we bend our rations a bit today?"

"For guests, of course."

Adonis strides from the room.

"What do you know about the ticklers?" I ask the father when Adonis returns with caviar and wine, which he pours to the brim of everyone's glasses.

The father empties half his glass in a single pull, smacks his lips. "Doubt anyone knows much—they sprang up too fast. But one rumor is that the spores were dormant in permafrost, then emerged as it thawed."

"I'd heard that, but don't you think we'd have found evidence in the fossil record? I don't know, maybe like *T. rexes* with plants growing out their asses?"

"We've talked about this," Dee cuts in, a bit impatiently. "Less than one in ten thousand species even makes it into the fossil record. And plants don't preserve well."

"Father," Adonis says, holding up his empty glass. "Can I get another bottle?"

The man nods.

"They could have been helped along, too," the younger son says.

"How do you mean?"

"I mean they could have been made in a lab. Father says it wouldn't be the first time."

The dad nods, stroking his beard. "Like HIV."

I feel my eyebrows climbing against my effort to keep a straight face.

The father notices. "You don't believe me? AIDS was Big Pharma's dream business model. Lifelong, dependent customers."

"Well I'm not sure killing 99.9% of your customers is such a good business plan."

His eyes flash as he leans forward. "I didn't say *this* was Big

Pharma. Could've been military, too. If they could orchestrate 9/11, you can't put this past them."

I close my eyes, try to be a polite guest and say nothing at this fucking idiocy, but the wine's in my head and Adonis is back in the room staring at my wife's breasts. "What's next, we faked the moon landings?"

"There *are* some things that don't add up," Adonis says. His frown melts into that million-dollar smile. "But really, we shouldn't argue with guests. Why don't we play a game?"

"Good idea," I say, exhaling a breath I didn't know I was holding. "What'd you have in mind?"

"You guys like cards?"

"Sure. What's the game?"

Adonis looks my wife up and down. "Strip poker."

"I'm not sure that's an appropriate joke," I say after a moment.

Adonis links his fingers behind his head, leans back in his chair, smiles. "Who said I was joking?"

"What is this, high school?"

"No," the father cuts in. "This is our home. And the game is house's choice."

"Dee, I think it's time to go."

She locks eyes with Adonis. "What are the stakes?"

"Dee, this is weird! Let's get out of here."

The father furrows his brow. "Don't be a poor guest. We opened our home to you. Just oblige us with a little entertainment."

"Yes, thank you for the food, but we're going." I stand up. "Now, Dee."

"You two on a team," the father presses, gesturing for me to sit down. "If you get us naked, you can leave."

"I don't care to see any of you naked. We're leaving."

"What if we lose?" Dee asks.

"Your husband leaves, and you stay with us."

I grab Dee's arm. "Let's go!"

She shrugs me off.

"Dee? What . . . "

She bites her lip and peers at Adonis.

He winks at her, turns to me. "She can't help it," he says, a stupid fucking grin on his pretty-boy face. "It's only natural for a woman to want a strong man. A man who can provide. And who can provide better than us? Certainly not someone who can't even keep his water clean."

My jaw clenched tight, I grab Dee by the arm and pull her from her chair.

From the corner of my eye I see a blur of speed from the father. When I look over, I'm staring down the barrel of his pistol. "Sit the fuck down and play."

I swallow and sit, so wired I barely feel the magma flaring in my ass.

"Can I get another bottle of wine?" Adonis asks, pointing at the empty glasses.

"We're past our ration," the father says. He waves his pistol at me. "But anything to calm this little meerkat."

"What would the lady like?" Adonis asks.

"Can I see what you have?"

"Of course. Come with me." He takes Dee by the arm and leads her away as the young son fetches the deck.

I want a clear head for the game, but I'm so on edge that when Dee and Adonis come back and pour wine, I empty my glass in one draught.

"House game is heads-up Texas Hold 'Em," Adonis says. He pulls off his shirt, throws it on the table. "Blinds are one article of clothing posted prior to each hand." His muscled chest is hairless. A dog tag necklace hangs just above his washboard abs. His brother and father remove their shirts. Dee swallows a mouthful of wine and starts taking off hers.

"Dee! It's *any* article of clothing—you can start with a shoe!"

She rolls her eyes and puts her boot on the table next to mine.

I draw high card. My deal. I shuffle and give two cards to the men, face-down, and two to us, then take a look at our hole cards. Queen, 9.

"We check," Adonis says.

"I bet two more articles."

The father grins. "Ah, the little meerkat's gonna make it interesting!"

"We call," Adonis says, starting to slur his words as he tops off everyone's glasses. The men all take off their boots. Dee and I remove our remaining boots, plus one sock for me. Dee, who doesn't wear any, puts her necklace on the table.

I flop three community cards: 9, Ace, 6.

"We check," Adonis says, staring at Dee with a feral glint in his eyes.

"I bet three articles."

"Oh this is so exciting!" Adonis says, clapping his hands. "We call!"

The men take off their socks and pants so they're just sitting in their underwear. Except for Adonis, who evidently goes commando and judging from the grin on his face as he leans back and spreads his legs, thinks it's the funniest thing in the world. I avert my eyes, but even from the corner of my vision it looks like a baby's arm reaching over the edge of his chair. Dee pulls off her bracelet, shirt, and pants, then stares at Adonis's member as he ogles her breasts.

"Dee, what the fuck?"

She looks away, but doesn't say anything. I remove clothing until I'm just in my underwear. Dee wears a silver Claddagh ring with a huge diamond, the band I gave her when I asked her to marry me. Aside from the ring, just a lacy black bra with matching panties. My favorites.

I flip the turn card. 4.

"We check," Adonis says.

I've got no idea what they have, so I check and flip the final community card. Jack.

The father takes another peek at their cards. "What do you think, boys, we're in this far, should we go balls deep?"

Adonis grins. "We're all in."

I stare at the cards on the table: 9, Ace, 6, 4, Jack. We've got a pair of nines.

"Can I get another bottle?" Dee asks, looking at me. "It'll help with his paralysis by analysis."

The men laugh.

I turn to my wife. "Why are you doing this, Dee? What is it, his fucking shredded abs? This isn't you!"

She ignores me and sashays to the wine room with the younger brother, swaying her hips for Adonis and his father, their eyes glued to her panties.

"You man enough to call?" Adonis slurs.

Dee comes back in with his younger brother, pours wine. The men drink and watch me mull the probabilities.

I meet Adonis's smirking gaze. "Yeah, I call." I flip our cards.

The men stare at the board, expressionless. Adonis flips one of their hole cards. Six. I shift in my chair. Our nines still win.

He flips the other. Ace of diamonds.

I jump out of my chair. "Bullshit! Why didn't you bet at the start if you had an Ace!"

The father levels his pistol at my face. "It's called slow play, little meerkat. Now a bet is a bet. Both of you, please make good."

Dee unclasps her bra, holds it between her fingers for a moment, lets it drop to her feet. When she steps out of her panties, Adonis licks his lips like a fucking snake.

"This is horseshit!"

"Sons, please help the man pay his debt."

They leap from their chairs, slam me into the wall, and then they're on top of me. Adonis pins me down, his cartoon dick flopping over my face while his younger brother tears my boxers past my kicking feet.

"That's the weapon you were talking about? It's a pea-shooter!"

The men laugh as they drag me up the stairs.

I look down at Dee just before they pull me through the hatch. "Are you fucking serious, Dee? After all we've been through, you're going to let them do this?"

"A bet is a bet," the father says.

Dee grabs his forearm. "He didn't bet his life, though. At least give him back his suit."

The father strokes his beard, narrows his eyes at me. "That is true. You'll get your suit. But if you *ever* come back here, it'll be the last thing you do."

Dee stays behind as the brothers drag me, kicking and screaming, up to the first floor. When they throw my hazmat suit at me, I'm smart enough to stop struggling and don it before they shove me out the blast door and onto their manicured fucking lawn.

I run down the street, waving goodbye with one finger. Each step feels like a lightning bolt striking up my ass. When I'm out of sight I loop back around and sit in the bushes across the street. The imprint from where Dee and I sat together in the weeds is still there.

TAKING ROOT

When Dee walks out the blast door two days later, I sprint to the porch and throw my arms around her. We go back inside, through the sterilization chamber, and down the stairs. The younger brother is dead, Adonis and the father not far behind. All three are naked.

Ticklers sprout from the father's cock like the fronds atop a palm tree. I stand above him, grasp the plants, and pull. They don't break free, but I do draw some pathetic whimpers from the bastard. "These things root so fast!"

He struggles weakly. I slap his hands away, step on his stomach, pull harder. The ticklers break free by tearing his dick in half lengthwise. "Haha! Splitcock! I saw that at Burning Man!" Blood spurts through his fingers as he clutches his double dick in a futile attempt to slow the last bit of life flowing out of him. I hop over his pooling blood and make my way to Dee, squatting beneath the table.

"You're going to love this," she says over the father's dying sobs.

I crouch beside her to see face cards of each suit taped beneath the table where Adonis sat.

I shake my head, stride over to the pretty boy. A tickler sprouts from his ridiculous pecker. "Don't be silly, wrap your willy! That's what I do. And never, ever go for open mouth kisses." I wink. "You never know what someone might be carrying!"

He blinks in pain, his breath coming in wheezes around the little jungle growing from his mouth. I sit on his chest, flick the ticklers, and whisper in his ear, "Are these from making out with my little Typhoid Mary, or did you go in for the clam dinner?" He whines like a sick puppy. "You're a dirty boy, Adonis. But look, you have a pipe cleaner in your throat! Let's see if this helps."

I place one foot across his neck, grab the plants in his mouth, and pull. The ticklers tear free with a *pop*, followed by gurgling screams and bloody vomit.

"Yuck." I toss the plants to the floor. "How was the safe room?" I ask Dee over Adonis's wet wails.

"Bulletproof." She nods to the steel floor door, now pocked with indentations.

Dee and I carry the men outside, one by one, and dump them in an overgrown yard down the street to fertilize the weeds beside a rotting Chihuahua. I think. Could have been a terrier. Hard to tell at this point.

We walk home hand-in-hand, and pause on our manicured lawn. "They weren't such bad hosts after all," I say, looking up at our new fortress.

Dee puts her arm around me, rests her head on my shoulder. "Best place we've found yet."

I squeeze my wife tight to my side. "Yeah. It'll be nice to finally put down some roots."

When not writing on dead trees, Christoph Weber works with live ones, as a certified climbing arborist. Before that he was a firefighter on US federal hotshot crews, and before that, an interpreter in China. "Taking Root" was his recurring nightmare. Now, it's yours.

A winner of the 2016 Writers of the Future Award, Christoph's work has appeared in Nature, Poetry Quarterly, *and other venues. He's now finishing* The Hangman, *his novel about a bee-less future in which de-extincted Neanderthals are enslaved to pollinate crops for modern humans. Though this arrangement may be reversed, if one clever Neanderthal has his way . . .*

Stay apprised by following Christoph on Facebook: www.facebook.com/christoph.weber and at www.christophweber.com

THE BLISS POINT

WRATH JAMES WHITE

"**S**OME OF YOU are not going to like what I have to say."
James paced back and forth behind the pulpit, possessed by an
abundance of energy and enthusiasm, a religious fervor that filled
his eyes with fire and his every motion with manic vitality. He was
filled with the spirit, the Holy Spirit.

"You'll call me a blasphemer, a pervert. Say I am promoting sin.
And I agree with you on the latter. I am promoting sin. Sin for the
glory of our Lord and Savior, Jesus Christ! But I cannot agree with
you on the former. I am no pervert. Obeying our natural instincts
and desires is not perversion. But denying them . . . *that* is the
perversion."

There were stifled gasps from the newcomers in the crowd. First-
timers found their way to the small but enthusiast church for all
reasons. Topping most lists was Reverend Doctor James Watson's
acceptance of those who felt unwelcomed and didn't fit in traditional
church settings. Those with alternative lifestyles, homosexuals, the
promiscuous, those who questioned, and those who didn't believe
in turning the other cheek.

Today, there were quite a few new faces. James recognized less
than half the congregation, but he knew better than to be overly
optimistic. Few of them would remain for the entire sermon. Not
when they found out the true message of his religion. As a
psychologist specializing in alternative sexuality, James spent years
counseling men and women wracked with guilt over how they were
wired, battling desperately to change, to conform to what the world
considered normal. Homosexuals trying to turn straight. Sadists and

masochists struggling to live vanilla lives. Transvestites and transexuals, adult babies, human puppies and kittens, every deviation imaginable from what religion and society had arbitrarily judged normal. Many of them had been shunned by their families and churches, and wanted desperately to find a place where they could be accepted, so James had given them that. He had opened his home to them and welcomed them in.

When word of his doctrine of acceptance spread, his study group quickly outgrew his one bedroom apartment. So, he'd rented space in what was a swinger's club in the evenings, and, with the help of a couple dozen volunteers, he'd transformed it into a real church by day. And it was no accident that the church was built in a sex club. Many of his congregants were swingers who'd stumbled in surprised to find it open during the day, expecting an orgy, and then stayed for the sermon, enthralled by James's words of salvation—just as he had hoped. Now, they returned every Sunday. They weren't the ones who stormed out of his little parish, accusing him of heresy. It was the walk-ins, spill-over from other congregations in the neighborhood who came in without a clue. He had learned long ago to use their outrage as a teaching moment for his flock.

James held up the Bible, closing his eyes and bowing his head as he continued. "I know my words contradict everything you've learned in church, but it isn't counter to this book." He knocked on the Bible with his free hand. "It is all in line with Jesus's teachings. That's right. You have been told to avoid sin, to deny your animal instincts, the very urges and impulses authored by the creator. But I say that you know the creator by his creations, by his works. And when you look at those animals so programmed that they cannot disobey their instincts, what do you see?"

His regulars smiled knowingly. One of them called out: "Sin!"

James grinned and pointed to the voluptuous middle aged woman in the front wearing a dress through which her black lace panties, bra, and garter were visible.

"That's right, sister! You see every act that mankind has determined to be sinful. And don't be fooled, it is man and not God who has proclaimed it so. You see homosexuality. You see promiscuity. You see polyamory and adultery. You see rape and sodomy. You see theft. You see greed, lust, envy, wrath, and deceit.

You even see murder, all throughout nature. And you have all tried to resist these primal urges. And you have all failed. Each and every one of you has failed. No human being in the history of mankind has resisted these urges. Not Mother Teressa, not Ghandi, not Dr. Martin Luther King Jr., no one. They have all sinned at some point in their lives. Because what you are attempting isn't possible! It isn't. It is not possible to live without sin, because God has preprogrammed you to be sinners. We are born in sin!"

"Amen!" a man shouted from the back of the room, ripping off his clothes and diving onto the woman next to him who was already peeling herself out of a skin-tight dress. The two of them began fucking in the aisle.

An overweight woman who had come with her thin, balding husband and two obese kids stood, knocking over metal folding chairs as she hustled them up the aisle and out of the church. "You're all crazy, and you're all going to hell!" She pointed an accusing finger at James.

"We're going to hell?" James chuckled. "No, I don't think so. Do you know the *only* way, according to the Bible, that you can go to hell now, after Jesus's sacrifice? It's to deny Jesus Christ as your Lord and Savior. Anyone here deny the divinity of Jesus Christ?"

"No!" The congregation replied in unison.

"Anyone here not accept the love of Christ into your hearts?"

"No!" They all replied again.

"Then how do you think a sin, or even a multitude of sins, would damn you to hell, if Jesus already died for your sins?" The family hurried out the exit as James continued, "How can anyone be damned who accepts Jesus Christ as their Lord and savior when he himself proclaimed that you were saved? That through him you would not die, but have eternal life—that you would sit beside him and his father, our God, in heaven? Jesus died in the knowledge that mankind was helpless before sin, unable to resist the instinctual drive to sin, because we are all, at our core, at our essence, at our primal nature, sinners."

James felt the energy coursing between him and his flock. He was vibrating as one with the majority. Most of them understood. "Now, how is it possible for a born sinner to deny his or her very identity? Can a fish *not* swim? An eagle refuse to soar? Jesus knew that you could not live without sin. That's why he died for those sins. He suffered to free you from the futile burden of trying to resist what you are. It would be a *waste* of that sacrifice for you to stop sinning now, even if you could, which you cannot—and he knew that too. It would be as if, after hundreds of thousands of soldiers fought and died for the freedom of African Americans during the Civil War, they refused to leave the plantations and chose rather to remain living in servitude. I am telling you now that you have been enslaved and you are choosing to remain enslaved by your own fear and ignorance and the lies of those who would use religion to subjugate you! You have been duped and deceived into wasting this precious gift, into believing that sin—which is the natural state of man—is an affront to the Lord who created you to sin. Now, does that make any sense at all?"

"No!"

Before the woman's outburst, Holly had considered leaving, but something about Reverend Doctor James Watson's sermon had resonated with her, filled her with hope. But now it was only making her tense. She looked at Toby with his pony tail and *Duck Dynasty* shirt, then to her friend still struggling with meth addictions, Jessie—Toby's wife. They looked concerned too.

Holly knew only a little about the storefront congregation known as Our Father of Perpetual Indulgence. Toby had picked it out—after a stint in jail and court-ordered anger management classes. Jessie begged him to find Jesus. Jessie and Holly thought church would end his abusive ways. Holly could appreciate Toby wanting to feel accepted, and had accompanied them today to show support to her best friend's husband. But this church seemed to be preaching about something beyond just acceptance of all life styles. Something was very wrong here.

"I tell you now that to go against your God-given nature is to go against God himself!" The Reverend said. "You honor and celebrate our Lord Jesus Christ when you sin! Now go forth and be sinful!"

Toby stood up and grabbed Jessie by the hand. "You ain't no man of God! You're twisting Jesus's words! This is sacrilegious!"

Toby had barely gotten out the words before a large man with a shoulder-length mullet stood and threw a right hook that connected with his jaw, almost dropping him.

"Dude, what the fuck?" Toby raised his fists, but the big guy with the mullet hit him again, driving an uppercut into his solar plexus, expelling the air from his lungs. Doubled-over, gasping for oxygen, wide eyes glistening with tears and shock, Toby raised one hand out in front of him in a feeble attempt to ward off further attack, while holding his bruised stomach with the other.

Holly dropped to her knees and crawled to a corner in fear while two overweight-middle-aged women had Jessie by the hair and were punching her repeatedly in the face, pulverizing her features.

"Stop! Help! Toby, help me!" Jessie screamed, but Toby was in his own world of hurt. A young blonde in a miniskirt with huge fake tits squeezed into an undersized pink tank top swung a hardback leather-bound hymnal at his head, opening a gash in Toby's forehead. More of the congregation joined in, striking the man with anything they could find. Toby and his meth-head wife wilted beneath a deluge of punches and kicks. Three young toughs, barely out of their teens, rushed the couple, two of them baring knives, pushing their way through the crowd of attacking parishioners.

"Oh, God! No! No! Stop! *Aaahhh!*"

Soon blood and entrails stained the church floor as the couple was disemboweled, their steaming purple intestines, like links of blood sausage, dragged out between the rows of folding chairs. James remained silent as his flock tore the couple apart.

As if on cue to start an orgy, several members around Holly shed their clothes and began fucking in the expanding pool of blood. They bathed their naked bodies in the red river of life pouring forth from their victims, licked it from breasts, cocks, and cunts, used the blood as lube as they filled each other's dripping orifices, adding their own sexual fluids to the tide, swallowing mouthfuls of semen and blood as the culmination of their lusts synchronized with the cessation of life. Toby's body still danced in its death throes, stiff limbs rattling spastically against the wood floor as he expired.

"Are there any others who would deny the word of God? Speak now or join in the celebration!" James looked out over the flock. It looked like he reveled in the horrified expressions on Holly's face as well as the other first-timers. "Come! Lie down with your brothers and sisters; bathe in the blood of the lamb! For Christ lives in all of us. This couple's sacrifice shall serve as your communion. Come and receive the sacrament! Be baptized and born anew without fear of sin!"

Each church member was led to the pool of blood in a line and made to strip and be baptized in red. Some came willingly, eagerly disrobing and throwing themselves down amongst the cavorting celebrants to join in the orgy of blood, others wept and offered token resistance, afraid to join in the sin of murder, but knowing that if they did not, they would certainly be the next sacrifice.

"Be not afraid, my children. Your freedom awaits! By joining us in the ultimate sin, you shall unburden yourselves of your guilt and fear. What is lust or adultery compared to the taking of a life? What is greed or covetousness? Obey your primal instincts, for they are the true commandments of the Lord written into your very genetic code by his divine hand! Look upon the lovely breasts of your neighbor, her supple thighs and sweet pussy. Look upon his firm pecs and biceps, his engorged cock. Feel the lust within you and know that it is good. Allow your desire for the flesh to take you where it will! Be not afraid, for you are children of the Lord made in his divine image. There is no sin but the denial of your natural desires!"

And one by one they succumbed to his word, joining the blood orgy, until only Holly remained, terrified and weeping.

Toby's death was no great loss. If anything, it was a blessing. Toby was an abusive asshole. Holly should have known a sexist pig like him would choose a sex church to find salvation. He'd probably been hoping he could get Jessie and her into some kind of *ménage à trois*. He was always trying to stick his little oily cock in her whenever Jessie wasn't around. And if that *was* his plan, boy did it backfire. But Jessie had been her friend since middle school. They'd both suffered through drugs and lousy men together. Helping when they could.

Now Holly cringed in the corner, eyes squeezed shut, bony fists pressed against her ears, while Jessie's screams wound down to a gurgling death rattle, and Toby's corpse finished its convulsions and lay still.

"Help me, Jesus. Oh, Lord! Sweet Jesus, please help me," Holly mumbled. She didn't know what else to do but pray. She was trapped with a cult of murdering lunatics, too far from the exit to make a run for it without being stopped by one of the Reverend Doctor's followers before she could reach the door, and there was no way she could fight them off. Already she was trying to imagine what it would feel like to be pummeled nearly unconscious and then repeatedly stabbed, dismembered, and disemboweled like Toby and Jessie. She wished she was high again, but even on meth she barely stood a chance of winning.

"Oh, Jesus. I don't want to die! Help me, God. I'll do anything you ask. You have to help me. Don't let them kill me. Pleeeaaase!"

Mascara ran down her face like black tears. She rocked back and forth in her little corner, still holding herself, paralyzed with fear.

Holly opened her eyes just as Reverend Doctor James Watson left the pulpit and walked toward her, removing his shirt and pants, a beatific smile spread across his rugged, handsome face. He looked a lot like a biker she'd dated in high school. He had been the quintessential "bad boy," introducing her to drugs and sex, encouraging liberal experimentation with both. Holly imagined he'd look a lot like the Reverend Watson had he not been immolated when his Harley slid beneath a fuel truck and exploded.

The Reverend paused and removed his underwear, revealing a thick, venous erection bobbing in the air, pointing right at her face like a divining rod. Seeing his huge cock gave Holly an idea. Perhaps Jesus had answered her prayers after all. It wouldn't be the first time Holly had sucked a cock to get herself out of a bad situation. She'd taken more than one cock down her throat for a hit of meth. If getting face-fucked by the good Reverend Doctor Watson would save her life, she'd gladly suck, swallow, and smile. Hell, she'd even gargle his cum if that's what he wanted.

It's your world, Doc. Just let me live, Holly thought as she crawled toward Reverend Doctor Watson on her hands and knees, affecting the most seductive dick-sucker pucker she could manage.

Holly cleared all thoughts of the carnage from her mind, focusing on the task at hand, her own survival. Suck a cock and live. It was pretty simple mathematics to her. As a past junkie, the economics of sex was something she could understand.

She wiped the tears from her eyes and beckoned the Reverend

Doctor forward with her index finger, then opened her mouth and touched the finger to her outstretched tongue before sucking on the tip. The reverend was now standing above her with his cock bouncing inches from the tip of her nose. She reached up and caressed it.

"Do you not believe? Do you not accept the word of God?"

Holly shivered, but managed to keep a smile on her face as she stroked the reverend's engorged member, then lightly licked the head. "I do, Reverend. I accept the word of God. I love God. Let me show you how much."

Slowly, as if the movements caused him discomfort, the Reverend Doctor shook his head. He sighed and a weary half-smile slid upon his narrow face.

"No. You don't accept the word of Christ our Lord. You don't accept me."

Holly slid the head of the Reverend Doctor's cock between her lips, flicking the underside of it with her tongue, licking away a glistening pearl of pre-cum, before swirling her tongue around it. The Reverend Doctor moaned and threw back his head. She continued stroking his cock as she lowered to lick and suck his balls, taking the wrinkled sack of flesh between her lips and rolling the testicles around in her mouth one by one. The Reverend Doctor's cock grew even harder, thicker, his moans deepened to a husky growl.

"Oh, how I wish I could believe you, my child."

She could feel he was only minutes away from orgasm when Holly took the Reverend Doctor's cock between her lips once again and inched his turgid flesh to the back of her mouth, past her tonsils, until she could feel his engorged erection pulsating in her throat. Then she grabbed the cult leader by his scrawny buttocks and encouraged him to fuck her mouth. He began with a few tentative thrusts, testing her gag reflex. Holly responded like a pro, breathing through her nose when his length clogged her windpipe, licking his cock and stroking it as he slid it back out so the head of his cock was encircled by the tip of her lips, before sliding it back down her throat with increasing urgency.

Tears streamed from Holly's eyes as the Reverend Doctor raped her throat. More mascara ran down her face, drawing long black lines, turning her cheeks into a spiderweb of dark shadows. The Reverend Doctor grabbed the back of her head in both hands, ramming his cock to the back of her throat, brutally fucking her mouth. His body tensed, and he threw back his head, staring heavenward as he began to jerk and spasm.

"Oh, God! Oh, my sweet Christ our Lord. I'm cumming! I'm cumming, Father!" His seed filled Holly's mouth and she gulped it down, licking spilled semen from her lips, scooping it from her chin with her hand and sucking her fingers clean. The Reverend Doctor reached down and, with a hand beneath each of her arms, raised her to her feet. He hugged her, brushed her hair from her face, then kissed her forehead.

"Oh, my child, you are a wonder!" He laughed, smiling joyously.

Holly forced herself to smile too, stifling her sobs. She wiped the back of her hand across her eyes, smearing dark make-up from eye to temples and blackening the back of her hand. She touched her bruised lips gently. Her mouth felt like she'd been smacked.

"I told you I'm faithful. I love Christ. I can love you too, any way you like," Holly said, congratulating herself on a job well-done. She had saved her life with the most basic of skills, a simple blowjob. Empires had crumbled, wars been won, marriages ended, and relationship born on the power of that one act. Her father may have been an asshole, but he'd saved her life today by teaching her the art of fellatio. *May he rot in prison forever*, she thought.

The Reverend Doctor's smile bristled with malevolence as he placed his palms on both sides of Holly's face and forced eye contact, peering deep into her bloodshot baby-blues.

"I believe you are the one. You and I are going to do something wonderful together. Come with me," the Reverend Doctor said. He gestured to two blood-drenched acolytes who'd been watching intently, presumably prepared to rush to his defense and end Holly's life had she been stupid enough to try something like biting off the Reverend's cock and spitting it in his face. She had certainly been tempted to do just that, but saw no way in which that ended well for her. One of the men was a stocky, hyper-muscular black guy with biceps as large as Holly's head. The other was a tall, lean but well-built blonde who towered a full head above his partner and at least a foot above Holly.

WHITE

The Reverend Doctor's other lunatic followers were still fucking, sucking, stroking, and licking on the church floor. They were all covered in tacky coagulating blood, but none of them seemed to mind. Holly stared at them as she was led to table the back of the church, wondering if she might have been better off just joining in with their orgy. Before she was pulled into another room, Holly cast one last glance at her two dead friends. Jesse had been completely decapitated, one of the congregants was fucking her disembodied head, while two other men raped her corpse, one was fucking her headless throat, grunting like a beast as he came down her vandalized neck-hole. Toby, who'd always been a racist, sexist, homophobic piece of shit, was suffering the most fitting indignity she could imagine as his corpse was brutally sodomized by the mullet-wearing brute who'd been the first to strike him. A morbidly-obese African American woman with huge pendulous breasts the size of watermelons and an ass like a beach ball sat upon Toby's lifeless face, grinding her blood-soaked pussy against his mouth. Holly could not tell if it was Toby's blood that coated the woman's dripping snatch, or if the blood was coming out of her. Holly turned away, and the door was shut and locked behind her.

She looked around the room she'd entered. There were a few candles glowing in the windowless room, but it was otherwise dark. Slowly her eyes adjusted to the gloom and Holly began to scream.

"No! No! Noooo! *Nooooo!*"

The room was filled with torture devices. Holly had seen BDSM dungeon porn before, and she recognized many of the implements hanging from the walls: whips, floggers, paddles, straps, canes. There was a chair with leather restraints at the arms and legs, a standing cross also affixed with chains and metal shackles. A dentist's chair filled one corner of the room with a tray full of sharp implements beside it. There was a stockade and a huge spider web of chains stretching between a wooden octagon frame large enough to suspend a human being from, as well as a leather bondage table, and many other terrible pieces of furniture.

Holly struggled to escape, tugging on the doorknob. The Reverend Doctor's two blood-soaked followers dragged her away from the door and toward a leather-topped table that had handcuffs at the top two corners and ankle cuffs at the bottom. The big black guy who was built like a linebacker took hold of her wrists, crushing them together in one of his huge hands. One at a time he locked them into the handcuffs. Holly thrashed and kicked at the tall blonde guy, catching him with a kick to the chest that staggered him back and seemed to knock the wind out of him. He recovered fast and seized one of her ankles, struggling to lock it into the cuffs as Holly continued to fight and struggle. This time she connected with a kick to the tall man's jaw that knocked him to the floor where he laid unconscious for several seconds before raising to a sitting position. Holly felt a momentary thrill of victory and hope before the big linebacker grabbed her by both ankles and, ignoring her kicks and struggles, easily wrestled her into the restraints. Once she was completely helpless, he stepped away then turned to help his tall friend up from the floor.

"Help!!" Holly cried out. "Heeeelp!"

"Shhhhh!" The Reverend Doctor said as he approached the table and ran a hand up her inner thigh. "You are about to experience something few people on earth ever have. Do you know what I did before I started this church? I was a psychologist. My specialty was addictions and so-called deviant sexual issues, but after several years counseling drug addicts, I developed my own opioid addiction. Just like you. I sank as low as a human being possibly can. I was living in the gutter, stealing, even prostituting myself to support my habit. Sound familiar? I went from prescription painkillers to heroin.

"It took finding God for me to finally kick my dependency. And, like so many of the newly saved, I began reading the Bible fanatically. I was addicted to God. He became my new drug. It was during my sixth or seventh cover to cover read of The New Testament that I had my revelation, that the true meaning of The Resurrection was revealed to me. I felt compelled to spread the good word. That's why I built this church."

Holly's brow knitted in confusion. Eyes wide, she shook her head.

"What? What the fuck does that have to do with me? Why am I chained up?"

Reverend Doctor James Watson nodded.

"I'm sure this must all be confusing for you. Let me try to explain. See, before my fall from grace, I was a respected psychologist. In addition to treating patients for their various addictions, I also did a lot of research studies, conducted a lot of experiments. I had a theory that I never got to test. Have you ever heard of the bliss point?"

Holly slowly shook her head.

"In the food industry, the bliss point is the most pleasurable, most addictive amount of sugar you can add to food before it starts to become less enjoyable, the point at which ultimate pleasure is derived. Too little, and it is good, but not as good as it could be. Too much, and you reach a point of diminishing returns where the experience actually begins to lose pleasure by degrees. It just becomes too sweet.

"See, I became convinced that all physical sensation had a bliss point too, not just taste but cutaneous and subcutaneous sensations as well—even sexual pleasure. There has to be a point beyond which pleasure becomes pain. And, conversely, a point at which pain becomes pleasure, where the endorphin levels reach a point that they overcome the pain. Did you know they have conducted experiments with monkeys where they hooked the pleasure centers of their brains up to electrodes and gave them a button to push that would send a current through their brains that would simulate an orgasm? Those monkeys kept pushing that button until it fried their brains and killed them. I believe those monkeys wanted to die. Even back then, when I was just a psychologist, before I had ever found God, I was convinced that this bliss point is what man calls heaven, nirvana, rapture . . . and hell. I believe those monkeys reached a point where they could see heaven, and I believe you and I will reach that point together today."

Holly began to struggle again. "What are you going to do to me? Please, just let me go! Don't hurt me! Please!"

"That's just it. I don't want to hurt you. I don't want to *only* hurt you. I want to give you true bliss. Oh, and don't think I'm arrogant enough to think I can do this all on my own. I have no illusions of my own sexual prowess. I have many wonderful devices here to help."

THE BLISS POINT

Holly screamed and moaned, thrashing against her restraints as one orgasm after another wracked her body with violent convulsions that were almost agonizing. The Reverend Doctor's two brutes had fixed a spreader bar between her ankle-cuffs and strapped her thighs down to the table with two big leather restraints—making it impossible for her to close her legs or move them much at all. Another thick strap, like an old-fashioned weightlifter's belt, went around her waist holding her firmly against the table, limiting her movement from the waist down. She had cried and pleaded the entire time, promising them all the best blowjobs of their lives if they would just let her go, an eternity of blowjobs.

"You can fuck me in the ass if you want! I'll take all three of you at once, double- penetration, ass-to-mouth, any nasty filthy fantasy you can imagine. We can turn it into a bukakke session. You can all cum on my face. I'll suck all of you dry then get you hard so we can do it all over again. I promise. Just let me go!"

She could tell that the tall guy and the linebacker were considering her proposal from the lengthening and thickening of their enormous cocks, but it wasn't them she needed to convince. They were just followers, and their leader had already cum once. His cock hung limply between his scrawny pale thighs. Holly wept, realizing that she'd played her only bargaining chip too soon.

"You are good, my child. So good. I can't remember the last time a woman worshiped my cock like that, but I could train any woman in my congregation in such a skill if that's all I wanted. We have a higher purpose here. I want you to enter heaven, to see the face of God."

A device Holly recognized as a Hitachi Magic Wand—the Cadillac of vibrators—was strapped into a leather harness. There was something different about it though. She had one of the powerful devices in her bedroom at home, and it didn't look quite like this thing.

"This is an electro vibe wand. It vibrates just as powerfully as the famous Magic Wand, but it also delivers powerful electric shocks. It has five different intensity levels. I believe we are going to hit all five. But first . . . "

The big muscular black guy, the linebacker, handed the Reverend Doctor a small black box with lots of wires hanging from it.

WHITE

"This is a TENS unit. They use it during physical therapy. It sends electric currents through your muscles to make them contract."

Holly watched hopeless as he affixed little metal alligator clamps to the ends of each wire. She cried out when he attached the clamps to her labia and nipples. He affixed little sticky pads to four more leads and slid two of them inside her, attaching them to the walls of her vagina, then fixing the last two to her anus.

The Reverend Doctor held up a pear-shaped metal device that also had wires attached to it. Holly recognized it as a buttplug—a vibrating buttplug.

"And finally, a simple metal vibrator . . . attached to a Violet Wand electro-stimulator."

He slathered the vibrator, the buttplug, her asshole, and her entire vagina with a conductive gel that also served as a lubricant, then slid both the metal vibrator and the plug inside her. The vibrations immediately did their job, sending delicious sensations throughout her sex. Jacked up on fear and adrenaline, her body began to betray her, rapidly approaching orgasm. Maybe they didn't want to torture and kill her, or fry her brains like those poor monkeys he spoke of. Maybe they only wanted her to cum her brains out like they said. Hell, she decided, she might even enjoy it.

Then the Reverend Doctor turned on the TENS unit, and her vagina began to rhythmically contract. Her nipples were buzzing like she was hooked up to a car battery. Unable to fight it, the first violent orgasm tore through her, surprising her, and stealing her breath away. Had she not been strapped down, she felt like she would have flown off the table. Holly could not remember when she'd last had such a powerful climax, if ever. She was panting heavily like she'd just sprinted a mile, but the Reverend Doctor was not done. She had forgotten about the Hitachi. He strapped the harness around her hips and thighs, holding the large vibrator firmly against her clitoris. Then he turned it on.

Holly's dilated rectum and vaginal walls were contracting around the vibrator and the buttplug buzzing inside her as the TENS unit did its job, the Hitachi vibrated against her clitoris, and her labia and nipples buzzed with electricity. Holly screamed as another orgasm ripped through her and she continued to cum, one bone-jarring climax after another, tumbling down over each other like an avalanche of pleasure buffeting her body relentlessly. Whenever she thought she could not experience any more pleasure, the Reverend Doctor would turn up the intensity on the TENS unit or the Hitachi, driving her further and further into a cocoon of overwhelming ecstasy.

Holly was delirious. She had no idea how long she'd been in the room or how many orgasms she'd endured. A river of vaginal fluid flowed between her legs, saturating the leather bondage table.

"Oh, my God! Oh, fuck! Oh, Jesus Christ! I can't take it anymore! Stop! Please stop! I feel like I'm dying!" Her eyes rolled up in her head, saliva drooled from the corners of her mouth, and tears flowed freely as she continued to cum.

"Do you see him? Do you see the face of God?" The Reverend Doctor asked, bristling with excitement.

Holly shook her head from side to side, then thought better of it and began to nod enthusiastically.

"Yes! Yes, I see him! I do! He's beautiful!"

The Reverend Doctor dropped his head, closed his eyes and let out a long sigh.

"No. You don't see him. You're lying. Don't lie to me. This will all go so much better if you are truthful."

Holly sobbed loudly, uncontrollably.

"Just let me go! Let me go! You have to stop! I can't take it!"

She could barely see the maniacal cult leader through the haze of salacious sensations. His voice sounded like it was a mile away. Holly was dimly aware that the two brutes were masturbating on either side of her. They splattered her face and breasts with cum that dripped down her forehead into her eyes. She tried to blink the sticky mess away. When she could see again, she saw that they were still masturbating, preparing to ejaculate on her again.

"Then you have to tell me the truth. I want to know when you pass through the gates of heaven. I want to know when you see the Lord's face."

"I'm not lying! I see him! I do!" Holly said breathlessly, another orgasm colliding against her like a wall, knocking her head back and causing her entire body to spasm and convulse.

"No. I'm afraid you aren't quite there yet. Let's turn it up a bit more shall we?"

WHITE

"Please! Please don't! I can't take anymore! I'll die! You're killing me!"

Electric shocks ripped through her loins, as the metal vibrator inside her began to crackle with electricity and the Hitachi strapped against her clitoris released its own electric charge, as did the metal buttplug vibrating deep in her anus. The pain was intense, but combined with the powerful vibrations, the painful jolts brought her to more thunderous orgasms that felt like they would break her in half. Her mind swam in a sea of agony and ecstasy, going under, slowly drowning in sensations beyond anything she could have imagined.

A joyous smile burst upon her face and Holly whispered, "More."

The Reverend Doctor leaned in closer. "What did you say, child?"

"Don't stop . . . P-please, don't stop. I want m-more! More!"

The Reverend smiled and nodded. "Ahhh, the bliss point."

He turned the intensity on the electro wand between her legs to the max, then increased the TENS unit and the Violet Wand until Holly's entire body vibrated with electricity and the smell of burning flesh filled the air along with the pheromone rich musk of sex. When the Reverend Doctor removed a scalpel and a cauterizing pen from a medical bag and began cutting and burning her, Holly could no longer distinguish the pain from the pleasure. It had all merged into one kaleidoscope of lubricious sensation. She was drunk, intoxicated with endorphins, only dimly aware that she was still cumming, that she was still in the dark room strapped to the table, who she was or had ever been, as the Reverend Doctor cut a circle around Holly's left breast then grabbed the edges of her skin with a hemostat and slowly removed the skin with a wet, sticky, ripping sound, peeling it like a grape and revealing the bubbly yellow fat and pink muscle tissue beneath. The two brutes were still furiously masturbating as they crowded in to watch their beloved religious leader skin Holly's breast.

"I see Him!" Holly shouted. "I see the face of God!" She repeated gleefully, smiling in profound joy, divine rapture, as semen rained down upon her ecstatic face.

Wrath James White is a former world class heavyweight kickboxer, a professional mixed martial arts trainer, distance runner, and performance artist, who is now known for creating some of the most disturbing works of fiction in print.

THE BLISS POINT

Wrath is the author of such extreme horror classics as The Resurrectionist *(now a major motion picture,* Come Back To Me*) Succulent Prey, Population Zero, and many others.*

Wrath lives and works in Austin, Texas with his three daughters, Isis, Nala, and Zoe, his son and co-author, Sultan Z. White, and his beautiful wife Tammy.

WOEFUL CITY

GARRETT COOK

1.

"Through me you come to the City of Woe,
Through me you reach eternal pain
Through me among the lost you go

Justice moved the maker who would reign
Unstoppable from year to year to year
Wisdom high and love that shall not wane

Before my coming nothing could appear
That's not eternal, eternally I endure
Leave your hope behind if you'd enter here"

IS IT DANTE?

This is not what I expect to hear from a woman riding me at an arcade booth at an adult videostore on 82nd. I am not at an arcade booth at an adult videostore on 82nd. I am elsewhere. I am drifting. She is grinding, she is gorgeous, she is glowing and I am drifting. I have come here for a reason, I know it. She's taking me back so she can take me forward.

2.

The sun is beating down hard on my shoulders, which are straining. There's a shovel in my hand and it's urgent. Dirt behind me, a hole in front, getting big enough for me to reach in for what I'd buried there a few hours earlier. Four hours and twenty-seven minutes earlier. You'd best believe I've been watching the clock. There's a right way to do this and a multitude of wrong ways. Hell, it's quite possible that there's no right way. Likely. Probable. But I wouldn't be doing this if this was something I should do.

Suddenly, paydirt. Literally. There it is, the big wooden box, a coffin with strategic airholes. I lift the lid like Peter Cushing at war with the dead. The smell of piss. The sound of heavy breathing. A tiny blonde, whose eyes are big and the color of seaglass. I lift her up. She's fine. Fine as she can be. I mean, she's not fine. If she were fine, she wouldn't be buried there in the back yard. It's a relief for sure.

I take her to the bathroom and run a bath. I pour her a big glass of water. She sits in the bubbles and the comfort. She relaxes into the bath, she takes in the water, then she slurps up the air just as greedily. She'd been in a coffin after all. I run the sponge and my hand over her. Getting the sweat and the dirt off her is a big job, but I savor it. Her body is precious to me, she deserves to be clean and comfortable and happy. From washing, my intention changes and I slide my fingers inside, and I wrap an arm around her waist and I play her like a violin, working over the surface seeking out the tones I want.

"I do this," she says, "for the moment I stop thinking you'll come back for me."

3.

I'm sitting at a booth across from an immaculately assembled middle-aged woman, a Frankenstein bride of Sephora, outlet mall Chanel and years of corporate degradation. This is not the kind of company I usually keep. And it's not because I don't feel good enough for these sort of people. She clearly does her damnedest to make sure I do and she has since I first sat down at this restaurant.

"I need you to get what this is about, okay? This is about shame. This isn't like a sex thing, not really. It's a thing I need to talk about."

I am starting to hate this woman. It's my fault for deciding to live like this though. I live for these experiences. What else is there?

"My son plays high school football. He's not very good at it, you see. He's actually really, really bad at it. You tell your kid to stick with it, you tell your sons to be strong and that this builds character, but he never seems to get any better. They mutilate him on that field. He's slow and he can't take a hit. He's small too. You'd think a boy his size would be hard to catch, but he isn't. I understand why they don't pass to him."

Why is she telling me about this? Is this something incestuous, something gross and scatological? I'm really hoping it isn't. I don't pop a boner from incest or cancer or anything like that. I'm ready to call this a night when I notice something. She is clutching her purse. There's something in there that she wants but isn't giving herself.

"This isn't a sex thing, okay? I'm not going to fuck you. I just want that to be clear. This isn't a date. Their rivals, their rivals are the Tigers. They never really beat the Tigers. They make fucking fools of themselves every homecoming. I'm a bad mother."

"You're probably not a bad mother," I counter. I don't like the face she makes when she says *I'm a bad mother*.

"Let me talk. I'm a bad mother. Everything tells me that who I am is this child's mother and that my value and my right to go on walking around in this skin is contingent about my doing this job well. I keep a tiny stuffed tiger in my purse. I bought it at a game. The other team's mascot is in my purse. All the time. And I watch from a corner of the bleachers at these games."

"Yeah, and?"

"And I never wear any panties when I go to these games. And I watch them as they grind his face in the dirt, as they pile on top of him. This isn't a sex thing, you understand? It's shame and I watch and I clutch my purse and I quietly get myself off at these games. It's not a sex thing. It's shame."

And then it really hits me. It occurs to me who she is and what she's about and why this turns her on. She's going to tell me, to go into specifics. But I pay for our drinks and I get the hell out of dodge.

4.

This one doesn't make me feel so bad. This one I almost don't mind going back to.

The catalogue model sits surrounded by the long, red hair that had been her livelihood. She is smiling beatifically. I hold in my hand the clippers, surprised that I went through this but not surprised when I see that smile, that skin, that body, that gratitude. Most of the time, I give a woman what she wants. That's what being a man's about, especially for me. I've never done anything they didn't want. Sometimes even when I didn't want to. But that smile, the relief. I'm glad she convinced me.

"I'm free now," she says, "they'll never want me again."

I hug her close, rub my face against hers. I had thought she was kidding but that serenity runs deep. This is a spirit liberated from bondage. I am proud of this pile of hair at my feet and what it represents to this woman.

She reaches into her handbag and pulls out a scalpel, then a pen knife.

"I need you to take off my nose. My ears. I want them to never look at me again."

I break into a cold sweat. I feel nauseous. Tears and the red wine from dinner alike are ready to explode from me.

"I can't do that."

She runs the scalpel across her doll-like skin, across the perfection that earned her paycheck.

"Any of this is another hole. Has anyone offered you their heart and actually meant it?"

5.

A blur of desperation and kisses. A dance whose beats end in bodies pressed against walls, allies and awnings and overpasses, all the way back home. We are all need. The first date fever. Groping, grabbing, nails almost breaking skin until the threshold's crossed. The bedroom cannot come soon enough. She hits the bed. It is impossible to undress her fast enough. My teeth find her throat and she cries out. Then suddenly her eyes are wide. Suddenly, she shakes her head. She begins to tear up.

"Not now. Not now. Not now."

She shakes, caught up in some kind of seizure. Her stomach widens and distends. A sound of something struggling to get out. I think back to Kelly and her coffin. This body it seems is not altogether unlike that coffin. Her skin stretches. Splits far, like an internal earthquake. And along, the fault line, a small body digs up, through yellow fat, through pink, through red, through splinters of bone and organs and emerges, slick and wet, a little girl around ten.

"He started when I was seven," says the intruder, "but I'm grown now. I'm a big girl. Come here, daddy, come touch me."

I flee screaming into the night. There is nobody to talk to about this.

6.

There are dreams, there are hungers, there is a somnambulant pulse of twitch that leads me down 82nd. And then I'm wandering past glass dildos and past plastic faces looking up at me in some semblance of seductive from a multitude of videos. And then I pass into the back, into the dark of the arcades and the booths.

I don't know what I'm looking for. You won't find comfort here. You won't find company here. Pornography is ubiquitous pretty much everywhere, yet I am here, about to walk into the dark of the booths and sit down. There are sounds of pleasure erupting from the TVs, but behind them, there is a sound of pleasure erupting from actual people: a man's moaning, wet slosh, bouncing bodies.

I sit down and I peer through the hole. There is one of the guys who came to the place to shoot up. The needle is still in his arm and on him, a lady phantasm is grinding. She is wearing an expressionless porcelain mask. Her hair is opium black, not unlike the shit inside the needle, she might well have seeped out from in the needle, were it not for skin that might be moonlight streaming into the room.

And as she moves on him, the light starts from him, the light starts to fade from his eyes, his breath starts to get constricted, he starts to gasp. He does not flee, he cannot move and I can do nothing to intervene. A rot starts to overtake him, grey green, leprous, his skin begins to putrefy, then to slough off, his fingers, his arms bony, his face tightening, shriveling into a skull, caught in a perpetual scream that will never happen. He lays dead.

And god help me, I knock on the wall. She seeps in like mist, ethereal as she is. All curves and lines and sacred geometry, she unzips me and she gets on top. She feels so warm and yet so very cold. It hurts inside her. I hurt inside her. And she speaks.

WOEFUL CITY

"Through me you come to the City of Woe,
Through me you reach eternal pain
Through me among the lost you go

Justice moved the maker who would reign
Unstoppable from year to year to year
Wisdom high and love that shall not wane

Before my coming nothing could appear
That's not eternal, eternally I endure
Leave your hope behind if you'd enter here"

And I float. And I feel these things that led me to the place, witness the moments, weigh my heart. And I get ready to drift.

But then there is laughter.

"So you come here and you think love and death are the same and you think pain and joy are the same and you come here and you're ready to sleep and you're so damn weary from all this fun you've had that you just want to relax like that mound of meat next door?"

My mind walks again to coffins, to dead girls, to models who want to be cut and though my head feels heavy, I manage a nod.

"Yes."

She shakes her head, she slides off of me.

"Walk it off, asshole."

Garrett Cook is an author of Horror, Bizarro and Cosmic Horror fiction. He has appeared in Best Bizarro Fiction of the Decade, Exquisite Corpse, Giallo Fantastique *and more. He is the editor-in-chief of the New Bizarro Author series and co-creator of* Imperial Youth Review. *Most recently, his novella* Archelon Ranch *was reprinted by Rooster Republic Press.*

RITCHIE

ERIC J. GUIGNARD

I'M BOUND IN a wheelchair now, a quadriplegic. No one survives this much paralyzation to reach old age, and I know my health will just keep deteriorating slowly and miserably until I die. All that's left is to wonder what will get me: Pneumonia? Septicemia? Suffocation?

Or will it be Ritchie? I can't say which is worse. My injuries will take me slow, which is lousy to imagine, but Ritchie would . . . *would what*? Sure as hell be quicker than this condition, but what he might do to me, I'm terrified to consider. He's probably picked up a list of ideas over the years to torture me with, maybe even some of them I've done on him. There's just so many possibilities, so many stinkin' ways of revenge he might pull off, half of which I can't even imagine.

See, I never was the brightest bulb anyway, which is maybe why Ritchie and I were always at each other's throats. We were too much alike, just dumb and angsty and unwilling to back down.

I knew Ritchie since I was twelve years old. I transferred across Texas to Eagle Crest Junior High that year, and he was in my class, a year older than the other kids 'cause he'd flunked a grade. He seemed to hold his failings against everyone else, especially me for no other reason than I was the new kid and my 'D minus' average was the envy of his 'F plus' aptitude. Ritchie was fat, and his zits were like little red candies stuck all over a cream pie face. He didn't look intimidating and he sounded even less so, whiny with a voice that cracked whenever he raised it, which happened pretty much every time he spoke. He wasn't a bully by your classic standard—no over-muscled build, no pack of leather jacket cronies—but he knew how

RITCHIE

to make your life a living hell. In that regard he was head of the class. Ritchie Turdamczyk was his full name. I called him Ritchie the Turd.

And Jackson Offerman is my name, so it's no great leap of junior high wit to bastardize that one.

"Hey, Jack Off," Ritchie said, and pushed me hard against the lockers. "What'd you bring me for lunch?"

"Your mom's scabies," I answered and pushed him back.

"That comeback's older than the crust in your underwear," he countered with a harder push, throwing his flab into it.

"And you're the one dreaming about what's inside my underwear!" I punched Ritchie in the jaw, barely fazing him.

He punched me in the stomach, and my air went out. I gasped, then I hit him harder, this time in the nose. That stung him. His face wrinkled up and he cried out. Then we were rolling on the ground, kid punches thrown that didn't amount to much but for scrapes and the calling of more names.

Teachers broke us up, but our fight carried over the next day, and the next after that. People said I had something to prove, being the new kid and all. But I didn't. I was just defending myself, not wanting to get pushed around by some lardass punk.

I heard later in life that if you stand up to a bully they'll leave you alone. Psychologists say the tormentor will either start to respect you or they figure you're not worth the trouble and go off searching for someone easier to pick on. But it wasn't like that with Ritchie. The more I stood up for myself, the more it incited him to get at me; the taunts and pranks became crueler, more frequent. It seemed like I was feeding him. Maybe in his case, if I'd just ignored him, he would have left me alone. Although maybe if I'd ignored him, he'd have thought me weak and found even more ways to torment me. Maybe he'd have killed *me* instead. Maybe it would have saved me from my present lingering torment . . .

One time Ritchie got a bunch of pictures of Mr. Bovard, the school janitor, doing normal stuff, sweeping the walkways, emptying trash, eating lunch on his cart. Ritchie stabbed the eyes out in each picture and drew red lines across the necks. He got into my locker somehow and taped all those pictures inside. Then he jammed a toothpick inside the lock so when it came time to go to class I couldn't get it open.

Of course, I had to get Mr. Bovard's help.

When Mr. Bovard got my locker open and saw all those pictures of himself inside, he nearly ripped my arms from their sockets.

Ritchie was a bastard, made my life Hell.

When I was sixteen, my folks got me a car for Christmas. I'm not saying we were rich and they whipped out a credit card to gift wrap a Camaro or something. My old man was tighter than a rusted lug nut, and I normally got socks and tighty-whities for the holidays. But it really meant something to him and my mom that I stayed in school and mostly out of trouble. They were both drop-outs. So they saved for awhile and surprised me with a used '78 AMC Pacer. Its timing belt squealed louder than a fire alarm, and it was missing its rear windshield.

On that last point, Dad clapped me on the shoulder and said, "Think of it as an instant convertible."

The car wasn't what you'd call a "chick magnet", but it made me grown-up. No more walking six miles to school, no more asking Mom for a ride to hang out at the mall.

But when Ritchie saw my ride, the leaking oil spots lost all their luster.

"*Ho-lee shit*," he said. "Look at Prince Jack Off. How's the weather up in your mansion on the hills?"

I flipped him the bird, walking from the parking lot. White exhaust fumes followed me from that rattle bucket, but Ritchie acted like I was a debutante.

He bowed as I passed. "Spoon-fed prince, coming through."

I wanted to punch him. But what had that solved before? For once, I tried the highest road I could manage. "What's your problem, Ritchie? Just get off my ass, okay? You go your way and I'll go mine."

"Sure, you'll *drive* your way out. Must be nice, getting a car from mommy and daddy."

"Prick," I called him.

"Rich bitch," he shot back.

Later that day I found an egg had been thrown at my car, its dried yolk splattered in a wide arc across the door. It was only the first of many to come.

Over the next year, we weathered our ups-and-downs, the "ups" meaning we weren't at each other's throats, the "downs" being the school principal or police getting involved. All this fighting culminated in Ritchie's death. And it was me who killed him. March 15 was the day, *the Ides of March*, the day men consider unlucky to die, as if you care about superstition once you're six feet under.

I was seventeen when it happened, nearing the end of eleventh grade. Ritchie the Turd must've kept the hen business running single-handedly, 'cause not a day went by that I didn't catch an egg with my car. Sometimes it'd be before school, sometimes at lunch, sometimes when I'd pull out of the parking lot thinking I'd made it yolk-free, an ovoid missile would come firing at my windshield. I'd beaten his ass a dozen times for it, but Ritchie never gave up. He'd even know when I was going to chase him, and he'd lay a trap. One time he hid behind a corner, and I raced after him only to feel the impact of a bag of dog crap shower my back after I passed his point of ambush.

This particular instance he'd been right in front of me when I was pulling out of the parking lot. Like a rabid dog he sprang from the school's hedges and smacked the windshield with another one of those goddamned eggs. My fury peaked, and I meant to hit the brakes so that I could get out and knock him unconscious. I really meant it . . . but I hit the gas pedal instead. I accelerated and spread Ritchie Turdamczyk all over the boulevard.

I didn't end up in jail or juvie afterward; the judge ruled it an unfortunate accident, but those knowing of his and mine's history still blamed me. All the years of suffering with Ritchie were for nothing: The guilt broke me, and I ended up dropping out of school after all.

A year passed, and life became the pits. I turned eighteen and my folks kicked me out. I still had the Pacer, but no home. I slept on a buddy's couch some nights and in the car's seat others. I was miserable and reviled and lonely. Worse even than Ritchie's taunts was the feeling of being ostracized. *The Classmate Killer,* I was called.

Then comes the following March 15, mid-afternoon, about the time I would have been pulling out of my school's parking lot had I still been in attendance. Only now I was in the kitchen of a flop house making a gallon of cherry-flavored Kool-Aid.

A voice I'll know 'til the end of days spoke. "Hey, Jack Off, I got an egg with yer name on it."

Ritchie.

I turned, fully expecting to see nothin' out of the ordinary. I was just hearing things after all, maybe a bit too much of the reefer . . .

But there he stood, same as he appeared a year ago, fat and covered in bad acne and smashed to hell from being run over. The right side of his face looked like an artist had painted it fresh in acrylics and then ran his thumb all the way across, so his features slid back two or three inches. A couple ribs broke through the rags of his chest and one arm was snapped in a dozen places, so it jiggled and shook as he advanced like a chain of iron links swinging in motion. But when Ritchie smiled, that was the worst; he bared a mouth of broken teeth like how a kid might draw the grin of an evil shark, all jagged angles.

I screamed. Swear to God, the only time in my life I've ever shrieked like a girl in a horror flick was that instant, seeing Ritchie shamble toward me, a ghost or ghoul or zombie or whatever you could call him. Ritchie raised his arms, fingers outstretched as if he was going to gouge out my eyes the way he did Mr. Bovard's pictures.

But there on the kitchen counter was a cutlery block and I grabbed the largest blade in reach. Without thinking, I thrust the knife out in front of me, fast into his chest, pulled out, thrust again and again, stabbing and stabbing, all the while still screaming.

And Ritchie screamed back. I *hurt* him. Here he was already dead, and me stabbing him was like I was killing him all over. Before his eyes rolled up, he showed a look of absolute perplexity, like maybe he was surprised that his vengeance had been checked, that he could still feel pain . . . I don't know.

Ritchie fell back, crumpling to the floor, his outstretched fingers now clutching his punctured chest, blood spurting from each knife wound, though how he could bleed after being run over—and already dead for a year—was a bewilderment. His cream pic face paled even more, and tears fell from his eyes, and he gasped out one parting farewell: "*Fuck you.*"

Then he was rotting away like watching one of those shows in science class, how they speed up the process of decomposition. His broken-ribbed torso melted into itself, limbs shrunk and withered away. He was drying up, turning to dust or vapor or whatever happens to . . . to things like that.

RITCHIE

Talk about a defining moment in life. If there was ever something needed to make a man rise above the maelstrom of his shitstorm life, it's having the kid he killed come back for revenge. I mean, there I'd fallen, sobbing on the floor of a flop house, and no one ever checked on me; no one cares about derelicts. So I decided right then, I'd never put up with crap like that again, never let myself fall to pieces, never again let my life be for nothing.

So I joined the army. They didn't care I was a drop-out, a loser with no prospects, *The Classmate Killer*. Did my basic at Fort Jackson, even went on to get a specialty as a cavalry scout at Fort Knox. One year after I'd been couch surfing in a flop house I was defending oil fields in Saudi Arabia.

March 15: the day arrived and I didn't think twice about it. Getting shot at and bombed by battle-trained soldiers can push yesteryear's recollections far from one's mind . . . I was so worried about the foreign enemy, I didn't think about that personal one.

But Ritchie came back. *Again.*

Over that past year, the seldom times I *had* thought about the return of his ghost, I decided it'd been in my mind. Madness, really, brought on by depression, dope, hunger. But I was clear-focused now. So clear-focused that when Ritchie appeared while I was on Forward Observation, I sighted and triggered two bullets through his forehead without hesitation.

Then I watched him do that decomposition thing like last time, and I couldn't stop trembling. *He'd come back . . .*

I promised myself the next time I wouldn't be caught unprepared. I took R&R the following year so I could be alone should Ritchie make his anniversary return.

Which he did.

I waited for him far off the grid, in the middle of a desert wasteland with a clear line of sight in all directions. A Beretta M9 pistol and a Ka-Bar knife were holstered at opposite hips. Good ol' bullets and steel, effective at killing Iraqis and, apparently, at killing haunts. Mid-afternoon and Ritchie just sort of materialized about twenty feet away, looking busted to hell and with an added pair of bullet holes in his forehead to top off the damage I'd done from previous years.

"Jack Off . . . " he said, his voice strained and wispy. "Jack Off, I'll get you back . . . someday, I swear . . . "

"It was an accident, Ritchie. You ran out in front of my car."

"Bullshit. You drove over me on purpose . . ."

Man, regret is a heavy load, a knapsack on your back that someone keeps dropping bricks into when you're not paying attention, until all of a sudden you stagger under its weight.

"I wish I could take it back," I said. "I swear on everything holy, I wish I could."

"Prince Jack Off . . . always thought you was better'n me, better grades, more money, more friends."

"Hell with that! I didn't have any of those things, Ritchie. I was the same as you, a nobody."

"No . . . you got what I wanted, all I ever fuckin' wanted was to leave that shithole town and start over, somewhere no one knew me . . . I was stuck there, trapped at Eagle Crest, trapped in east Texas, everyone despised me for years . . . " Ritchie's wrecked face quivered like he was going to cry, his pale, lopsided eyes bulging, than narrowing, unsure whether to let the tears flow or not. "Nothing worse . . . knowing every single person around you has cut you somehow, and you got to see them day after day, the jeers echoing on each face . . . and here you come, someone with a fresh slate . . . should've been me . . . should've been me . . . "

"I was only a kid, I didn't have any say in the matter!" I felt shocked, beyond overwhelmed at what he'd said, the asininity of what people lay on you for fault. "My old man lost his job, we had to move so he could start work again. I *hated* moving, I had friends I left behind—"

"Oh play me a fuckin' fiddle, you had friends. I *never* had a friend!"

And when Ritchie shrieked, I saw those broken teeth inside his mouth, all ivory razors with stains on them from drinking too much cola or chewin' bubble gum or maybe it was dried blood from being run over, I don't know.

He raised his arms at me again, fingers outstretched like how he did in the flophouse kitchen, like he was going to gouge out my eyes, rip out my tongue, tear my face the way a raptor rends its prey with talons.

I pulled my Beretta. "This is how it's gonna go, Ritchie. This haunting business is done. Go back to whatever pit of Hell you crawled out from, or I'm going to pop you again, first in the knees, then the elbows. I know you still feel pain."

"I do," Ritchie said. "Pain and loneliness . . . " and he started blubbering. Fat tears poured down his smashed face, rolling over zits, falling into gaping wounds. He sunk to the ground, crying and crying.

"Oh God, man, I'm sorry," I said. I holstered the gun and took a step tentatively to him.

Ritchie looked up to me and bawled like a baby. "I'm sorry too . . ."

He held his arms up wide, offering a hug, one of those arms jangling around from all the busted bones. I suddenly felt he was just this broken doll-child I wanted to comfort, wanted to relieve of all his hurt, all his torment. I moved to Ritchie and accepted his embrace.

. . . and he grabbed the back of my head and bit into my throat with those shattered teeth. I screamed, not from fear, but from rage: *Even in death, Ritchie the Turd had laid a trap for me.*

I wrenched backward, a geyser of blood freed at my throat. Next came those fingers slashing for my eyes, as I'd expected all along. I twisted away in time, but as his hand trailed past my face, he caught my ear. Those talons trenched into my temple ripping my left ear half off my head. If I would have backed from him anymore, I'd have completed the dismemberment myself.

Instead I drove forward with my head, smashing it into the bridge of Ritchie's nose. He yelped, and let go of my ear and his hand went to his face. For a moment we were kids again, trading punches that didn't amount to much. This time though, it'd be brawling to the death.

Ritchie laughed, a horrible twang coming from his busted nose, his ruined mouth, his chest full of holes. "How's that taste, Jack Off?"

I already felt weaker, blood flowing from my neck, wondering if he'd chewed out an artery. But I wasn't done yet. "Tastes like this, douchebag!"

I pulled my gun but didn't shoot—naw, that'd be too easy. I held it by the barrel and started pummeling his face. He went to screaming and crying and beggin' for mercy, but I remembered those crocodile tears from earlier, and by then it was too late anyway. Once I started, I couldn't stop. Ritchie's head was a jack-o'-lantern that'd been left on the porch a month after Halloween's passed, just all rotten and pulpy inside. The Beretta went up and down, up and down into him, crushing it all, what was left of his face, his skull, 'til nothing remained but how a candle looks on its holder after it's melted out: a bit of wick and a puddle of red wax splashed all around.

I let Ritchie fall, and his body started withering and fading as it'd done before. I felt about to faint, but my heart was pounding, and adrenaline alone got me moving. I managed to get to my jeep and make for help.

When I came to, I had thirteen stitches in my neck and the top of my left ear was missing. I told the doctors I'd been attacked by enemy insurgents and fought them off, and saved a kidnapped boy in the process.

Of course, no one could find that boy or any of the four soldiers I'd claimed to have killed. My story didn't make sense, but it'd be even less sense should I tell the truth. I was called a War Hero and returned to active duty.

Besides that one fib, I was a good soldier, but six months later the war ended, so I was discharged. Went home to Texas and became a deputy sheriff in the very same town I'd first killed Ritchie Turdamczyk. People didn't call me *The Classmate Killer* anymore; I was now *War Hero*, I was *Sir*.

And as a deputy, I protected others and I served as obliged, but all the while thinking about March 15 . . . dreading March 15 . . .

It came, inexorably and dreadfully, just like Ritchie himself. No one else would have known it was Ritchie but me, that lardass wobbling toward me on shattered limbs, blood and guts smeared everywhere, his head gone. Above his neck was just a broken jaw; everything higher than that mashed away to oblivion.

"Anything to say to me this time, Ritchie? Any parting jabs, any more taunts?" I asked. "You got anything, *Turd?*"

Ritchie didn't reply as he staggered toward me, just nodded the remnants of his jaw up and down the way a chicken waggles its gullet.

"Here's an egg for you, Ritchie, a big shiny egg," I said and showed what I'd brought for his fourth unholy visit: a felling axe with a five-pound head on a thirty-two-inch hickory shaft.

"This is for my car." I swung that axe into his leg, right at mid-thigh. The blow knocked Ritchie over, and he fell like a sack of potatoes, all lumpy with things rolling around inside. I chopped again, severing off the leg entirely. Crimson poured out, regardless that I'd killed him four times already.

I sank the axe into his chest, shattering whatever ribs remained. "Let's see you come back next year on one leg."

And he did.

The fucker came hopping for me while I was on an emergency call. I told my partner, Deputy Reaves, that I was going to circle around an alley to flush out a burglary suspect. Instead, when I was alone, I used my taser gun to incapacitate Ritchie, then my baton to beat the shit out of him until he dissipated for another year, all the while wishing I'd chopped off the other leg and both his arms last year when I had the axe.

Are all men somehow haunted by those they've slain? I never spoke to any of the other soldiers about it, and I didn't know any killers—accidental or otherwise. Guessin' everyone deals in their own way, not like there's a support group for vengeful ghost murderers. But why did only Ritchie come back? I'd killed a dozen or more in the army, and put down a rapist with a knife while on the police force. *But only Ritchie . . .*

Like I said before, I never was the brightest bulb. I do know it's considered unlucky to be killed on the Ides of March, so maybe that was it, the day Caesar got murdered by the people he was closest to . . . only had Ritchie been closest to me, the one who paid him most attention?

And that got me thinking about old *MAD* magazines. There was a comic strip in each issue, a recurring gag called *Spy vs. Spy*, in which two beak-nosed characters were always fighting each other, tricking the other until one got killed.

You never knew why they were at odds against the other, just took for granted they were mirror images of themselves, but that one was colored white and one was colored black, so that made them enemies, always at each other's throats, like me and Ritchie. Every month one of them would die by a new means, a new trick or taunt: gun, bomb, pit of sharks.

Next year I'm gonna dissolve Ritchie in a tank of acid . . .

And I would have, but would even acid have ended it?

See, as the next March 15 approached, something snapped in me. I'd been having a shitty few weeks: A man who beat dogs got freed in court over a technicality I loused up. A girl I was dating left me, because I screamed Ritchie's name every night in dreams. I was sick and miserable with politics and foul weather and heavy debt.

When the Turd next came hopping for me, I'd cleared out the garage and welcomed him in. I handcuffed him to a chair bolted to the floor and took out all my angst and aggression and despair that had bottled up over recent events. A pair of his fingers went off with gardening shears; salt was poured over the stump of his head; I used an electric drill in the small of his back, then a welding torch, then a stapler. Ritchie writhed and spasmed but didn't make a sound. Man, I had more planned, using him as the outlet for my unhappiness, but then he gave that final shudder and rotted away from the chair. I guess that was all his undead body could take for the year.

Next time, I'll draw it out even longer.

And I did. Years passed in that way, and it became easier, more thrilling, something I grew to look forward to, the way a child might look forward to the adventure of opening gifts come Christmas time. Oh, March 15 in my garage came a time to cherish, just cleansing and renewing me for a new year.

For a decade that went on, and Ritchie kept coming back for more, what was left of him anyway, crawling to me like a great rotten worm. I'd find new ways to torture him, new ways to kill him, and still he'd return. And maybe that was me in school, in Ritchie's eyes: Thinking I'd just go away if he tormented me, yet I came back day after day, 'cause that's what a kid in school does, isn't it? That's what a cursed soul does, the terribleness of having to repeat that which we loathe, which we fear, which causes us pain.

And I thought: *I beat you, Ritchie. I killed you, and I'm still living. I kill you every year, and I love it. I'm a war hero, an officer of the law, people respect me, I make good money . . . I* am *better than you!*

But then he got me back, like he always did. I had a good run toppin' him, though like *Spy vs. Spy*, the adversary keeps returning until he gets his revenge, and then the battle wages on another day, and there ain't any end in sight.

Truth be told, I'd taken to doing some crazy shit, and my sanity probably would have soon snapped anyway. I'd amputated his good arm and taken his other leg, jammed bottle rockets up his ass, flayed him, and worse. Only limb he had left was the arm that'd snapped in a dozen places when I ran over him, the one that swung loose like a chain of iron links when he lifted it. Only two fingers remained in its hand, one of those missing the knuckles and held in place with a twist tie. Really, he was half a skeleton by then. I could lift him same as a baby, and I did, dressing him in doll clothes and carrying him around the house.

I'd prop him up on the couch, watch football on TV together, use him for a dartboard. I'd pour beer down his throat, try and make Ritchie's remains get drunk, and then masturbate in his lap. *Jack Off*, I'd imagine him whispering, and that'd make me smile.

See, lording it over a monster makes you feel invulnerable. I'd grown lax, taken for granted his scheming ways.

That day I had to take a piss, and I left him unattended in the living room. I mean, what could he do, right? But when I returned, the room was in shambles. Tables upended, a crack in the TV screen, books, cushions flung everywhere, the telephone knocked over, the beer knocked over, plates thrown, everything broken, spilled, trashed. And there was Ritchie just laying in the middle of it all, his chest thumping like he'd exerted himself too much, one of those last two fingers upraised to flip me the bird.

"Oh, Ritchie, you done it now. You fuckin' turd, I'm going to hurt you. I'm gonna rape your stumps, rip out your bowels and strangle you with them. You're a screwed pooch when you suffocate by your own intestines, huh? The last smell by your own crap, even if your nose is gone, *ha ha*! I'm gonna boil you in vinegar, piss on your bones . . . "

I grabbed his hand and dragged him into the garage and went to work on him.

That sneaky bastard . . . little did I know, when Ritchie wrecked the living room, he'd dialed 9-1-1 with the last good finger of his shattered arm. The rest of the destruction was just camouflage so I wouldn't notice the phone's receiver had been knocked off the cradle.

Seems the 9-1-1 operator heard my rant and dispatched an emergency alert to the police right away.

Ironic thing, they were my own department that showed up, officers I'd been working alongside for ten years tipped to the fact that someone was being tortured and killed in my house.

Ritchie's final trap. They kicked down the door right when I had a scalpel inside the Turd's lungs, all covered in his blood. I still don't know where his blood came from, but it was everywhere. My partner, Deputy Reaves, was among the responders, and his face paled white as Ritchie's exposed thighbone.

"Jackson, drop the knife!"

"No, no, he started it!" I cried out defensively, pulling the scalpel free.

Ritchie started convulsing and his hand jerked up, like he was trying to jab me.

"Not this time, Turd," I said, and slid the blade through his shattered ribs into the black lump that was his heart.

To their credit, my brothers in blue used rubber bullets. Better though, they'd have used live rounds.

One of the first shots spun me, and another round smashed the fourth vertebrae of my spine. It was a fluke, doctors told me afterward, a freak accident that turned me into a quadriplegic.

But I'd gotten Ritchie again, at least for another year. He withered and vanished so fast that the officers—my friends and partners—saw nothing more than one of their own, lying perfectly still on the floor and raving half-mad.

So here I wait, as another year's passed, all the while thinking 'bout the ghost that's coming and not knowing what it's going to do when it gets here, only that it'll be bad, real fuckin' bad, a whole lifetime of bad that it thinks it owes.

And maybe I do owe it to him, whatever's coming, maybe I owe him a whole lifetime that he didn't get. Maybe if I don't suffer it now, I'll pay more the dearer in Hell. Or maybe Ritchie'll have learned mercy, finally give it up, let bygones be bygones, though that's as likely as me walking again. Like it or not, I'll wish I was dead as him, and if there was a way to kill myself I would.

So here I sit in this wheelchair, frozen from the neck down, waiting for tomorrow to come. He's got no head, no legs, one busted arm, only one good finger. I don't know how he'll get his vengeance, but he'll come up with something.

After all, it's Ritchie.

Eric J. Guignard is a writer and editor of dark and speculative fiction, operating from the shadowy outskirts of Los Angeles. His works have appeared in publications such as Nightmare Magazine, Black Static, Shock Totem, Buzzy Magazine, *and* Dark Discoveries Magazine. *He's won the Bram Stoker Award, been a finalist for the International Thriller Writers Award, and a multi-nominee of the Pushcart Prize. Outside the glamorous and jet-setting world of indie fiction, Eric's a technical writer and college professor, and he stumbles home each day to a wife, children, cats, and a terrarium filled with mischievous beetles. Visit Eric at www.ericjguignard.com, his blog: ericjguignard.blogspot.com, or Twitter: @ericjguignard.*

I'D GIVE ANYTHING FOR YOU

JACK KETCHUM AND EDWARD LEE

"**PLEASE, PLEASE DON'T** do this to us, Clare!" Roderic pleaded from the imported flagstone steps of the great house.

Us, Clare thought. *Thirty years old and still living with his mother. Jesus!*

His voice called out nasal and forlorn behind her. "I'd give anything for you!"

How many times had she heard that in the last nine months? Big deal! She wanted to shout. *Can't you take a hint? There's nothing I want from you!* Instead, she turned.

"Look. It's not working out," she said.

He looked befuddled.

"What are you taking about? Things are great! You said you'd marry me!"

"Oh Roderic, I did not," she lied.

Early on, eight long months ago, that was exactly what she'd said. At thirty-one, she wasn't getting any younger. And Roderic had millions. Or, rather, his mother did.

"I'm sorry. I just can't see you anymore."

He went utterly vapid. "Is it . . . another guy?"

"Of course not!" she lied again. How dare he accuse her of sleeping around!

Anyway, Wardell wasn't just another guy. He was everything Roderic wasn't. Strong, handsome, assertive. And hung like fucking Dillinger.

She opened the door to the 300ZX—a birthday present from Roderic—and slid in.

"But what about Paris?"

She'd considered it. Paris might be fun. Except that Roderic's mother was going, too, and so was Fudd—that old lady's hoodlum manservant.

To hell with Paris. Wardell would be taking her to Cancun anyway after his next big score.

"Roderic, forget Paris. Our relationship is over. Get it?"

Obviously he didn't. But Fudd did. The guy was lurking by the side of the house in his long leather jacket, stacking a cord of firewood, dividing each round cut with one of those automatic log splitters. And the look he shot her said he'd be happy to split her neatly down the middle too. If anything, Fudd was loyal.

Mama apparently got the message, too. Clare could see her distain pouring through the sitting room window.

Goddamn crinkled old weirdo.

Hell, they were all weirdoes.

"Darling, please come back inside. We'll sit by the fire, I'll open the Louis XIII. Please!"

For God's sake, he was crying now.

"Please, I—"

"I know, Roderic. You'd give anything for me. No, thanks." She slammed the door and started up the car.

"Tell me!" He was sniffling outside the window. "Tell me what I can do to prove my love for you!"

Go play in traffic, she thought. *How about that? You romantic putz.*

She pulled out of the driveway. In the rearview mirror she saw him fall to his knees in Shakespearean anguish, his mother coming through the double oak doors and down off the porch to comfort him. Fudd glaring.

Poor Roderic, she thought. The man just didn't have a clue.

Wardell did.

She'd just walked into the apartment and already the deft, strong hands were unbuttoning her blouse, his tongue roving her mouth in greeting.

"You break the news to the wimp?"

She nodded. Now that it was over she felt a little guilty.

"God! He was devastated. I'm surprised he didn't take back the car."

His hands shucked off the blouse and pawed her naked breasts. "He can't take back the car. He put it in your name for chrissake, remember? The dumb little creamcake asshole."

"Well, you can bet he won't be paying the rent anymore."

Wardell had his penis out already, which he often referred to as "Papa Fuck" or "Mr. Meat Missile." Wardell was not subtle.

"Fuck him and fuck his mama's money. Couple days, my next big score comes in and we'll be rollin' in it. Gimme that ass, babe. Over here."

He stripped off her jeans and led her onto the couch, got down on his knees, and began those oral preludes which never failed to grease his skids. His tongue was not particular about which orifice it tended. It tended each and it tended well. In moments she was lost in raging heat.

It launched her into another world—a great big wet wonderful tongue world where she was the queen and sensation was her daily homage. The cleft of Clare's ass became a playground, and Wardell's tongue was the troupe of kids swinging from the monkey bars. It was hard to think of butt-licking with any notion of sophistication; nevertheless, Wardell proved a master, wielding his skills with a brazen expertise. His hot tongue laved, and prodded, licked and titillated, drew sloppy, wet swirls about that sensitive little starburst.

"Like it when I lick your asshole, huh?"

Clare staked to the couch with her feet pinned back behind her ears, could fathom no response to her lover's less-than-urbane inquiry. Instead, she moaned and sighed, then abruptly shuddered when—

"But now I think I'll have me a taste of this here pie."

—his tongue re-navigated itself to a northerly direction. Her anus, evidently, was but an appetizer; now it was time for the entree. Clare whined at the avalanche of feeling, a sudden spike of swoony, pulsing pleasure which staked her hips fast to the couch. Her pussy felt separately enlivened, a furred, pink-blushing icon which revealed at the worship of its congregation—in this instance, Wardell's mouth. His tongue slid hard up and down over the olive-sized clitoris; his mouth sucked the free-flowing fluids out of her pussy like fruit juice from a straw. He sucked so intensely that Clare thought the delicious suction might actually relocate her uterus to the couch cushion.

"Ooo, you big hot wonderful love-tongue, you!" she wailed. "Eat my pussy till I'm cross-eyed!"

But, of course, she already was cross-eyed. She was stupefied, enraptured, enfrenzied. Currents of pleasure speared her ass to the couch. Her clit felt plugged into a wall socket as she moaned her bliss to an empty ceiling. Her first climax erupted with the impact of a five-ton wrecking ball striking a dam. The dam broke, and out gushed its reservoir. Her pussy pulsed like a cock coming, like a great big throbbing dick shooting wild plumes of sperm . . .

"Here's a little something to help you forget that mama-rich dickhead, honey."

This, of course, was a meiotic—it was not a little something. Clare often thought of Wardell's crotch as a Burger King: Home of the Whopper. His cock was a masterpiece, a thing of mystic beauty while at the same time frightening because of its size.

He flipped her to hands and knees and, with no further overture, buried himself in her.

"I dare you to think about him with my dick stuffed up your snatch," he said.

And she couldn't. Not with Mr. Meat Missile prodding the bulb of her cervix. Not with Papa Fuck plumbing the deepest regions of her womanly hole. She reached down under him and fondled testicles which felt as large of cue balls.

What a fuckin' man! she thought.

Machinelike, his cock pistoned in and out. Each stroke quaked her, retracted her sex and beat the air out of her lungs.

"Oh yes," she moaned. "Yes! All the way in as hard as you can!"

With a snide grunt, Wardell obliged. To Clare it felt as though Wardell had just unreeled another three or four inches of hard cock into her slot. It was an excruciating mix of pain and mind-boggling pleasure. His cock was coring her like an apple.

"Uh-huh," Wardell promised. "I'll be bustin' my baby a big nut up this cooze. Honey, I'm gonna crack a load in you so hard my spunk'll be squirtin' out yer nose. You'll need the biggest hanky in the world."

Then—

Mid-stroke and midway to the gate for both of them, the telephone rang.

The answering machine kicked in. "Hello, this is Clare, I'm not home right now so please leave a . . . "

"Jesus Christ, you gotta be fucking kidding me," Wardell said.

BEEEEEEEEEEEEEEEEEEP.

No, no, no, thought Clare, *please, please don't let it be . . .*

"I'd do anything, darling," Roderic said, his voice drippy, weepy, sniffly, and disgusting. "I'd give anything for you . . . "

Wardell hadn't much cared for the telephonic coitus interruptus. So he'd worked off his lack of amusement at the expense of Clare's physical real estate. Not that she objected. Her orgasms ensured without abatement, in multiple fashion. What Wardell lacked in sophistication he more than made up for in cocksmanship. Other than that, she knew next to nothing about him. He'd never elaborated on his occupational pursuits, claiming simply to be a "salesman," and Clare never asked what he sold—though she doubted its legal status. He was muscular and brusque and incredibly handsome. Also very . . . enduring. And for her, right now, that was enough.

That night, though, she slept fitfully.

Roderic consumed her dreams. Roderic, who wrote poetry all day long and doted on his mother—whose wealth, she had once read in *Forbes*, ran to the mid-eight figures—who would pick her up in his conservative gray BMW and take her to the best clubs, restaurants, and shows, who would bring her gifts every week—jewelry, mostly—pay her rent, buy her a car, and leave delightful little cash envelopes beneath her pillow. Not bad for a girl nearing the far side of the hill, but . . .

. . . she guessed it was his mother. Crimp-faced, rouged, and paper-thin. Eternally sarcastic. He'd bring her home to the mansion sometimes for "romantic" little chats by the fire, snifters of Cordon Bleu, and—disappointingly for Clare—pre-ejaculatory sex, and his mother would always be there when they arrived, nodding curtly from the sitting room and offering some cryptic remark like "I hope you're taking good care of my boy," or "Good boys like my Roderic are easily taken for granted, missy," always calculated to be discreetly rude. *Fuck you,* Clare would think, and offer up a smile instead. For Mama.

It was no way to live.

To make matters worse, Fudd was always there too—about as cheerful as a mugshot. Never saying a word, all black glances and subtle scowls, skulking around in black leather driver's cap, mitts, and long-tailed jacket. She wondered how much the old hag was paying him to keep her ancient pussy stocked with pork.

The implication was clear: Mama Roderic would overlook Clare's gold-digging as long as she "took good care" of her "boy."

It was difficult, and it wasn't. On the one hand, Roderic was a loving, compassionate, romantic man. He was also fat and slack-muscled, pale as a fish belly, with a small, pathetic weenie that tended to give up its seed long before any serious amalgamation of genitals could be made.

Once while necking she had made the mistake of brushing his groin with the tips of her fingers. *Oooops,* he'd said. And showed her the wet spot on his custom-made Italian slacks.

On nights they actually made it to bed, he would usually have to apologize for the milky puddle on her belly moments after getting naked. "You excite me so much I just can't help it," he would tell her. There was no point sucking a dick that had spent its freight before she could even get it into her mouth. So that was out. And his own oral gestures proved equally futile, usually like a kitten lapping milk.

Which left her with her finger.

No. After nine months, restaurants and cold cash simply didn't cut it anymore—and Fudd and Roderic's mother coming with the package as they so obviously did only hastened her decision.

Besides, by then she had met Wardell. Who knew how to fill all the places Roderic left empty. *I owe it to myself,* she thought, *as a modern woman, to pursue my spiritual, sociological, and personal well-being. As well as the gigantic cock.*

Why couldn't Roderic understand? They simply weren't right for each other.

She didn't wish him any harm. She truly hoped he'd meet some frigid little blue-blood one day and live happily ever after. But . . .

She knew that some men would pine over a lost love for years. Become obsessive. Go to . . . extremes.

She hoped that wouldn't happen here. But maybe that was what scared her a little. Because there was something about poor little jilted Roderic that haunted her. Something deep in his eyes and in that forlorn, desperate promise of his . . .

. . . I would give anything for you.

Please Roderic, she thought, *whatever you've got to give, take it elsewhere.*

"Hey, love muffin," Wardell had awakened and was nudging her with something other than his hand.

It was an excellent distraction, and Clare was grateful. She provided a welcome silo. Her mouth. All that burgeoning cock inside her, the glans big as a baby apple.

"God, woman! You sure can suck good peter! Get it, sugar! Suck all that red-hot pecker-snot right out of that cock!"

Quaint.

But she did. Slipped a pinky into his ass to prod the overlarge prostate as his testicles jettisoned yet another copious ration of semen. And, at exactly the same moment, thought of Roderic.

Jesus, Roderic! Go away!

I'd give anything for you.

That goddamn promise. What did he mean?

What would he give?

His fortune? His inheritance?

His life?

Jesus Christ, she hoped not. She didn't think she was ready for that at all. Definitely not. But you had to think about it. Was the crazy little sonofabitch going to try to prove something?

Was Roderic suicidal?

Nah.

Even if he was, there'd be Fudd and Mama to tie him down for six years if necessary. Until he got over it.

No problem.

Except that he phoned every day. Luckily, he tended to do that while Wardell was out, taking care of his "salesman" duties. But she started to hate the sound of her phone ringing.

Please come back darling, darling please, please, we were meant to be together, I would give anything in the world for you darling please . . . Good God!

Clare would never answer. But his calls were crowding her answering machine.

And at night he haunted her dreams.

Roderic in a tub, his slit wrists leaking cloudy red. Blue-faced in his BMW in a closed garage. Gunshot, poisoned, hanged by the neck.

His mother made scowling cameos. Shadowed by leather-clad Fudd, gloved hands opening and closing into creaking fists. "You take good care of my boy, missy," the dream-crone nattered. " . . . you take good care of my boy, good care of my . . . "

Each nightmare ended the same. Roderic's corpse, the black mouth opening wide, filled with pus and maggots, the death-rattle voice. "I'd give anything for you."

Wardell became the vehicle of her oblivion. She resolved to fuck and suck the little twerp right out of her brain. And that was fine until, exhausted, she eventually fell asleep. There he was.

"I'd give anything . . . "

One morning Wardell was in the shower, whistling "Love Me Tender," when the phone rang. Clare snatched it up.

"Roderic, stop calling me!"

"Clare, please," he whined. "Talk to me. Listen, I want you to come over."

"No!"

"Wait! Don't hang up! Listen to me. Mother and Fudd have gone to Paris for two weeks. We'd have the whole place to ourselves. Please!"

"I don't want to come over. I don't want to ever see you again! Get it?"

"Buh-buh-but . . . I love you! At least tell me why—"

"You're fat, okay?"

"I'll lose weight."

"You're pale as an albino."

"A tanning booth—I'll buy one."

"You've got no muscles."

"I'll join a gym. I'll start working out. I promise."

This was going nowhere. No choice, she thought.

"You come in ten seconds flat, and you've got a little dick!"

Cruel, sure. But Jesus, what could you do?

"A sex therapist. I'll go to a sex therapist! And I'll get one of those penile implants and . . . "

She was going to scream. She knew it.

"Because, darling, I'd give anything for—"

Suddenly the phone was snatched away. Wardell stood there buck naked and dripping from the shower, his dick bouncing like a springboard.

"Look, you little creamcup fuckhead. Don't ya call here no more, understand? I'll kick your ass so hard your balls'll pop out your ears. I'll come over to that fancy mansion and burn it to the fuckin' ground and piss on the ashes and bury you up to your neck and shit on your goddamn head and when I'm done blowin' a nut up your mama's tired old ass I'll bury her right next to ya and shit on her too. You take my message, dickbrain?"

God, Clare hoped so.

Wardell slammed down the phone.

The next day Wardell's "big score" came in. They flew to Cancun that evening. A month in paradise. Clare expected to work on her tan but it quickly became apparent she'd be working on her libido instead. She didn't mind. Wardell's cock was a boom that never lowered, his balls a veritable sperm factory that remained in production round the clock.

The nightmares stopped.

And so did all thoughts of Roderic. She realized that one night with Wardell's cock stuffed so far down her throat she was wearing his balls like sunglasses. Indeed sex had proved her release. And it was a release she couldn't help but pursue.

If variety was the spice of life, then each day and each night of their vacation offered Clare another bellyful of ripe red peppers. And, to stretch the metaphor to its absolute limit, Wardell was never reluctant to pour liberal volumes of cream into Clare's coffee. Where does it all come from? She wondered . . . And best of all, Roderic was gone. Out of her mind.

Forever!

Wardell had to leave a week early; a sudden "business deal" had arisen. A "customer" had an interest in his "product." Clare lounged on the beach all day. Each night, in bed, she masturbated well into the night. All she could think about was her lover's interminably stiff cock, the plumy hot balls, her thoughts forever and solely of Wardell and his earthly love for her. Getting fucked by Wardell was akin to dropping a box of Godiva into the lap of a chocolate addict.

Clare left Cancun four days early.

On the flight back she was so antsy to see him she could hardly keep her hand out from under her skirt. Once she got into the cab, she didn't try.

His car was there in its parking space. Bags in hand, she dashed into the apartment.

"Wardell? Honey?"

No reply. "Love-muffin's home." She dropped the bags and ran into the bedroom. Stared.

And shrieked.

Wardell lay sprawled on the bed, his face a dark shade of scarlet.

"Parachute cord's the best." Fudd emerged from the corner, leather-capped-and-gloved. "Piano wire's too messy. And nylon's unreliable. Last broad that dumped Roderic, I was doing a job on her with nylon, and the damned thing snapped on me. It got ugly."

Clare could see the deadly ligature sunk deep into her lover's throat. His face had swollen to a queer balloon, strangely distended.

"You should listen to your messages," Fudd said. "The old lady's not happy, let me tell you."

He stepped forward and she screamed. Last broad that dumped Roderic, I was doing a job on her . . .

But it wasn't a garrote that Fudd held out to her. It was a chloroform-soaked towel.

Clare awoke in Roderic's room. She knew it instantly. Even though her senses skittered like autumn leaves in the street.

"Oh, missy." His mother sat erect in a fine cane chair opposite. Fudd was standing behind her. "You were supposed to take care of my boy." Clare's tongue felt thick and sour. "We . . . we broke up."

"Broke up? You dumped him, you silly, selfish horse's ass! My boy is a gift to the likes of you! You know, you're not the first to treat him similarly, and Fudd always has been kind enough to give them what they deserve. But you? For some reason, I haven't the heart. Roderic loves you so." She sighed, pigeon breast heaving beneath the frumpy dress. "You should listen to your phone messages, missy."

Clare trembled. "I—I was on vacation."

"I know. Cavorting, no doubt, with that detestable narcotics dealer. Unfortunately Fudd and I were on vacation, too. But if you'd phoned in for your messages you might have prevented all of this."

"All of what?"

"Poor Roderic. He's a nice boy but admittedly an eccentric one— with some odd ideas about proving his love. Fudd found him . . . outside."

Clare's mind swam in muck. Her nightmares all came back to her. Roderic shot. Poisoned. Hanged.

"He's . . . dead?"

"No," she simpered. "No, thank God, he's not."

Fudd scowled and plugged a cassette into the tape player on the sideboard and walked off into another room. *Hi, this is Clare! I'm not home now so please . . .*

Then Roderic's voice. "Clare! My love! Why won't you believe me? I'll prove it. I'll prove my love for you, prove that I'd give anything for you! Listen!"

A pause. A snap. A brief scream.

"That," the old woman informed her, "was my son cutting off his pinkie with a pair of tin snips."

The tape continued. Roderic sobbing. "There! Here's my proof. For each day I'm without you I'll cut off another part of myself. Goodbye, Clare." Clare did her math, paling. She'd been away over three weeks. Fudd reappeared with a blanketed bundle in his arms. He set the bundle on the bed. Undraped it and stepped aside.

Clare gasped. Her eyes bugged. She bent over and vomited.

"Clare! You're back! I knew you'd come back to me!"

Roderic's bright face beamed at her.

"Ten fingers, ten toes." Roderic grinned proudly. "And the rest, I pre-applied tourniquets and used a hacksaw. The legs and the left arm were easy. But the right arm . . . I bet you can't guess how I did it!"

She vomited again onto the plush Persian throw rug.

"I crawled out to the woodpile, tightened the tourniquet with my teeth—and stuck my arm under the automatic log splitter. It did a nice, clean job."

She knew that for the rest of her life she would never escape the sight. Roderic swaddled on the bed. No arms and no legs. Just a living, talking torso.

"Do you believe me now? Do you believe me when I say I'd give anything for you?"

She could only croak a single word. "Yes."

"You've got your entire lives to spend together," said the old woman.

She got up and shuffled toward the door. "In time I'm sure things will work out nicely. For now, of course, Fudd will remain. To see that you comply."

"Cuh—comply?"

Fudd smiled. His gloved hand twirled the garrote idly.

"Assume your responsibilities," said Roderic's mother. "And without a fuss. It's only fair." Her stern eyes held her fast. "I expect you to take very good care of my boy."

Fudd locked the door behind her. It took Clare a moment to realize exactly what the old lady was saying.

"Get your clothes off and get to it," Fudd directed. "You don't want to keep him waiting."

"Oh, darling," Roderic said, "Till death do us part! We'll have such a splendid time together."

For there was one part of himself Roderic hadn't cut off, and that part now throbbed erect for her.

Sort of.

Jack Ketchum is the pseudonym for a former actor, singer, teacher, literary agent, lumber salesman, and soda jerk—a former flower child and baby boomer who figures that in 1956 Elvis, dinosaurs and horror probably saved his life. His first novel, Off Season, *prompted the Village Voice to publicly scold its publisher in print for publishing violent pornography. He personally disagrees but is perfectly happy to let you decide for yourself. His short story "The Box" won a 1994 Bram Stoker Award from the HWA, his story "Gone" won again in 2000—and in 2003 he won Stokers for both best collection for* Peaceable Kingdom *and best long fiction for* Closing Time. *He has written over twenty novels and novellas, the latest of which are* The Woman *and* I'm Not Sam, *both written with director Lucky McKee. Five of his books have been filmed to date—*The Girl Next Door, The Lost, Red, Offspring *and* The Woman, *the last of which won him and McKee the Best Screenplay Award at the prestigious Sitges Film Festival in Spain. His stories are collected in* The Exit At Toledo Blade Boulevard, Broken on the Wheel of Sex, Sleep Disorder *(with Edward Lee),* Peaceable Kingdom *and* Closing Time and Other Stories. *His novella* The Crossings *was cited by Stephen King in his speech at the 2003 National Book Awards. In 2011 he was elected Grand Master by the World Horror Convention.*

Edward Lee is an American novelist specializing in the field of horror who has written 40 books, more than half of which have been published by mass-market New York City paperback companies such as Leisure/Dorchester, Berkley, and Zebra/Kensington. He is a Bram Stoker award nominee for his story Mr. Torso, *and his short stories have appeared in over a dozen mass-market anthologies, including the award-winning* 999. *Several of his novels have sold translation rights to Germany, Greece, Romania, and Poland. He also publishes quite actively in the small-press/limited-edition hardcover market; many of his books in this category have become collector's items. While a number of Lee's projects have been optioned for film, only one has been made,* Header, *which was released on DVD in June 2009.*

HOSTILE

JEFF STRAND

A DIM, BUZZING fluorescent light on the ceiling was the only illumination in the windowless room. Mold covered the concrete walls, and the cement floor was decorated with a generous variety of stains.

A man was strapped to a chair, struggling, absolute terror in his pleading eyes.

Harry stood facing him, wearing a clean white apron. He gazed into the man's eyes, grinned, and held up a hunting knife.

With one quick swing, Harry slashed the knife across the man's throat.

The man gurgled and twitched, then his head lolled forward as he died. Only a few spots of blood tarnished Harry's apron.

Satisfied, Harry walked to the door. He pressed a button and a buzzer sounded.

About fifteen seconds later, the door opened. Adam, who was young, immaculately groomed, and dressed in business casual attire, walked into the room.

"Done already?"

Harry nodded.

"How was it?"

"Incredible. Absolutely incredible. Worth every cent."

Adam smiled. "Good to hear, good to hear. I'm glad you had a satisfactory experience." He looked at the corpse, then his smile disappeared. "Did you slash his throat?"

"I sure did."

"That's it?"

"Yeah."

Adam gestured to a shelf that was filled with a huge variety of weapons. "All this stuff to choose from and you just cut his throat with a knife?"

"It's what I wanted to do."

"Yeah, but . . . I mean . . . " Adam walked over to the shelf and started holding up items. "You had a power drill. You had a hacksaw. You had a baggie filled with thumbtacks."

"I was happy with the knife," Harry insisted.

"You had a weed whacker! When do you ever get the chance to use a weed whacker on somebody? You had a bear trap! You had ninja throwing stars, for God's sake!" He picked up a large metal contraption with lots of moving parts. "You had this thing. What is it? I don't know. But it could sure do some damage!"

"That didn't interest me."

Adam, shaking his head in frustration, walked over and examined the corpse.

"You didn't even cut him anywhere else! Why bother with the soundproofed chamber if all you're going to do is slice his neck? Why not just stab a junkie behind a fucking Dumpster? You don't go to an ice cream shop with dozens of flavors and order a single scoop of vanilla!"

"What difference does it make to you?"

"It's disrespectful. A lot of work went into acquiring these resources, and it's like you don't even care."

"Look, all I wanted was to take a human life. That doesn't mean I have to turn into some depraved freak. Sorry, but I don't need to torture somebody for hours with a cheese grater to feel like a big man. I'm sure you get plenty of whack-nuts in here who are all like 'Ooooh, look at me, look at me, I can rip out a woman's toenails one by one!' But that's not what I'm about." Harry walked over to the shelf. "And you know what? Your selection isn't all that great." He picked up a hair dryer. "What am I supposed to do with this?"

"You set it to the highest heat, hold your victim's eyelids open, and blow it directly onto their eyeball until it completely dries out and starts to cook."

"Okay, yeah, that would be pretty effective," Harry admitted, setting the dryer back down. "But that's a mentally ill thing to do.

That's for somebody who drools and wears necklaces made out of body parts. I don't wear necklaces made out of body parts, I will never wear necklaces made out of body parts, and I don't appreciate you trying to make me feel guilty about not wearing necklaces made out of body parts."

"All I'm saying, sir, is that you didn't really take advantage of our service."

"Again, stop acting like your service is so great." Harry pointed to the dead man. "He only *barely* looks like my father. So my daddy issues are still unresolved. Thank you for that! Thank you for failing to resolve my daddy issues!"

"Well, maybe if you had provided us with a high-res photo like we asked, he would have looked more like your father."

"Well, maybe that wasn't practical because I never get to see my father! If he were ever around for me to take pictures of, I wouldn't need your crappy service!"

"It's not a crappy service," Adam muttered.

"It sucks. I should've listened to the reviews."

Adam grabbed a butcher knife from the shelf and quickly moved toward Harry.

"C'mon, seriously?" Harry asked.

Adam realized what he was doing and dropped the weapon.

"Gonna stab me with a butcher knife, huh?" Harry asked. "Oh, that's *sooooo* creative."

"It was in anger."

"After that big long lecture, you come at me with a knife."

"It was an act of anger. It's not the same thing."

"A completely generic butcher knife."

"Anger! It was in anger! These are two completely different sets of circumstances. Apples and oranges."

Harry sighed. "I don't want to argue any more. What if I used the weed whacker on him a little bit?"

"You want to mutilate him after he's already dead?" asked Adam, appalled. "Sir, that's messed up."

"So what do you want from me? How do I fix this?"

"You could pay for another session and do it right."

"Not gonna happen."

"The discount coupon would still apply."

"Nope. I don't have that kind of money."

"Whatever."

They just stood there for a very long, very awkward moment, avoiding eye contact. They shifted uncomfortably, looked at the floor, checked their watches, scratched imaginary itches, and so on for about thirty seconds.

"Okay, fine," said Adam, wanting the socially awkward moment to end. "Grab the weed whacker."

Jeff Strand is a four-time nominee (and zero-time winner) of the Bram Stoker Award. His novels are usually classified as horror, but they're really all over the place, from comedies to thrillers to drama to, yes, even a fairy tale. His book Stalking You Now *is being made into the feature film* Mindy Has To Die. *Because he doesn't do cold weather anymore, he lives in Tampa, Florida with his wife and cat.*

METAL HEAT

JAAP BOEKESTEIN

THE BASEMENT OF the building was huge, Pam reckoned, and almost completely dark. The single light of a strong industrial lamp formed a near perfect ten-foot circle, just touching a concrete pillar. Down the pillar hung two chains: shiny promises in the harsh white light.

She licked her dry lips but did not waste any breath with a "Hello?" or "Are you there?" That guy Doc was either here or not, and if he was, he had heard the clanging of the heavy steel door and her footsteps when she came down the metal stairs.

Instead Pam walked to the pillar and turned around, facing the lamp. She could see nothing but the light. Outside the empty circle the darkness was full of potential, either for ecstasy, or danger—which sometimes was the same as ecstasy—or disappointment. Without noticing herself, Pam licked her lips again. So many possibilities!

Finally, she started to strip.

Jacket first, she threw it to the edge of the light and the dark. The heavy leather landed with a soft thud.

Faded black blouse, iron skull button by iron skull button. *Never strip with something you have to pull over your head, it looks ungainly,* she had once heard a burlesque artist tell in some documentary.

Skirt. That was easy, just a zipper. Gravity did its work and she stepped out of the red imitation leather.

It was warm in the cellar, thank God. Pam took off her boots.

Stockings, garter belt. Down they went.

What's up, Doc? Your dick? Are you getting hot? she thought. *I am not.* That was a lie, but only a little.

Bra. Almost naked now.

Panties. Naked now.

She stood, waited. *Here I am. Come and get me, Doc. Or not.* Should she be terrified? Here alone in the basement of some anonymous building, without anyone knowing? Maybe she should be, but she had lost the ability to fear things long ago. Do what you want, world. Either I get stronger or I die. Do whatever you want, I refuse to fear you.

"Your piercings. Remove them, all of them," an unseen man—Doc?—said. There was some New York Irish in that voice, a slight singsong twang. It was a tense voice, a bit haunted maybe.

My piercings. For a moment she hesitated.

Then she began.

Now she was really stripping. Her metal! Her markings! Her medals of valor and endurance! She had to give them up.

Nose, eyebrow, nipples, vulva, clit. She took them out, one by one. She carefully placed her darlings on the leather jacket. For the first time she felt vulnerable and naked.

"Your ears," Doc commanded.

Oh... They were hardly piercings, still she took them out. All of them. Finally, she was naked. *Really* naked.

Pam leaned with her back against the rough concrete. She breathed heavily, her fingers played with the chains and cuffs. Metal. Trusted, lovely, solid, dependable metal.

"Cuff yourself. Feet first."

She did. The metal embraced her ankles and then her wrists. When she was finished she looked up. *Come on.*

He kept himself in the darkness, circling her, his steps were like heartbeats. He stopped somewhere behind her, on the other side of the pillar.

Chains rattled. Her wrists were pulled up. She had expected that. The chains stopped, her arms hung high. Not uncomfortable though. He knew what he was doing and so did she. She was not a chain virgin.

Feet. Her legs were pulled apart, a bit. Not really far. She still stood steady.

A figure stepped into the light. It was Doc, the guy from the picture he had sent her. A wiry man, bald, small jaw, deep eye sockets. Old dragon tattoos covered his chest and back. He only wore a pair of old jeans, no shoes.

What's up, Doc? Pam really wanted to say that, but somehow she couldn't. Her only thoughts were: *Metal. Metal. Metal.*

Oh the promises he had made!

He looked at her, nodded.

His hand was fast, but landed softly on her face.

Sour animal smell, and more. *Metal!* She knew the smell of metal, the feel of metal. She knew all about metal.

His hand did not move, it was really warm.

Suddenly she felt it.

A hundred pin pricks, coming from his hand.

Electricity?

No. The flesh of his hand grew, transformed. Tiny needles grew into bigger points which grew into not too-sharp studs. Metal studs. Oh, Pam really knew all about metal. This was metal on her skin, growing directly from that guy's hand.

It is true! It is really true!

His hand moved over her nose, her mouth (she licked, *metal, warm, alive*) down over her throat, one of her breasts (nipple-touch-metal-pleasure), stomach, belly, thighs (*Touch my pussy! Please! Awww*), and finally her ass.

Pam panted, looked at Doc, opened her mouth to ask a thousand questions.

She did not get the chance. He kissed her.

Tongue on tongue, no reconnaissance, no hesitation.

Flesh on flesh.

The first few seconds.

His tongue changed. Two tongues, three, four, more . . .

Metal, all of them. Warm, living, writhing, sucking, pinching, twisting metal. Her mouth was full with taste and sensation.

She moaned, his hands (metal and metal) were everywhere, touching and kneading. *Metal on her skin! Oh, metal on her skin! Touch and scratch. More! Harder! There! And there! And there!*

Pam fought in her chains, fought him. Not to get free, hell no! Just so he touched her more, touched her harder, made her feel more of those fucking hot hands.

The bald, wiry guy got out of his jeans, without letting go of her (still mouth on mouth, his hands were back, everywhere) and kicked them away. The next moment he entered her.

Oh yeah. Pam already was soaked. How could she not be? *Fuck Hell Jesus Yes!*

Pounding.

Between a rock and a hard place . . . Okay, between a concrete pillar and his pounding hips. The hard place was *in* her.

Giggle. Nice. Fucking nice. Nice fucking.

His dick grew.

It *grew!*

Bigger, stiffer even, no *rigid. Metal* rigid!

Flesh rod to metal rod.

Yeah! Fuck! Yeah!

Pam knew the feeling of metal in her pussy. She had had all kinds of . . . She knew the feeling of metal.

Studs, knobs, scratching, searching, expanding, filling every crevasse, touching every nerve end in her. *Metal touch!!!*

Fuck, fuck, fuck, fuck.

She came, she screamed, with a mouth and pussy full of God-fucking sweet metal. She came again, she screamed again. His hands, his whole body now, was metal.

Fucking a metal man!

She was in Heaven. Metal Heaven.

Pam came and came and came.

Years ago.

"L . . . L . . . Love you!" Pam sung, very drunk.

The love of her live, her fiancé, smiled, only slightly less drunk. Outside the New Jersey night sped by.

Pam unlocked her seatbelt.

"What are you doing?"

"I'm gonna give you a . . . present!" She giggled.

"Fuck yeah!" he said when her hands found the zipper of his pants. "Yeah baby! I love you!"

His dick was hard and alive in her hands. Pam bent over and took the love of her life in her mouth.

"Owww, baby!" he moaned while he hit the gas. "Yeah, quicker."

The car accelerated, and so did Pam.

Warm lips and tongue, hers.

Warm dick, his. Soft flesh, so hard.

He put one hand on the back of her bobbing head, she liked that. With his other hand he steered.

Dark highway, New Jersey night.

Fast, faster.

Hot engine, hot lips.

Speed, speed. Almost there.

He came. His penis shocked, the sticky sperm covered the inside of her mouth, ran over her tongue.

"Hmmm!" she said with her mouth still around his penis.

"S . . . Suck it," he panted. His glassy eyes were on the road, his hand forced her head down once more.

Pam sucked and swallowed. Warm sperm went down, revolting and exhilarating at the same time. She liked to be forced.

He liked to force her and came one more time.

He didn't have to tell her anything.

Pam repeated her part. With pleasure.

Dark New Jersey night.

They parked outside a diner, in a dark spot. He killed the light.

"I want you to come," he said.

She looked at the love of her life. *How?*

"Touch yourself."

Touch myself? Here, in the car?

He only looked at her.

Pam blushed. She had never done this before. *I . . .* Her hand went to her skirt.

He put on the radio, some easy listening channel.

She used her fingers. Her eyes were almost closed and through her lashes she watched him watching her. Never had she done this while someone watched. It was weird and wrong and fucking sexy.

The love of her life took out his dick again. He used his hand. "Go on."

Pam did go on. The fingers of one hand circling, rubbing, dancing over her pussy. With her other hand she unbuttoned her shirt just enough to reach her breasts. She was quiet, except for her breathing.

Oh, yes! Her excitement got him excited. His penis grew, hardened. He did not take his eyes from her. A slight nod encouraged her to go on.

Fuck. She was getting wet. *He must be able to smell me.* She wanted to feel ashamed, but didn't. Her lust was getting too strong.

Fingers, fingers. In and out. Pinching, touching. *God, yes.*

She was getting there. She was getting herself there. While he watched and touched himself. There, on that dark parking lot of the New Jersey diner.

The windows of the car had all steamed up.

She felt her own flesh, hot, hard, wet. Nails, the engagement ring, scratching a little inside her. Strange. Good.

Dry throat, clammy hands, she was almost there.

He smiled, he knew.

Eyes closed now, her hands, her body, fuck yes.

Yesss.

Orgasm. Forced, while he was watching. Wrong. Good.

She came again, in her car seat.

An endless moment of oblivion.

Pam never heard the truck.

One moment of sweet total mind and body shut down, no thoughts, just glowing peace. The next moment total chaos, the sound of breaking glass and screeching metal, being thrown around by a giant's hand.

The truck ran into their car at full speed, they later told her. A stupid accident, a drunk driver, a truck full of reinforcing steel bars. He went to jail for that. But that was later, afterward. After the hospital and therapy. After her body recovered.

Now Pam opened her eyes, hyper alert but still feeling the hot afterglow of two seconds ago. A high octane mix of adrenaline and endorphins.

The smell, the hot iron smell of blood filled her nose.

The love of her life, her fiancé, sat beside her. The steel bars of the truck had impaled him a dozen times. He was dead, very much so. His eyes were still on her.

Forever watching.

"What is it?" Pam asked. "Where did it come from?"

They were standing before the coffin-like contraption. The sides were thick and black and dull, the inside . . . The inside looked like a mix of a medieval and sci-fi torture device: shiny metal tendrils, slowly waving in creepy lifelike patterns, protruding thickly from the sides and bottom. The smell of ozone hung in the air and the inside of the coffin radiated heat.

A power cable and a fat water hose were fused with one of the black sides.

"Dunno, I found it just like that." Doc scratched his nose and looked away.

"But you have to know *something*," Pam insisted. "Is it military, or . . . or . . . *alien*?" Her words sounded ridiculous, she knew. But fuck, what else could this thing be?

"I don't know, I don't care," Doc replied. "Could be a time-traveling pink bunny left it here. All that matters is what it can do."

Ah, yes. What it could do.

Pam looked at the machine (*It is some kind of machine*, she had decided). Did she . . . ?

Doc did not ask, did not help in any way. He had explained the how and the consequences. That was it. The rest was up to her. Doc was a great fuck. Human skills? Not so much. Pam did not mind, she had met her share of broken cuckoo clocks over the years. It took one to know one. Doc could deliver, that was what was important. He already had delivered plenty, and now he was offering a chance at her wildest dreams.

Thanks, Doc! Pam really meant that.

She was still naked. She stepped into the coffin.

The warm metal tendrils welcomed her. The experience was not exactly like stepping into a warm bath. Not at all, no. It was like thousands of tiny hot fingers touching her all at the same time. Metal fingers. They supported her, caressed her. She sat down, her legs and buttocks got massaged by hundreds of hands. *Owww*, and her anus and pussy, and the sweet part in between. Tickle, tickle.

Pam laid down, arms along her sides. She fitted easily.

Millions of nerve endings all over her body, all stimulated at the same time.

The tendrils touched her cheeks, her ears, combed through her hair.

Some people would have panicked. Pam didn't. Sensory deprivation, being wrapped in shrinking plastic, being locked up in the smallest of underground cages, water torture. She had experienced all of it, and plenty more. She never had any fears, just could not fear anything. She didn't feel any fear now. Not even when the tendrils started to creep further, covering her mouth, her eyes, her nose. As well as the rest of her body.

Warm living metal, she was in a shell of made of the sweetest of all things in the world.

I want this forever.

The metal tendrils started to enter her. Her ears, her mouth, her nose, her pussy, her ass. Every orifice. *Owwwwwwwwwwwww*. Warm flexible metal fingers inside her, searching, growing longer and longer, not stopping.

Yesyesyesyesyesyessss.

Double penetration and deep throat and breath play and wet tongues in ears all rolled into one, only a thousand times stronger. No, make that a million.

The metal held her head, her body, she was a prisoner unable to escape.

Like hell, she did not want to escape. Never ever. She was in Heaven.

The second wave of penetration started. The one with all the pain.

Over her whole body a hundred thousand needles punctured her skin, all at once. A dozen or so tendrils slithered into her eyes, through lids and skin, over and under the eyeballs. The metal that was already in her, in her pussy and ass, and throat and lungs and skull, branched out.

PAIN.

She screamed, well tried to. Not out of fear, no because of the *pain.*

Pam did not fear, but she damn well felt the pain.

Every birth is painful, but usually not for the child.

Ah, tough. This birth was.

Like every birth one had to leave the womb eventually.

Pam was on all fours now, on the concrete floor just outside the contraption. She was coughing, trying to make sense of all the impulses that overloaded her brain. She could feel the metal in her body, a fine network of molecule-thick tendrils, reaching everywhere inside her. It was like a million eyes, a millions hands, a million of millions she suddenly felt. And they were all hers.

Doc approached her, she could sense the metal network in him, the same as hers but with its own distinct signature. He had a hard on. Pam could tell without turning her eyes and seeing his erect penis. He grunted. It was clear what he wanted.

He wants to fuck me in the ass. In her mind she saw what he would do: take her ass, push her buttocks apart. His penis a loaded gun with her shithole as a target.

Pam tried to speak, but could not find the right instructions in her brain to do so. It was all so much! She wanted to look at Doc and shake her head. *No.*

Like he cared. He had one thing on his mind. He wanted to fuck. That was why had initiated her. To fuck someone like himself.

No. Goddamn NO! She desperately tried to shake her head, to do *something.* It was impossible. There was just too much.

He took her in his arms and lifted her up without any trouble. She tried to fight but her garbled brain just did not know the right commands anymore.

"Shhh, take it easy. I know what you are going through," he said. "You need to sleep. I will put you to bed."

No fucking no fucking no fucking, Pam pleaded in her mind. He could do anything he wanted with her, she was completely helpless.

For the very first time since a car ride in the Jersey night, years ago, Pam felt fear.

She did not like it.

Doc carried her down a corridor into a small barren room that had a bed. It looked like a prison cell but apparently it was the place he slept. Carefully he put her down.

"Rest now. We have plenty of time, later."

He did not fuck her.

Not so many years ago.

It was so quiet in the S&M club you could hear a pin drop. All looked at the Master and His slave.

Her feet were on the floor, her arms high above her, cuffed and chained. Her body was full of needles. The flesh was punctured a thousand times, the needles forming beautiful patterns on her back and thighs. The whole was decorated with colorful ribbons. Needle play could be about fear, but it also could be an art form. In His hands it was.

Fear did not work on her. But they were not alone. One could share fear. The arty-farty part of the demonstration was over, now it was time for the nasty things, the shit that made the audience hold their breath.

He held the long thin pins with latex gloves. Shiny metal, about ten inches long. He had dozens of them.

The Master looked at his slave girl—Pam—and asked her permission with His eyes. *Are you sure?*

Do it.

He took her right breast and pushed the pin in, far above her nipple.

In and in it went, and out it came again, on the other side of her boob.

The audience was silent, except for a few gasps. Yeah folks, *needle play*.

The pin was in her boob, about five inches covered by her flesh, about two and a half inches on either end were outside her.

He took another pin and again He looked at her.

Do it. There was no fear in her eyes. Only a strange kind of longing.

Metal, metal, metal.

He pushed another long pin all the way through, and another and more and more, in each boob until they looked like porcupines and were completely stiff. Blood trickled down. You never could avoid hitting a few veins.

They did not stop here. She wanted to go on, and although He was the Master, He also was the slave to her longing and His need to shock an audience.

The pins through her vulva closed off her pussy. There was more blood there. More veins.

The pins through her lips closed off her mouth. Blood ran down her chin.

More, her eyes demanded.

He hesitated.

More, her eyes begged.

He started to push pins through the skin of her throat.

Quite a few people in the audience turned away. Some hardcore sadists and masochists were still looking, but nobody felt comfortable.

Metal. More metal. More metal.

Pam cried when the Master finally ran out of pins.

Hot tears mixed with dried up blood.

Later, back in the car, Pam said: "Next time you need to bring more pins."

He shook his head. "There won't be next time. I won't do that shit with those pins anymore. Needles are okay, but pins . . . No."

"But I want *those!*"

The guy turned at her. "Pam, this can't go on. You need help. What you want is not healthy."

First she was quiet, then: "You are a fucking pussy."

He ignored her challenge. "I am not using those pins on you anymore."

She cursed, called him names. Faker, wuss, Daddy Dom (he really hated that).

"Stop the car. I will find my own way home," she cried.

"Hell no!" he shouted. "Dressed like that you'll be raped and murdered in five minutes." She still wore here slave outfit under her shiny rain coat: nothing but a collar, a girdle, stockings and heels. He liked it that way.

"I don't care. I am not afraid."

"No, but you are behaving fucking stupid. I will take you home."

"No!"

"Yes."

He took her to her home and they broke up. Later on Pam sometimes thought back. He wasn't a bad guy, especially not compared to some of the guys she met along the way, but he could not give her what she wanted. No one could, until one night she met a guy online who called himself Doc and who promised some really weird shit that sang to her heart.

"How long have I been out?" Pam asked between the chewing and swallowing of the food. Tinned stuff, she did not care, it tasted wonderful. She was famished.

"Three days," Doc replied, sitting on the only chair (an old crate) in the room. Pam sat on the bed. "Did you dream?"

"Uhm . . . I don't remember."

"I watched you, your body changed. You adapted to the metal."

Pam chewed and checked herself. She could feel the metal, it was a part of her, it felt *natural*.

Doc held up his hand. The skin got a metallic glow, crooked silver thorns started to grow out of the palm and back of his hand. "Can you do this?"

Pam held up her hand, looked at it. *Thorns*. She pictured dagger-like thorns growing from her hand.

She felt the change immediately. Metal moved inside her.

Pam gasped, the feeling . . . This is what she had longed for. The feel of metal in her flesh. Really *inside* her, a part of her.

The thorns grew out of her hand. Just like that.

"Cool!" Doc said.

Fucking cool! Pam thought.

He grew a pair of horns, soot black.

In response she opened her mouth and grew vampire fangs. Growing them was the weirdest feeling in her mouth. Like . . . like . . . Like the *inside* of her teeth being pulled, but without the pain. *Weird*.

He grinned. He held out his hand. *Do you want to . . . ?*

Pam hesitated, for the whole of half a second, maybe less. She had metal inside her. He had metal inside him. *Oh yeah!* Of course she wanted to know how that felt.

"In the big room, where we first did it," she demanded. She didn't have a clear picture of what she wanted to do, but at least she wanted to be able to move around. This tiny room was too *limited*.

Doc nodded and rose.

She followed him.

It was dark, but he turned a switch and the industrial light came back to life. Again the white circle in a sea of darkness.

Neither of them was clothed. Pam walked into the circle, swinging her hips. Swinging the metal tail she had grown the last few seconds.

He howled, wolf like.

Pam smiled. *What's up, Doc?*

He jumped her, like she was a bitch in heat.

She was.

He was all over her, arms, hands and body, and his touch almost took her breath away. The living metal inside her sensed the metal in Doc. It did not vibrate, but it felt like it did. It recognized its counterpart and responded to it.

"Whoa! That's new!" Doc experienced the same.

The sensation did not stop them. Far from it.

Wrestling, kissing, biting, clawing. They danced in the light.

Finally he had her, one hand on her neck, his other hand held her arm behind her back. She growled, lashed out with her tail and her hair writhed like a nest of metal vipers.

Yesyesyes! shouted her mind. Excited her metal glowed.

He pushed her against the pillar, where it all began. Her face grazed the rough concrete. The chains clinked aimlessly. They didn't need them, they had their own metal.

Doggy style, that was what he wanted. He had to let go of her neck to pull her ass toward him.

You can't always get what you want, boy. Twist and turn.

Now they were face to face. She flung her arm around his neck, her legs around his pelvis.

Take me like this, against this pillar.

BOEKESTEIN

His metal rod nailed her against the concrete. His mouth on hers. Tongues . . . both metal, both twisting and mutating and grasping and pulling. Little hooks growing from his hands and arms penetrated her skin, she did the same to him, with larger hooks, and deeper. Her heels dug into his buttocks.

Up! Up! He pushed her upwards, the rough concrete scratching her back. Pam thought he lifted her so she could ride his thick metal dick better, but suddenly she felt the real reason.

A second penis, long and flexible, growing right under his real one, moved up, finding its way to her anus. It entered as a living snake.

Fuck, asshole!

Indeed.

He started to move, filling her twice.

Asshole! Asshole! Assssssshole!

Pam bit him in the neck, he head-butted her.

A laugh escaped from her clenched teeth.

Two can play that game.

Her metal tail flung around his double penis, all the way. The thin end entered his ass quickly only to expand deep inside him.

Doc grunted, looked at her with big eyes. But he did not stop, he just quickened his movements, pounded her harder and deeper.

Pam responded in kind, letting him fuck her and fucking him with the tentacle between her legs. She matched each of his movements, push for push.

He cursed her, called her names, begged her to go on.

She had no plans of letting go. On the contrary. She concentrated with all her mind on the real penis inside her. It was metal—of course! —and bigger and with more *things* then a normal penis, but basically it still was a penis: a tube with an opening at the end.

Penetration time, baby.

In the blink of an eye the thin metal rod grew from the wall of her uterus. Her aim was perfect. It entered the opening of his throbbing penis and glided all the way in.

He felt it, oh yeah, he did. He tried to let go of her, but that was impossible. To many limbs and hooks and *parts* were intertwined. They were as good as one, he could not get lose.

Meanwhile she did not stop fucking him. Her hips grinded his.

"Oh god! Oh god!" Doc cried. "Nasty fucking bitch!"

She only laughed, while she fucked him in his ass and his penis. *Sucking time, baby.*

The thin metal rod in his penis grew fatter and hollow.

How . . . ? She figured out how to arrange her muscles.

Push. Push. And with every push the needle inside his dick started to suck.

"Hnngh!" Doc was unable to speak anymore, his eyes glassed over. "Hnngh!"

Pam laughed. *Fuck yeah!*

They fucked each other.

Metal on metal.

Metal in metal.

Metal around metal.

Metal *fusing* with metal.

Pam and Doc didn't notice. They fucked.

His metal. Her metal. It wanted to be one. It wanted to fuse.

It started to fuse. And the meat was in the way.

Blood trickled down their shiny bodies. Slowly, at first. The metal cried dark tears.

"Owwwww . . . "

"Hnnngh!!!"

Pam and Doc did not notice. They fucked and fucked and fucked. Their whole world existed of fucking. There was no room for anything else.

Blood, bile, pieces of flesh started to drop.

They cried in ecstasy, metal forms—no *form*—rocking and pounding.

Pain. If they had been human, they would have felt the pain. Whole slabs of shredded flesh fell down to the floor in an ever growing pool of oozing filth.

They did not feel any pain. They fucked.

Bones. Pulverized. It rained splinters.

Doc and Pam did not fall, metal kept them upright.

Pulsating metal, metal tentacles throbbing in metal orifices. Metal claws digging into metal skin. Metal heads locked in an everlasting violent metal kiss.

Metal fucking metal.

Piece by piece the meat was shredded and rejected. Living metal slithered, entwined, became one. Skin, flesh, organs, bones, molecule-thick tendrils cut it to pieces in their urge to become one.

Only the outline was still vaguely human. And the movements of course.

Fuck. Fuck. Fuck.

The brains, those squishy parts, were the last to go. Maybe at the very end, during a fraction of a second, they realized what was happening, or maybe they didn't. Probably the didn't. Pray they didn't.

The separate mashes of metal sliced merciless through brain tissue to embrace each other.

Blood and tissue fell to the floor.

Dead.

For a moment the metal continued fucking, an echo of a memory. Then it stopped.

The metal followed the way of the meat: down.

All was quiet in the basement.

At the foot of the concrete pillar, in the harsh circle of light, there was a dark pool of blood and filth.

And metal, of course. Living, writhing metal.

Slowly, snakelike, the collection of tendrils slithered out of the pool. By some instinct it was moving in the direction of the coffin-like contraption hidden in the darkness.

The metal left a trail of gore on the floor. By the time it oozed back into the machine, the metal was clean again.

Down in that basement, in that strange machine, the metal tendrils moved in creepy lifelike patterns. Sometimes, just for a moment, the face of a man, or a woman, seemed to appear. Other times a hand, a leg, a pair of breasts or buttocks were visible.

Of course there was no one to witness all that.

Alone in the dark the metal machine dreamt its dreams of flesh and fucking.

METAL HEAT

Jaap Boekestein (1968) is an award winning Dutch writer of science fiction, fantasy, horror, thrillers and whatever takes his fancy. Five novels and almost three hundred of his stories have been published. His has made his living as a bouncer, working for a detective agency and as editor. He currently works for the Dutch Ministry of Security and Justice. http://jaapboekestein.com/

REPULSIVE GLAMOUR

JOHN MCNEE

THE GIRL HAD the most unbearably beautiful body Agbal had ever seen. But of course, Sherda wasn't happy with her natural appearance.

Her dark skin was unmarked except for those regions where she had pierced herself, making pin-holes for tribal jewellery and fashionable clusters of gemstone and silver. Agbal had asked her to strip them from her body, along with her boots, clothes, and underwear. She had willingly obliged before sliding her naked limbs into the restraints.

"Sherda," he said, placing the ashtray under her head. It was the name she had offered, though likely not her given name. One she had chosen for herself. "Are you ready?"

She nodded.

"Can you speak the vow?"

She took a deep breath then intoned: "This body is given in service to the Goddess. Let flesh be the vessel of her abundant light. May it inspire awe."

"Word perfect." Agbal smiled before setting a match to the dry grass in the ashtray and the ruby-red seed underneath. He then retreated to a corner of the cellar where the smoke wouldn't reach him.

The grass burned quickly, but the seed took longer. It sizzled for a while, then steamed, before finally flaming and turning to ember, disgorging thick plumes of scarlet smoke. It moved at a strange pace, curling slowly upward then suddenly spiralling its way into Sherda's mouth and nostrils. When it touched her throat she gagged before something overrode her reflexes and she inhaled deeply, sucking it down into her lungs.

When she exhaled, her breath was clear.

She went limp, head pitching forward, chains pulling taught to hold her aloft. Agbal didn't have to go near her to know she was unconscious. He took the hip-flask from the pocket of his cardigan and drank from it—a way to pass the time before the transformation.

Twenty minutes passed before she moved again. Just the smallest twitch of a muscle in her shoulder, barely enough to rattle the chain. But Agbal saw it, and knew the process had begun.

Something shuddered between the girl's ribs and jolted her awake. She gasped, eyes going wide, whipping her head toward Agbal. She caught herself before she cried out, as though suddenly remembering where she was, and turned her face away from him.

Her reaction was not what he'd been anticipating. Inside a feeling of doubt spread through his gut. "Sherda?"

Her body quivered once more, vibrations tinkling up the chains.

"Remember your training," Agbal said. "Keep your focus."

She clenched her fists hard, then released them. Her breathing was slow, considered, but far from relaxed.

Agbal crawled back toward her. The doubt in his gut curdled into fear as he approached, seeing the signs of her distress. Tension and strain were not a part of the ritual. Nor was pain. Not for those who had been properly prepared.

"Sherda . . . look at me." He leaned in toward her, putting his face in front of hers, though she did her best to hide it. Her eyes were squeezed shut, veins standing out on her temples and neck. She gave no indication that she'd heard him, instead letting out a whimper as muscles in her thighs twisted, announcing their movements with quiet pops that echoed in the basement chamber.

"Sherda," he repeated, with some urgency.

She opened her eyes. They were bloodshot, desperate, ringed with tears.

"No one prepared you for this?"

She hesitated, as though afraid to admit the truth, but another blast of pain convinced her. She shook her head. "It hurts," she whispered, teeth red, blood on her tongue. "Help me. Please."

He moved without another word, running past her toward the stairs.

"Help," she cried again. It was all she said before a fit tore through her body, clamping her jaw shut.

Agbal raced up the stairs, away from the furious chorus of the chains and the sounds of spattering blood, up into the tattoo parlor where Pox and Degredatia waited. They were in conversation as he approached but were quick to silence themselves as he threw open the door.

"Devils!" he yelled. "What have you done?"

Neither was quick to offer a response. Pox, reclining in a repurposed barber chair, swivelled slowly to regard Degregatia. She, idly toying with a piercing gun, met his gaze.

Then both burst out laughing.

It made for quite a sight. From a distance, with her white skin and stretched limbs, Degradatia resembled a wigless store mannequin in a gown of blue leather, but a closer inspection of her body revealed a network of bloodless scars, halfway concealing the biological machinations just below the surface. Up close, the open wounds in her face quivered like a dozen thin, puckered lips, connected as they were to folds of sinew just below the skin and the long cavities by which her breath filled them like bellows. When she laughed, the folds inflated and burst from her wounds, giving her head the appearance of a blossoming red rose.

Pox, by contrast, could offer no grand displays with the flesh on his face, but his frozen features were grotesque enough without embellishment. Branches of blue and purple veins were pronounced beneath skin so stretched it was almost translucent, pulled taught by spears of bone at the back of his skull. With the light behind him, his head wore a halo of glowing webbed skin. The result of this extreme facelift had left him with lips that wouldn't close far enough to kiss and eyelids he couldn't blink. The latter problem had been solved by fusing glass lenses to the outer rim of his eye sockets. Their red tint was purely cosmetic, but they protected his eyeballs from the elements and ensured that even when he was guffawing with laughter, his mad gaze never left Agbal's.

"Stop that!" Agbal cried, grabbing the first thing that came to hand and hurling it across the room—a tub of disinfectant. It bounced against a mirror then landed on the counter, spinning for a moment before settling, upright, almost as though it had been placed there by gentle hands.

The siblings looked to each other, both trying to judge whether this pathetic display was worth another round of laughter, but thought better of it.

Pox coughed and sat up, steepling his long, intricately-tattooed fingers, making a show of trying to compose himself. "Something, um . . . something wrong, old man?"

"No games," Agbal said. "You swore to me that the girl had been properly instructed."

Degradatia, imitating her brother, tried to cough, but let out a giggle instead. "We may have exaggerated. Just a touch."

"Yeah . . . " Pox's thin lips could do nothing to hide his grin. "Fact is, we don't really know the silly bitch."

"You tricked her?" Agbal was horrified. "You tricked me?"

"Thought it might liven up your evening," said Pox, with casual disregard. "You don't need to worry about the girl. Just one of the hangers-on from the club, been following us around for weeks."

"Odious little cow was kissing arse because she wanted the seed," said Degradatia. "Wanted that because she couldn't afford surgery, but it wasn't like she could even afford our services, was it? I mean, how am I supposed to run a business with every tedious tart expecting special favors?"

"We told her as much, but would she listen?" said Pox. "Trust me, if the stupid cunt knew how to take a hint she wouldn't be here now."

"We gave her what she wanted in the end," said Degradatia, wet flesh shivering through the wounds in her neck. "We may have . . . skipped a couple of steps, but at least it means she won't be boring us to death anymore."

"Monsters," Agbal cried. "You tricked me!"

"And it was easy," she yelled. Shouting, for her, employed different muscles to laughing and pushed air into different passages. Raising her voice in anger caused fleshy red sacks to burst from her neck like tumors. "If you'd bothered to sober up for five minutes maybe you'd have seen she didn't know what the fuck she was getting herself into! Don't blame us for that."

"But how could you?" Agbal asked, appalled. "You swore to me. We made a pact!"

"What we've got is an arrangement, old man," said Pox. "One you've done pretty well out of, up till now. Free room and board, free food, free booze—"

"And you drink a skinful," Degradatia interjected.

"You drink and babble and pray for a time you can barely remember, and we've tolerated it all. When you got too lazy to even handle the inductions, we stepped up. But we're a bit sick of it now."

"We've better things to be doing. There's a whole world out there desperate to worship at our feet. If you'd seen it, you'd know. It would be cruel to deny them."

"You talk of cruelty?" Agbal pointed behind him, toward the sounds of Sherda's torment. "Do you have any idea what will happen to her?"

"Some fucked up shit?" Pox suggested, sniggering.

"She'll die!"

Pox shrugged. "So what?"

"Good riddance," said Degradatia. "The world won't mourn her."

For a moment, Agbal was too incensed to speak. He turned from them, bowed his head into his hands. "Why would the Goddess bring me here? I thought I could trust you."

"You can, up to a point," said Pox. "But we're not your slaves."

Agbal peered at the siblings through his fingers. It felt like he was seeing them for the first time. "What are you?"

Pox rose from the chair, ascending to his full seven feet, blue velvet robes unfurling beneath him. "We're devils," he said, throwing Agbal's own insults back at him. "We're monsters."

"We're tired," said Degredatia, sounding like she meant it very sincerely. "Tired of you." She turned toward the exit.

"Harsh lesson I know, but think on it," said Pox. "Maybe you'll take your end of the deal more seriously in the future."

Agbal wasn't looking at either of them as they walked away. His eyes were on the floor. "You'll pay for this," he said, his voice barely a mumble. "You can't offend the Goddess so."

"Threats?" Degredatia turned back and threw up her hand toward him, curling her fingers as though to clasp his face. He saw the small crosses in the flesh of her fingertips. "Your threats mean nothing. Nor do your prayers. It's time you realized that we are the closest things to Gods this miserable world has. You want to pray to something, you should join the flock and pray to us." With a flick of the wrist she straightened her fingers, pulling the flesh tight. When she did, needles of sharpened bone slid through the crosses. The effect was like a cat exposing its claws.

She held the pose, like a looming threat, long enough for him to respond. When he failed, she said no more, didn't spare him another glance as she strode away.

As Pox turned to follow, Agbal crossed the distance between them and snatched at his arm. "Wait," he begged. "Please, just . . . her name. Her real name. What is it?"

Pox hesitated, eyeballs shifting behind red glass, then shrugged. "You know what? I actually can't remember." He put a hand on Agbal's shoulder. "Do me a favor? Take a picture, before you clean it up? I'd like to see what's left."

The girl's blood had hit the bulb above it, spattering the glass with red polka dots. Its light cast a pattern of greasy brown splotches across the room.

Agbal was slow making his descent, afraid of what he'd find, whether the girl would still be alive. She was, but the fact brought no relief.

In his absence, she had broken free of one of her restraints, slicing through the leather with a sharpened tendon. It, and the hand it was attached to, now appeared so mangled as to be beyond use. The tangle of knotted flesh quivered on the floor, at the end of an arm with at least five more joints in it than when he'd left. Yet this was far from the worst she had suffered.

The muscles on her back were now exposed to the open air. Her flawless skin had split along her spine and divided, peeling away to hang in two great flaps over the sides of her body. Sinews glistened in the weak light, contracting like a stack of crimson snakes. Agbal kept watch on them as he edged around the side of the room, reluctant to look at her face till he was standing in front of it.

When he did, he found there wasn't much left to see. The right side of her skull had crumpled into itself. Her right eyeball was swollen, pupil dilated, and appeared ready to pop from the socket.

Her left eye was intact, but glared at him between tendrils of flesh that sprouted from her cheek and curled upward, like black flowers searching for the sun. Her jaw looked distended, having stretched to accommodate her growing teeth. The bottom set had shot up like reeds, spearing through her cheeks and the roof of her mouth, rendering her mute. Blood trickled from the wounds, pattering upon the mess on the floor—bloody clumps of hair and most of her scalp.

Agbal tried to speak, but the breath shot out of him in one high-pitched gasp. Fighting for composure, he swallowed and tried again. "I'm . . . sorry this happened to you."

By the look in her eye, she hardly appeared comforted.

"They tricked both of us. It shouldn't be like this, but when an untrained mind is exposed, fear and panic have their way. You can't be afraid, because then . . . "

Something bubbled and burst on her arm, spraying blood and pus across the bricks.

Agbal sighed. " . . . this." He crouched down to snatch up the ashtray from the floor beneath her head. It was brimming with ash and blood. He walked over to a corner of the cellar hidden by grey tarpaulin and ducked beneath it.

"You're going to die, Sherda," he said, when she couldn't see him. "The Munzur will tear at you till there's nothing left. I can't halt it. I can't reverse it."

The girl twitched. Another piece of her splashed on the floor.

Agbal emerged once more, still clutching the ashtray—now clean—in one hand, and a half-dozen grey-green buds in the other. He squeezed his fist and crushed them. They crumbled like ash, but in the debris he spied the seeds, gleaming with the promise of strange magick. He strained them with his fingers and dropped them into the ashtray, layering dry grass on top for kindling.

Crouching back down in front of her, he stared pleadingly into her one good eye. "Sherda, there's no hope of going back. But I can offer you . . . something else."

There was a sound of skin tearing under her breasts. In the shadows beneath her belly, something dropped, wet and heavy.

"You don't have much time left. So tell me. If it were possible, would you live again?"

She shuddered, snorting blood from ragged nostrils. It sprayed across Agbal's face, but he didn't care. He kept watch on her deformed head as she raised it slowly up and down, conjuring all her strength to nod *yes*.

He sighed. "I was afraid of that." Agbal placed the ashtray under her head and struck a match. Touching its flame to the kindling—and the dozen seeds nestled beneath—he returned his gaze to the girl's bloodshot eye. "You're not going to like what comes next."

"There's a drug. But instead of altering your mind, it alters your body." This was what Pox had told the girl. He could remember the words, but he couldn't remember her name. He didn't know why this bothered him, but it did. "Problem is, the only guy with access is this head-case who made up a whole crazy religion about it. So if you want the drug, there's some weird shit you've got to do and say to make him think you're as fucked in the head as he is."

"Cathedral", at one time in decades past, had been exactly what its name suggested. But over the years the congregation thinned and the building crumbled, till finally it was gifted to the whims of private enterprise. Now it was a nightclub where pale, odd creatures in black leather and lace could cavort to industrial rock in hazy Gothic opulence.

Pox's home was a silver caravan connected to a spiral staircase fifty feet above the dance floor. Tricks of its design—half-hidden supporting columns and cables—made it appear at a glance to be hovering in mid-air, close to the cathedral roof, floating on a cloud of dry ice.

It was a sanctuary to retreat to, a relatively quiet space even in the midst of one of Degredatia's excruciating DJ sets. It was a place of comfort where he could sit, drink and think, while one random clubgoer applied fresh ink to the tattoos on his chest and another sucked at his forked penis. Unsheathed from his robes, his genitalia resembled a two-headed albino snake—an entirely unintended consequence of his own spell under the Munzur's influence. It amused him to think how even a mind as well-trained as his could still be outdone by those mischievous seeds.

Sherda, as Pox and Degredatia had explained to Agbal, was

nobody. She was nothing worth exerting any thought over. That he should have forgotten her real name was of no consequence. He could barely recall his own. Truly, his life—and his sister's—had only begun when a tattered stranger had shown up at their door carrying nothing but a plant in a polythene bag.

At any other door he'd surely have been turned away, but he'd chosen theirs. He'd spent the preceding months stalking the vaults and basement bars of their city, searching its neon-bathed enclaves for someone willing to believe the story he had to tell. Amongst all the pierced and painted citizens of the night, the implanted and modified, he'd spotted Pox and his sister and recognized within them the desperate longing to become something more than human.

"Half the world feels that way," Degredatia had said, on hearing him describe it so. "Why come to us?"

"Simple," he'd replied, clutching the plant to his chest. "The Goddess told me to."

Against better judgement they had listened attentively to his tales of the far-flung land and obscure culture from which he had fled—and the prize he had smuggled out with him. Too intrigued to dismiss his outlandish claims, they had given him a place to stay and submitted to his tutelage.

"I can teach you how to use it," he'd said. "You can become angels."

And so they had, uniting with the seed, letting it lead them on a journey that twisted their bodies beyond the limits of earthly science. They had been overwhelmed by the results and quickly their minds had turned to profit.

Agbal had seemed disappointed by their attitude. He hadn't expected the "chosen disciples of the Goddess" to be so capitalistic. But trusting in Her judgement, he agreed to help them.

The potential was obvious. *Want bigger tits but scared to go under the knife? Come to Pox and Degredatia. Want to be taller? Thinner? Better looking? All cosmetic enhancements handled at a fraction of the retail price!*

Agbal had assured them it didn't work that way. There was nothing cosmetic about the Munzur. It engaged with the user on an intellectual, emotional, and spiritual level. The ritual worked wonders on flesh, but it didn't always do what it was told. Pox proved this for himself on his third and final trip.

Still, there was money to be made, especially within their community. It thrived with men and women who had paid surgeons thousands to contort their flesh, sculpt their muscles, break and reset bones, all in the hope of outwardly displaying their internal otherness to an uncaring world.

Soon the siblings gathered a flock of admirers, strangely receptive to their unique brand of repulsive glamour. And from such small beginnings they had, over the subsequent weeks, months, and years, built an empire.

"More teeth," Pox told the girl at his crotch, the first words he'd spoken to her since their introduction. She obliged, grinding her incisors along the thick skin of his shaft, paying no attention to the thin trails of blood streaming down his belly, caused by the electric needle of her companion.

Pox liked his tattoos to be retouched frequently—daily if possible. He didn't want to let them heal. Better that they bled, always. The girl at his side was no artist, but was no more squeamish at the sight of blood than her friend. That had to count for something.

Both girls were white with dyed fluorescent hair and the contents of half a make-up counter smeared across their faces, but in many ways they weren't unlike Sherda. Just as cloying, just as eager to please and dazzled by his monstrosity. Like her, they hoped to taste the Munzur. They longed to become something more. Like Sherda, they couldn't afford the asking price. But unlike her, they were willing to trade in favors.

In this regard at least, Pox thought, they were smarter than she had been.

A child's plastic sippy cup was in his hand, half-filled with ice and vodka. Attempting to drink from anything else usually led to spillages. Raising it to his over-wide mouth he realized that as with Sherda, he couldn't remember these girls' names either.

A pounding fist on the caravan wall spoiled the moment. The girl with the tattoo gun sat up and turned it off. The other withdrew her lips from around Pox's cock and gazed up at him with blank eyes.

"Answer it," he told the first. When she stood, he passed the sippy cup to the girl on her knees. "Here. Best keep in practice," he told her, adjusting his robes to conceal his genitals.

Sound flooded the room as the door swung open—the cacophony of the crowd coupled with the screech and shriek of Degredatia's latest mix. Agbal stood in the doorway, backlit by strobe lights and lasers.

For all the unpleasantness of their earlier meeting, Pox was pleased to see him, immediately waving him in and the girls out. As she made her way past him, the second girl handed the sippy cup to Agbal, then slammed the door behind her.

The caravan wasn't entirely sound-proofed, but it was at least possible to converse at a civilized volume. "Come to make amends?" Pox said.

"That's right."

"Good sense not to hold a grudge."

Agbal put a hand in his pocket. "What happened to Sherda was my fault. I shirked my responsibilities to the Goddess and that got her killed." He produced his phone and held it out. "You asked for a picture."

Pox immediately leaned forward and stretched out his arm. "Give us a look then."

Agbal handed the phone over and turned away. Pox ignored the apparent show of disgust and put the screen up to his bulging eyes. What it showed him was a grey husk. Sherda's body appeared desiccated, frozen in the midst of a back-breaking lurch, as though she had been instantly fossilized at the height of her agony. From the angle at which the photo had been taken it was possible to make out the second mouth that had opened in the centre of her head, its black throat promising smooth passage to the very core of her being. To Pox, it looked like she had died while regurgitating her soul. "I didn't know the seeds could do that to a person," he said, making no attempt to conceal his awe.

Agbal said nothing.

If Pox could have blinked the vision away he would. Instead, he wiped the sleeve of his robes across his glass-covered eyes and held out the phone, swapping it for his sippy cup. "You disposed of the remains?"

"Not my first time." Agbal's hip-flask was in his hand, the top unscrewed.

"I didn't think so. You're not angry, are you?"

Agbal shook his head. "I lost my way, but I feel I've found it again."

Pox's hideous smile widened just a fraction. "Hey, it's like you always say. The Goddess picked us for a reason, right?" He raised his cup in toast.

Agbal tapped his flask against the rim and raised it to his lips. "That's what I'm hoping."

Pox threw his head back and drank. The vodka was halfway down his gullet when it revolted—an explosion of icicles in his throat. He choked, froth spraying from his lips, and jerked forward on the couch, sputtering, straining to make words through the pain. He popped the lid and found the liquid brimming with something oily and red. "What did you put in here?"

Agbal's flask was still at his mouth, but his lips hadn't touched it. Now he tipped it upside down, emptying its bloody contents onto the floor. The dark red puddle quivered, then spread liquid tentacles toward Pox, who retched, hands clawing at his throat.

"The Munzur can do more than you realize," Agbal told him, as the blood trickled up his legs, dividing and subdividing into needle-thin rivulets. "A single seed misused wreaks bloody havoc and certain death." The slivers of blood climbed Pox's thighs and crossed his belly to reach and mingle with the trails from his tattoos. "But an overdose? That's a different matter entirely."

Pox screamed as Sherda's blood invaded the open wounds on his chest. He felt it twisting in his veins, poisoning his flesh. He leaped from the couch and staggered toward the door.

The crowd roared when he appeared on the platform outside the caravan, but he barely heard it through the blood in his ears. He felt a lump in his throat, something churning with the mad panic of a suffocating eel. Gripping the hand rail, every muscle straining, he pitched his head forward and tried to puke it out.

The thing that forced its way up wasn't vomit. It brought half his esophagus with it as it emerged—a slimy red rope of skinless flesh and sinew, snapping his jaw loose from his skull. He saw it pour from his lips, scattering teeth, yet it did not drop. It hung from his mouth, something anchoring it deep within his stomach, then bent in half, the cluster of knitted red fibers at its end curving back towards his face. He recognized their shape in the instant before they speared his eyes.

They were fingers.

Degradatia, concentrating on her music, was late to the party. Sounds of confusion and concern from the crowd had erupted into screams before she glanced up from her position in the DJ booth and saw her brother—or what remained of him—hanging from the platform high above the dance floor.

Spotlights found the thing that had a hold of him—the thing that appeared to be *hatching* from him, tearing its way through his head, neck and chest like a blood-smeared baby lizard bursting from its egg. Flesh, bone, and red glass showered the revellers below, each violent movement revealing a little more of the red, writhing thing within.

It had too many arms. Too many claws. Its head was a complicated cage of intersecting bone and sinew topped by a cluster of thin horns, snaking their way around each other to form an elaborate crown. With a tug, it tore itself free of Pox's mutilated body, let it tip over the rail and drop.

Degradatia screamed to see her brother fall, sending jets of air into every bellow in her body, the sacks bursting from her skin like a thousand blood-filled blisters.

She kept screaming as the creature he'd birthed reared up, crossed its myriad spiked limbs over its torso and spread its wings. They were ragged and pock-marked, like sheets of scarlet leather that had been savaged with a rake, but they worked well enough. The crowd scattered as the beast launched into the air and swept down toward the stage. Degradatia dove beneath the DJ booth, but it offered no protection. Her brother's killer ploughed straight through it, then through her—bone and armored muscle smashing wood and plastic, skin and organs to shreds. It swung back through the crimson cloud of debris, snatched what was left of Degredatia up in its talons and cast her broken body out into the flock. Torn fragments pattered the room like bloody hailstones.

No music now. The hiss of stereo feedback and whimpers of the crowd played background to the whipping sound of wings as it rose higher, up to the roof of Pox's caravan.

Agbal had retreated only a few steps down the stairs. There had been no time to go farther. The siblings' destruction had taken only seconds. And it had been beautiful.

The newborn's body was coated in blood. It streamed from the ends of its riveted limbs and painted elaborate patterns in the grooves of its chest. Digging is talons into the caravan's roof, it raised itself up to its full height, threw its head back and unleashed a howl of tormented ecstasy.

No man or animal alive could match it.

In the gore-spattered hall below, the flock ceased their whimpering. Still clinging to each other, too much in shock to run for the exits, they lifted their heads to regard the shrieking miracle high above. Like Agbal, they beheld Her magnificence. They beheld Her glory.

Humbled by the sight, Agbal dropped to his knees.

A moment later, the crowd followed.

John McNee is a writer of strange and disturbing horror stories, published in a variety of strange and disturbing anthologies. His debut novel, Prince of Nightmares, *was published in 2016 by Blood Bound Books. He is also the creator of the diseased sludge-city Grudgehaven, and author of two books detailing the adventures of its freakish inhabitants:* Grudge Punk *and* Petroleum Precinct.

He lives in Scotland and is gainfully employed as editor of a trade magazine, writing mostly about the horrors of tea and biscuits. He can be easily reached via Goodreads, Facebook and Twitter @THEJohnMcNee).

THE BITCH

KRISTOPHER TRIANA

"Be still, and know that I am God."
—Psalms 46:10

HE CAME IN closer to her lips as he fiddled with his belt buckle.

Already she could smell the accumulation of his days without bathing. The front of his jeans were stained with food specs and old cigar ash, the material tightening as he lifted his semi-hard cock out of them. As he shook it out, a waft of groin-musk entered her nostrils and she felt her balance slipping even in the confines of the chair. Before her now—right in her face—was his beige cock, slung out like a raw sausage. It wasn't very long, but thicker than any other that had ever been inside of her mouth or body. She watched as a single vein twitched beneath the brown rim of his circumcision scar. Beyond it was a black bush that glistened with sweat.

"Now remember our deal," he said. "You be nice to me and I'll be nice to you. Do this and you won't have to worry about the cops."

Emma tried to nod in agreement but a dizzying nausea had made it hard to do so. The warped head of his dick came closer and she felt his fingers sluice through her hair and bind a fistful of it up into a ball. When the tip of his cock grazed her shuddering lips, she hesitated slightly and turned her head, only to feel the ball of her hair tighten as he pushed her back into place. Already she could see that he was growing harder, excited by this sadism. He pushed his manhood toward her and it touched her mouth, bumping slightly on her teeth as she closed her eyes.

A hard hand slapped her and she gasped. The other hand still held the hair and it jerked her neck back toward him after the catapult of the slap.

"Open your fucking mouth!"

The cock came at her again and she did as she was told, her jaw stretching wide to receive it. He had the salty beef taste of a stick of jerky, and his wet pubes crawled up her nostrils as he forced her face to his waist, pushing every bit of his coke-can cock into her head. Then he pulled it out, only to thrust it back in. This time his dick was a little harder. Each time he did this the shaft inflamed. He pinched its base with his thumb and index finger and began slapping her in the face with it, getting her own drool all over her rosy cheeks, and then he plunged into her again and began fucking her face, his hips rocking as he jack-hammered his cock in and out of her skull. Her tongue pushed out over the rim of her bottom lip as a drain to let her saliva spill out, washing his balls and slathering her shirt. The bottom roll of his paunch surrounded and then released her nose so she could grab only short breaths between his thrusts. Normally when a guy would get over-excited like this she would put her palms up on his thighs to push him back just a bit, but with her hands tied behind her all she could do was lock up her muscles and brace herself against the chair, waiting for the beast to just cum and get it over with.

Her wish was soon granted as he exited her throat and snapped her head back again. She gasped and felt mascara tears falling from the corners of her eyes from the pressure. He was on his tippy-toes now as he milked his cock, his face equally flushed and coiled into a grimace of ugly ecstasy. Hot ropes of sperm spurted out of his hole and splashed across her face. One wad slapped into her eye and she shut it against the burn as he continued to baptize her in dick-snot. Once done, he began slapping her with his erection again, stirring the goo, an artist with a painter's board.

He popped it back in her mouth and let her taste what remained.

TRIANA

Just a few hours beforehand, Emma had been driving through the winding back roads that led to the mansions hidden in the lush forests at the edge of Wayland. She knew the area well, having spent the past year doing dog pickups in the company van. She worked for a small kennel that offered boarding and daycare services; one of the extra services they provided to their richest customers was free pickup and delivery of their dogs to attend a day or more at the facility. It was her job to take the van—which was filled with crates and had cartoon pictures of paw prints all over it—and drive to these clients' homes in the morning, pick up their dogs and then deliver them in the afternoon. The work wasn't too bad, but seeing how these elitists lived filled her with sour envy; unnecessarily huge homes plopped down in the center of several beautiful acres that were well-kept by professional landscapers, massive swimming pools and Jacuzzis, snowmobiles in the garage and expensive-looking antique furniture inside the houses.

She'd been inside these homes many times and always had to bite her bottom lip to keep from cursing. The owners would often still be in their pajamas when she'd do these pickups, having nowhere to go, but still they'd ask for her to come out to them in the snow and sleet and pissing rain to get their pups. Some of them had even allowed the business to make copies of their house keys so that they could have her get the dogs when they weren't home.

She even had a list of alarm codes.

She'd been working at the facility for months, building a good reputation. She worked hard, never complained or let her disdain of the rich show. She never called out and never even came in late. Emma worked when she got sick, was hung over, or was strung out, and she covered other peoples' shifts even if it meant she'd have to work over seven days in a row. Best of all, she beamed when she talked to customers and let her voice rise to a near squeal when she took their dogs.

It wasn't a dedication to hard work and a general philanthropy that made her toil and always show great customer service. Emma did this so people would put their guard down and never suspect her of being a criminal. And the ruse was an easy one to upkeep. All she had to do was keep on smiling. Then, once nobody would ever suspect her, she'd move in, take what she deserved, and leave them wondering who would have done such a thing.

She felt no remorse. It wasn't like these people didn't have all their expensive luxuries insured. Or the money to replace anything that wasn't. In her mind, you had to take what you needed when you could get it. You had to always be on the alert for opportunities and sure as shit ready to act upon them before it was too late.

Which was exactly what she was doing now.

The Harringtons, a particularly wealthy family who Emma knew had just had their first baby, were going on vacation. She knew this because they'd canceled their usual routine. Every weekday she picked up their butterball bulldog, Zoe, and their aged and decrepit terrier, Ellie, and brought them home at night. They kept this schedule unless they were going away on one of their extravagant vacations, during which they would board their dogs. Fourth of July weekend was coming, and Emma's boss told her to strike the Harrington dogs from the list. They were going to be staying with Mrs. Harrington's mother in Belmont. The family was planning to go to the Bahamas for a full week of relaxation, margaritas and scuba diving in gorgeous, blue waters that Emma could only dream about, being a poor girl from shit-ass Lynn. Jealousy and hate burned through her at this news, but a plan had formed as well, creating knocks on that golden door of opportunity.

The Harrington's house was an exceptional display of how the upper one-percent lived. Mr. Harrington, although he was only in his early 30's, was one of the top surgeons in Boston. His wife was a gorgeous and wealthy socialite, having been born into old money, and she always came into the kennel wearing staggering rings and necklaces that would have taken Emma a year to afford—provided that she didn't spend a cent of any of her paychecks. Of all the houses she had a key and code for, this one was the fucking jackpot.

Her plan was simple.

She would enter the house on the day after they left for their flight. She'd already made her own copy of their house key and had memorized their house code. She'd asked for the day off. Going there on her own time in her own beaten down El Camino, she would load up on expensive clothes, jewelry, the home theater system, authentic art and whatever else would catch good scratch. The house was isolated enough that no neighbors would catch sight of her with their prying eyes. Despite their high-tech alarm system, the Harrington's had no security camera on their property like the Abbotts and the Forziatis. She would wear latex gloves to avoid prints and when she was finished she would bash the doorknob to bits with her crowbar and pry apart the seam where the deadbolt was so it wouldn't be obvious that she'd used a key. She'd let the Harrington's blame the alarm's failure on a faulty unit. She didn't want to fuck with that.

The day of the heist she drove out to the Harrington house around noon. The way she figured it, if someone did see her, they'd probably think she was a house sitter, whereas a night visit would look suspicious. Her El Camino struggled on the hills. It was pushing on thirty years and hundreds of thousands of miles. The noon sun was pulverizing, so she pulled her platinum blonde hair back in a ponytail as she drove, glad that she'd worn cut-off jean shorts and a tanktop. She bopped her hands on the steering wheel to the sound of the Judas Priest cassette in the tape deck. It was out of date technology but tapes were cheap and she liked older metal anyway.

She was getting pumped now, the excitement of the game giving her a rush along with the buzz she'd gotten from the ice she'd smoked earlier. She was cautious about how much meth she allowed herself on "break-in" day. She was a functioning drug user; always well-groomed and pretty at that. She was fit and healthy, and hadn't deteriorated like some soup kitchen scrounge or the overblown junkies you see in movies. She was stable, and she knew she had to be to keep up appearances. You can't be good at what she did and allow herself to get angry and over-pumped the way so many drug users did.

On the floor was her crowbar and on the passenger seat she had two duffel bags to steal clothes in. She'd never seen Mr. Harrington, but Mrs. Harrington had a very similar frame to Emma's. Emma had seen some of the immaculate dresses and blouses that the woman owned but was more interested in her casual wear—the four-hundred-dollar jeans and the galaxy of shoes from around the world.

When she reached the house she waited for a few minutes, scoping it out. There was no car in the driveway. The garage was closed. No lights on. She peered through the slats in the gate that surrounded the backyard and pool. All looked clear, so she got out and headed up the driveway, walking quickly. She reached the front door, opened it, and walked through the hallway to the mounted alarm system. She went to punch in the code but saw that the system was unarmed. This puzzled her. Every day when she picked up the dogs they had set the alarm. *Why was it off now?* Maybe they'd been in a hurry to catch the plane, she thought, and their minds had been too preoccupied with not forgetting toothpaste and cell phone chargers.

She shrugged it off and looked around. The house was still and silent as she made her way back down the hall toward the living room. There was plenty in here she would take, but first she was going to wrap around to the dining room where she'd seen the expensive china that was displayed on the walls. Those were a top priority and she wanted to get the most expensive items into the car first so she wouldn't have to bother jettisoning things when she ran out of room.

She walked into the kitchen, which was dim with the blinds drawn, and put her bags on the table, wishing the solid oak masterpiece could come with her. She reached for the first plate and as she brought it down she heard something click behind her. Although she was not a gun person, she recognized the sound from watching movies.

A hammer was being pulled back.

Fuck, she thought without turning around. *I'm not alone. Must be a security guard or house sitter. Maybe even a family member. Fuck, oh fuck.*

"Turn around," a man's voice barked.

She did so slowly, and when she looked up she saw a middle-aged man with a paunch standing in the doorframe with a revolver in his hand. He had a giant head and a horseshoe mustache that underlined his shaggy, curly hair. His eyes were beady and mean, caves in boiled meat.

"Whatcha doin' in my house?" he asked.

Mr. Harrington? she wondered. *He's still here?*

He didn't look the way she would have imagined him. He had on an old, pilled pocket tee and a pair of worn jeans with a hole in the knee. His railroad boots were covered in scuffs and around his waist, hiding somewhat under his gut, was a belt with a big, shiny cowboy buckle that read *cockfighting* with a picture of two roosters going at it. Tucked into the belt was a length of yellow rope. All she could figure was that he'd been working in the garage. She'd heard that Mr. Harrington had a '69 Chevelle that he'd restored. Emma figured he must have been perking up his engine when he'd heard the front door open.

"I said, *what are ya doin' in my house*? You better speak up, girly."

"I'm sorry," she said, near a whisper.

"Sorry, huh?"

"I, um, I made a mistake."

"A big one, I'd say."

He moved closer, looking her up and down.

"What's your name?"

"Amy," she lied.

"You tryin' to loot my house, Amy?"

"Um . . . no."

"Well then, why're you here?"

She didn't have an answer to that.

"I thought so," he said. "You're fulla shit. You were just about to steal my dishes. Betcha wasn't gonna stop there either, huh?"

"Listen, I'm really, really sorry. Please, just let me leave and I promise I'll never come back."

"You ain't goin' no place, girly. Not until the cops get here."

She swallowed hard. This was not something she could afford.

"Sit down," he said, pulling out a chair.

She sat and he moved behind her.

"Arms behind your back," he told her.

"Please, Mister . . . "

He smacked her upside the head and repeated the order. It jolted her, and this time she complied. His hands went to work on hers, tying them at her wrists and looping the rope through the back of the chair. When he was done, he turned around to face her and put the gun on that fancy kitchen table.

"Please," Emma said again. "Don't call the cops."

"Why shouldn't I?"

"I can't go to jail. I have two priors. This'll ruin me. I'll be nailed to the wall."

'"Oh yeah? What're your priors?"

"Drug possession . . . and shoplifting."

"What'd you steal that time?"

"MP3 players."

He sniffled and sneered. "What kinda drugs they bust ya on?"

"Some prescription pills."

"You some kinda dope fiend?"

"No, just dabbled in it."

They sat there in silence for a beat, just staring at each other, the room like a yellow coffin closing on her.

"Please, just let me go."

"I don't see why I should."

"Look, I won't ever bother you again."

"Seems there aughta be somethin' in it for me. You don't go to jail, that's what *you* get outta this. What's in it for the big man?"

Her eyes fell to the floor.

"What do you want?" she asked. "I've got maybe thirty dollars in my purse, in my car. But I could get more from the bank."

He just glared at her, and she instantly regretted the offer. What did he need with her chump change?

"Well then what do you want?"

He stood up then, moved closer to her. Putting out his hand he let it glide across her cheek. Then, slowly, he slipped a finger into her mouth. It was salty and calloused and had a hint of the gun metal taste to it. Hating herself for it, she closed her lips around the digit and let him slide it in and out of her mouth.

She knew what was coming next. This is what the rich did. They took advantage whenever they could. That's how they got and stayed fucking rich. She would just have to bear whatever sick fantasy he wanted of his new slave girl, whatever depravity he couldn't convince his spoiled little wife to partake in.

When it was over he just left her sitting there, still tied up, his jizz dripping down her forehead. He zipped himself up and went to the fridge, pulled out a Heineken, and then came back. He smiled at her, as if proud of the paint job he'd given her face. He picked up his pistol, tucked it into his jeans, and then he started to walk away toward the living room.

"Hey!" Emma said.

"What?"

"Where are you going?"

"Upstairs for a bit. I wanna relax now with my beer and a nice cigar."

"You're supposed to let me go! That was the deal."

"No it wasn't. I said I wouldn't call the cops. Never said nothin' 'bout lettin' ya go."

"You bastard!" she shouted, shaking in her chair. "Let me the fuck outta this chair!"

"Maybe later."

He walked into the living room as she continued to scream. She heard his footsteps on the stairs and then the soft closing of a door and she rocked in the seat and looked around the room, fuming as panic started seeping into her veins. The rope was nylon but tied tight. She tried to find a metal edge or some kind of sharp corner she could rub the rope against and wondered if she scooted close enough to the wall if she could bang on it and get a dish to break. But it would be nearly impossible to get a shard from the floor the way she was tied, and the noise would just bring *him* back down the stairs.

His cum ran down her face and slithered onto her lips. She spat against its snotty flavor. Emma had tasted her share of semen in her life, but this guy's nut was particularly rancid, salty as seawater. She wasn't happy to have it all over her, but she was relieved that he hadn't made her swallow such sour spunk, sure she would have gagged on it.

"Hello?" she called out.

Emma had been sitting in the kitchen for some time. The sunlight beyond the curtain had shifted and the cum had dried to her face like glue paste. The only clock was on the microwave, which was behind her, so she had no clear idea of just how long she'd been there. It could have been an hour. It could have been three.

"Hello?" she cried out again.

"What?" he hollered from upstairs.

"Can I please go now?"

"No."

"Can I at least go pee?"

"Go right ahead."

"I can't, I'm tied up!"

"Piss your pants, stupid."

She cringed. "Come on, I'm not going to piss my pants!"

She heard him laugh. "Yeah, you will."

"No, I *won't.*"

"Ya can't hold it forever."

The sadistic son of a bitch.

"How long are you going to keep me here?" she asked.

"That depends on how well ya take orders."

Emma gulped sourly. The suggestion made her skin go gooseflesh and her bowels churn. The grim nature of the situation was slowly becoming clearer, no matter how much she tried to deny the harsh reality of it. The thought of him getting his rocks off in any part of her body again made her shudder—it was enraging, terrifying and goddamned sickening all at once. She'd blown Tommy for a gram once and used her looks to score cheap deals, but that was different than this. This man was her goddamn captor. She had no choice. Once again, the upper 1% was taking advantage.

She breathed in an effort to calm down. She'd talked herself out of some tight spots before. There had to be some way to reason with this fucking pervert. She believed that if she thought hard enough and showed patience and respect, she could convince him to let her just get in her car and go home.

She'd meant it when she said she'd never come back. Hell, at this point she didn't even want to get back at him for making her suck him off.

She just wanted out.

That wasn't so much to ask was it?

Night fell and he still hadn't come downstairs. She heard no television or any other noise and she wondered what he could possibly be doing. Her only guess was that after his blowjob and beer he'd acted like most guys she knew and had taken a nap. But no matter what he was up to, she needed to urinate—*badly*. She'd been crossing her legs but now they were bouncing and dancing in an effort to keep the levee from breaking.

"Hello!" she called out again, frustrated, frightened, alone. "I need to piss!"

She received no reply but heard something stirring above her. The floorboards creaked, followed by feet stomping down the staircase. A light came on in the living room, lighting up some of the kitchen but keeping most of it stuck in heavy shadow, and the man emerged and stood in the doorframe. He lifted his shirt and scratched at his hairy belly.

"I'm hungry," he said.

"I need to pee, seriously."

"I done told ya that you could."

He walked to the fridge and looked inside, the light from it breaking the darkness like an axe blade. The room had grown hot and stuffy as the sun had set, and Emma was sweating. Her hair was sticking to her and her underarms had moistened her nearly to her waist. The fridge closed and he came back around and sat at the table beside her with two frozen pizzas.

"I know ya like pepperoni," he said and snorted a laugh.

"Please let me use the toilet. I promise I won't run away."

"Ain't ya hungry?"

She thought about it and, admitting to herself that she might not be leaving anytime soon, she decided not to pass up the chance. She wasn't sure when he'd offer her food again or for how long he'd retreat to upstairs the next time.

"Yeah, I'm hungry."

"Piss your pants for me and ya can have some pizza."

You fat motherfucker, her mind hissed.

He snorted a laugh that made her seethe inside.

"I'm not gonna—"

He stood and belted her with the back of his hand. Before she could even collect herself he did the same thing to her other cheek. She gasped each time and trembled against her will.

THE BITCH

"You gonna make me beat it out of ya?" he asked.

She took a deep breath and closed her eyes, her face pinching as she resigned herself. Deeply uncomfortable with him standing there, it took a few moments, but then the seal broke and her panties slushed. The piss flowed out of her shorts and dribbled into her seat, riding down her legs and sopping into her socks. She fought the urge to cry, not wanting to give the bastard the satisfaction.

When she finally opened her eyes she saw that he had knelt down. He smiled at her wet crotch, then ran his fingers through the puddle on the floor. She watched him lift his wet fingers to his nose then, and he inhaled the scent of it before he popped them—one by one—into his mouth and licked them clean. She turned away in disgust.

"Who the fuck are you?" she asked. "You're not Mr. Harrington. You *can't* be Mr. Harrington."

He wasn't listening. He had gone back for seconds.

The first night she spent in the chair he left her alone.

He kept her sitting there with her piss chilling her while her back ached and her ass went numb. Her shoulders hurt from being pinned backwards so long and her hands were rope-burned from struggling against her restraints all those hours. He hadn't let her clean up. He hadn't even been decent enough to wipe her face clean of his cum-crust. All he'd done was slurp up her piss puddle, throw the pizzas in the oven, and fed her three burnt pieces.

She did not sleep, so she tried to concentrate on an escape plan, but still she pondered the man's true identity and tortured herself with horrifying scenarios of things to come. She cried quietly for a short while, alternating between terror and anger. This could have been her last job. The money she would have scored would have given her the ability to relax, lead a normal life—cut back on hours and maybe buy a brick of the good stuff. Why the fuck did the Harringtons have to go on vacation when this sick fuck was stalking the neighborhood?

She forced the self-pity from her mind, then refocused her attention on the back of the chair where she'd felt just a slight splinter. She picked at it diligently, trying to remove enough of the wood to make a jagged edge she could rub the ropes upon. It was slow-going work, but it was hope, however small, and she clung to it to keep her out of the jaws of panic.

As the sun rose it filled the room with instant heat and she couldn't help but wonder why the air conditioning wasn't on. The summer morning was already blistering outside but inside the kitchen was worse. The trapped air was stagnant and reeked of piss, a rancid reminder of her shame. Her body odor grew stronger.

When he finally came into the living room he was wearing nothing but his tighty whities and they weren't all that white anymore. He smiled, baring the yellow teeth that held a cigar between them. He took a puff and then blew the smoke into her face. She turned away from it, coughing, and that made him laugh. But he didn't say a word. He merely walked up to her and pulled his underwear down, letting his fat, semi-hard cock plop before her.

"Ready for your breakfast sausage, girly?"

"Go to hell."

"Open wide now."

"I'm not sucking your disgusting cock again!"

This time he punched her in the stomach. The wind left her, and for a moment the sensation made her feel like she was dying. She struggled to regain her air as he grabbed her jaw, wrenched her head up, and puckered her lips together like a fish. She could feel the veins pulsing in her taut neck, pumping the terror on a main line through her heart. He stared into her face and she couldn't stand to look him in the eye, so he puffed more smoke in her face and then walked out of the room. She began to breathe again but now she was shaking so hard that the legs of the chair clicked upon the tile like a tap dancer.

When the man came back in, she saw that he had Zoe's leather leash in his hands. At the end of it was a prong training collar. It was a small length of chain with several prongs—V-shaped pieces of metal that were spread out in links. Zoe had been trained on one to keep her from dragging her owners around on walks. Emma knew these collars well. They snapped together and when you pulled on the leash they tightened, giving the dog a pinch when tapped lightly and a harsh correction when you really pulled.

But this was not what the man had in mind when he adjusted it to fit her neck.

He popped a few prongs off and let them hit the floor. Zoe's neck was much fatter than Emma's, so he adjusted it to fit her. She went rigid and even held her breath whereas moments ago she'd been worried she'd never have any again. She was afraid of the prongs because one time she had gotten curious and put one around her bicep and tugged. It wasn't too bad and so she'd pulled harder. That's when it hurt and it even left a tattoo of small, pink dots where the prongs had sunk in, not breaking the skin but bruising it. Dogs had much thicker hides and a much higher tolerance for pain than humans. But the prong collar would be very unforgiving to a woman's delicate neck, and she knew it. She felt it snap into place and the man stepped back holding the end of the leash in his hand. His cock was now fully erect and pointing at her in an upward curve like a nasty thumbs up.

"Ya startin' to get the picture?" he asked.

She nodded.

"I am your master," he said. "You'll do as I command, because you're my bitch, bred just for me."

He moved in closer and her eyes began to water. He then tapped on the leash and she felt the collar pinch ever so slightly in a warning. He came closer still and she felt his cock glide across her face. He smelled even worse than yesterday, his night-sweat collecting to form a pungent tang. He tugged once more, harder this time, and she got the message. The command had needed no verbal cue.

She closed her eyes and opened her mouth.

Over the past day or so—she was unable to keep count in her sleep-deprived state—a heavy layer of dried cum had formed a plaster mask upon her face. At one point it had taken her great effort to pry her eyelids apart, breaking the glue of the semen in her lashes. He had continued to force her into oral sex several times a day, and each time he fucked her face with more ferocity, as if he was using the head of his dick as a battering ram to get through the back of her skull. She'd gagged several times and had vomited once but he'd just kept on going, thrusting his pink and engorged member in and out of her with the leash held high in his hand.

The leash went on and off but the collar stayed on her at all times, a vicious reminder. It claimed her, much like his shot wads marked his territory as he jerked them onto her crusty face again and again. She was given little opportunity to move and increase her circulation, only being released for bathroom breaks, and her body betrayed her, twitching and pinching, and only grew more painful when she struggled in vain against the ropes. The man fed her only at night, and only if she had obeyed. At times she had to fight the urge to bite down on his man-meat and tear it right off of his fat-fuck body. But she knew the satisfaction of that would not last long. At the first hint of teeth the prong would yank, sending small knives of pain through her, and that would be just the beginning.

When she did get those bathroom breaks, the man made snide jokes about how much her shit stank. And as soon as she was done she was walked back to the kitchen while she fought the urge to make a run for it, knowing it would only get her a bullet to the head. She'd sit back down and he'd tie her up once more, not noticing the chip in the back of the chair that had grown so much bigger.

It was at night when she first heard the crying.

It was distant but high pitched. At first she'd thought it was a cat in heat but as she listened more closely she knew it was something else. The house was very big and the sound was echoic, as if it was coming from the other side of the world entirely. It started as a quiet murmur but built to a wailing that was unmistakable.

Jesus, there's a baby in here.

She stretched her ears and leaned towards the noise. The sound grew louder and reverberated through the house in a haunting cacophony. It seemed to circle all around it like a poltergeist, a spooky thought that sent a mean chill through her.

Suddenly she remembered Mrs. Harrington having just had a baby last fall and she wondered now, more than before, just what the hell was going on in this house. She tried to listen closer as she heard footsteps moving about. They thumped above her like bass drums and then wandered off to where she could no longer hear them.

But the baby's crying went on, at least for a little while.

Exhaustion had pummeled her now and as the sound faded she began to wonder if it had truly been there at all, or if the hallucinations of sleep deprivation and confinement were finally kicking in.

Another sound she would sometimes hear came during the day. She heard a car start and then drive off, and she would call out to the man after that but would get no reply. She knew he was going somewhere, doing something. It made her wonder where the car had been when she arrived.

Probably the garage, she thought.

She tried to use this time to pick at the chair with more gusto. She'd developed a notch but it still remained too smooth to make any progress on the rope. She tried to tear away small fragments in the hope that it would splinter.

After these brief absences the man would usually return with some groceries, mostly cold cuts and beer. One day he came back with a small pharmacy bag and a big bottle of bourbon.

He poured two shots and lifted one to her lips.

She sipped at it, just glad for something wet.

When she finished, her poured her another.

Then another.

"Ya said ya like pills, didn't ya?" he asked.

She didn't answer. He reached for the collar and popped it.

She twitched, gasped. "Yes."

"Well, I got my little bitch a doggie treat today," he said.

He opened up the paper bag and retrieved a prescription bottle. He shook it before her face, making the pills inside rattle like raw pasta.

"Doc says I need valium," he said. "It keeps me from gettin' too stressed. I tell ya, they've been workin' too. I'm just as happy as a pussycat in a tuna factory."

With this line he used his finger to flick at the zipper of her shorts. Then he popped the cap off the bottle with his teeth and put four of the blue pills into his hand. He came towards her with them and another shot of whiskey.

"That's too much," she said.

"No it ain't."

"I know valium. I've taken it. Nobody takes four and washes them down with whiskey."

"You're wrong. *My bitch* does. She always does what she's told sooner or later. Don'tcha, bitch?"

"Why do you keep calling me *bitch* anyway?"

Her tiredness was making her extra cranky and daring.

"You're a female on a leash ain't ya?" he said. "Therefore, you're the bitch."

"I'm just a female dog to you, huh?"

"Just a female dog that doesn't wanna be kicked in the belly."

He held the pills up closer.

"I could O.D. on those," she said.

"Or I could shoot ya in the face. With the gun this time, instead of my pecker."

He snorted a laugh and, as always, she ended up opening her mouth for him. A helplessness had befallen her and it sluiced through her body like a nest full of snakes. Her anger faded to a vacant despair and her exhaustion just dragged it further down, burying it in her very core. She hoped now that the valium backed by the booze would at least make her pass out.

Maybe just for a little while, so I can finally sleep.

Pain woke her.

She was in thrall. Her body was fully nude and she was bent over the coffee table in the living room. Each of her legs were tied to a leg of the table while her hands were still tied behind her back. The collar was tight and the leash lay upon the floor in front of her, pinned under the table. Her back felt like it was burning. Something was gliding across it, sinking into her flesh and separating it. Its touch was cold but piercing, and each stroke, while gentle, created hot new wounds.

THE BITCH

The son of a bitch is cutting me up.

She could turn her head just enough to see him behind her, also nude. He was masturbating with one hand and held the bowie knife in the other. With each slice he brought the blade up to his face and lathered it with his tongue. Seeing this horror, she screamed louder than she'd ever had in her life, her cries raking her throat like sandpaper. She shuddered at the sight of this human vampire drinking her blood and playing with himself right behind her bare bottom. Aroused by the scream, he slapped her ass and started making barking noises. She cried out and he replied with mocking wolf howls.

"What are you doing? *You sick fuck!*"

He just kept howling and she felt the knife pierce her again, this time at the base of her spine. But it didn't end with a soft slice. This time he stuck the tip into the wound and twirled it, opening the hole further. The pain burned and she felt her blood pouring out more thickly, spilling down into the crack of her ass. He ran his finger through it, making little swirls on her buttocks as she tried to kick and shake herself free to no avail.

"You'd better relax," he said, and she felt the tip of his finger, lubed with her blood, start prodding her anus.

She shook harder and screamed and screamed and screamed.

The finger moved in, sinking to the middle knuckle.

"Ever been fucked in this pretty ass of yours?"

"*Fuck you!*"

She began to sob.

"Ya tellin' me this here is a virgin butthole?" he asked. "Ya never let one of your boyfriends fill up your poop shoot?"

"No! *No!* Get away!"

Emma wiggled, popping out his finger. She heard him laugh and she turned her head around to see him unscrewing the cap to a large bottle of vegetable oil. He upturned it on her ass and slathered it across her cheeks, shaking them and slapping them together. He dabbed her anus. Then he poured some oil on his dick and worked it till it was full and hard. Knowing what was coming she turned away. She felt the wetness around her asshole, then the first probing of his cock's head.

"You weren't kidding," he said. "You're sealed up like Fort Knox."

But he pushed on, squishing his way into her. A sick, hollow feeling overcame her stomach. The head eased in, his girth expanding her asshole wider than any turd she'd ever passed.

She hadn't been lying. She'd never had so much as a finger in her butt. Some of her boyfriends had tried to coax her into it, but it was one sexual act she found utterly disgusting. He moved in deeper and she struggled not to vomit as she felt the rim of her anus begin to tear. He pushed on, pummeling the end of her intestines, her colon filling up with his fat meat.

"Don't you shit now," he said. "A bitch that shits is doin' so in self-defense, and I don't take kindly to that."

He took it slow and she cursed herself for appreciating it, but she did. He slid in and out very tenderly—much gentler now than whenever he fucked her face. With one hand he began to rub her clitoris but he still played with the knife in the other, this time making thin cuts on her ass cheeks. With each sluggish expulsion of his dick it came back harder and thicker. She felt it stretching her further and further and his breathing became more rapid as his sweat began to fall upon her back. She grit her teeth against the nauseating pain and revulsion and just tried to go limp.

As this sodomy continued, she felt herself retreat inside her own mind. This defense gave her a feeling that was otherworldly, something she had experienced a few times when high. When life was too much too bear, she had always been able to escape with the aid of drugs, and sometimes, though rarely, she would even hear a voice in this state, one that was both her own and not her own, that would guide and advise her, coaxing her. As his cock tore her open, she was able to find that far away place without any snorting or smoking, and she heard the first faint murmurs of that old, familiar friend. The voice beckoned her from the edge of consciousness, just barely audible, a lover's whisper in the dark.

But this time the voice did not calm her, did not soothe her with promises of relief. Instead it was angry, its whispers seething, fueled with hatred for the man, for her lot in life, and for what the Harrington house had so easily offered her only to take away. Rapid and mad, a message wove its way around her brain, taunting her with malevolence and lust for revenge.

As the man came closer to climaxing, he moved faster, plunged deeper, shocking her back to this bleak reality. She heaved and swallowed a hint of vomit. The thrusts intensified and the swirl in her stomach overpowered her, making her dizzy, and without making any effort to she suddenly shat, uncontrollably, and the noise was wet and flatulent. Fecal stink instantly soured the air and she felt her waste run down the insides of her thighs. Before the man realized what had happened he made two more quick thrusts, further spattering the feces before he yelled out in enraged disgust.

He exited her. "Ya nasty little cunt!"

The man came around in front of her and she could see her shit all splattered across his groin and belly. She was surprised at how much this pleased her, but the vengeful satisfaction didn't last long. Still tied, she could do nothing to resist the stomping. His foot came down on the small of her back and she feared that he might shatter her spine. When she screamed he reared back and kicked her in the face again and again. Some of her teeth loosened and her mouth overflowed with blood.

"Ya wanna shit on me, bitch?" he said. "I'll fix ya of that."

She tried to turn away as he came in close, but there was nowhere for her to go. His shit-covered cock moved towards her face, still hard, and he began smacking it against her lips. The awful stench of her own waste filled her nostrils. Then he forced his way into her mouth, the shit swishing around with the broken teeth and blood, creating a foul, hellish brew for her to wretch upon.

"Don't shit where ya eat, bitch! Don't *shit* where ya *eat*!"

That night dinner was a little different, but she was glad to have something to wash the taste of feces and semen out of her mouth. Her lower back was in agony, as was her swollen lips and bruised face. Her tongue dug into two holes where her front teeth had been. She would have cried had she anything left in her.

He dropped the dish down in front of her and she cringed at the sight of the red, rubbery mess. She'd heard him cooking something in a pot but had been unable to see what it was, her chair facing the wall in a dunce's punishment. The stuff was spongy tubes covered in some kind of sauce—like some exotic squid. It reeked and couldn't look less appetizing.

"I made ya my specialty tonight," he said. "I feel bad about stomping ya like I did. I reckon ya didn't mean to shit yourself. It just happens sometimes."

He forked a length of the goo and cut off a small segment and brought it up to her mouth. As nauseating as it was, she was damn hungry, and anything would be better than the current aftertaste.

"What is it?"

"Tripe."

"What's that?"

"It's guts."

She blinked at it, seeing the dish now for what it was—blood-soaked intestines and what looked like some kind of organ she couldn't identify. She hoped she could keep it down.

Christ, the things some people eat.

She bit into it and was surprised at the acidity. The goop was even more rubbery than it had looked. The blood was rich though, like a rare steak, and she savored it, sucking on the goop so that the flavor would cleanse her mouth out. The man shared the meal with her and he wolfed it down like it was a stacked hamburger.

"Ya can't beat good tripe," he told her.

That night she started fading in and out of consciousness. And though pain ravaged her entire body, from her torn anus to her busted-up face, her accumulated insomnia finally gave way to her overpowering exhaustion. Yet even in her dreams the man tortured and debased her. Her nightmares had him on top of her, belching cigar smoke into her mouth as he raped her, cut her, laughed at her.

And circling through these dreams like a singsong narrator was that same voice. It had grown louder and deeper and still held that malevolent tone to it, sardonically laughing, mocking even, as she was brutalized. It spoke of dark, twisted things with a thirsty sense of bloodlust, plotting something that hinted at fatal violence—maybe murder, but maybe suicide. These dreams were bad enough that she was grateful to snap awake.

THE BITCH

During one of those waking moments, she heard the distant crying. It was low at first but then grew louder and louder until it roused the man. His footsteps moved overhead and then reached the room on the other end of the house. She heard him murmuring but was unable to make out his words. The sound of the crying baby turned to cooing.

The man was singing a lullaby.

She awoke to the feeling of something pushing into her vulva.

The man was crouching in front of her with what appeared to be a length of hose in his hand. The weather had turned to rain, making the light in the room grow faint and gray, and so she had trouble adjusting her weary eyes. She blinked rapidly to regain her vision and saw that the hose was plastic. It ran back to a large barrel behind him. He seemed to be trying to put the length of hose inside of her.

"What the fuck are you doing?" She shifted in her seat, trying to close her legs at the knees even though she was tied too tight to the chair to do so.

"Time for your cleanin'." He spat into his hand and rubbed it on her vaginal lips. Then he probed a finger in and out to dampen her. She hissed and cursed at him, but he seemed oblivious, focused on the task at hand. As her eyes adjusted she saw that the barrel was on wheels and it had a length of electrical cord running from it and into the wall socket. She'd used these appliances enough times at work to recognize them.

It was a shop vac, a heavy-duty vacuum used for both wet and dry messes.

"What the fuck are doing with that, you bastard?"

The man attached a new head to the hose, a smaller piece that was used to get into corners and small areas. He spat on it as well, then moved forward and worked it into her. She squirmed, popping it out, and he rose in a rage and pulled straight up on the leash. The prong contracted like a metal noose, sending little stabs into her throat as it choked her. Her vision started to waiver, a blackness surrounding her, and the voice found purchase and shrieked.

Find a way out of this or die!

"Bitches need cleanin'!" he shouted.

He let her go and the leash smacked the floor, now covered in her terror piss. Instead of lapping it up like before, the man just forced the hose back inside her—harder, meaner. Once it was in he went to the power switch.

"No!" she said, gasping from the loss of air. "Please! I'll do anything!"

"You'll do that anyway," he said, giving her a mocking smile.

Then he hit the switch.

It was during the daytime that she managed to get the rope loose.

She was beaten, exhausted. Every inch of her body hurt. Her face was raw from abuse and covered with god knows how many cum-baths. The only time the semen had been washed away was when he'd pissed on her head and let it run down her face, all warm and putrid. Her anus bled every time she had to relieve herself, her vaginal walls were raw, and her mouth was so torn that one whole side of her head had swelled up. One eye had puffed up so black that she could only open it a crack. Numbness, caused by being tied in place, kept her from feeling certain parts of her body.

But now there was hope.

The chip in the wood had gotten bigger. She'd been working on it so feverishly that her fingernails had cracked and bled; one she had accidently bent backward and ripped it completely off and she had to bite her lip to stifle her scream. But now there was a sharp and jagged edge that was more than just a splinter that would break away.

The man had gone out for his regular shopping so she'd had some time to work without worrying about him coming into the kitchen. She'd been sawing away for a while, not sure just how far she had gotten, when the rope suddenly came loose, bringing tears to her eyes and making her whole body shake. She pulled her hands free and then rubbed her wrists where the red rings had been made. Her arms felt like they were moving through clay. Because of the dull ache, she struggled undoing the ties at her feet, but the man was clearly no boy scout. The knots were simple and she was free in less than a minute. Delirious with relief, she began to laugh uncontrollably.

Focus, the voice said, above her laughter. *You have to move fast.*

The voice was right. Sometimes the man was back in twenty minutes, other times it was two hours. She looked down at her naked, ruined body to her weak and tingling legs.

Now!

Emma moved through the kitchen, stomping to wake up her feet and legs, and sprinted up the stairs, leaning on the walls for balance, taking the steps two at a time. Her vagina still ached from being vacuum sucked, but she ignored it, letting the voice drive her past the pain and into a frantic hurry to find clothes, shoes, and hopefully her car keys. It warned her that her body might not make it down the long winding roads on foot, especially barefoot, and even if she could, god forbid *he* be the first car that saw her. And if she was going to trek through the thick forests of Wayland she had to be somewhat clothed. What if she passed out exposed and died of dehydration?

Once upon the second floor she looked around and saw the two big doors that led to the master bedroom. Barging in, she saw the king-sized canopy bed, lavish dressers and shimmering, new entertainment center. But while this was the room she'd been looking for, she wasn't happy that she'd stepped into it.

The odor hit her first—a reek that was overpowering and yet familiar. When she'd shared a house with some girlfriends, one day she had detected a similar odor, which seemed to come from the floor. Finding nothing, she'd gone into the crawl space beneath the house and discovered the rotting carcasses of a few alley cats who had gotten trapped in there. It seemed that they had gone in during the recent blizzard and that the raging winds had slammed the door to the crawlspace behind them, latching it in place. Each of them had been eviscerated and had had their eyes scooped out. Emma had heard a rustling in the shadows and when she'd looked closer she noticed a bigger cat, still alive and covered in blood, and she knew what had happened to the other two.

Now it looked as if something very similar had happened here.

Spread out on the bed, with her legs propped open and her arms slung over the headboard in a Christ-like pose, was Mrs. Harrington.

She was torn from her breastbone all the way down to her vagina. All of her internal organs where gone and Emma wretched and shuddered, recalling her meals.

Bile boiled in Emma's throat.

Mrs. Harrington's face was spattered with old semen, and so was her husband's. He lay on the floor before the bed, on his belly with his pants at his ankles. His butt was bare and the crack was caked in dried blood, his evacuated bowels in a crusty pile beside him. He wore no shirt and Emma could see that all the flesh of his back had been removed in one perfect square. The muscle and sinew was shredded and each of his lungs had been pulled out from behind his broken ribs. They lay draped across his back like rubbery wings, and Emma wondered if the man had allowed Mr. Harrington to die before this horrible act.

Vomit sprayed out of her and spilled across the expensive carpet. She gathered herself as quickly as she could and opened up a dresser drawer, finding Mr. Harrington's t-shirts. Not wanting to waste any time, she threw one on. It was backwards but she didn't notice, let alone care. Going to the closet for a pair of shoes, she grabbed a pair of Mrs. Harrington's sneakers and jammed her feet into them even though they were a size too small. She ran out and went to the stairs—

The sound of soft cries stopped her.

The fucking baby.

Emma had been so frantic that she'd forgotten all about the wailing she'd heard so many times and hadn't been sure if it was a hallucination or not. It certainly sounded real right now. She looked to the front door, which she could see from the top of the stairs. But the crying echoed, sizzling her nerves.

She shuddered and turned back to find the baby.

The hall stretched all the way across the giant house. It was lined with door after door, all of them closed, making her feel as if she was in some sort of nightmarish fairy tale. She moved quickly, on tippy-toes, struggling to find where the sound was coming from as it reverberated through the hollow hall, trying to listen over the sound of her heart thudding in her chest and still stay alert for any sound of a car coming into the driveway or the front door opening.

When she reached the end of the hall she found the nursery and opened the door. Pink walls surrounded a fluffy crib where the noise blasted from. A terrible thought raced through her then—maybe it was a recording, a doll or some other horrible ruse made to trap her. But when she looked over the edge she saw a tiny baby wrapped up in fleece beneath a spinning mobile. She stared at it a moment, and strange thoughts, dark and confusing, seeped into her head.

What the fuck do you have to cry about? He's sung to you, cared for you. She tried to shake the thoughts loose.

Concentrate!

She snatched up the infant, blanket and all, taking no time to be gentle. Once it was scooped against her, she carried it out and jogged down the hall in a hurry, stopping only when she heard a car door slam.

Emma made it downstairs just before he reached the front door, and bolted through the house in search of a back exit, cursing the mansion's ridiculous size.

Why the fuck do two people and a baby need all this space?

She heard the front door open and tried to hush the baby, which was still crying.

Ah, just toss the little shit, that strange, dark part of her said. *It's gonna get you caught!*

She continued to run, making lame attempts to coo the squirming mass, and as she reached the kitchen she spotted the large cutlery set on the counter. She slid out the butcher knife, then ran through to the den where the sliding glass door led out to the pool. She went to open it just as she heard the man cursing, obviously having heard the baby crying.

The vicious voice came back. *Throw the baby down!*

She shushed the infant, but it began to shriek.

Emma pulled hard on the handle after unlocking it, but the door didn't budge. She looked it over and saw that there was a steel bar at the bottom that kept it in place. She knelt to get it out of the groove, and this was all the time the man needed to spot her from the kitchen and come raging forward.

He charged like a mad bull and as he dived for her she raised the knife high and brought it down into his chest as hard as she could. He yelled out and crumpled into her, the momentum he had built up sending her crashing through the door, which exploded in a crystal spray. Instead of trying to break her fall she held on to the baby, shielding its face from the flying shards. The concrete slammed into her back but she was used to pain by now and got to her feet quicker than the man, who groaned on the ground, clutching at the knife in him as blood poured from the wound.

Emma kept on running as the man struggled to pull the knife out. She exited the screen overhang of the porch and looked back and forth, seeing that she was trapped by the surrounding wooden fence. The yard was enormous and she realized she had to completely circle the pool again from the outside to get to the gate.

She ran on and as she did so she saw the man getting up. By the time she reached the gate he was at the screen beside her, just a few feet away, and was slashing it apart with the gore-slathered knife. He growled like an animal as he did so, smashing the bar that divided the upper and lower screens so he could walk through the hole he'd created.

Emma burst through the gate, discombobulated, and saw that she was on the side of the house where the garage was. The small door that led into the side of it was ajar. She hoped she could duck in there long enough for him to run out through the front yard and into the street, giving her a moment to maybe sneak away through the woods. She slipped in and put the door into place and locked it, hearing the man raging as he ran past it a moment later.

She put her hand over the baby's mouth, finding herself growing increasingly angry at it for giving away their position.

Privileged fuck! Can't you see I'm trying to help you?

It wasn't until the infant began to writhe that she realized she'd been holding her hand all away across its nose as well, cutting off its air.

Good, her new dark side snarled.

She released her grip and made a grunting noise in an effort to shake the black thoughts loose.

The gloomy light of dusk filled the garage. She saw that locking the door had been futile, for the large garage door itself was wide open. She thought about hiding behind the Chevelle, but the fucking baby started crying again the moment it had air. Soon the man would be in front of the garage and she'd be cornered. She plopped the baby on the hood of the car, then went to the workbench where an enormous variety of tools hung on the corkboards above it. She grabbed a sledgehammer with a long handle and then hid herself behind the towering 80-gallon air compressor.

When the man reached the front of the garage his head snapped around at the sound of the crying baby. From where he was standing, Emma knew that he could hear but not see the baby. She crouched and waited, using the baby as bait, watching the man through the small space between the compressor and the edge of the door. He came sprinting up the driveway and she reared the sledgehammer back over her shoulder.

Just as the man reached the foot of the garage, she stood up, and as he walked past the compressor she came roaring forward with the hammer's head and landed it square into his chest with a thunderous crack. He tried to scream but only a wheezing came out as his mouth went wide and his face went white. He fell backward and landed flat on his back, hard, and the knife flew from his grasp and slid underneath the car.

Wasting no time, Emma swung the hammer up again and brought it down on one of his knees, shattering and dislocating it. Now he did scream. He tried to roll over but she was too quick, cracking him in his other knee, shifting it too far, breaking it. The man howled as the kneecap popped out of place and the baby cried louder in unison.

Emma basked in the sounds of pain that for the first time weren't coming from her.

She was tempted to bring the hammer down onto his face, but she didn't want to kill him.

Not yet.

Crippled, the man couldn't go far, so Emma flung the hammer away and turned to the workbench to see what she could find. She wanted to restrain the fat bastard's hands first, so he couldn't make a grab at her, but she felt that the ropes and chains coiled in a crate weren't exactly what she was looking for. She wanted something more befitting of her former captor. Finding the vice grip mounted on the workbench, she grabbed his wrist and lifted his right hand to it, giggling. The man was still overcome by his broken knees and ribs, so he didn't put up a struggle as she placed it into the vice's teeth. She wheeled it upon his hand and he cried out as it tightened upon his knuckles. She had to put all her body weight into the turning bar to make his knuckles snap, but it was worth the extra effort.

She looked down at him, a mad rictus grin on her puffy face.

"Who's the *bitch* now?" she asked.

He started to babble an apology and she reared back and kicked him in the balls. He gasped, his eyes going even wider with pain. She savored the moment—Christ, she *really* enjoyed it—then reared back and gave him another dick shot. He tried to cover his nuts with his free hand and she backhanded him.

"Move your hand, bitch!"

He refused, so she went to the workbench.

Emma grabbed the machete at first and tested the blade. It was dull; too dull. She tossed it aside and kept looking.

The baby was bawling, and it sent a weird quiver through her.

Shut up! Shut up goddammit, or I'll give you something to cry about, you silver-spooned little fucker!

She found a small hatchet that looked brand new. She pulled it off of the board and swung it up with both hands. The man didn't even have time to react. She brought it down upon his free arm, cutting through to the bone. He shook and flailed but the vice grip refused to let go of the other arm. She kicked him in the balls again and again, and when his hand returned to defend them she hacked another gash in his forearm. She realized that removing it completely would take too long and, worse yet, would cause him to pass out and probably bleed to death.

That's no kind of send off for my bitch.

Blood gushed from the man's wounds and he had begun to shake violently. Emma slammed the hatchet's blade down into the workbench so that it stuck. Then she slid open the largest drawer of the tool chest, giddy as a girl with a large box on Christmas morning. Inside she found a power drill that already had a drill bit inside of it, a battery for it, and a nail gun that already had its battery in it. She smiled picking it up, suddenly glad that she'd been made to do all the handiwork at the kennel. She picked up the nail gun and grabbed the man's free wrist with her other hand. He tried to pull away but his wounds made it too painful to do so. She placed his palm on the bench, pressed the nail gun to the back of his hand, and fired before he could get out his plea. Just to be sure, she fired two more, securing him.

Now she had him pinned to the bench, twisted at the waist, his legs lying crooked and useless. She thought about all the awful things he'd done to her and wished she was able to cum on his face; but knowing this piss-slurping, ass-fucking freak, he'd probably enjoy it. She thought about how he had raped, tortured and beat her and the urge to snatch the life right out of him was pitch black and powerful. She envisioned splitting his skull with the hatchet or beheading him with the table saw. She thought about using the soldering iron on his nipples and filing down his teeth. But then, remembering how he had sucked the tender insides of her vagina raw with that vacuum, a new plot suddenly popped into her brain.

With the bicycle pump attachment tip at the end of the compressor's hose and the man's jeans unbuttoned, she pulled his flaccid cock out and licked the tip of the needle. She pointed the head of his dick up and then spat on his pee hole, rubbing it with her thumb. He stirred slightly, dazed by pain, whimpering. The needle was a little wider than his dickhole so she had to force it in. The man squealed like a warthog being butchered. He thrashed but the two-inch long needle was already stuffed into his urethra.

"I know how much my boy loves his blowjobs," she said.

"No . . . don't . . . "

"That's what she said."

Emma gave him a crazed smile with all the teeth of a jack-o'-lantern. She turned the compressor on high, giving his dick enough pressure to inflate a monster truck tire.

She realized that the prong collar was still around her neck, so she removed it and attached it to his. It was too tight for him but she was still able to latch it by pinching his neck flab together. He had passed out from the agony of his dick inflation and put up no resistance. The leash wasn't still on the collar, so she went to the workbench and retrieved a length of the same nylon rope that had bound her to the chair she'd been in for days. She made a tight knot in the chain's loop and tested it out with all her might, pulling *hard*.

The man came awake, screeching as she yanked the rope up into the air. His face turned purple as the prongs sunk in, sending sinister quivers of joy through Emma's heart. Watching him suffer like this filled her with an elation that was beyond mere pleasure. It was otherworldly in its euphoria—more powerful than any drug she'd ever known. She grew hysterical torturing him and couldn't resist giggling.

Her nipples stiffened.

I can see why he likes this so much.

Not only did she thrive on giving him his comeuppance, she also marveled at her sheer creativity as she turned the garage into a little shop of horrors. Above all, she savored the sick delight of totally dominating him. Here he was, crippled, pinned by nails and a vice, his arms half butchered, his dick swollen and bleeding, his nuts engorged and his neck inflamed, and still she pondered what to do next.

Some part of her knew now that she had been warped, perhaps forever changed. But her utter dominance over him gave her a twisted thrill that was beyond any drugs, theft, money or even sex. But this power was sexual in nature. She knew that by the way her pussy had gone moist as she'd sent the air up through his urethra and into his bladder, where she wondered if she had caused any tearing. She imagined the bladder popping like a child's balloon and his body going toxic from his own piss.

That's when she remembered how he'd made her taste her own shit a few days ago, the same day that he had bashed her front teeth out. She stood up and looked around. The baby was crying so loudly now that it was hurting her concentration, so she paused her game and went to it.

"What the fuck's wrong?" she yelled.

As she picked it up the stink wafted up her nose and she knew why it had been bawling all this time. Laughing, she laid the baby down on the workbench and unbuttoned its one piece. She rolled it up and then ripped the tape away from the diaper, pulling it away slowly, smiling wide at the foul, green treasure waiting within. She slid the diaper out from under the baby, leaving much of the filth still smeared on the baby's genitals.

She tried not to breathe as she stepped closer to the man slumped against the workbench with his head resting on it. She moved to him with the diaper in hand, then took him by the nose and pinched it shut as she used it to lift his head. When he opened his mouth to breathe she smashed the nasty end of the diaper into his mouth and let the swampy feces pour in and sluice through the gaps between his teeth. With his head still tilted upward, she worked his Adam's apple to make the runny dump slide down his throat. Once he swallowed it he began to heave, his belly contracting. Knowing the vomit was coming, Emma slid the oil pan out from beneath the workbench to collect it. It came out in a savage spray, both from his mouth and his nostrils. The puke fell and splattered and she applauded him.

"Good boy!" she said, patting him on the head.

Then she upturned the pan over his head.

"Even better than cum." She laughed as the shit-vomit dribbled down his face.

"Please," he said. "You've had your fun . . . ya got your payback. Please, just let me go. I won't chase ya. I can't even move. I need a hospital."

"Ohhh . . . does my little bitch have a tummy ache? Well, we can make you think about something else instead."

He began to cry now, still begging.

She walked back to the toolbox, took out the power drill and slapped in the battery. The drill bit seemed too small though, too thin. She pulled open the top drawer and found the largest one—about three inches around and nine inches long with sharp curves. Knowing she'd need some assistance, she grabbed a can of WD-40 and sprayed the drill bit until it was dripping. She buzzed it into life with two quick taps of the trigger.

This thing has some serious power.

Emma went over to the man and stood behind him. Pinned to the bench and slumped over on his stomach, he was unable to turn back. He had no leverage and was too wounded to thrash.

TRIANA

"Whatever you're thinkin' about," he said, "please don't do it."

His pants were already undone and it was easy to slide them down over his butt. His fat, hairy, pasty ass greeted her with a big, black smile. She dragged each leg to the side, causing him to whine as his broken limbs scraped against the concrete. She poked around for his asshole and, finding it, she put her thumb into it, dry, and was pleased that it was a nice, snug fit.

"Looks like you've got an ass cherry to pop too," she said.

She wiggled her thumb inside of him, letting her long nail scratch the tender flesh. His flabby cheeks shuddered. She slid her thumb back out and moved in with the drill. She forced the bit up into his anus and slid it up slowly, inch by inch, letting him wonder at what point it would end. She got it all the way up and knew that its edges must already be cutting him because he had gone very still and was holding his breath.

"Dear god . . . " he whispered.

"Don't you shit now," she said. "A bitch that shits is doing so in self-defense, and I don't take kindly to that."

She pressed the trigger and held it down.

The drill spun to life and ravaged his colon, blood pouring out of his gaping asshole, slicking her hands. She spun it around inside of him, first clockwise and then counter clockwise, making sure that every bit of his rectum was torn apart.

Sure enough, he did exit his bowels, but it didn't even faze her. A bizarre state of consciousness had flushed her now, her sanity flaking away like old paint. She pressed her crotch against the body of the drill, letting it vibrate against her vulva as she thrust the drill in and out of his ass, fucking him with cold spins of the steel. Her nipples grew so hard that she thought they may burst, her sopping pussy soaking her crotch.

Now own him, the voice said. *Make him yours, forever.*

As the man screamed in agony and shuddered in his death throes, Emma screamed in orgasmic pleasure and shuddered in her newfound rapture. Her breathing grew rapid and the smell of gore and feces filled her snorting nostrils like spring rain. She moaned and moaned, screaming to the heavens, then came harder than she ever had—actually squirting for the first time.

She fell backward, twitching in her intoxicating delirium.

THE BITCH

When Emma came out of her orgasm, she scooted over to the man who slouched there in a large blood pool. More had poured out of his open mouth and his eyes had rolled back so that they showed solid white. She checked for a pulse, which he no longer had.

Wanting just one more giddy, little thrill, she went back to the sledgehammer that had saved her life and let it have the honors. She brought it down on his head, splitting it open like a melon. She gave it two more whacks until the head came apart, exposing the grey, rubbery meat of his brain. She reached in with her hands and dug into it with her jagged nails, tossing it like a salad, half wondering why, half transfixed by the depravity of it. At last when she was finished playing with it she sniffed her fingers curiously and then wiped them on her shirt.

The baby had stopped crying and was in the deep sleep that comes after the wailing and fright of not being heard or helped. She was not surprised to find that something about its sleep soured her stomach. Emma looked down upon the infant and for a moment she was mesmerized by its beauty and innocence. It was clean, pure and untainted by the cruelty of the world, the very cruelties Emma had unjustly had to endure, the ones that had shaped her into the deranged woman who now looked down at this child with an all-new perspective.

How fair was it that Emma had suffered, while others remained untouched? How fair was it that she was born to nothing, and this little brat born to wealth and privilege? How fair was it that the man had enjoyed torturing her for days while she had only enjoyed about an hour of torturing someone, and now craved so much more?

Someone would have to level things out. Someone would have to show this baby what the world was really like, to teach it good— *really fucking good*.

She went to the man's body, snapped the prong collar free and popped off several prongs, fitting it, then placed it around the baby's neck and sealed it tight. The infant's face twisted into a hot pink ball of discomfort that sent a warm ripple across Emma's flesh. She picked the baby up and held it close, feeling its tiny body pushing away from her, rejecting her, rejecting everything, and she walked out of the garage and into the pitch-black night beyond.

She'd come here for treasure.

Now she'd gotten it.

Kristopher Triana is the author of Body Art, The Ruin Season *and* Growing Dark. *His next horror novel,* Full Brutal, *is slated for release next year. Triana's fiction has appeared in many magazines and anthologies. Some of his stories have been translated to Russian, and* Body Art *is scheduled for a German edition. His fiction has drawn praise from* Publisher's Weekly, Rue Morgue Magazine, Cemetery Dance *and more. Triana is obsessed with all aspects of the horror genre, and has amassed a staggering collection of cult films, horror books, movie memorabilia, busts and Halloween masks.*

He works as a professional dog trainer and lives in North Carolina with his wife.
—

IT'S *HELLRAISER* MEETS *BOOGIE NIGHTS!*

KRISTOPHER TRIANA

HORROR

HI-FI
STEREO

BODY ART

RATED X

"DEFINITELY POISED FOR A PLACE ALONGSIDE
THE LIKES OF WRATH JAMES WHITE AND
MONICA J. O'ROURKE."
- THE HORROR FICTION REVIEW

In *400 Days of Oppression*, Wrath James White pushes the boundaries of race and sexuality—easily his most controverial and erotic novel yet!

Would you accept the challenge of the craziest BDSM experience imaginable? And could you survive . . .

400 DAYS
OF
OPPRESSION

WRATH JAMES WHITE

THE RESIDENTS OF THE BALLADOR HOTEL CAN'T WAIT TO MEET YOU...

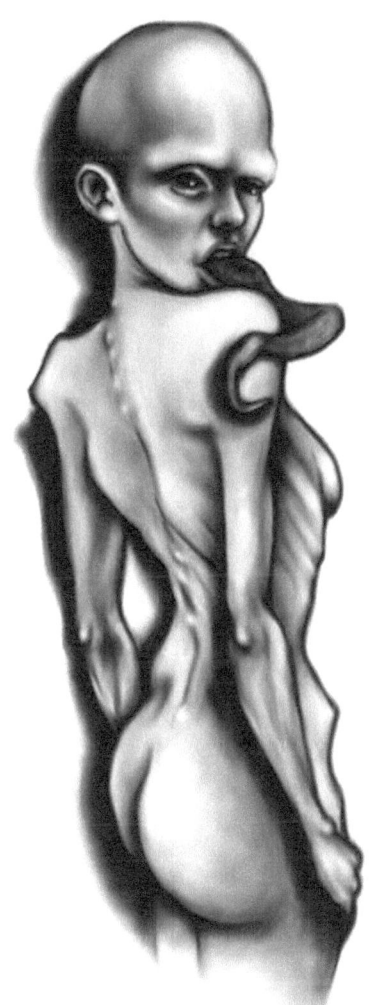

"BRUTALLY VISCERAL."
— CEMETERY DANCE ONLINE

●

"FRESH AND DISTINCTIVE."
— HORROR AFTER DARK

●

BLOOD BOUND BOOKS PRESENTS THE DEBUT HORROR NOVEL FROM AUTHOR JOHN MCNEE

Prince of Nightmares

"Transgressive and hard-edged"
~ Jeff VanderMeer, Nebula award winning author of the *Southern Reach* trilogy

"Flabbergasting Black Metal New Weird"
~ Edward Morris, author of the *Blackguard* series

"Death, violence, and inappropriate sex"
~ Neil Williamson, author of *The Moon King*

BleakWarrior

Alistair Rennie

"*Pretty Pretty Princess* is disgusting, offensive, and absolutely hilarious."
~ Sci-Fi and Scary
"Shane McKenzie has the kind of imagination that should take a license to operate."
~ Ray Garton

DON'T MISS THIS TWISTED FAIRY TALE FOR ADULTS!

Extreme Horror meets Hardboiled Fiction in a world deep below our own . . .

"Take one part Sid Vicious, one part H.P. Lovecraft and shake. Throw in a dash of the thrill kill thug life and you have *Mother's Boys*."

~ David C. Hayes, author of *Cannibal Fat Camp*

Follow Author T. Fox Dunham

"Part medical horror, part supernatural suspense, MERCY is a hard-hitting fever dream of a novel. I enjoyed the hell out of it!"

~ Tim Waggoner, author of *The Way of All Flesh*

Wrecking civilization one story at a time . . .

Blog:tfoxdunham.blogspot.com

Twitter: @TFoxDunham

Facebook.com/tfoxdunham

www.ingramcontent.com/pod-product-compliance
Lightning Source LLC
Chambersburg PA
CBHW030544260626
47157CB00006B/2184